EVILS OF A SECRET PAST

ERICK ISKERSKY

ISBN: 1542365147
ISBN 13: 9781542365147

DEDICATION

This book is dedicated to Samantha McCarthy, a girl who died from a terminal illness at the tragically young age of 11 years old. In her memory, all royalties from the sale of this book will go to Sam's Fans, an organization dedicated to providing music therapy to critically ill children who are confined in hospitals.

Sam's Fans was started by Nickki McCarthy, Sam's mother. Music therapy provides joy and peace to children fighting for their lives while undergoing treatment and rehabilitation. It is a source of hope. For some, music therapy provides moments of happiness while they spend long, lonely hours in hospital rooms. Please go to www.samsfans.org to read about this very worthwhile organization. If you have bought this book but would like to provide more financial assistance, simply follow the instructions on the website.

Two of my favorite things in life are music and tennis. I teach tennis for a living, and through one of my students I learned about Sam's Fans and all of the wonderful things this organization is doing for critically ill children. I have also had the privilege of meeting Nikki McCarthy and have been greatly inspired to do all I can to help. Hopefully my book project will raise some money and assist Sam's Fans in bringing joy to children suffering from life threatening illnesses.

Erick Iskersky
Author of "Evils Of A Secret Past"
Tennis Instructor
Bad piano player (but lover of music)

PROLOGUE

I awoke from the stupor. My hands were tied behind my back. Duct tape was wrapped across my mouth preventing me from screaming. I was uncomfortably upright in the seat of a prop plane. Two of my captors sat across from me, while the third one was obviously flying the plane. It was definitely a situation that was not only alarming, but was also unfathomable. What increased my anxiety even more was the fact that the two men responsible for guarding me now strapped a parachute onto my shoulders, said something in Hebrew that I didn't understand, and then enjoyed a hearty laugh – clearly at my expense.

I didn't know for how long we'd been flying, nor how long I had been out cold. My hope was that this was all a nightmare and that all would end at any moment. Just like in the movies. Or that this was all a joke and that at any moment my captors would shout out, "Smile, you're on Candid Camera." Which, of course, would have been quite impossible in light of the duct tape covering my mouth. However, the events that happened in the hotel earlier now started coming back to me as the fog in my brain lifted, and I knew this was real.

Suddenly one of the men yanked me up out of my seat, and with the help of the American sounding man, dragged me toward the cabin door. This did not look promising. I tried to put up what, in my mind at least, was a valiant struggle. I was much too weak to fight against the two men, especially with my hands tied behind my back. I kept thinking of some clever maneuver I could pull off and stall what appeared to be the inevitable. They held me against the wall by the door and then one of them turned the handle on the door and opened it.

Almost simultaneously, as the pressure changed dramatically and the wind whipped furiously in the cabin, the other captor sliced the tape off my hands, tore the tape off my mouth, and shoved me out the door. As I hurled towards Earth and felt the wind ripple with great force against my face and body, I knew I had to do something.

Amazingly at that very moment thoughts started to enter my mind that had nothing to do with my predicament. My life actually started to flash through my mind even as my body careened out of control and kept plummeting. It seemed that my life was about to end, I could do nothing about it, and everything that transpired leading to this moment was coming back to me at lightning speed. At least I still possessed some of my mental faculties and did the one thing I could do – I pulled the rip chord on my parachute.

CHAPTER 1

It all started in the summer of 1976. My summer had gone wonderfully. I was a member of the United States Junior Davis Cup team, which meant I was one of the best eighteen-and-under tennis players in the entire nation. Earlier in the spring, as a senior, I won my second consecutive Ohio state high school singles championship. Not only had I won as a junior, I also lost in the finals as a sophomore and the semi-finals as a freshman. All of this was accomplished while I was attending Toledo St. John's High School.

In early June I was invited to play a tournament in Tulsa, Oklahoma. I was really looking forward to the start of the summer tennis season. I had just graduated from high school and was looking forward to playing some tournaments to get ready for my upcoming college career. At the tournament in Tulsa, I won my first two matches and then had to face John McEnroe in the semifinals. Needless to say, McEnroe became one of the best players in the world. However, also needless to say, he had not yet achieved his lofty status. Playing one of my best junior tennis matches, I defeated McEnroe and reached the finals. In the finals I defeated Larry Gottfried, who at the time was the top junior tennis player in the nation.

From there my summer only got better. At tryouts for the United States Junior Davis Cup team I lost my first two matches, but rallied to go undefeated the rest of the way and consequently I was named as a member of the team. That meant I would get all of my expenses paid for the entire summer and would travel with the rest of the team members. Those members included John McEnroe, who became number one in the world; Eliot Teltscher, who reached a top ten world ranking as a pro; Tony Giammalva, who reached the top 50; Robert Van't Hof, who reached the top 50; and Van Winitsky, who also reached the top 50. It was certainly exciting to be a part of such a talented group.

Our summer started out West at a tournament in San Jose. I reached the semifinals and had the joy of playing John McEnroe once again. It was always a "special" treat to play McEnroe because I knew there would likely be some sort of confrontation over a call, or angry outbursts by John, or basically just the knowledge that the match would be a general pain in the ass. In this particular instance, McEnroe got revenge for my Tulsa win and ended my run in San Jose.

After San Jose we headed to Burlingame (a suburb of San Francisco) for the National Hard Court Championships. I was upset by Marty Davis, who at the time was not highly ranked as a junior, but would eventually become a top college player and a successful pro. I was beaten by Marty in the second round so spent the rest of the week hanging out and practicing.

Our next stop was in St. Louis. I lost to Tony Giammalva, a future college team mate of mine, in the quarterfinals. Wouldn't you know it? In the consolation bracket I ran into McEnroe yet again, who defeated me in straight sets. One of the players in the tournament was Vince Van Patten, who at the time was known for his child hood acting career and not his tennis. Vince, however, ended up being very successful as a tennis pro, reaching a top 50 ranking in addition to being an actor.

Then we were on to Louisville for the National Clay Court Championships. In this tournament I got revenge by beating Marty Davis in the second round and eventually had to play McEnroe for the third week in a row. He defeated me in straight sets in the semifinals. In the quarterfinals I defeated Eliot Teltscher, which was always enjoyable because Teltscher was not known for his good sportsmanship, but more for his confrontational and brash style.

Something noteworthy occurred at the club in Louisville. Two men were watching some of the matches, which of course in itself was entirely normal. What made it strange, however, was that I was certain that I had seen both of them at the tournament in St. Louis. It was possible, I suppose, that they were fathers of two of the players in the tournaments. Not many parents traveled to all the tournaments, which made me think these two men were not with any of the players. Somehow to me they seemed out of place, although I couldn't quite put my finger on why I felt that way.

I noticed one of the men because he walked with a limp. He looked to be average in height with a full head of hair. He was quite thin and had a scar that ran across his cheek. The scar was quite prominent because I could see it even from twenty feet away, which is as close as I got to him. The other man was fairly fat and quite short. He was balding and was wearing a long sleeve shirt and dress pants, even though it was extremely hot outside. His complexion was quite pasty so perhaps he was trying to protect his skin from the sun.

Ultimately I decided that the two men were of no real consequence and even convinced myself that I may have been mistaken about seeing them both in St. Louis. Or perhaps they really had connections in some way to the junior tennis circuit and I would be seeing them every week for the rest of the summer. The man with the limp stood out in my mind because of his scar and the fat man stood out in my mind simply because he looked really weird.

Nonetheless, I didn't see them anymore in Louisville and I quickly forgot about them. From Louisville we traveled to Springfield, Ohio for the Western Open. This tournament turned out to be the best junior tennis tournament of my entire junior career. I was seeded eighth going into the tournament and was trying to become the first Ohioan in the history of the Western Open to win it. Because I was born and raised in Toledo, Ohio this was definitely a special tournament to me and I really wanted to do well in my final appearance.

I won my first three matches in straight sets without too much trouble. In the fourth round I faced Jonathan Paley from California. He had upset fourteenth seeded Peter Rennert. In a long and memorable match (for me anyway) I pulled out a victory by the score of 7-6, 1-6, 7-5. That victory provided me with a lot of momentum heading into the quarterfinals. In the quarterfinals I faced third seeded Van Winitsky, who hailed from Florida. To my relief, after winning the first set rather easily, I managed to win the second set 7-6 and avoided a three set match. In the semifinals I had to play eleventh seeded Chris Dunk from California, who was compared by many to Stan Smith, in both appearance and playing style. Dunk was certainly a confident individual and I knew it would be a tough match. I defeated Dunk 7-5, 6-2 and was on the verge of making history. And who was my opponent in the finals? The one and only John McEnroe, who was seeded fourth and whom I would be playing for the fifth time that summer.

The beginning of the match was not good for me. I lost the first four games and looked to be in trouble. McEnroe cruised to a 6-3 first set. I wasn't giving up, however. This match was to be a three out of five set match, just like the finals of the National Junior Championships would be the following week. Consequently dropping the first set wasn't a disaster. I rallied to win the second set 6-3 after going up 4-1. Then came the all important third set. With my confidence growing and McEnroe's temper flaring, I cruised to a 6-1 third set. One more set and I would become the first Ohioan to win the Western Open Championships! As McEnroe started to wilt in the heat I kept the pressure on and finished the match off 6-1 in the fourth set. The final score was 3-6, 6-3, 6-1, 6-1. A huge victory for me and a real boost heading to the National Junior Championships in Kalamazoo, Michigan.

After about a six hour drive, we arrived in Kalamazoo. I was elated. This was my first championship in a national caliber event and could not have come at a better time. For one of the rare times my father Vladimir had watched me play. I always thought I got nervous when my father watched me so gradually he stopped coming to matches except every once in a while. This had been one of those occasions, although he and my high school tennis coach, Jack Dewey, had stayed hidden from view until after the match was over. I was quite thrilled that my father got to see me play the best tennis match of my career to date.

Unfortunately, after winning my first match very easily in the first round at the National Junior Championships, things got a lot tougher. And, once again, I saw the two men who I had previously seen in St. Louis and Louisville. This time there could be no mistake. And what made it more unnerving was that both of them were watching me play my second round match against Reid Freeman. Partly, because of that distraction, I dropped the first set and hoped that I would be able to recover my concentration. Fortunately I did and won the last two sets 6-1, 6-1.

After the match I tried to find the two men and talk to them. At least I wanted to try to find out who they were. Perhaps they were college coaches who were scouting me, although it was probably a bit too late for that. I was already planning to go to Trinity University in San Antonio. Or perhaps they were simply tennis fans who liked to watch tennis, but that seemed a bit strange to me that two grown men would follow the junior tennis circuit around.

I talked to Bill McGowan, one of our Junior Davis Cup Coaches but he convinced me that there could be nothing sinister about the presence of the two mysterious men. In any case, I described the two men and asked him to talk to them if he saw them.

"Look Bill, I know that it's unlikely that these guys could be up to something, but just in case I want to try to find out who they are. They really broke my concentration in my last match."

"Okay Erick, I'll keep an eye out for a couple of guys who match your description, but I would think the odds are going to be fairly slim that I spot them. I really don't think there's anything they could be up to. Who knows why they've been at three of the tournaments, but there's gotta be a legitimate reason."

In the third round I played Lloyd Bourne, who would go on to play at Stanford and have a fairly decent career as a pro. I had another three set match. Once more I dropped the first set, and once more I rallied to win the last two sets. These long matches were certainly not ideal because of the long week I had in Springfield but luckily the excitement of advancing towards a possible national championship kept me going.

Next up was Jai DiLouie, to whom I had lost in the semifinals of the National Indoor Championships way back in November. Jai was going to attend SMU, which had one of the best teams in the nation, and was going to become one of my big rivals in college tennis. I avenged my previous loss by pulling out a real nail-biter by a score of 6-2, 2-6, 7-5. My dream of claiming a national championship was still alive and kicking!

My opponent in the quarterfinals turned out to be top-seeded and defending champion Howard Schoenfield. Howard was a very unusual human being, but was also a very gifted player. He had sat out the summer junior circuit for personal reasons, but was certainly going to be a very difficult opponent. The match I played against Schoenfield ended up being one of the biggest disappointments of my entire tennis career.

I initially handled the pressure of playing the defending champion on one of the stadium courts in front of a large crowd, wonderfully. Kalamazoo College, the site of the national championships, has a beautiful facility with three stadium courts. The tournament is a huge event in the city and attended by a lot of tennis fans. To play a featured match at the event is really exciting. I won the first set 7-5 and was playing some of the best tennis of my life. I jumped out to a 3-1 lead in the second set and it very much looked like I was going to pull the big upset. And then the painful reality of the moment sunk in and I simply choked. It had to be the biggest choke of my life and could not have come at a worse time. I lost five consecutive games and blew the second set by a score of 6-3. Somewhat rattled, and no longer playing my best, I could not reverse the momentum, and I lost the third set 6-3. My chance at a national championship was gone! I would never have the chance again. When it really mattered, I folded. At that time, I felt like it was the lowest point of my life.

Bob McKinley, my future college coach, consoled me with words of encouragement. "Hey, it was a great effort and you were really close to defeating the defending champ. You had a fantastic summer and I think you'll do just fine in college."

"But how do I overcome blowing such a big lead in the biggest match of my life?"

"Well, you know it just takes time," Bob replied. "When I was a senior I served for the match against Jimmy Connors in the quarterfinals of the NCAA Singles Championship and I blew the match. Connors was just a freshman. And obviously we all know what a great player Connors became within two years of my match against him. I eventually got over it but I have to admit that I've always wondered if my career would have turned out differently had I won that match."

Of course Bob's career didn't turn out too badly. He had reached a world ranking in the top 50 at the height of his career, however he got tired of the traveling and ended up quitting the tour to become the Head Tennis Coach at Trinity University in San Antonio. Receiving advice from someone as experienced as Bob was certainly what I needed after my disastrous defeat at the hands of Howard Schoenfield.

After a few days I was able to put everything into perspective. My conversation with Bob was extremely helpful and made me realize that I had much to be thankful for, and that I potentially had a bright future ahead of me. Even though the summer was winding down, there was still some tennis to be played before I headed off to San Antonio to pursue my college education and tennis career.

We finished off the summer playing tournaments in Tuscaloosa, Alabama; Philadelphia; and finally in Long Island. Because we were members of the United States Junior Davis Cup Team, we received invitations to the pre-qualifying event for the US Open. In 1976 the US Open was being played on a clay court surface (officially known as Har Tru) so the pre-qualifier was held at the Windy Harbor Tennis and Yacht Club in a beautiful section of Long Island, close to the Hamptons.

The summer had been a long one. We played a tournament virtually every week for ten weeks, this coming on the heels of a week long try-out for the Junior Davis Cup Team. Physically most of us were tired. Mentally we didn't have much to give. However, the thought of having a chance to get into the main draw of the US Open provided me with the energy and incentive I needed to give it my all for one more tournament.

It was late August, so the weather was hot in New York, and also rather humid. My first match was against Walter Redondo, a player with a lot of talent who didn't quite live up to expectations. He had once been the very best player in the nation, but now, although still very good, was a player I should have beaten – especially on a clay court surface. However, it was not to be. I couldn't seem to get going in the early stages of the match. I dropped the first set rather easily and even though I made a valiant attempt to come back in the second set, I ended up losing in straight sets. My summer was now over.

I was definitely disappointed with my performance, but I was also quite proud of my overall summer record. I would end up being ranked as the number three player in the nation behind Larry Gottfried and John McEnroe. Larry, who would be a college team mate of mine, had defeated McEnroe in the National Championship finals at Kalamazoo. All in all I had to be pleased. Here I was, a kid from Toledo, who didn't get to play that much tennis in the winter months, yet I was able to compete with the very best. I would have loved to have finished as the number one player in the nation, but certainly being number three wasn't too bad.

After my match I told Bill McGowan that I was going to walk back to our hotel to take a shower and have some lunch. The walk to the Kennington Inn was about five blocks. The Kennington was a beautiful, old hotel with large rooms, a great view of Long Island Sound, and a restaurant that served up some of the best food I'd had all summer. My spirits picked up considerably on my walk to the hotel because of the great view and the sunshine beating down on me. I loved summer and this was truly a wonderful day, not withstanding my defeat.

I walked into the lobby and made my way towards the elevator. I got on the elevator and pressed the button for my floor, the fifth, and waited. The elevator was quite old and seemed to take forever just to climb five floors, but finally it shuddered to a halt and the doors opened up. To get to my room I had to turn left out of the elevator and walk about fifteen feet, before turning left down the hallway. I approached the corner with my head down and made the turn. I looked up as I turned the corner just in time to avoid running into a man. It was the fat, balding man who I had seen in Saint Louis, Louisville, and Kalamazoo. Now I knew for sure that something strange was going on.

"Hello Erick," said the weird looking man in a thick accent. It sounded like a German or Swedish accent. I wasn't sure which. "It is so good to finally meet you. Someday, you know, you will be the most famous and powerful man in the world."

After the initial shock wore off I was able to speak, although I really didn't know where to begin. "Who the hell are you and what in the hell are you talking about? Have you been following me all summer?"

"Erick, Erick, I am your friend and wish you only the best. Yes, it's true I have been at some of your tournaments. But in time you will understand why I had to do so. Let's have some lunch and I will explain everything. Then it will all be clear. My car is downstairs. We can go to a little cafe I know just a mile or two from here."

If the situation wasn't so eerie I probably would have been laughing. The man's thick accent, the way he looked, and the way he acted really was funny. Of course there was no way I was going to go anywhere with this loon and I told him so.

"Look, buddy, I don't know what you are up to or who you are. But I'm about to call the police and report you for harassment."

"Erick, I assure you there is no need to take such action. Just let me tell you what I have to tell you. I know once I explain everything you will be as excited as I am. You don't know what a great opportunity you and I now have to do really fantastic and powerful things."

The man started to sound crazier and crazier to me and I was beginning to worry just a bit. I was hoping some hotel guest would show up at any second but didn't hear the "ding" from the elevator door, nor did anybody come out of any of the rooms in the hallway.

Just then I heard a loud shout from behind me.

"Vorsicht, Herr Gruber!!"

I whirled around to look at the opposite end of the hallway. I recognized the language that had been shouted as German because I took the language in high school. What I did not expect was who shouted the words. The thin man with a limp and scar who had also been in Saint Louis, Louisville, and Kalamazoo was quickly making his way towards us.

"Ah, du bist es!" yelled back the fat, balding man known as Gruber.

"Halts du jetzt," replied the man with the scar.

"Nein, nein," Gruber shouted back and quickly reached into the breast pocket of his blazer. I hadn't thought of it at the time, but considering how hot it was, it was indeed very strange that someone would be wearing such an outfit.

Meanwhile I instinctively started to panic and quickly bolted towards the corner a few feet away to try to turn right to the elevator. Just as I was turning I saw Gruber pulling a gun out of his blazer. Almost simultaneously, as I reached the corner I saw the man with the scar pointing a gun in our direction.

Three loud shots rang out in rapid succession as I dived around the corner to the momentary safety of the elevator hallway. I heard a shout of pain and a tumbling body. I heard quick steps coming down the hallway. The man with the scar quickly passed by me down the hall. I heard one more shot. In a matter of seconds while I was pushing the elevator button, he passed back the other way.

"Do not worry," he exclaimed, "you are now safe."

With that he went back down the hallway. Just as the elevator door opened, I heard the exit doorway that the shooter had originally come through, close loudly. I quickly entered the elevator and, with my breathing and heartbeat at a feverish pitch, pressed the close door button. It seemed like a long time, but finally the door closed and I headed down to the lobby.

By the time I reached the lobby it was obvious someone had heard the loud commotion on the fifth floor and called security. A hotel security officer greeted me as I came out of the elevator.

"Hey kid, where have you just been? I don't want you going anywhere until I have a chance to talk to you. I also need to make sure you aren't armed because someone called down to say they heard shots."

Still breathless, I tried to calm down. "Look, I was just on the fifth floor. There was a shooting. I was able to get on the elevator. But I saw what happened right before the shots were fired."

After the security guard patted me down to make sure I didn't have a gun, he yelled to the manager, who had appeared on the scene at this point. "Have this kid sit down and keep an eye on him. I don't want him going anywhere until the police have a chance to talk to him."

With that, the security guard got on the elevator and presumably headed to the fifth floor. The manager, apparently named Mr. Tom Kincaid if his name tag was correct, came over to me. "What's your name? I think I've seen you in here before."

"Yeah, my name's Erick Iskersky. I'm here playing a tennis tournament over at Windy Harbor Tennis and Yacht Club. This is where my team is staying."

"Okay, come on over with me to my office and have a seat. I'm sure the police should be here any second."

With my legs still shaking, but now with a calmer heartbeat, I followed Kincaid to his office and sat down in the sofa that was against the wall in his office.

"Can I get you anything to drink?" asked Kincaid.

My mouth had suddenly become very parched and I realized that I was very, very thirsty and needed a drink badly. "I could use a Coke if you have one."

Kincaid left the office and came back a couple of minutes later with my Coke. "Look, I guess I'll leave you in here until the police arrive and talk to you. Are you staying on the fifth floor? Is that why you were up there?"

"Yeah, that's why I was up there. I was just going to my room to shower and then I was going to eat lunch."

"Well if you want I can get you something to eat."

"You know, all of a sudden I'm not all that hungry. I just want to find out what happened. I don't get it. Obviously I was scared out of my mind but I still don't understand what that guy named Gruber wanted from me."

After Kincaid left the office, I pondered the situation. Clearly Gruber knew who I was because he addressed me by my name. I, however, had no idea who he was except for the fact that I saw him briefly at the tennis tournaments in Saint Louis, Louisville, and Kalamazoo. For some reason he had been following me, as was the man who shot it out with Gruber. Yet the man with the scar obviously felt he had spared me from danger by having the shootout with Gruber. It also was clear that the man with the scar came down to my end of the hallway by the elevator to take one more shot at Gruber. My guess had to be that Gruber was not going to be alive when the police found him.

Minutes later a uniformed policeman walked into the office and identified himself. "I'm Officer Corrigan, young man. I understand you witnessed the shooting upstairs."

Inwardly I chuckled when Corrigan called me "young man". He could not have been more than four years older than me. He was acting in a very official manner, which I'm sure he was required to do, but I felt like he was not yet experienced enough to gain the respect of older peers.

"Yes I did, at least some of the shooting. For the most part I was just trying to dive out of the way to safety."

"Well, I'm going to ask you some questions and after that we'll wait until the detective on the scene, Detective Jason sends for you. Unfortunately we may have to take you up to the fifth floor so you can positively identify the victim."

My instincts were right, apparently. Gruber did not survive the shooting.

Corrigan asked me for my name and other personal information. I then recounted as best I could what had happened on the fifth floor. By this time I had somewhat recovered my poise, although I still was thinking about how close I had come to being injured or killed had I not dived into the elevator hallway. The man with the scar may have thought he saved me. On the other hand, if he'd never shown up, there would not have been a shooting in the first place. I wondered if he really knew something about Gruber that convinced him I had been in danger.

Suddenly a voice spoke loudly into Corrigan's walkie-talkie. "Corrigan, it's Detective Jason. Bring the young man up to the fifth floor so he can take a look at the body. Before you do, make sure he knows that it's not the most pleasant sight, but I think it will be useful for us if he checks the body out."

"Alright Erick, let's head on up. You heard what Detective Jason said. Have you ever seen a dead body before?"

"No, I never have. Other than at a funeral, that is."

"Well, at least it's a fresh body so you won't have to worry about the smell of decomposition."

Oh, goody, I thought. I get to see a dead body that's nice and fresh. Just what I needed after going through the trauma of the shooting. It looked like my summer was coming to an end with a bit more excitement than I bargained for.

I followed Corrigan out of the office and we headed towards the elevator. It had been less than an hour before that I was contemplating my defeat and looking forward to going home before I took off for college. And now I was on my way to see a murder victim who had spoken to me seconds before he died.

We rode up the elevator and were greeted at the door by a plump, cheerful looking guy. What he had to be cheerful about I wasn't sure, but he definitely looked like he was pleased to see me. He was dressed in a gray suit, his tie pulled away from his neck. He was sweating, but not profusely.

"Corrigan, introduce me." He stuck out his hand to shake mine. It was a firm handshake, but also a quick one.

"Detective David Jason, this is Erick Iskersky, the young man who saw the shooting. He's in town for a tennis tournament being played at Windy Harbor." Instead of pronouncing my name properly as Iss-ker-skee, he pronounced it Iz-er-skee.

"Erick, a pleasure to meet you. Obviously, I wish it was under different circumstances, but at least you were not hurt. After you take a look at the body, and you contact your parents and whoever is in charge of you here, I'd like to take you down to the station for some questions. Hopefully, you'll be able to help us out so we can get working on finding the shooter. I'd love to get down to the bottom of this mess. We don't get a lot of shootings in this area."

"I certainly want to do whatever I can," I replied. "Especially, because I don't know the two guys who were involved in the shooting, yet they seemed to know me."

"Alright, take a deep breath and let's go around the corner. It's a bit gruesome."

I followed Jason's advice, took a deep breath, and walked around the corner. I looked down. The body of Gruber lay splayed out on the hallway floor. His eyes looked up at me. I almost gagged. Hallelujah! I had now seen a murder victim for the first time in my life.

CHAPTER 2

Officer Corrigan gave me a ride to the Fourth Precinct, Long Island Division after I calmed down a bit. Even though I didn't know who Gruber was, it still had been quite a shock to see a dead body in person. Before we made our way to the Fourth Precinct we had stopped by the Windy Harbor Tennis and Yacht Club so I could inform Coach Bill McGowan about the incident at the Kennington.

"Hopefully I won't be too long, Bill, but you know where I'll be. Obviously after I'm done I'll get in touch with you and maybe we can take care of my travel arrangements so I can head on home."

"I still can't believe what happened to you. And here I thought you were being paranoid about seeing those guys at the tournaments. In retrospect, I should have taken you more seriously and done something about it."

By now it was well past lunch time so I asked Corrigan if there was anything he could give me to munch on. Just like on all of the television shows I watched as a kid, like Rockford Files and Dragnet, there were vending machines in the hallway of the Fourth Precinct. Corrigan got me a bag of chips, a Three Musketeers bar, and a Coke. I followed him to one of the interrogation rooms where I chowed down and patiently waited for Detective Jason. Earlier I had indicated to Corrigan that I didn't want to call my parents and tell them about the incident until after I had talked to Detective Jason.

Minutes later, Detective Jason walked in. He still looked cheerful, even though it was obvious that he was sweatier and hotter than he was at the hotel. Now I noticed that he had a twinkle in his eye despite the fact that his job could not have been all that pleasant. He greeted me when he saw me and his voice sounded like a really smooth baritone. I could envision him as a singer in a church choir or as a member of a barber shop quartet. To me, those images were much more believable than the image of him as a detective. I wondered if he always seemed to be cheerful or if there was a special reason he was so upbeat.

"Corrigan here has informed me that you don't want to call your parents until after we're done here, which is fine. Except, we could be here for quite some time."

I wondered why he didn't have a New York accent and decided to ask him that very question.

"Well, it's a long story, but to give you the short version, I'm originally from Columbus, Ohio."

"Really," I interrupted, "I'm from Toledo."

"You don't say. I came to New York with a great dream. I wanted to sing and act on Broadway. So after I finished my bachelor's degree in music at Ohio State, I came to New York to fulfill my great dream. As you can tell, I'm not quite doing what I thought I would be doing when I came here over twenty years ago."

I guess my instincts about Detective Jason had been right after all.

"Now, let's get down to it and see if you can fill me in on what transpired earlier today and maybe get some sort of feeling from you on why it happened."

I proceeded to present my lengthy story on what happened. Jason had turned on a tape recorder and encouraged me to provide all the information I could think of. I started from the very beginning (which seemed like a good place to start) and described everything that had happened with precise detail. All in all I must have spoken for close to an hour. Jason asked me quite a few questions, but for the most part let me tell my story like I wanted to. By the end of my presentation, Officer Corrigan had gone and I was in the room alone with Jason.

"I must say Erick, your story is a strange one. For the most part, the homicides I've dealt with around here involve domestic disputes between the rich folks of Long Island, or a shooting during a robbery. But your story is unusual because the two men involved in this incident clearly seem to know you, but you don't know either one of them."

"That's what makes it so creepy," I explained, "because I can't think of a single reason that these guys would be following me around. I've certainly done nothing notorious in my life, nor have I ever been to Germany. And obviously, whether or not these guys live here now, or in Germany, they were definitely shouting in German. That much I'm sure of."

"Well, we don't have much to go on. I would suggest you call your parents now, and after that we'll bring in a sketch artist and at least try to get an idea of what the shooter looks like. Use the phone on the desk and I'll go get the sketch artist. By the time you're done with the sketch artist, I should be able to fill you in on what we know."

I dialed my home phone number. It was a Wednesday and was approaching 4:30 so I knew there was a good chance my mother would be staring dinner and would be home. After three rings the phone was picked up.

"Hello."

"Hey, Boris." It was my brother, who was almost three years older than me.

"What's up?"

"Is Mom home? I assume Pa is not home from work yet."

"Yeah, he's not going to be home till later. He's playing tennis this evening. Mom's here. I'll get her for you."

My mother Helen got on the phone and greeted me warmly. In Russian, of course. My parents were originally from the Soviet Union and so we grew up speaking Russian at home, although as Boris and I got older we tended to answer in English, even as my parents spoke to us in Russian.

"Well Mom, the good news is I will be home tomorrow. I'll let you know a little bit later about my flight time. The bad news is I lost to Walter Redondo in the first round of the pre-qualifier."

"That's alright. You had a wonderful summer and I'm really quite proud of your performance."

I knew my father's opinion would not be totally the same. Even though he was always very supportive of my efforts, his stern Russian upbringing had deprived him of the ability to be patient. He expected us to work hard and be the best. Success was expected, failure was not an option. Consequently, if I performed well on the court, things were as they should be and I received minimal congratulations. If I performed poorly, it was time for more work and more focus. Fun was not always the ultimate goal.

"There's also something else I have to tell you. Now don't worry when I tell you this, Mom, because everything is just fine. But earlier today, when I was heading up to my hotel room, a man came up to me and wanted to tell me something. He acted very strangely and I didn't know him – yet he knew my name. He said something crazy, like I was going to become famous and powerful and he was going to be along for the ride."

"You have no idea who it was?"

"Nope, not a clue. But here's the thing. While this guy was talking to me in the hallway, another guy came up behind me and shouted at the crazy guy. Next thing I knew, these guys are having a shoot out and the crazy guy got killed. The other man intentionally shot him one more time after he was down to apparently make sure he was dead. Then he ran off, but not before he told me I was safe now."

I heard my mother gasp and then there was silence.

"Mom?"

"Oh, Erick, I am so thankful you are okay, but I am also so nervous and worried. Did the crazy man try to hurt you?"

"He claimed he would explain everything and then I would understand. But there wasn't much time and then he was shot. All I know is that both men were shouting in German and the one who was shot was named Gruber."

I sensed a slight hesitation before my mother spoke again.

"We can only thank God that you are alright. Are you in a safe place now?"

"Yes, Mom, I'm at the police station. They've asked me some questions and then I'm going to try to describe the shooter to the police sketch artist."

"You say the man who was shot was named Gruber? Are you sure? Could you have been mistaken?"

"No, Mom. I'm sure."

It was time for us to end our conversation. My mother told me to call home later to talk to my father. He was supposed to be home by 8:00, so hopefully I would be done at the police station by then. Overall, even though my mother was naturally very shaken by the incident, she was also very relieved that I was okay. We hung up and I got up to go look for Detective Jason.

I walked down the hallway and to the information desk.

"Where is Detective Jason? Could you tell him Erick Iskersky is ready for the sketch artist?"

The officer at the desk got on the phone and called Jason. "Detective Jason, Erick Iskersky is here at the desk and ready for the artist. Alright. I'll do that."

"Go down to the end of the hallway and look to the left. You'll see Detective Jason's office. He's in there with the artist."

I made my way down the hallway and spotted Detective Jason and a woman sitting in Jason's office.

"Erick, come on in. This is Officer Maggie Tannenbaum. She's going to draw the picture of the guy you saw based on your description. I've got some things to take care of, but I'll be back. Germany is several hours ahead of us time-wise, but hopefully I'll be able to get at least some preliminary information on Gruber. Assuming, of course, that he indeed lived in Germany."

With that Jason left his office and I walked in.

"Hello, Mrs. Tannenbaum."

"Miss," she replied. Maggie Tannenbaum looked like she was in her forties, although I must say she aged rather well. Even when she was sitting, I could see that she had a great figure. Obviously an eighteen year old male like myself could not resist a peek at her breasts, which were rather prominent, despite the fact that she wore a rather plain business top and knee length skirt. Her name tag was clipped on. Her hair was pinned back in a bun. I wondered to myself why she was a "Miss" and not a "Mrs".

"Let's get started," she said. "It's probably going to take a couple of hours, depending on what details you remember about the man you saw. Try to be as detail-oriented as possible and don't hesitate to make changes as we go along."

I started to think of what the man with the scar really looked like and described those details to Miss Tannenbaum. Obviously the scar across his right cheek had to be a prominent part of the drawing. But I also remembered his full head of hair, which was brown and parted on the left side. His face was fairly narrow and was well shaped and not all that unusual. His ears were above average in size, but by no means grotesque. Overall he was not a bad looking man and I had to guess that his age was in the early fifties.

The process I watched was rather amazing. With deft strokes of the pencil, and making constant adjustments to her drawing based on my comments, Miss Tannenbaum started to catch the essence of what the man with the scar looked like. It did take some time, but ultimately after about one-and-a-half hours the drawing was done to my satisfaction. I now had a picture in front of me that looked very much like the man who had shot Gruber.

"That's unbelievable Miss Tannenbaum!" I exclaimed. "That looks almost exactly like the guy with the scar. I really didn't get that many good looks at him, but I really think the image you drew matches my memory."

"I'm glad I could help out. With any luck this will give us a chance to identify who the shooter is and hopefully apprehend him."

Miss Tannenbaum picked up the phone and called the information desk to find out where Detective Jason was. After hanging up, she put away her drawing equipment and got up.

"Erick, it was nice meeting you, although I'm sure you would prefer not having to be at a police station."

"The pleasure was definitely all mine," I proclaimed, with probably more enthusiasm than I should have shown.

With that, Miss Tannenbaum left the room. Just as she was leaving, Detective Jason appeared at the doorway to the office. A final glance at Miss Tannenbaum from behind, as she walked away, confirmed my earlier thought – she definitely had a great figure. Something that Detective Jason must have noticed that I noticed.

"Uh, let's try to concentrate at the business in hand," he said with a grin breaking out. "After we're done here you can worry about the usual things guys your age think about."

"Oh, definitely," I replied, somewhat embarrassed that my leering was so obvious.

"Erick, I'm going to try to summarize what we know for you and kind of fill you in on what we're going to do. The first thing, of course, is to confirm that the drawing by Miss Tannenbaum looks like the man with the scar."

"It really does, Detective Jason. At least it looks like I remember what he looks like."

"Well good. We'll make copies, circulate it throughout all of the precincts, and make sure that security at the airports get copies in case he tries to fly out. We'll put out an APB on this character and hope that we luck out. Other than that there is not much more we can do about the shooter. I'm also going to send a copy of the drawing to our German counterparts to see if this guy was notorious enough to be in one of the files of the German police departments. You never know – he might have a criminal background that will enable the German officials to ID him for us. I also assume Germany has an organization similar to our FBI that can help us in trying to track this guy down."

Based on his comments, it was now clear that Jason knew that Gruber was German for sure. While he'd been talking, Jason had sat down and then he took a sip from the cup of coffee he had brought into the room with him. "Oh, do you drink coffee? Or you want something else to drink? I know it's been a long day."

"Nah, I'm fine. I'm just ready to get out of here."

"Okay, I think I have all of the information I need from you. I can tell you, from our preliminary investigation, who was shot back at the hotel. I'm going to have to wait until early tomorrow morning to get in touch with the proper authorities in German for more details about Gruber. The man who was shot was Gunter Gruber. We know that because he was staying at the Kennington, just like your team. We found his passport in the hotel safe assigned to his room. We know he entered the country in New York on July 6, so it sure looks like he would have been around when you were playing all those tournaments. Looks like it's certain that you weren't imagining seeing him in all those cities. Based on his passport, he was sixty years old and lived in Munich. Other than that, I won't know more until tomorrow at the earliest. I have your contact information and I'll get in touch when I have more to tell you."

Jason made a call to the information desk and then hung up. "Officer Corrigan is still on duty. I'll get him to give you a ride back to the Kennington."

Corrigan walked in shortly afterward and nodded in my direction. "Detective Jason here tells me it's time for you to go back to the hotel. You all set?"

"I sure am." I turned to Jason. "Detective Jason, thanks for all of your help. I don't know what the hell happened today but I sure hope that you'll be able to solve this puzzle. I guess I feel kind of lucky to be unharmed. Who knows what could have happened during the shootout?"

"Hey, don't thank me yet. We've only just begun our investigation. At least this didn't happen in the city – otherwise your case would probably get a lot less attention. They have so many murders to investigate, and they're stretched thin. Because of that a lot of cases are put on the back burner if there aren't any promising leads. Like I said, I'll be in touch."

I followed Corrigan down the hallway and out of the Fourth Precinct. It was approaching eight o'clock. I was getting really tired, but I was also hungry. I wasn't sure which I wanted more – sleep or food. It only took us a few minutes to get back to the Kennington because traffic was really light. I thanked Corrigan for the ride and wished him well in his career. He told me he'd look for my name in the newspapers if I ever got famous. I chuckled at that one and walked into the lobby after shutting the cruiser door.

The first thing I did was go to the lobby phone and call Bill McGowan. "Bill, this is Erick. I'm back from the police station. Everything seemed to go fairly smoothly."

"Did the police have any idea who the guy was that got shot?" asked Bill.

"They have a complete name – Gunter Gruber – and they know he lived in Germany. But other than that they don't have anything. They're going to check into it further and they are also circulating a drawing of the other guy. Hopefully he'll be spotted and get picked up. I don't imagine the odds are real great on that."

"It certainly wasn't the greatest way to end your summer, but at least you weren't hurt. I'm sure the police will do a good job. I've got your flight for tomorrow booked. You'll be leaving La Guardia Airport on a flight at 8:30 in the morning, connecting through Pittsburgh. You'll get into Toledo at 11:45."

"Sounds good. How do I get to the airport?"

"I've got a spot on the airport limo from the Kennington reserved for you. I guess now is as good a time as any to say goodbye, because a couple of the guys are still alive in the pre-qualifier and I'll be busy dealing with them in the morning."

I thanked Bill for all of his help during the summer and then headed up to my room on the fifth floor. When I got off the elevator and then turned down the hallway toward my room, I stopped dead in my tracks. I could see the blood stains on the floor where Gruber had been shot. Although it was obvious an attempt had been made to clean the carpet, I could still see the darkened areas upon which Gruber must have bled. Unfortunately, I was jolted back to the reality of the early part of my day and I realized that I was still somewhat shaken by what had transpired in that hallway.

I got to my room after gingerly stepping around the darkened stains. I entered my room and noticed that it was after eight o'clock. Chances were pretty good my father was home by now, so I decided to give him a call. On the first ring, my father answered the phone.

"Hello."

"Hello, Pa. I'm back in my room so I thought I'd give you a call. How was your tennis?"

"Never mind my tennis. How are you doing? Mom, of course, told me what happened. Are you sure you're alright?"

I was a little surprised about how worried my father sounded. I expected his usual stoic Russian demeanor. Instead it was obvious that he was really concerned and it made me feel good. My father was not always that great about openly expressing his feelings.

"I'm really okay. Nothing happened to me physically, and I think I've recovered fairly well. The biggest problem I'm having is figuring out why these two guys involved in the shooting were, at least from what I can gather, following me around this summer. I never told you and Mom about it because I figured I was imagining it all."

My father let out an audible sigh. "We're just so thankful that nothing happened to you. That of course is all we ever want as parents. We want to do all we can to protect you and shield you from the realities of the world, but it can't always be done. Do the police have any leads or ideas?"

"I think we'll hear more from Detective Jason in the next day or two. All they know now is what I've told them and who was shot. The man who got killed was a man named Gunter Gruber, from Germany. They got that from his passport."

I proceeded to fill my father in with all of the information I had about the two men and everything that had happened during the summer. He sounded very edgy, on the one hand, but very relieved and happy on the other hand. I imagine it would be quite a shock to learn that your son was involved in some mysterious shooting and that two men had seemingly been following him around for a number of weeks.

For now, I had nothing more to tell him, and he had nothing more to tell me. We would both have to wait for the police to do their thing and hopefully ascertain what Gunter Gruber and the man with the scar were all about. Personally I don't know how much confidence I had in Detective Jason. He seemed to be a capable detective, at least based on my interaction with him. But I wasn't sure he had to deal with too many murder cases, so I wasn't all that sure about his level of experience.

I started packing for my trip home tomorrow and really was looking forward to taking a break from my tennis and seeing my family. Meanwhile, because some difficulties had developed over my college decision process, it was likely I would have to take the first semester off until I headed to Trinity University. Mainly, I had signed a National Letter of Intent to attend the University of Michigan in April and then changed my mind. Because Michigan wouldn't release me from the Letter, I would have to sit out the first semester until I could start attending Trinity. It looked like my family time at home would be a bit longer than I had originally anticipated.

CHAPTER 3

The next day I got up nice and early to catch the airport limo to La Guardia. I can't say I slept very well. I was anxious and uneasy. The events of yesterday had really come back to haunt me. When I did sleep, it was fitfully. My dreams were bizarre and every time I woke up I felt like I had just experienced whatever I dreamed, for real. Gruber's dead eyes kept staring at me, yet his face kept changing into various grotesque shapes. Out of his unmoving lips came words of familiarity. "You are my friend. Together we will be great. Erick, won't you come by and visit me?" At the same time, the man with the scar kept chasing me. But all I could see was his scar. The only way I knew it was him was because of the exaggerated limp. He could never catch me, but he kept waving a gun and insisted he would save me. All in all I was thrilled to get on the limo.

My flight left La Guardia on time and I was on my way home. I reflected on my college situation and decided it wasn't all bad. I would have four months to recuperate, play some tournaments, and get ready for my freshman year in college. Trinity University was one of the top tennis programs in the nation and was also a good school academically. Plus the weather was going to be a lot better than we would have in Toledo. I felt certain that I would enjoy my college experience.

I also reflected about how lucky I was to be in the situation I was in. In terms of my lifestyle, I was very fortunate. My father was a family physician and made a very good living. We lived in Rossford, a suburb of Toledo, on the muddy Maumee River. I was brought up strictly, but fairly. Boris and I pretty much got what we wanted and my parents had taken care of the expenses of my tennis and Boris' music. Boris was a very talented cellist and had been studying pre-med at Marquette University for the past three years. For his fourth year of studies he was going to go to Germany. His chances of getting into medical school were going to be a lot better overseas, so it made sense for him to finish up his undergraduate studies in Germany. In fact, he was going to be leaving for Germany by the end of September.

My mother no longer had to work. When my parents first arrived in the United States in New York City, they were struggling mightily to get by. At that time there were very few positions available for foreign medical personnel, especially young doctors. Consequently my father was doing everything he could to find work at any hospital in the New York City area that was short of staff. To help make ends meet, my mother worked as a dishwasher in the delis that were willing to hire immigrant labor. It did not help that when they first arrived in America they barely spoke any English.

There was no doubt I was lucky I wasn't living under the strong armed communist government of the Soviet Union. My parents were born during the beginning stages of what would become the Soviet Empire, my father Vladimir in 1920, my mother Helen in 1925. They are of Russian origin, even though they lived in Kiev, which is part of the Ukraine. Kiev is one of the largest cities in the Soviet Union and is located on the Dnepr River. The Soviet government of the Ukraine was formed in December of 1917, and by February of 1918, Kiev was declared as the capital of the Soviet Ukraine. My parents met while Vladimir was studying pre-med at the University of Kiev and Helen was in high school. Pa was twenty-one and Mom was sixteen. Two years later they were married in 1943. The circumstances of their escape from the Soviet Union were truly remarkable and only with the grace of God was it possible that they ended up surviving World War II. It was what my parents went through that made me feel so fortunate to be an American and have the life that I have.

By 1939 in the Soviet Union, the standard of living had somewhat improved over the last ten years, although by Western standards life was still grim. At least there was no more rationing of food, and there was food in the shops as well as more jobs available in the factories. Joseph Stalin, the leader of Russia, entered into a neutrality pact with Adolph Hitler, the leader of Germany, but this was done mainly to placate Germany while Russia built up its armed forces. Stalin fully expected that Germany would eventually invade the Soviet Union. This was the atmosphere my parents faced as they tried to forge some sort of existence in their early lives.

It turned out that Stalin was right, although he didn't believe it would happen so fast. On June 22, 1941, Germany attacked the Soviet Union while my father was studying in medical school and my mother was not too far away from finishing high school. Germany planned to use over 3 million men, 625,000 horses, 600,000 motor vehicles and 3,600 armored vehicles in the attack. It was to be a massive undertaking, especially since the Soviet Union covered an area of over 8.5 million square miles, a million square miles more than the United States and China put together.

My parents faced the terror of war well before my father finished medical school. The German army was making swift progress and was destroying the Russian army. By the end of August, the Germans were within ninety miles of Kiev. The Russian army was in disarray. By the end of September, the Russians had abandoned the city of Kiev and the Germans had captured 650,000 prisoners. Life would no longer be normal for my parents.

They now were living in constant fear for their lives. Water had become scarce. Food was being rationed, power was out in much of the city, and conditions were becoming unsanitary. The German army left thousands of soldiers in the area of Kiev, but for the most part left the civilian population alone. Most of the army was now headed northeast in a race to Moscow. Because the house where my father lived was destroyed in the fighting, my parents were now living in an apartment occupied by nine people – my father, my mother, my father's parent's, my mother's parents, my father's brother, and my mother's brother and wife. Needless to say life was bleak. Everyday was spent foraging for food and water, hoping the electricity would return, and figuring out ways to productively utilize time.

Ironically, this also gave my parents their first taste of freedom from the communist regime of the Soviet Union. Under Stalin the government controlled everything. Where you worked, where you lived, how much food you received, when you could go out in public, and with whom you could fraternize. Basically the citizens of Russia had no rights to speak of, and if citizens chose to speak out against the government they were either imprisoned or simply executed. The people of the Soviet Union lived miserable lives and were living in constant fear. Family meant everything, because other than that there was no joy.

Then after the invasion by the Germans, my parents actually had some freedom. Germans were placed in positions of power in the local government and were in charge of administering the mechanics of running Kiev. Gradually the electricity was restored and water and food became more plentiful. My father returned to medical school and my mother returned to high school. For the most part life was slowly returning to normal, but without the horrible yoke of the Soviet regime. The Germans didn't bother those Russian citizens who were cooperative and submissive. By many, the Germans were almost seen as saviors. The dreaded life under Stalin was over, at least for the time being.

Of course life was still not easy. All nine family members continued to live in the same small apartment. My mother's parents, Daniel and Sofia, were not able to find work because the factory in which they both worked had been destroyed by the Russian army. In fact the Russian army destroyed as many large buildings as they could in Kiev before they fled. This was done so the Germans would not be able to utilize the city's infrastructure for their own good. My mother's Uncle Dmitri tried to eek out an existence as a ballet teacher at the Kiev School of Ballet, but naturally during a war there was little emphasis on cultural activities. My mother's Aunt Marika washed dishes whenever she could at a local restaurant. My father's parents, Mikhail and Svetlana had fairly good jobs. Mikhail was a family physician, which had inspired my father to go to medical school.

Svetlana was an elementary school teacher. Ivan, my father's younger brother was in his last year of high school. This family unit of nine became very close and their love for one another greatly helped them get through the misery of war and life in the Soviet Union.

Meanwhile, the war was not going well for the Soviet Union. By October 1941 the German army was poised to take Moscow, which was located approximately in the center of Russia. The Germans were also making great progress in the Caucasus located in the south, and were besieging the city of Leningrad in the north. Interestingly it took Napoleon only two months to get to Moscow when France invaded Russia, but took the Germans five months to do so. Of course the German army was five times larger than Napoleon's and was fighting on several fronts at once, whereas Napoleon only faced one battle on his way to Moscow and was not fighting on several fronts.

By November 7 the Germans were within fifteen miles of Moscow and the German offensive looked like it would break the backs of the Russians. But then there was a dramatic reversal of fortunes for three reasons. Even though the Russian army was being defeated in every encounter with the Germans in the vicinity of Moscow and was suffering huge casualties, the Russian commanders were able to find replacement soldiers and keep the war going. In addition, the Germans were finding it increasingly difficult to supply the troops with food and armaments because of the great distance from which these supplies had to come. And finally, the weather turned nasty. It became brutally cold and started to snow furiously. By December, temperatures had fallen to zero and as many as 100,000 German troops suffered from frostbite in the month of December alone. The tide started to turn and the Germans would never get closer than fifteen miles to Moscow.

Because the Germans were now forced to dig in and defend their positions, Stalin decided it was time for the Russians to mount a counteroffensive against the Germans on all three fronts – center, north, and south. By this time the cold had taken its toll on the German soldiers who lacked warm clothing. The German air force also had great difficulty flying in the freezing weather and could not adequately supply the army with air attacks. The Russian army was also better equipped to fight in the extreme conditions and supplies for the Russian army were, of course, much closer to the fronts.

By May 1942, the Germans had staved off the Russian offensive and the Russian army had once again suffered huge casualties. But the Germans had failed to capture either Moscow or Leningrad. The Germans had also suffered tremendous casualties. Between November 1941 and May 1942, the Germans had lost 900,000 soldiers killed, missing, or wounded, but had only had replacements of 450,000 soldiers. This was a devastating blow to Hitler's war machine.

Despite logistical problems and increased difficulties with troop deployment, Hitler ordered another offensive attack, once again with the aim of capturing Moscow and Leningrad. The goal was to complete this strategy well before the winter of 1943 set in. Despite huge losses, the Russians still had plenty of manpower. Though the Germans were better soldiers, the Russians fought fiercely with greater confidence than they had exhibited earlier in the war. The Russians fought out of hatred of the Germans, fear of being shot by their commanders if they refused orders and genuine patriotism. The Germans fought through professional pride, trust in their leaders, and a belief that the great Hitler would lead them to ultimate victory.

During this time period of vicious fighting to the east, north, and south of Kiev, life for my parents had become a bit more predictable, if nothing else. My father was finishing up medical school, my mother finished high school, and as Kiev was slowly being re-built, my mother's parents were able to find jobs in a factory once again. My parents also got engaged and were looking forward to their marriage, which they planned for September 1943. Life was certainly still miserable and Kiev was still an occupied city. News from the war fronts was not reliable, frequently censored by the Germans. The citizens of Kiev were clearly under the impression that the Germans were in the process of conquering Russia.

I remember vividly how emotional my father would get when he would discuss this memorable and frightful period of their lives. "Boris and Erick," he would say, "do you realize that, despite all of our troubles, we never gave up hope? But our hope was not that Russia would win the war. Our hope was that we would someday be able to escape the horrible chains of communism. Life under a communist regime was like no life at all. If not for my love of your mother and the rest of my family, there would have been no life at all. It was right before we got married that your mother and I decided we would do anything we could to escape from our life in the Soviet Union."

It was at that point that they made the distasteful decision to side with the Germans, mainly because they believed that the Germans were winning the war and would eventually become the rulers of the Soviet Union. There were opportunities to have contact with German soldiers who were still stationed in Kiev and my father, at great risk to his life, would surreptitiously engage in conversations with some of the officers in command. He indicated his willingness to help the Germans as a medic when he completed his residency at one of the hospitals in Kiev. Of course, had Russian officials discovered my father's treasonous activities, he would have been instantly executed. Such was my parents hatred of communism.

Because of my father's activities, the entire household in the small apartment was living on pins and needles. They started to formulate a plan. At some point my father would join the German army as a medic. If the Germans were victorious, the family would all stay in Kiev. Hopefully their loyalty to the Germans would be rewarded and their lives would improve without the terror of communism. If the Germans started to lose the war, the family would retreat with the Germans back to Germany and start life anew.

"Trust me," my father told me once, "it was a situation that we feared either way. Staying loyal to the Russians meant that we would never experience any sort of freedom, which I can't even imagine now that I have lived a life of freedom in America. But siding with the Germans meant we were entering the world of the unknown and risking everything that we had. We may not have had much, but at least we had life. I was also so very fearful that I would somehow lose your mother – once I joined the German army, who knew what would happen."

And now, as the winter of 1942/1943 approached, the Germans were in a precarious position, although most of the generals still believed they would be able to soon crush the Russians. What the Germans didn't realize was that the Russians were building up huge manpower reserves to replace the hundreds of thousands of men who had been lost. Russia had a huge population and consequently by the summer of 1942 the Russian army was once again at full strength and poised to strike. The Germans had truly bit off more than their available manpower could chew. The unnecessary attack on Stalingrad, Hitler's refusal to listen to the advice of his generals, the over-extended supply lines, the need for security in the rear areas of the German army, and the failure of the German industrial machine to replace vehicle losses put the German army in a dangerous situation.

The Russians counter-attacked in November of 1942 with over one million men, 900 tanks, 12,000 artillery pieces and 1,200 aircraft. The Russians slowly but surely started to encircle the mighty Sixth Army of the German military machine, while cutting off the supply lines from the west. Hitler refused to allow the Sixth Army to retreat and as the winter grew colder and colder, the Germans were getting into deeper and deeper trouble.

By February of 1943, as my father neared graduation from medical school, the Battle of Stalingrad was coming to an end and the invasion of Russia had reached a real turning point. This battle really destroyed and wrecked the dominant fighting force of the German army in Russia. The German soldiers could not overcome the weather, the starvation, and the vast number of Russian soldiers. In that battle alone the Germans lost 120,000 men and another 90,000 spent years in Russian prisons. Additional losses of 874,000 dead had been incurred since the beginning of the invasion against Russia. It was now apparent that the Russian army was capable of fighting back the Germans and that Russia was much too vast a country to successfully invade.

Now, in August of 1943, as my parents prepared for their September wedding and the family entourage continued to try to survive as best they could, the Russian army had started to try to take back the Ukraine, where Kiev was located. My parents and their families now had to decide once and for all what they were going to do if the Russians came in and re-captured Kiev.

"You know, this was such a difficult choice," my father would tell Boris and me when he would recount our family history. "Your mother and I were just about ready to be married and my residency was going well at the hospital. And now, potentially, this was all going to come to an end if we decided to flee from communism. After a lot of consultation with all of our family members, all nine of us in the apartment agreed to escape from Russia. Making that decision was dangerous, but so was staying. If any-one ever found out that we were thinking of abandoning Russia in favor of Germany, and reported us to the authorities, we would all be executed. Ultimately, our hatred of communism overcame our fear of death."

My parents were married on September 19, 1943. From all accounts the wedding was a joyous success and under the circumstances was memo-rable for not being interrupted by the sound of fighting or by news of the war. Many distant relatives and friends attended the wedding and in their hearts my parents knew that they might never see these people again. Nothing really changed for anyone in the small apartment. Life continued as it had for the past couple of years, but now my parents were husband and wife.

The Russians continued to counter-attack and were getting closer and closer to Kiev. As the Germans retreated they practiced the in-famous scorched earth policy. Basically this meant that the Germans destroyed everything that could be of value to the advancing Russians. That included destroying buildings, roads, and crops. In early November the Germans evacuated Kiev, and for my parents life took a sudden di-sastrous turn.

Because the Russians basically drafted anyone old enough to be in the military as soon as they recovered an area of Russia, the German army imprisoned all of the young men they could gather as they retreated in order to keep these men out of the Russian army. My parent's plan to escape to Germany was no longer an option. The Germans simply stormed into my parent's apartment late one night and forcibly removed my father and his brother Ivan, while the rest of the family cowered in fear.

My mother always recalled that this was the most frightful night of her life. "Suddenly without any warning, our door was crashed open and several German soldiers charged into our apartment. We had time to do nothing. They simply pushed all of the women and older men aside and grabbed your father and Ivan. They tried desperately to resist but, of course, were greatly outnumbered and had no weapons. Within seconds they were gone. We were all in shock and had no idea what would become of your father and Ivan, or what would become of us."

Now for my father, Vladimir and his brother, Ivan, life became a living hell. The Germans imprisoned thousands of Russians in Kiev and started the march westward back towards Germany. Although Hitler insisted that the German troops not budge, the German infantry was outnumbered at this point by two million to 350,000. The Russians also had 8,000 tanks compared to 700 operational German tanks. The German retreat was inevitable and was slow but steady.

The distance from Kiev to Berlin, Germany was nearly 800 miles and now these Russian prisoners were being forced to march this distance with little food or water. They were treated inhumanely, to say the least. Those who could not keep up were simply left to die when they could no longer walk, or shot. Winter was also approaching and the weather was getting brutally cold. The Germans knew that a large percentage of the Russians would never survive the march to Berlin, but those who did would be forced to work in the labor camps in an attempt to keep the German war machine sputtering along. Consequently it was vital to get as many of the Russians as possible to Berlin.

The 800 mile march started to take its toll on my father and Ivan, but my father seemed to be physically stronger and was surviving the elements much better than Ivan. He was also treated somewhat better than the rest of the men when it was discovered that he was a doctor in training. Sometimes that meant he received a bit more food or water, because the Germans needed men with medical training to tend to their wounded. Tragically, Ivan's health started to fade in February as the human convoy of Russians and Germans was approaching the Russian/ Polish border. My father tried in vain to share some of his food and water with Ivan but was not allowed to do so by the German guards.

I remember my father tearfully telling my mother about his futile efforts. "Here was this young nineteen year old man, and really just a boy, who had once been so full of life. He was such a wonderful brother and looked up to me. And I could do nothing. The pain of that winter will never go away, no matter how many years have gone by. Why couldn't I have done something? Why did I never get to see Ivan grow up to be a man? All I could do was cry everyday and pray that I would survive the horrific march. During that winter I prayed everyday that I would see you again and that I would somehow save Ivan."

But it wasn't to be. As Ivan became weaker and weaker, and sicker and sicker, he had to support himself on my father merely to take each step. This also weakened my father and slowed them down. Everything came to an abrupt end when one of the Germans shot Ivan as he was being held by my father. My father had nightmares for years, of the blood gushing from Ivan's head wound, of the deep snow turning bright crimson, of Ivan's collapsing body and his last breath. Yet, because his lust for life and for seeing my mother was so strong, he had to simply leave Ivan's body lying there in a pool of blood, and march on. As if nothing had happened.

The dreaded 800 mile trek ended in late March. Of the 85,000 prisoners who had started the long crawl from Kiev to Berlin, 40,000 survived. My father survived and had actually been ordered to join the German army as a medic. Refusal to do so would of course mean certain death.

Thus, the plan to escape to Germany was quite a failure. Out of my nine ancestors who planned to escape to Germany, only one had made it – my father, and he was in Germany taken by brute force. Ivan, who would have been my uncle, was tragically dead. My mother's and father's families were now stuck in Kiev. By April of 1944, the Russians had actually re-captured all of the Ukraine and had reached what was once the Russian/Polish border. To escape to Germany, my ancestors would now have to find a way to cover the 800 miles to Germany. There would be virtually no food available on the trip, conditions in Germany were sure to be disastrous as the Russians continued to advance on Germany, and they had no idea where my father was. In addition, on June 6, 1944 the Allies landed in Normandy, and Germany would now have to fight on another front. Things were bound to get worse.

CHAPTER 4

I snapped to when I heard the voice of the pilot. "Ladies and gentlemen, we are now preparing to land at the Pittsburgh International Airport. Please make sure your seat belts are buckled and your seat is in the upright position. We should be landing in about ten minutes."

I was back to the present moment, at least temporarily forgetting about the travails that my parents had experienced in getting to America. I realized how much I missed my family and how glad I was to be coming back to Toledo, at least for the short term. It wouldn't be long before I got to eat some home cooking for a change and take a bit of a break from my tennis.

We landed without incident and I disembarked from the plane. I had about an hour layover before my flight to Toledo so I headed to a snack bar located in the terminal and grabbed a hot dog and a Coke. After gulping down my food I checked the monitor in the terminal hallway to see what gate I needed to go to in order to board my flight to Toledo. It worked out that my next flight was in the same terminal so I didn't have to go very far to get to gate number four, where flight number 7641 was taking off for Toledo at 10:45. I grabbed a seat in the waiting area and read the newspaper I had purchased at the gift shop.

My mind started to drift once again. I thought about how difficult it must have been for my mother when she was suddenly alone in Kiev, without my father. Of course, there was still the support of her family to help through the crisis they were all experiencing, but she had only been married for a very short time and the love of her life was torn away from her by the Germans.

The winter of 1945 arrived and my mother had heard nothing from my father. It had been over a year since my father and Ivan had been kidnapped. Then, a miracle!. A letter arrived in the mail. My father was alive!

"My dearest Helen. It is so hard to believe, but I am alive and well, at least as well as I can be. I am a medic in the German army and had been stationed in Poland, but now that the German army is being pushed back I have been sent to Berlin where I help tend to the sick and wounded who have been brought from the eastern front. I am doing my best to try to appear loyal to the Germans so that I have a better chance of being treated well. Because of my cooperation I was permitted to start writing to you. Hopefully my cooperation will also make it easier for when you arrive in Germany. I know that it will be so very risky for you and the family to travel here, but I certainly can't live without you. If you decide you are not able to come to Germany, let me know and I will do everything I can to make it back to Kiev. Ivan died a horrible death on our way to Germany. He was brutally shot by a German guard. I still remember the guard's name – Colonel Joseph Erdmeister. He is such a cruel man. I wish there was something I could do to him because he is stationed in Berlin with me and I occasionally see him at the local tavern near the army base. He has no idea that I am Ivan's brother. But enough about me. I miss you so very much and love you more than life itself. Please be careful and safe. I pray for your safe arrival. Love, Vladimir."

Years later, my mother showed me that letter. Although the ink had faded somewhat by the time I saw the letter, it was a real testament to the strength of love and hope and resolve. Whenever something happened to me that was unlucky, or unfair, or unpleasant, I would think about the letter and realize that it was miraculous that my parents were able to re-unite. Without that miracle, I would never have been around to experience the joy and love I shared with my parents.

After my father's letter arrived, my mother's family decided it was time to make their escape to Germany. Several more letters arrived before they began their escape that described where my father lived in Berlin and how they would re-unite in the German city. It would not be easy. They had to figure out a way to traverse the 800 miles to Germany through war torn Russia and Poland. Now that the Russians were once again in control of their country, they would be very suspicious of any travelers heading in a westward direction. Officials of the communist controlled government were fully aware that the Russian people were patriotic, but they were also aware that the average Russian citizen detested the torture of living under the Stalinist regime. If my mother's family was suspected of trying to escape from Russia, death would be instantaneous.

They decided to begin their trip in the beginning of April, when the weather would start getting warmer. They would head west to the city of Lvov, which was about 300 miles away. This part of the trip they could go by train. By now the railroad tracks had been repaired and travel had been restored to near normal. If confronted by communist officials they would assert that the trip was a visit to relatives. Luckily, that part of the story could be true because my mother's Uncle Dmitri had a distant cousin who lived near the city of Lvov. After scraping together all of the money that was in their possession and packing as if they were going on a short trip so as to not arouse suspicion, my mother's family boarded the train in Kiev. Their trip was nerve wracking. Although they had no concrete reason to believe anyone knew what they were planning, every time someone in a uniform, be it conductor or soldier, walked by them on the train, my mother's family held their collective breaths. Fortunately the trip ended uneventfully and they made their way to Dmitri's cousin's house.

Now the tricky part of the trip was to begin. Their next step was to get to Krakow, Poland, located about 150 miles away. There was no train available. Poland had not yet been rebuilt, however the Russians were now in control of the country and my mother's family would have to find a way to escape detection. If the Russian communists confronted my mother's family in Poland there would be real trouble. There could be no logical explanation for why they would be traveling in Poland and so it was of the utmost importance that they avoid any contact with any Russian soldiers or officials. Consequently the decision was made to travel by night and to avoid the roads as much as possible. As a guide, they used an old compass and continued their journey northwest.

Luckily the weather stayed warm during the day and not too cool at night when they walked. During the day they slept in any wooded areas they could find, or if near a river, along the bank of the river. Progress was slow because Mikhail, my mother's father-in-law was not in good health and he had to go slowly, with many breaks. They averaged around ten miles per night. If it was cloudy or rainy, their progress was even slower. Food was almost non-existent. Usually they ate bread that they purchased in small towns that they passed through on their journey. Frequently they had to drink water from the rivers they walked along. Several times they saw Russian soldiers in the distance, but luckily they were never spotted. They crossed the Russian/Polish border with no problem because there had yet to be a re-establishment of Poland as a country and only the main roads were being patrolled by the Russian army. By the middle of April, they reached Krakow. Now they had to travel another 350 miles to reach Berlin.

This last part of the trip turned out to be absolutely treacherous. Fighting now raged everywhere as the Russians continued to push the Germans back towards Germany through Poland. Food was very hard to come by. Water, when it could be found, was not always clean. But my mother's family persisted and crawled ever so slowly towards Berlin.

By staying away from the roads, this group of freedom seekers avoided most of the skirmishes that were going on all around them. However, once in awhile they would encounter an actual battle, and each time they would huddle together and pray – pray that God would somehow see them through this horrible war and deliver them safely to Germany.

Luckily, the soldiers involved in the intense fighting had little time to engage with the civilians they came across during the moments of shooting, and running, and shooting again. The Germans desperately out-manned and lacking the necessary firepower. The Russians, with hugely superior numbers, simply overwhelming the Germans with sheer mass humanity. Thousands were dying, but there were so many thousands that the Germans did not stand much of a chance.

Unfortunately, Mikhail's health continued to worsen. Even though he was only in his mid fifties, the journey across Russia and Poland with little food and water had begun to really take its toll. He contracted what was most likely pneumonia and slowly but surely became weaker and weaker. Now his health became a real issue, because my mother's family could not risk the time or energy to look for a doctor, nor was it likely that a doctor could have helped much at this point. Poland was over-run and in ruins. The Germans destroyed the countryside as they fled and the Russians used up any resources they came across for their own benefit. Hospitals were full with the wounded and dying, and conditions in these hospitals were abhorrent. Many died from infections or simply because medicine was not available for many illnesses, that if treated, would not have been deadly. Under these circumstances, a dreaded decision had to be made.

"Can you imagine what it is like to have to sentence a loved one to death?" my mother once asked me when we were discussing her horrible memories of the war. "Mikhail was dying. There was no doubt about it. If we stopped, it would have been likely that we never would have made it to Germany. We might have been caught behind the Soviet lines and then, for sure, we would never be able to rendezvous with your father. We had heard, from many of the Polish peasants we encountered in the rural areas, that the Americans and British were attacking Germany from the west and were basically in a race with the Russians to occupy as much of Germany as possible. So we had to make the decision to leave Mikhail. We simply left him, sitting in a tavern in a small village. The village was partially destroyed and had little signs of life. That was the last we ever saw of Mikhail. We could not stop crying as we slowly trudged away from the village, abandoning Mikhail so we could live."

The anguish in my mother's voice was palpable when she told that story. While it was true that Mikhail insisted that they leave him, my mother's family could never forgive themselves for the action they took. Yet it really was the only thing they could do. A frail, dying man, sitting in a chair, waving goodbye and praying for their good fortune, while knowing he would never realize his own dream of experiencing freedom. The ultimate tragedy. A tragedy that could not be erased, even by time.

Once they had left Mikhail, progress on foot became quicker. Even though they were hungry, and tired, and depressed, they kept going. The thought of reaching Germany and seeing my father drove them. Their thirst for a new life, a life without the constant menacing hand of the Soviet government in their lives, was all they had to motivate each other. They prodded each other, encouraged each other, did everything they could to try to keep their spirits up. They tried to convince themselves that Mikhail's death would not be in vain.

By early May Hitler was dead, after committing suicide in his fortified bunker. His mistress turned wife had also committed suicide. The Germans were just about done. The Russians had reached Berlin from the east. The Americans and British had reached Berlin from the west. There was chaos in the streets of Berlin. The Russian soldiers were cruel and unyielding as they exacted revenge on members of the German army and even the civilian population. For the Russians, victory had to be unequivocal and absolute.

Germany's official military surrender took place on May 9, 1945, but this didn't stop the Russian forces from continuing their punishing forays into areas formerly occupied by the Germans. The Russians started to take control of Poland and Czechoslovakia, and also attempted to set up a provisional government in Austria. They even slaughtered thousands of Russians who had been prisoners in Germany, simply because the Soviet government viewed then as traitors who chose to be captured and remain in Germany, rather than commit suicide. This really was an attempt to cleanse the population of any Russians who were viewed as less than loyal to the Soviet regime. My parents and their family members were now in grave danger. If captured by the Soviets, they were sure to be executed as traitors to the great Soviet communist empire.

Unfortunately, my mother's family wasn't sure what to expect as they got closer and closer to Berlin. They had very little information about what was going on in Berlin. It was quite apparent to them, however, that the Soviets were now firmly in control of Germany. They saw very few German soldiers as they stealthily made their way through the countryside. On the other hand, they saw thousands upon thousands of people being marched eastward by the Soviet troops. These were clearly Russian civilians and former soldiers who were now being treated as enemies of the state. My mother's family was getting ever so close to the final objective – get to Berlin and find my father. Just getting to Berlin itself seemed like an impossibility at this point. Even if they got to Berlin, was there any real chance my father would be at the address from which he had written his last letter?

"It was amazing. We were finally no more than ten miles from Berlin. We could see the skyline of downtown and the smoke rising from the rubble of the suburbs as we got closer and closer," my mother would recall later. "We literally were moving from building to building. Chaos was everywhere. People were running all over the streets. Some were running away from Soviet soldiers; some were being grabbed by Soviet soldiers; and some were being shot by Soviet soldiers."

What happened next was truly a miracle. Without, what my mother insists was divine intervention, she has always believed there would have been a painful and deadly end to the journey from Russia. Even with divine intervention, there would be more tragedy. Apparently divine intervention could go only so far.

As my mother's family was walking down, what once was, a vibrant and crowded thoroughfare of Berlin, they spotted a tank. The tank was in the middle of the street. Roadblocks were set up on either side of the tank. The soldiers were spread out across the street. At least a hundred of them. All dressed in drab olive uniforms, wearing drab olive helmets. The uniforms were not totally familiar to my mother's entourage, although most of the Russian soldiers they saw during their journey wore green looking uniforms. This was the moment of truth. They were hugging the buildings as they made their way down the sidewalk, afraid to step away from the protection of the walls. It felt safer that way. What should they do? If the soldiers were Russian and spotted them, all was lost. If they were not Russian, then there was hope.

Without warning, they heard a loud roar from behind them. Several tanks were rumbling down the center of the street. Hundreds of soldiers were marching behind the tanks. Soldiers dressed in green. In front of the tanks ran a mass of people, almost looking like a herd of cows being driven to slaughter. People with fear in their faces. Panic filled the air. The flags mounted atop the turrets of the tank were red, with a sickle and a star in the upper left hand corner. It was the Soviet flag.

Suddenly the soldiers started to run past the tanks and started to fire in the direction of the fleeing and desperate civilians. My mother's family immediately started to run, down the street toward the one tank, sitting at the other end of the street. They were either headed into a trap, or they were headed to possible freedom. Thunderous waves of sound started to echo off the buildings lining the streets as the number of shots being fired increased dramatically. The soldiers were gaining on the fleeing crowd that was dashing furiously as one to avoid capture. The crowd started to engulf members of my mother's family, who were tired and weary and not able to run all that fast.

Bodies started to fall as people were hit by the shots fired by the Russian soldiers. People screamed loudly, screaming almost more because of the realization that their quest for freedom was ending than because of their injuries. Somehow my mother's family stayed fairly close together, and were able to continue running away from the soldiers without being shot.

Then absolute and utter chaos and desperation broke out. Shots were fired from the direction in which the crowd was stampeding toward the solitary tank. But these shots were different. They were being fired in the air, not at the fleeing mob. In a matter of seconds, those who recognized that these new shots were not intended to hit them, continued to run forward. Those who didn't recognize the nature of the shots being fired, froze and stopped.

The solitary tank lurched forward. Two jeeps came around from behind the tank and slowly accelerated towards the sea of people. The flags mounted on the jeeps had red and white stripes, with white stars mounted on a blue, square background in the upper left hand corner of the flag. It was the American flag! My mother's family was no more than a hundred feet from freedom.

As the American soldiers started forward to greet the hysterical and frenzied civilians trying to escape the Russians, the Russian soldiers started to slow down their advance, but had overtaken many in the crowd. The soldiers started to pull away as many of the civilians as they could before the freedom seekers could reach the Americans' position. At this moment there was real potential that fighting would break out between the American and Russian soldiers. Tension was high, danger was real, and for my mother's family, freedom and life hung in the balance.

Sofia and Daniel, my mother's parents, clung to each other as they pushed their way past the approaching American jeeps. Dmitri and Marika, my mother's uncle and aunt, also managed to cross over to the end of the street occupied by the Americans. My mother had a fairly firm grasp on Svetlana, my father's mother, but then the unthinkable happened – from nowhere a Russian soldier grabbed Svetlana from behind. She struggled. My mother instinctively pulled back as hard as she could. The soldier swung the butt of his rifle at my mother's head. He struck only a glancing blow, but it was enough to knock my mother off balance. She lost her grip and the soldier pulled a screaming Svetlana away from my mother. Almost instantly Svetlana and the soldier disappeared back into the mass of bodies, of Russian soldiers and panicking civilians, people who would never taste the sheer joy of freedom. My mother never saw Svetlana again.

Suddenly my daydreaming was interrupted. "Flight 7641, now boarding at gate four. Please have your boarding pass ready to show to the boarding agent. We will board first class passengers and those needing assistance first."

With that announcement, I realized I was going to see my family quite soon. Walking our dog, sleeping in my own bed, riding my bike, hanging out with friends. It was going to be fun. Eating at Tony Packo's, a place made famous by Klinger from the television hit M.A.S.H. Eating at Schmucker's, a great little diner located near the University of Toledo. Play a little tennis with one of my true friends, Jim Davis, affectionately known as J.D. He had quite a bit to do with my success in tennis. All of these things I looked forward to greatly. The freedom to do what I wanted to do. It's amazing I took that for granted, when doing such simple and fun things wouldn't have been possible without the brave and amazing journey my parents had taken over thirty years before.

After a few minutes I was on board the jetliner for the final leg of my trip home. The flight to Toledo was going to be a little bit under an hour. The weather was sunny and warm, so I was pleased that there would be no weather delays of any kind. We took off without incident and ascended quickly into the bright and blue horizon. I took out the newspaper I'd carried onto the plane with me to double check the baseball standings. My beloved Baltimore Orioles were in second place in the American League East Division, but were only four games over five hundred at 64-60. They were twelve games behind the first place Yankees. It didn't look like there was going to be any play-off appearance this year. The draw for The US Open was announced. It would start on Monday. Connors was seeded first, Borg was seeded second, Vilas was seeded third, and Panatta was seeded fourth. After Connors, the highest American seed was Arthur Ashe, seeded seventh. By changing the surface of the US Open from grass to har-tru in 1975, to supposedly keep up with the world trend to go to a slower game with more rallies, the United States Tennis Association had compromised its integrity, in the views of many. Americans tended to do better on faster surfaces, so in order to satisfy world opinion the U.S.T.A. had lowered the potential for success by American players in their own national championship.

I looked out the window at the landscape below. We were over thirty thousand feet above earth, yet I could swear I saw what probably was the

Ohio River as we flew in a northwesterly direction. The view was breath-taking, with the sun glinting off the wings of the jet and the reassuring sound of the hum of the engines kept reminding me I was almost home. Then we started to descend, slowly and evenly. The flight was one of the calmest I had ever experienced, which only added to my feeling of serenity. The flight attendants went through the usual announcements and prepa-rations for landing and soon I could see the downtown skyline of Toledo. As we got lower and lower I started to recognize neighborhoods below me. Then we flew over Airport Highway, past my high school, Toledo Saint John's. Within minutes we touched down softly on the tarmac.

As soon as we stopped at the gate, I got my carry-on luggage out of the luggage bin above me and headed down the aisle. The flight atten-dant wished me a good day and I clambered down the stairs propped up against the jet's fuselage. The air was crisp and clean. It was cooler here in Toledo than it had been in New York. Apparently a cool front was passing through. I walked quickly towards the terminal and made my way down the hallway to baggage claim. As I approached the baggage area I craned my neck eagerly, trying to spot my mother and brother, who were going to pick me up at the airport. There they were! I finally spotted them near the carousel where my bags would be delivered.

I hurried over to my mother and gave her a big hug and kiss. She is only five feet, four inches tall, so I'm several inches taller. My mom has red, brownish hair with soft facial features. Her skin was fairly dark un-like many Russians who have pale features. Although she was already over fifty years old at the time, she was not overly heavy. Most people tended to say that she looked more like her father, who had died in 1966 than her mother, who had died in 1970. Most people also tended to say that my older brother Boris looked like my mom.

I greeted Boris next, with a hug and a handshake. He has wavy brown hair and a nose that, although not prominent, is fairly noticeable. He's about an inch shorter than I am and has a broad smile, when he chooses to smile. As he got older his hair seemed to get wavier and wavier, almost to the point of having the appearance of a perm. Although not very good as a tennis player, he is a very good skier and a fantastic cellist. We hung out together quite a bit when we were younger, but once Boris headed off to college there was a natural parting of the ways and our interests became less common as the years progressed.

"Wow, it's really great to see both of you again," I proclaimed. "It seems like it's been forever since I left for the summer."

"Yes, we have all missed you so very much, Ericek," (my mom's Russian nickname for me pronounced like err-ee-czech). "We obviously are very thankful that you are safe after that ordeal in New York." Of course, what my mom said sounds a lot different when spoken in Russian.

"Hey, that must have really been something when that guy started shooting in the hallway," Boris interjected. "Were you scared that you might get shot?"

"Not really. I didn't have time to be scared. After it was all over I got really shaky and was wondering what the hell was going on, but at the time of the shooting I guess I was more stunned at what was happening than I was frightened."

"Enough about that, enough about that," my mother said. "Let's get your bags and talk about something more pleasant. Detective Jason called this morning and talked to your father, so there will be plenty of time tonight to discuss the incident in New York."

With that we waited for my luggage. When it came off the conveyor belt, Boris and I grabbed the two bags, and with my rackets and carry-on luggage we headed to the parking lot. Once there, we loaded up the car and Boris turned east on Airport Highway in the direction of I-475/I-23, the loop that encircled Toledo. We got on the expressway, crossed the Maumee River and after we passed through Perrysburg we got off at the Rossford/Buck Road exit. Eventually we made our way down Lime City Road, that turned into Colony Road, and then headed into the development we lived in known as Eagle Point Colony. This was an upscale neighborhood in an otherwise blue collar town. Rossford was home to Libby Owens Ford, a major glass manufacturer. One of the largest glass factories in the United States was based right there in my home town and employed a considerably high percentage of the men from Rossford. A large segment of the population of Rossford was of Polish heritage, so in some ways my parents felt right at home in a town heavily populated by immigrants.

Our house had a long, winding driveway leading to a California style, tri-level house. California style meant a house with a flat roof, a car port instead of a garage, and very large windows facing the river on the backside of the house. We also had an in-ground swimming pool, which my father cherished. Perhaps not the ideal style house for a cold weather climate, but the location on the river made up for it, regardless of the occasional stench that emanated from the muddy and polluted Maumee River. It also was a far cry better than our first house which was located in the Toledo suburb of Oregon. That first house was within a couple of miles of the Sun Oil Refinery, so when the wind was right (or wrong as the case may be) the odor was unspeakably bad.

I was back in my familiar surroundings. I dumped all of my stuff into my room and immediately headed out to the pool to take a swim. By now it had warmed up considerably and the water felt great when I dived in. Boris and I cleaned up for lunch and headed to the kitchen. My mom had prepared one of my favorite meals consisting of a variety of Russian cuisine. First came some pickled herring in sour cream sauce. After that I had a hearty bowl of borscht, basically a Russian beet soup. Finally I dug into an ambitious portion of Russian cutlets, made with ground beef and veal, smothered in a flavorful mushroom gravy. The perfect side, potato pancakes with applesauce, topped off the meal. Fully satiated, Boris and I took a break and then played some baseball in our large front yard.

Although I was keeping busy, time was dragging because I was anxious to talk to my father about his conversation with Detective Jason. I couldn't wait any longer. I decided to call Detective Jason in Long Island to get the scoop on Gunter Gruber. At first my mother insisted that I wait and talk to my father first, before I bothered Detective Jason, but then she acceded to my wishes. Just in case we needed to get in touch with him, Jason had left his phone number with my parents. I anxiously dialed the number and waited for someone to pick up the phone.

"Fourth Precinct, Long Island Division. This is Officer Cornwell. May I help you?"

"Hi, my name is Erick Iskersky. I'm calling from Toledo, Ohio about a case I'm involved in. Detective Jason is the lead detective. I was hoping I could speak with him."

"Sorry, he's out right now. I can take a message and he'll call you back when he can."

After I hung up I looked at my watch. It was close to four o'clock and I wondered if Jason would even bother calling back. I was an 18 year old kid. He probably was busy. He probably had a lot of cases to worry about. Plus, he'd already talked to my father. I went back outside and entertained myself by shooting some hoops.

No more than an hour later, my mom opened the front door and yelled out to me as I was practicing foul shots. "Erick, come here right away. Detective Jason is on the phone." I immediately dropped what I was doing and sprinted toward the house so I could talk to Jason as soon as possible. In fact when I got on the phone I was still breathing hard.

Gasping for air I greeted Detective Jason. "Thanks for calling me back Detective Jason. I'm sure you're busy and I know you talked to my father earlier today, but he's at work and I haven't talked to him yet. I really want to know what you have on Gruber."

As usual, Jason was in a jolly mood. "No problem at all, Erick. I'm sure all of this is real exciting, being part of a homicide investigation and all." I thought to myself that it wasn't all that exciting when I was diving for cover when Gruber was being shot, but I had to admit I was getting into the spirit of being involved in a mysterious shooting and trying to figure out what was behind it all.

"Unfortunately, as I told your father this morning, there isn't much I learned from the German authorities that seems very useful. They also struck out, so far at least, on any identification of the shooter based on the drawing we faxed to them. Gruber was sixty years old and served in the German Army during World War Two. He was with the Seventh Division of the Eighth Army. This force apparently was involved at one point in the invasion of Russia, but eventually pulled back and was stationed back in Germany at the end of the war. Gruber was tried for war time crimes at the Munich Trials. These trials didn't receive nearly as much publicity as the Nuremberg Trials, because at Nuremberg they tried the most notorious Nazi war criminals. According to the German authorities, at the Munich Trials they tried those with lesser positions of power and those whose crimes were not perceived to be as heinous. Gruber was merely a lieutenant. He got convicted for his role in the treatment of prisoners of war, and even some private citizens. Overall, his crimes were not serious enough to warrant the death penalty so he got sentenced to thirty years in prison. He was released in May of 1976, just a few months ago. There was no record of what he was doing after his release, so he must not have crossed the law before he came over to the United States. All of that info does little to help us figure out precisely why he confronted you and why he was shot."

I was definitely disappointed by the news. I suppose I expected information on Gruber that would explain his weird actions and at least provide some hint as to why he was following me around and why he was shot by the man with the scar. The information given to me by Jason merely added to the questions I had. It did nothing to help solve the mystery.

"So now what?", I asked Jason. "Do you have any leads to follow? You're not giving up, are you?"

"Look Erick, I'll have to be honest. We have no eyewitnesses, other than you. We have no fingerprints that do us any good. The German authorities really don't care about Gruber because he was in prison all these years, has no family members as far as they can tell, and for them it's almost good riddance. They assured me they will do all they can to identify that guy with the scar, but of course the crime itself occurred on American soil. I don't know what to tell you. I'm not a betting man, but if I were, I wouldn't bet a whole lot that we're going to solve this thing. But, I'll keep your family posted as best I can, and you let me know if there are any developments at your end that could help us out. Hey, good luck with your tennis and we'll hope this was just some freak occurrence."

With that, Jason said goodbye and left me wondering if there was anything I could do to resolve the nagging uncertainty I had about what happened in New York. I hated the not knowing more than anything else. Sure, I was glad I wasn't hurt and I was glad to be home with my family, but damn it, I wanted to know what the hell was going on. Just then, I heard my father pull his car into our car port. I quickly forgot about my conversation with Jason and headed out the door. It would be great to see my father after all of these weeks.

"Hi Pa," I shouted as my father got out of his BMW. I came up to him and gave him a big hug. He hugged me back and smiled. He's about two inches shorter than me, at five feet eight. Dark slicked back hair, that is thinning. For someone who is fifty six years old, he's in good shape. He has piercing eyes and sharply defined features. Most people say that I look like my father, or even more so like his deceased brother Ivan. "Welcome home, Erick. It's wonderful to see you. Too bad you couldn't do better at the last tournament. It would have been great if you could have qualified for the US Open."

Well, that's typical, I thought. What a Russian response. Good to see me, but before we get too jubilant let's remember I didn't quite perform up to expectations. On the other hand, I knew my father loved me very much. He just wasn't very demonstrative about it and he expected me to do well. Maybe that wasn't such a bad thing. I also suppose, after what my father had gone through in Russia and during World War Two, it was natural for someone with that background to be a tough character. We headed back inside and got ready for dinner.

CHAPTER 5

Dinner conversation that evening seemed very boring to me, mainly because I kept wanting to talk about Gruber and my father's phone call with Detective Jason, and my mother kept steering the subject matter in a different direction. First we talked about my summer, which to my parents was exciting, but to me was rather mundane – at least in my state of excitability about the Gruber affair. Then we talked about my brother's impending departure for Germany to continue his studies. Boris was going to be leaving within the next couple of weeks. Finally we gossiped about the local tennis scene and what was going on in the town of Rossford. As usual, not much was happening.

After what seemed like an interminable amount of time, dinner ended, and while my mother and brother cleaned up the kitchen, I cornered my father in the living room and made him tell me about his conversation with Detective Jason.

"Look Erick, Mom told me you phoned Detective Jason earlier today. You really shouldn't have bothered him. I'm sure he's a busy man and he already told me all he knows. You should have waited to talk to me. Mainly because I have some information about Gruber which seems to somewhat clear up the matter. Other than why the man with the scar shot Gruber."

"Come on, Pa, there has to be some reason that Gruber followed me and then tried to talk to me in New York. Even if he was a wacko, somehow he tracked me down."

"That's what I'm trying to tell you. After I talked to Jason this morning, I called Sergei in Stuttgart to see if he had any ideas about what happened to you. My talk with Sergei was very enlightening. In fact, it was so enlightening that I will call Detective Jason tomorrow and fill him in on what I found out."

Sergei is my father's cousin. He is the only one from my father's side of the family to get out of Russia during the Second World War and to settle down in Germany. I met him one time when I was eight. He and his German wife Anna visited my parents soon after we moved into our home in Rossford. I didn't have any vivid memories of him and my father didn't really keep in touch with him all that often.

My father then explained. Apparently Sergei knew Gunter Gruber. Towards the end of the Second World War, after Sergei had already arrived in Germany, he witnessed some of the acts of violence perpetrated by Gruber against innocent civilians and prisoners of war. Although these acts were quite violent, the Munich Trial inquisitors decided there was not a totality of evidence sufficient to sentence Gruber to death. That was why he was sentenced to thirty years in prison instead.

"However," as my father indicated to me, "Gruber had the right to confront the witnesses called against him during his trial. There were quite a few witnesses, but Sergei's eyewitness accounts were some of the most damning. To a great extent, Gruber was convicted as a result of Sergei's testimony. Gruber was very vociferous in his denials and apparently put on quite a show in trying to discredit Sergei and the other witnesses. Unfortunately, he also showed his unstable side. Although Sergei wasn't present when the war court convicted Gruber, he later heard that Gruber vowed to get even with all of those who testified against him. Of course, at the time it didn't really seem possible that Gruber would really be able to carry out his threats."

As it turned out, after Gruber was released from the prison in Munich, where he had been held in captivity for thirty years, he did try to carry out his plots of revenge. At least that's what Sergei told my father. Gruber had found a way to track down Sergei, which in itself seemed remarkable. How he could remember the names of witnesses who testified against him, or if he was even provided with the names, my father wasn't sure. Nonetheless he made contact with Sergei on Sergei's farm outside of Stuttgart.

"Here's what happened, according to Sergei," my father continued. "Gruber arrived on the farm and demanded to know why Sergei had testified against him. He got very angry and threatened Sergei and his wife. He didn't have a weapon so Sergei felt somewhat safe, but he also didn't doubt that Gruber was serious. Gruber told Sergei that he knew he couldn't do anything to Sergei right then and there, because he didn't want to go back to prison if the police suspected him and caught him. However Gruber vowed that he would go after members of Sergei's family. His main goal was to cause Sergei pain, and his best strategy would be to harm people close to Sergei."

Apparently Sergei reported this incident to the police. Sergei thinks that Gruber knew he had to tread carefully around Sergei because the police were on notice that Gruber was accused of making threats. Because of his police report, Sergei felt somewhat safe, although he always made sure that his wife Anna was never home alone.

My father elucidated further. "Sergei believes that Gruber came after you as a way to get back at Sergei. Sergei doesn't have any children and no relatives in Germany. I guess the next best thing was to try to kidnap you and cause grief that way. Sergei and I were never very close, but in his warped mind Gruber must have thought kidnapping you, and causing your parents grief, would ultimately be some sort of revenge against Sergei. That's what Sergei thinks, anyway. If you believe Sergei about how crazy Gruber seemed to be at his trial, and how crazy he sounded when he confronted Sergei at his farm, Sergei's theory seems quite plausible."

"Come on Pa. Gruber didn't act like he was going to harm me when he talked to me. He acted like he wanted me to join him on some journey, or power trip, or I don't know what. But it didn't seem like he was really threatening me. Besides, what about the man with the scar? Who is he, and why did he shoot Gruber?"

"I don't know Erick, but I think Sergei's version of events makes the most sense and that's what I'm going to tell Detective Jason. I imagine that Gruber made a lot of enemies before he went to prison. The man with the scar must have been an enemy of his who wanted to eliminate Gruber. For whatever reason he decided to do it in New York, and not in Germany. At least based on what you heard, we must assume the man with the scar is also German."

"I don't know, Pa. I'm just not convinced, but obviously I can't say it's not possible. In any case, with Gruber dead it seems it's going to be impossible to figure out what was going on – unless the police track down the man with the scar."

It was getting late. I had gotten up early and had a long day with the flight and all. It was definitely time to get to bed. I said goodnight to everyone and headed to my bedroom on the lower level of our house. I stood at the window with the lights off so I could look out across the Maumee River without any glare. I could see the lights from the yacht club across the river, as well as the outline of Frank Uncle's illuminated against the dark background. Uncle's was one of the top restaurants in town, one that we frequented both for the food and for the gorgeous view of the river. Of course the view was always great, you just wanted to make sure you never stepped foot into the muddy, polluted water. The Maumee wasn't quite as bad as the Cuyahoga in Cleveland, where legend had it you could light the river by dropping a match in it, but you definitely didn't want to get baptized in the river that flowed past downtown Toledo.

I turned on the light in my room and closed the door. After getting into my pajamas I did what I used to do almost nightly during the baseball season when I was a young kid. I turned on my transistor radio to station WJR out of Detroit and listened to the baseball game with the radio tucked under the pillow against my ear. The Tigers were playing a home game. It wasn't against my Orioles, but it didn't matter. I loved hearing Ernie Harwell do the play by play of the games. He was a real pro and painted a great picture so I almost felt like I was right there at Tiger Stadium. Paul Carey was pretty good as the color analyst, although I preferred Ray Lane, who had been the analyst until 1972.

That night the Tigers were playing the Cleveland Indians. The legendary Mark "the Bird" Fidrych was on the mound for the Tigers. He was quite a sensation and the fans loved him. He talked to the ball and had a ritual he went through whenever he pitched. He was facing Dennis Eckersley. The game was real tight for the first few innings with the Indians clinging to a 2-1 lead heading to the bottom of the sixth. Then the Tigers broke it open against Eckersley. They scored four times that inning, including a two run homer by Ron LeFlore, and a double that drove in two more off the bat of Mickey Stanley. The Indians replaced Eckersley with Dave LaRoche. As I got sleepier and sleepier, the Indians had only managed the two runs against Fidrych, driven in by Buddy Bell with a double. As I drifted off to sleep, the Indians were mounting a bit of a threat after a walk to Ray Fosse and a pinch hit single by Boog Powell, one of my favorite players of all time when he had played for the Orioles. But I never made it out of that eighth inning. My eyes shut and a dream foggily floated across the TV screen of my mind.

I suddenly found myself flapping a large pair of wings and looking down over a city. I could see my father wandering the streets, calling out my mother's name. "Helen, oh my one and only Helen, where are you? I can't find you." He kept wandering and wandering. Asking people he ran into if they knew where his wife and her family were. But they didn't understand him. Or if they did, they wouldn't tell him where his precious Helen was. Then I flew lower and lower. I could see my mother! She was huddled around a fire with my grandparents. They looked very sad. I yelled to my father. "Mom is over there, she's over there. Keep walking. You'll find her." Just as my father was getting closer to where my mother was, a man walked up to my father and said something to him. He then pointed in the opposite direction from where my mother was. I yelled. "No Pa, no! You're going the wrong way. Turn around. You'll never find Mom if you don't turn around. You've got to find her." But he didn't hear me. The man who pointed my father in the wrong direction looked up to me in the sky, and grinned. It was Gunter Gruber. Then he started to laugh uncontrollably.

I awoke with a start. The radio was still on, but the game was over. There was some late night news show going on. I shuddered slightly, feeling really eerie that Gunter Gruber had forced his way into my dreams. I clicked the radio off and then quickly my mind shifted gears. I contemplated about how lucky I was that my father had actually managed to find my mother during the chaos that was everywhere in Germany towards the end of the Second World War.

After my mother, her parents, and her uncle and aunt were "captured" by the Americans, they were railroaded from Berlin to a refugee camp outside of Munich. They had to sleep outside on the ground until they were eventually supplied with sleeping bags. The Americans treated them well. Although there wasn't a lot of food, there was enough to survive on. Water was also somewhat scarce, but again, the Americans took care of the needs of the refugees as best they could. Of course, what my mother feared the most was that they would all eventually be sent back to Russia and their horrific experience would all be for nothing. And most importantly, she feared she would never see my father again. Every night she went to sleep, praying that my father was still alive and that he would somehow manage to find them. Of course, she was worried that my father, if alive, would be looking for her in Berlin and would have no idea that she was in Munich. Little did she know that my father was indeed alive and trying his best to get out of a precarious situation.

Fortunately for my father, he was captured by the British while tending to the wounded. He was in Berlin and was dividing his time between working with the doctors and medics taking care of the soldiers and civilians injured or dying on the front, and working at the local hospitals taking care of whoever needed attention. Consequently when the British and Americans were capturing German soldiers and imprisoning them, they treated the German doctors and medics less harshly, realizing they were performing a valuable service. Unfortunately, for those captured by the Russians, any sense of civility was ignored. The Russians treated their prisoners with brutality and vengeance.

As the resistance by the German forces lessened, my father found himself working almost exclusively at one of the local hospitals. There was much less fighting in the streets and it was clear that Germany was on the brink of collapse. Luckily my father ended up treating a British soldier, who happened to speak German. He discovered information about refugee camps and the fact that these camps were not only in Berlin, but also located in Munich, Frankfurt, and Stuutgart. He knew that the only hope he had was that my mother, her family, and his family had ended up in one of these camps. Sadly, he of course had no idea that his father Mikhail had been left in Poland and most likely was dead, and that his mother Svetlana had ended up in the hands of the Russians. Where she was, no one knew.

My father started his quest to find my mother by searching the camps located in Berlin. Each camp had a log that listed the names of all those imprisoned, although how accurate these logs were my father had no idea. There were a total of five refugee camps in Berlin and it took my father at least two weeks to complete his search. It was not easy toiling at the hospital for hours each day and then wandering to the camps to look through the refugee camp log books. Although his confidence level wasn't real high, my father decided my mother was not in Berlin, if she was still alive.

Now he had to figure out a way to visit the camps in the other three cities. Berlin was in northwest Germany. Of the three cities, Frankfurt was the closest to Berlin. It was located roughly in the center of Germany. Stuutgart was in the south of Germany, and Munich was the farthest from Berlin, located in the southeast corner of Germany. By this time, as the war was almost completely over, my father was on the medical staff at his hospital and was no longer even being treated like a prisoner. Although he had his doubts, he asked the British administrators, now functioning along with the Americans and Russians as temporary government officials, for permission to leave Berlin and search for my mother. He was pleasantly shocked to be granted permission and was provided with the necessary travel papers that would allow him to travel without being treated as an enemy combatant. By now the Allies had almost total control of the entire country of Germany.

With his papers in hand, my father first traveled to Frankfurt. Although the description of my father's experience during this time might be somewhat boring to the casual observer, for my father this was the ultimate journey with the ultimate stress. If he couldn't find my mother in one of these camps, it was very likely he would never see her again. And he also had to face the desperate uncertainty of not even knowing if my mother was alive. If she was alive, could she still be in Russia? If my father didn't find her in the camps, would he have to go back to Russia?

Although I never pressed my father for details of his search for my mother, he recounted some years later what it was like to wander through the camps and search the log books. "There were so many people. Thousands and thousands. Most were thin from the hunger they faced each and every day. Some were injured or sick, but not considered so sick or injured that room in a hospital bed could be spared for them. I felt very sorry for them and of course many were Russians. I was always hesitant to speak with the Russians because I was afraid the guards, who were mostly Americans and British, would ignore my papers and force me to stay in the camp I was visiting. They might think I was a Russian citizen who was going to be shipped back to Russia. They didn't know that I was granted asylum by the provisional government to stay in Germany."

Of course, because my mother was in Munich, my father had no success in the camps located in Frankfurt and Stuutgart. Now there only remained the four camps situated in Munich. If he didn't find her there, my father would have to decide between abandoning his search, starting a new life alone in Germany, or risking his life and traveling back to Russia to continue his search there. Everything changed so dramatically in that moment of truth when my father visited the second of the four camps in Munich.

"It was quite amazing. I started reading the log books, which were not in alphabetical order. They were simply listed in order of the arrival dates of the refugees. The book I was looking through must have had over 300 pages of names listed. It was thick, obviously written by hand, and the printing was not always clear. But there it was. Your mother's name. Helen Iskersky. She entered her married name. Can you imagine? That was the first time I had ever seen your mother's last name as Iskersky, instead of her maiden name, Beloblodsky. The tears of joy wouldn't stop flowing. Over two years, and I would finally get to see your mother again. Listed below her were her parents, Daniel and Sofia Beloblodsky. Below that, her uncle and aunt, Dmitri and Marika Constantinov. But then my heart skipped a beat. I didn't see a listing for my parents, Mikhail and Svetlana."

Needless to say my father was ecstatic that he had found the camp where my mother was located, but also was crestfallen that his parents were not listed. He hoped that they were simply in another camp or had accidentally been left off the list in the log book. Because there were so many people in the camp, and because it was rather spread out, it took my father over seven hours to finally find my mother. But when he did it was a re-union for all ages. Tears, laughter, hugs, kisses, astonishment, joy. Emotions that I can't even imagine. Yet here they were. Together again after more than two years of doubt and fear. And of course the re-markable feelings of joy mixed with the crushing feelings of despair and agony when my father learned of his parents' fate. More crushing because there was not real certainty that either, or both, were dead. But probably a likelihood that my father would never really discover what happened to them. He would go on not knowing if his father had died in that village in Poland, and not knowing if the Russians had killed his mother or shipped her back to Russia.

With all that happened in my mind that night I felt overwhelmingly exhausted. Not physically but just plain tired of thinking of the past and trying to figure out why it was that Gunter Gruber had somehow become a part of my life. It didn't seem right somehow. I was just about ready to embark on one of the most exciting journeys of life – going to college and also playing college tennis to boot – and now I had this intrusion.

Luckily my mental tiredness and my contentment with finally sleeping in my own bed led to deep sleep without any more dreams or interruptions. I awoke in the morning feeling surprisingly refreshed. My biggest task in life for the next couple of months was going to be keeping my tennis game sharp. Unfortunately I would have to do so without the benefit of the high level of competition I had experienced during the summer. Needless to say my practice opportunities were going to be quite limited in Toledo. However, I resolved to keep my game at a high level. I also resolved to pretend I was Sherlock Holmes and try to make some sense out of the "Gunter Gruber saga." I needed to get to the bottom of why Gunter Gruber had become a part of my life. With that thought in mind, I got out of bed and headed to the kitchen. I was famished and wanted breakfast.

CHAPTER 6

My life now became a routine. After I resolved to figure out the Gunter Gruber mystery and become an amateur sleuth, I settled into a predictable pattern. I would get up in the morning and work out. Usually I jogged three miles and also did some interval training, where I would jog for one-hundred yards and then sprint for one-hundred yards. This was great training for tennis. I also would do push-ups and sit-ups, and then I would finish the workout with some stretching.

After that I would shower and then head to the kitchen for some breakfast. I was lucky. My mother didn't work so she was usually home to make my breakfast for me. Talk about being spoiled. But she loved to spoil me and I didn't object. She was a really good cook and prepared all sorts of various egg dishes, or pancakes, and sometimes french toast. For the first couple of weeks of this routine Boris was still home before leaving for Germany, so he would join me in my workouts. He also was a good cook and frequently was the one who ended up preparing breakfast.

One day, while we were jogging, I asked Boris what he thought about the entire incident involving Gunter Gruber and whether he thought I could figure out the mystery. "I just don't believe that what happened to me had that much to do with Father's cousin Sergei testifying against Gruber in the Munich Tribunals. If he was that thirsty for revenge, why didn't he just do something to Sergei?"

"Look Erick, it does seem strange to me too. I don't know if I buy Father's explanation of why Gruber came to the United States. He came after you for a reason and it seems illogical that he followed you around all summer and did nothing to you. If he wanted revenge on Sergei by hurting you, why didn't he do so earlier? And could he really believe that hurting you would be that upsetting to Sergei? He and Father are not really that close."

I had to agree with my brother's assessment of the situation, but no matter what I asked my father about Gruber and Sergei, he would offer no other explanation. At least no other explanation that he would share with me. The thought certainly entered my mind that my father was not being entirely up front with me. But on the other hand, I had not a scintilla of evidence or even a logical theory that refuted what Sergei purportedly had told my father.

Fortunately my tennis kept me fairly busy and my lifestyle was, without a doubt, one that most people would envy. Usually, after my breakfast I would read for awhile and then I would head off to one of the tennis clubs. I would either play with Jim Davis at the Toledo Racquet Club, or drive up to Monroe, Michigan and play against another friend of mine, Mickey Schmidt. After I practiced I would eat lunch at Schmucker's, or Bonanza, or Barry Bagel's. This lifestyle also became somewhat boring because I was itching to play some real tennis, against stronger competition. For that reason I signed up for some weekend men's tournaments in the Midwest that had prize money. I surmised that the competition would be fairly strong even though first prize in most of these events was only around $1000.

One tournament was in Fort Wayne, Indiana. It was held at the Wildwood Racquet Club and I actually played quite well despite my lack of any real competition for a period of a few weeks. I got to the finals, where I lost to Tim Gullikson. Tim was about six years older than me and had only recently started playing on the tour. At the time of the Fort Wayne tournament he was ranked around 120 in the world so I didn't feel too bad about losing to him in three sets.

Another tournament I played was in Detroit. Once again I had a fairly successful run as I got to the semi-finals before I lost to Gene Scott. He was considerably older than me and was no longer playing full time as a pro. But he was experienced and quite savvy on the court. My inability to serve well and to figure out his crafty style of play doomed me, and I lost in straight sets.

My last tournament that fall was in Muncie, Indiana. I continued my string of strong performances and ended up losing in the finals to Tom Gullikson, Tim's twin brother. Once again I lost in three sets and Tom, like Tim, was also ranked in the top 120 in the world. The twins went on to great success in doubles, becoming one of the top teams in the world. Tim would someday reach the top 20 in singles, and Tom wasn't too far behind, reaching the top 50.

Meanwhile, Boris left for Germany to finish his undergraduate studies and to get ready for medical school. Of course I was saddened to see him go, but I had also gotten used to the notion of being home without a sibling because Boris had already spent three years at Marquette University in Milwaukee. The only difference now was that he would not be coming home on most holidays and, of course, never on weekends. For that reason, my parents thought it would be a great idea for me to visit Boris in Germany, sometime in early December. I also thought it was a great idea – not only would I get to see Boris before I left for Trinity University in January, I would be able to search for information about Gunter Gruber in his home country. There was bound to be something I could discover about my mysterious assailant (or whatever one would call him).

However, before I went to Germany I had some investigating I could do while I was still at home. Consequently, after I would play tennis and eat lunch, I would head to the library and conduct some research about The Second World War and, in particular, anything I could find out about the Munich Tribunals. Finding out information about Gunter Gruber turned out to be quite elusive. Usually I went to the main location of the Toledo Public Library, which was located in downtown Toledo, on Michigan Street.

This ritual ended up being a very frustrating experience. I literally looked at every single book I could find about The Second World War. It took me weeks to look at every book and hours upon hours of reading. I was bound and determined to dig something up about Gunter Gruber. In my mind I was hoping that he was a significant enough historical figure that he would be mentioned in at least one of the books. I have to admit I learned an incredible amount of information about The Second World War. If I entered a trivia contest about The Second World War there is no doubt I would have prevailed.

I learned about Hitler gaining dictatorial powers in Germany by 1933. How he plotted to take over Austria and Czechoslovakia. How he invaded Poland in 1939, which prompted Great Britain and France to declare war on Germany. What I learned was certainly fascinating because my study of "The War" in high school had not been nearly as detailed. Clearly the European countries had underestimated Hitler's desire to create a new world order and to what lengths he would go to in order to achieve his objectives.

After Poland, Germany invaded Norway. Then the Netherlands and Belgium. Then the successful invasion of France, which led to the famous evacuation of Dunkirk by British, French, and Belgian troops. A total of 340,000 troops were able to evacuate. By June 1940 the French surrendered. This simply reinforced my notion about the French. What a bunch of weaklings! They lost their country in a matter of weeks. No wonder I had such a low opinion of France.

After France fell, Germany took out Greece and Yugoslavia. Then followed the invasion of Russia in 1941, which I earlier described in great detail when documenting my parents' escape from Russia. This invasion led to the Anglo-Soviet Agreement of 1941, in which Great Britain and Russia agreed to assist one another in the war effort against Germany. Germany was also occupied with warfare in Africa and Hungary. Eventually, as is well known, the Germans could not sustain their early success. They were slowly but surely pushed out of Russia, as I indicated before, and then came the invasion of Normandy by the Allies, famously known as the D-Day invasion. Officially the war in Europe was over on May 8, 1945. Hitler's successor was at least successful in getting 55 percent of the army that had fought against the Russians to surrender in British-American areas of control, rather than to surrender in Soviet areas of control. That had been a miracle for my parents and my mother's parents. Sadly, it did not work out for my father's mother.

So all of that reading and studying and not a single mention of Gunter Gruber. Obviously he hadn't been infamous enough to get a mention in the history books written in America. The truly infamous members of the Nazi Party had been prosecuted at the Nuremberg Trials. I found information about the Nuremberg Trials in almost all of the books I looked at. I read up on those trials out of a grim fascination with the cruelty these Nazis had perpetrated against totally innocent people. I suppose I justified my interest by convincing myself that gaining knowledge about the Nuremberg Trials would help me learn something about what had happened at the Munich Tribunals, where Gruber had been convicted. Maybe it would give me some insight about what made a man like Gruber tick.

The Nuremberg Trials were held in order to prosecute the most prominent members of the political, military and economic leadership of Nazi Germany. The trials were held in Nuremberg, Germany – thus the name. Three major Nazis – Hitler, Himmler, and Goebbels – were not tried because they had all committed suicide, however there were 23 other major defendants who were tried. They were tried on one or more of the following charges. Participation in a common plan or conspiracy for the accomplishment of a crime against peace; planning, initiating and waging wars of aggression and other crimes against peace; war crimes; and crimes against humanity.

It was very eerie for me as I read the accounts of the trials. It was so hard to imagine that humans could be so cruel and indifferent. These Nazis were the worst of the worst. They were responsible for acts of inhumanity that led to the death of millions of people and for ruining the lives of millions more. As I viewed the photos of these Nazis in the books I read, chills ran up and down my spine. It sickened me to think about what these men did. If there is a hell, these men were definitely the first in line to be subjected to purgatory.

Of the 23 defendants, three were acquitted. The rest were found guilty. Four were sentenced to 15-20 years in prison. Walter Funk, Hitler's Minister of economics, Rudolph Hess, Hitler's Deputy Leader, and Erich Raeder, Commander in Chief of the German Navy, were sentenced to life in prison. The remaining defendants were all sentenced to death. Men like Martin Bormann, Nazi Party Secretary, Hans Frank, the Governor-General of occupied Poland, Wilhelm Frick, Hitler's Minister of the Interior, and Herman Goring, Commander of the German Air Force. All in all twelve of the 23 were sentenced to death. It was really scary to think about what would have happened if somehow Germany had won The Second World War. These crazy bastards would have been running Europe and probably killing millions more.

I investigated the Nuremberg Trials further and finally discovered a book that mentioned the Munich Tribunals, the trials where Gunter Gruber was convicted. Apparently there were over 500 defendants indicted at the Munich Tribunals, with 428 convictions. The indictments were primarily based on war crimes, crimes against humanity, and violating precepts of war for perpetrating violence against civilians. The Munich Tribunals received much less publicity than the Nuremberg Trials and those convicted were not nearly as notorious as the twelve defendants sentenced to death by the Nuremberg Trials judges. Nonetheless, those convicted at the Munich Tribunals had committed some very serious crimes punishable by terms of imprisonment of up to thirty years. Clearly, Gunter Gruber had committed some very serious crimes himself because he had only gotten out of prison a few months before. Right before he came over to the United States to follow me.

I also wondered what it had been like for my father to serve in the German army. Yes, he was a medic. He was trying to save lives, not end them. But he still had to serve under a Nazi regime and follow the commands of officers who, I'm sure in many cases, were devout Nazis. Perhaps some of those officers did not believe in the Nazi cause and were merely following orders because they feared for their safety. Regardless, my father had experienced the horror of war. He always reminded me that he was just trying to stay alive and re-unite with my mother. To him, the politics of war at that time were irrelevant. My parents hated communism so much, that they were even willing to face the prospect of living in Nazi Germany. My father always semi-joked that they were escaping one crazy despot named Stalin to live in a country run by another crazy despot named Hitler. What a choice!

I finally had made some progress in identifying Gunter Gruber. But I wanted to know more. My next idea was to go visit the University of Toledo History Department and to see if someone there could provide me with a road map of discovery. Someone with a PhD in history, with a specialization in World War II. By this time it was near the end of October so I had to get all my research in by the end of November. After that I was visiting my brother in Germany and then spending Christmas at home before I headed off to San Antonio.

I drove over to the University of Toledo on a Tuesday morning and parked in the visitor's lot. Earlier I had called for directions to the History Department and for suggestions on which of the professors would be the most knowledgeable about World War II. Based on that information I made an appointment with Dr. Phillip Berry, who taught classes with a concentration on The Second World War, with an emphasis on the European front. When I arrived at his office, Dr. Berry was sitting at his desk and reading the Toledo Blade, our local newspaper.

"Dr. Berry? I'm Erick Iskersky. I phoned earlier to set up an appointment through the department secretary."

Dr. Berry got up out of his chair and extended his hand. "Pleasure to meet you." His grip was firm and steady. He was tall, at least six feet, five inches, and he had floppy hair that lay messily to the side. Clearly his wardrobe was not a major concern. His pants were old looking khakis and his polo shirt had seen better days. Of course it was possible he didn't teach classes on Tuesdays. Nonetheless he seemed pleased to have a visitor and graciously offered me a seat in his office.

"How may I help you? You know, I'm a pretty big sports fan. Your name sounds familiar."

"I do play tennis. For St. John's. Or did play. I'm off to Trinity University. In January."

"That's right. Now I remember. I read in the paper that you originally were going to attend the University of Michigan, and then you changed your mind. From what I remember, you've had a pretty good tennis career so far."

"Not bad. But you know, I think I want to be a history professor. That is, if I can't make it as a pro tennis player."

"I hope you do better in your athletic endeavors than I did. I thought I would make a great NBA basketball player, but I quickly learned I wasn't all that good."

Over Dr. Berry's shoulder I could see his diplomas displayed. PhD from the University of Pennsylvania. BA in history from Purdue University. There were also various photos of Dr. Berry in what looked like academic situations. But one photo was a basketball photo, showing Dr. Berry taking a jump shot in his Purdue uniform. His hair was even floppier back then. His face, then chiseled sharply, was now a bit puffy. Lean and slim in the photo, now a bit of a paunch. Then athletic looking, now, very much looking like a professor of higher learning.

"How long did you play for Purdue?" I asked while pointing to the photo.

"For only two years. Then I hurt my knee and then I realized I wasn't really any good anyway. So I devoted myself to my real passion. The Second World War. Ironically I was born on Pearl Harbor Day. Not only on the day of the month, but the exact same year – 1941. I guess it was my destiny to love history. Enough about that. What can I do for you?"

"I want to learn everything I can about a certain Nazi by the name of Gunter Gruber. I've combed through all of the books I can find at the Toledo Public Library and have found precious little information. Other than identifying Gruber as being one of hundreds convicted at the Munich Tribunals, I can't get more specific stuff about him."

"Interesting. Why do you have such a strong curiosity about this Gruber character?"

"Well it's quite a long story. I'll give you a short version so I don't take up too much of your time," I replied. I then recited the events that occurred in the summer, without going into great detail.

"That's certainly a fascinating tale. And your father is unable to provide you with the answers to your mystery?"

"He knows of Gruber because his cousin supposedly testified at the Munich Tribunals. His cousin Sergei believes that Gruber approached me with the goal of carrying out retribution. Because German police were aware that Gruber made some threats against Sergei, Sergei believes Gruber decided to seek revenge by harming his relatives. Personally, I don't buy that story. My father can think of nothing more to add to the mystery."

Dr. Berry scratched his head thoughtfully. Then he propped his chin on to his folded hands and let out a sigh. "You know, I think I can help you. The Munich Tribunals were certainly not as publicized as the Nuremberg Trials. And, of course, the so-called famous defendants were tried at Nuremberg. But plenty of hardened and nasty Nazis were convicted at the Munich Tribunals. Let me think. Your best bet would be to go to Germany and read about the Munich Tribunals at the University of Munich. They have volumes and volumes of detailed history. As does the Munich War Museum. Of course everything is in German, and it's a bit far."

"Actually, my brother Boris is finishing his undergraduate studies at that university and will be going to medical school in Munich. I'm going to visit him in a few weeks so I'll definitely take a look at any books you recommend. Plus he knows German very well, so he'll be able to read things for me."

"Fantastic!" Dr. Berry exclaimed. "I'll prepare a list of books that I think will be very helpful to you. When I have the list, I'll give you a call. In the meantime, our library here at the University of Toledo has several volumes that have been translated from German to English. They are excellent books and have greater details about lesser known events and characters from The Second World War. These books will at least provide you with some additional information before you fly over to Germany."

Dr. Berry went to a notebook located on one of his bookshelves. He took the notebook down and leafed through several pages. He wrote down several items on a sheet of paper and handed it to me. He also reached in his desk and pulled out, what looked to be, some sort of pass. He signed it and gave it to me.

"This pass will allow you to use the library as my guest for the next week. You'll have to read in the library, however. You won't be able to check the books I listed for you out of the library. So bring plenty of paper for note-taking."

I got up, shook hands with Dr. Berry, and thanked him profusely. He gave my quest new hope. I felt excited. First I would get some information about the Munich Tribunals in the translated books at the University of Toledo. Then Boris could help me out in Munich, where I could broaden my search even further. Suddenly I didn't feel like I was at a dead end. I immediately walked to the university library as fast as I could, totally forgetting about the fact it was lunch time.

Once I arrived at the university library and showed my pass, I was shown to the section of the library that contained the list of books Dr. Berry had given me. Although hungry, I started to peruse the books one by one, looking for a reference to the Munich Tribunals and, in particular, Gunter Gruber. The first three books had fairly in-depth descriptions of the Munich Tribunals, but no mention of Gruber. It was fascinating to read the history of The Second World War from the German perspective. Two of the translated books were clearly written by authors who had been somewhat sympathetic to the Nazi cause. The implication in those two books was that the Allies were unjustly punishing Germans who had not really committed any serious crimes. The third book, however, seemed a bit more objective in its descriptions of the Munich Tribunals.

Then in the fourth book I hit pay dirt. The translated title of the book was "World War II – The Shameful Aftermath". It was a book that described the trials of war criminals and the effects of the war on the German citizenry. The author, Matthew Becker, wrote from the viewpoint that Germany had shamed itself greatly in following a crazed leader like Hitler, and that the people of Germany got what they deserved. In his mind, the war criminals were justly punished. He also believed the Allies (excluding the Russians of course) had treated the innocent defeated German people very generously.

There was an entire section of the book devoted to the Munich Tribunals. For each and every one of the 428 convicted war criminals there was a description of why the war criminal was charged, what the charges were, and what kind of punishment was handed out. I finally found some concrete information about the man who had stalked me throughout the summer.

Gunter Gruber was charged with "war crimes" and "crimes against humanity". He was charged for two major reasons. First, at one point he was in charge of a prisoner of war camp in Poland, soon after the Germans had conquered that country. He was convicted of mistreating the captured Polish and Russian soldiers who were under his care. Although not specifically charged with killing any of the prisoners, he was blamed for the horrendous conditions in the prison that led to the deaths of hundreds of soldiers. Supposedly there was physical abuse of the prisoners and the quality of the food and water was abysmal. The food was also in very short supply. Ultimately it was determined that Gruber couldn't necessarily have provided more and better food and water. This would have been the responsibility of those higher up the command chain. However, he was held liable for the treatment of the prisoners in general – for this he was sentenced to ten years in prison.

Gruber was also sentenced to an additional twenty years in prison. That part of the sentence caught my eye. After leaving Poland, Gruber was sent to Berlin to be an attache under General Rolf Maurer. Then he became an administrative assistant under Ernst Kaltenbrunner, who was one of the leaders of the dreaded German SS (comprised of the Gestapo and Criminal Police). As Kaltenbrunner's assistant, Gruber formed the infamous "Inner Circle of Five".

The mission of the "Inner Circle of Five" was really quite simple. Gruber and his co-horts became suppliers of women and sex for Hitler and his close Nazi peers. Gruber's group carried out search missions to find young, beautiful German girls in Berlin and elsewhere. They would simply "kidnap" these girls and take them back to Nazi headquarters for the pleasure of Hitler and his associates. Apparently there would be all sorts of sex orgies and the young girls were raped over and over. When the Nazis got tired of a particular group of girls, the "Inner Circle of Five" would get rid of the "used" group and find another group of girls. Apparently it didn't matter how young the girls were and the pain and anguish that these girls faced was indescribable.

At this point I became disgusted. Gunter Gruber had truly been a horrible human being. In my mind he should have received the death penalty. Now I looked at the man with the scar as a hero. He had rid the world of a monster. I still didn't really know what Gruber wanted with me but my speculation was that the man with the scar was seeking some sort of revenge against Gruber and decided to kill him.

But I also was very excited when I realized the description about Gruber's conviction included a list of who belonged to the "Inner Circle of Five". Along with Gruber there was Dr. Hans Friedrich. He was responsible for taking care of any medical needs of the kidnapped girls, or drugging them when appropriate. Apparently he also performed abortions if it was decided to do so with the girls who became pregnant. He died in 1944, before the war had ended.

Peter Brenner and Alfred Rheingold were members of the "Inner Circle of Five" who would actually go out and do the scouting to find the young, beautiful girls. They would also carry out the "kidnappings", with back-up from members of the SS. Neither Brenner or Rheingold was captured after the war, nor were they dead as far as anyone could tell. Speculation was that they might have escaped to Brazil or Mexico where a fair amount of Nazis fled to after the war. For some reason these countries had agreed to harbor some of the Nazi war criminals.

And the final member of the "Inner Circle of Five" was the reason I was really excited about what I was reading. It was Joseph Erdmeister. I knew that name for one very good reason. Joseph Erdmeister was the man who shot and killed my father's brother Ivan. I remembered his name from the letter my father had sent to my mother during the war when he was already in Germany. This was amazing. The coincidence seemed to be uncanny. The man who caused such grief in my father's life had a connection to Gunter Gruber. According to the book, Erdmeister was not taken prisoner after the war because he could not be found. Speculation was that he was killed or captured by the Russians because he was last seen in the Russian sector of war torn Berlin.

These new facts provided me with the motivation to continue my research when I visited my brother in the not too distant future. Clearly Gruber had come after me for a very specific reason. And somehow this reason must have had some connection to my father. Unfortunately I started to wonder about how truthful my father was being. There was no way Gruber randomly stalked me. And it seemed like a real stretch to believe he came after me because of something my father's cousin Sergei had done to him. I headed home with a bunch of questions for my father.

That evening I impatiently waited for my father to get home from work. He didn't get in until after seven and I immediately accosted him when he walked through the door. "Pa, you have not been telling me the truth about Gruber, have you?" I demanded to know. "There is no way you didn't know who the guy was."

"Erick, what are you talking about? I told you I knew about him because of Sergei."

"I don't believe you. I went to the University of Toledo library today and a professor over there gave me a list of books to look at. I found out about Gunter Gruber and the 'Inner Circle of Five'. And guess who else was part of that group? Joseph Erdmeister. The man who shot and killed Ivan."

My father took a deep breath and let it out. He bowed his head and then looked up. "You are right. I have been hiding the truth from you because I felt ashamed. I'm actually the one who testified against Gruber at the Munich Tribunals. I didn't want you and Boris to know too much about my past. For that matter, I didn't want anyone to know. Can you imagine what would happen to my reputation and my career if people started to think I was some sort of Nazi? That's why I told you the story about Sergei. So no one would ever know about my involvement with unsavory characters like Gruber."

"What about Erdmeister? And the man with the scar who killed Gruber?"

"You know about Erdmeister. He killed Ivan and painfully I had to see him during the rest of our march through Poland and to Berlin. And then of course I also saw him when we were both stationed in Berlin at the end of the war."

"And the man with the scar?" I asked again.

"I suspect that he was someone from Gruber's past who harbored a real grudge. Obviously he wanted to kill him out of some sort of vendetta. The world is certainly better off without Gruber."

There didn't seem to be much more to say. I could understand how my father could feel ashamed of his past and be very protective of his reputation. His life had been full of struggles and tragedy and now he had finally achieved success. I decided not to press my father further because I could see it was difficult for him to talk about. Particularly because he was fairly stoic in nature and usually didn't reveal many emotions.

That night I went to bed feeling a lot better. But I still wanted to investigate Gruber and Erdmeister some more. And I definitely wanted to discover who the man with the scar was if it was remotely possible to do so. Besides, my sleuthing had actually become fun. Who knows? Maybe I was destined to become a private eye, just like those guys on TV, Jim Rockford and Mannix.

CHAPTER 7

The next few weeks passed fairly uneventfully as I looked forward to my visit to Germany. Just in case I called Detective Jason in Long Island to see if there had been any progress made in the homicide investigation of Gunter Gruber. Jason informed me that there was no news of any consequence. The detectives were pursuing cases with much better leads. The man with the scar was never found, of course, and Jason candidly admitted that without some sort of spectacularly lucky break it was likely the case would soon become cold, if it hadn't already.

Meanwhile, by the middle of November it was miserably frigid in Toledo. Now more than ever I was thrilled that I had chosen to go to Trinity University instead of the University of Michigan. Not only was I heading to one of the best tennis programs in the nation, but I was heading to a warm climate, one that I had never gotten to experience on a permanent basis in the winter. A thin layer of ice started to form on the Maumee River and the days got darker earlier and earlier, making things seem dreary even though there was nothing to be dreary about.

I also received a call from Dr. Berry. He provided me with a list of books he recommended that I look at when I was in Germany. Most of the books could be found at the University of Munich Library. A few of the books could be found at the Munich Museum of War. I was very grateful for Dr. Berry's assistance. Without him I probably never would have tracked down Gunter Gruber's background. Now I had a plan in place.

My mother decided to visit my god mother in New Jersey and was going to be gone for about a week, but would be back before Thanksgiving.

My god mother Vera was from Latvia and had escaped from there during The Second World War with her husband Erik. Boris and I were treated very well by Aunt Vera and Uncle Erik. When we were little we always took a family vacation to Rova Farms, New Jersey, where we would meet up with Vera and Erik. Rova Farms was near the ocean, which my father dearly loved. It was a small community that was populated mainly by Russian immigrants. Thus, the reason for our trips there. My parents enjoyed the camaraderie they shared with other Russians, particularly because there were very few Russians in Toledo.

I kissed my mother goodbye as she boarded the Amtrak train. We had a station located in downtown Toledo and the train traveled overnight to New Jersey, before stopping in New York, so it was a very convenient trip. My mother reminded me to behave, which I invariably did anyway, and to make sure that I ate well. That was less likely because neither my father or I knew how to cook. That pretty much meant that we were going to be eating out most of the time for dinner. We waved to my mother as the train pulled out of the station and headed home just as some snow flurries started to fall. I was definitely ready to head southwest to San Antonio for some sun, blue sky, and warm weather.

Two days later I was waiting for my father to come home so we could go out to eat dinner, when the phone rang. I picked up, assuming it might be my father. Instead, after I had answered the call, I was greeted by a nasal sounding voice and a very thick accent.

"Is this the home where Dr. Iskersky lives?" the man asked, in what seemed to be a European accent, although I couldn't say for sure.

"It is," I replied. "May I ask who's calling?"

"This is Ricardo Diaz, a friend of Dr. Iskersky. Is this his son Erick?"

"It is. Pa is not home right now but I expect him anytime."

"Good. Please say to him I call back later."

"I can have him call you," I said, "if you give me a phone number where you can be reached."

"No, no. I call back. I am here in Toledo. I want to come see your father. I call back."

With that, Ricardo Diaz hung up. I had to admit he had a very strange accent. I didn't know who he was, because my father had never talked about a friend by the name of Diaz. I would have thought his accent would have sounded more Spanish, but on the other hand, maybe that's exactly what it was. I'd never met anyone from Spain. Only from Mexico.

My father came home a couple of hours later. He looked tired and didn't seem all that cheerful. I figured if I told him about a call from an old friend of his, it would lighten his mood. Instead, it did just the opposite.

"Pa, guess who called awhile ago? An old friend of yours'."

"Who was it Erick? I'm tired, and hungry, and I could use a beer about now. So don't keep me waiting. Just let me know who called."

"A guy by the name of Ricardo Diaz. He said he would call back."

I expected my father to brighten up and express some happiness that his friend had called. But, he let out a string of Russian expletives that made it quite clear that he wasn't thrilled with the idea of speaking to Ricardo Diaz.

"He calls himself my friend," my father said bitterly, "but he only calls when he wants something. And, truth be told, he is not really my friend. I just happen to know him because we met his parents after the war. His father is Mexican and his mother is German. They were doing some sort of export/import business in Germany while visiting Ricardo's relatives. We got to know the parents who eventually introduced us to Ricardo. But I have no use for him. Let's go eat, and if we're lucky, we'll miss Ricardo's call."

We drove out to Van's Colonial Steak House, located on Monroe Street near the Franklin Park Mall. It was one of my father's favorite places to eat. He could have a cold beer and a nice rib eye steak. I always looked forward to the relish plate served with hot bread. Then I would order the chopped steak with mushroom sauce and Van's special french fries. They were cut nice and thick, crispy on the outside, tender on the inside. The meal seemed to perk my father up, although maybe it was more the beer than the food that accomplished the mood swing.

We got home quite late and we both headed to bed. Soon after I fell asleep I was awakened by the sound of the telephone. It rang two or three times before my father answered it. I could hear his muffled voice as he spoke rather animatedly, but I couldn't understand a thing. My parents' bedroom was on the top floor of the house so the sound from his phone conversation didn't drift down sufficiently for me to catch any of the words. The conversation lasted for about five minutes. Then it was over.

The next morning I queried my father about the phone call. As I suspected, Ricardo Diaz had called. Once again my father voiced his displeasure about having to converse with his "good friend".

"It will be wonderful when Ricardo stops bothering me. Luckily he spends most of his time in Mexico and makes rare visits to the United States. Unfortunately he insists on visiting me so I'm going to bite the bullet and let him come over tonight."

I didn't press the matter further and headed out the door to carry out my training ritual. Today I was first playing some racquet ball with Tim Tierney. Tim had a friend who was getting us in to play at the University of Toledo Recreation Center. After I played with Tim I was going to play some tennis with Jim Davis at the Toledo Racquet Club. Lunch would follow at Schmucker's with Bob Obert. All in all another easy day in my idyllic life. By the time I was eating lunch with Bob, I'd totally forgotten about Ricardo Diaz.

But that would soon change. I drove down Reynolds Road from Schmucker's, turned onto Airport Highway, and then hopped on the expressway. When I got home I saw that a black Mercury Marquis was parked in our oval driveway. I also saw that my father's car was parked in the car port. My guess was that Ricardo Diaz was on the premises. I walked in the door, heard voices in the living room, and climbed the stairs to the second level.

When I got up there I saw that my father was sitting in his favorite living room chair. Across from him, in our L-shaped couch was a man who I surmised was Ricardo Diaz. The man was tall and just a bit overweight.

But he had golden blonde hair and was rather dashing. Handsome for a man who appeared to be in his fifties. Not what I expected from one of Mexican heritage, but I quickly remembered that his mother was German. When he saw me, he immediately leaped up and hurried over. Before my father could even say anything, Diaz grabbed my hand enthusiastically and spoke.

"Hello, Erick," Diaz said in his thick accent. "Very good to see you." He spoke like he was a long lost friend who I hadn't seen in years. He spoke like he expected me to recognize him. I didn't even have time to reply. "Vladimir has told me so much about you. It is good to finally meet you. My English is not good but I try hard to speak good."

"Nice to meet you too," I politely replied, while trying to extricate my hand from Diaz' grasp. His hands were long and boney. Clammy too. Certainly there was every reason to dry my hands on my pants after our hand shake, but out of a sense of courtesy I resisted.

My father spoke up. "Ricardo has been telling me all about his export business and how well it is going. Why don't you go do whatever you want right now and let us continue our conversation?"

"Oh, let him stay," intoned Diaz, with way too much flair. "It makes me so happy to finally meet my good friend's son."

I could almost see my father wince when Diaz called him a "good friend". I wasn't about to hang around any longer with this smarmy character. He acted way to convivial and falsely charming. He reminded me of some of the tennis instructors I knew, who oozed that repulsive sweetness that, for some reason, the ladies being taught actually believed was genuine. Or maybe they chose to believe because these instructors made them feel so special.

"No, no, Mr. Diaz. I wouldn't dream of interrupting you and my father. I'm sure you have a lot to talk about. I have some things I need to get done, so I'll just mosey on downstairs. It was definitely my pleasure to meet you," I said with as much sincerity as I could muster.

I quickly went down to my room and turned on the television. Talk about an ass. I'd only met the man for a few brief moments, but I immediately realized why my father couldn't stand Diaz. He epitomized the type of character, who while acting like you were so important to him, actually was mostly impressed with himself. Outwardly it was about you. Inwardly you knew it was about him.

I watched television for a few minutes but then decided I wanted to hear what Diaz and my father were talking about. I walked to the end of the lower level hall way and then crept up the stairs that led to the dining room. The dining room and kitchen were on the same level and from that level the stairs went up to the living room. I could crouch down on the stairs leading up to the dining room without being seen, but would also be close enough to hear Diaz and my father.

Unfortunately, I discovered that they were talking in German, which obviously made sense because Diaz was fluent in German and spoke horrible English. I assumed he learned German from his mother and I also assumed he needed to use German for his business. Although I had taken four years of German while at Toledo St. John's, it was obvious the Jesuits had not taught me very well (or perhaps I simply didn't have a flair for languages like Boris did). I could only make out a few words here and there and really couldn't follow any of the conversation. I thought I heard a reference to Hitler and some discussion about The Second World War, but I couldn't be sure. Of course, in light of my father's past history, it wouldn't be unusual for my father to discuss the war with a man whose mother was German, and who supposedly traveled to Europe on business. I gave up and went back to watching television. Roughly two hours later my father called me from the dining room.

"Erick, come say goodbye to Ricardo. He is about to leave."

With hesitation I headed upstairs. I didn't look forward to shaking hands again with Diaz. To my horror, not only did he shake my hand he gave me a big hug. He proclaimed, in that same sickeningly charming way, "Erick, so very, very good to see you. I hope I see you again before I leave back to Mexico. My business here is almost done." I avoided saying anything, just so he would be on his way as soon as possible. Diaz shook my father's hand, buttoned his coat, and went out the front door.

"My God," I loudly said to my father, "no wonder you can't stand that guy. He seems to be the most false personality I've ever encountered. Is he always like that, or maybe just when he speaks English?" I thought I would make a last ditch effort to give Diaz the benefit of the doubt. Perhaps his lack of familiarity with the English language made him feel he had to make an extra effort to make a good first impression.

"No," my father replied with a sigh and a shake of his head. "Ricardo always acts bombastic and overly enthusiastic. I just have never believed anything he tells me because I've always thought of him as a false weasel. Nobody can genuinely be that glad to see everyone and kiss up to everyone all the time. I'm so glad he's gone. Let's go eat. I'm hungry."

That night we ate a simple meal. We drove a couple of miles to the Buck Road exit off I-75 and dined at Denny's. Denny's always delivered quality, greasy, fast food. But they also had salads and vegetables so you could get a nice variety. We had a tasty meal followed by some dessert. It was the perfect way to end the evening after having to put up with Ricardo Diaz.

The next day went fine as usual. I did nothing exciting although I did talk to my future tennis coach Bob McKinley over the phone. He filled me in on the progress the Trinity tennis team was making in the fall and gave me an idea what the schedule looked like for the spring. Soon after I would arrive in San Antonio in January we were scheduled to play the National Indoor Team Championships at the University of Wisconsin Nielsen Tennis Center. That was a bit ironic. After heading south to escape the cold I was going to come back north to a place even more miserably cold than Toledo. So it goes!

That night my mother called from New Jersey. She was coming home in three days and gave us her train arrival information. She was having a great time with Vera and Erik and was thrilled that they had gone into New York City and eaten at the Russian Tea Room, a truly authentic Russian restaurant. They met my mother's uncle Dmitri and his second wife at the restaurant. Dmitri taught ballet and his wife Dortha Duckworth was an actress. They lived on West 54th Street, right near Carnegie Hall. The

Russian Tea Room was frequented by celebrities and my mother was excited to report that they had spotted Raymond Burr of Perry Mason fame eating at the restaurant.

Later that night after I had already fallen asleep, I heard the phone ring again. I looked at my clock. It was eleven o'clock. Who the hell was calling so late? I heard my father talking. And then he started talking much louder. I knew that it was wrong, but I was curious. I turned on a light and went to the den where I stealthily picked up the phone. I pressed my ear to the phone and listened.

I heard loud voices. In German. Nasal sounding. It had to be Ricardo Diaz. I listened for a bit longer but couldn't understand much so I quietly hung up the phone. After a couple of minutes it grew quiet, and then I heard more noise. It was obvious my father had gotten up. I grabbed my robe when I saw a bit of light in the hall reflecting from the dining room and heard my father coming down the stairs. I quickly made my way up the stairs to the dining room.

My father was fully dressed and had on his heavy coat. I couldn't help but notice the butt of his revolver sticking out of the side pocket. Of course I knew my father owned a gun, in his words, "for protection", but I never knew he carried it with him when he left the house.

"Where are you going Pa?" I asked.

"Oh, Erick. Sorry I woke you. I got a call from St. Charles Hospital. Apparently one of the doctors on call in the emergency room had a family crisis and couldn't come in, so they called me to take his place."

"Why the gun?" I inquired.

"Well, you know, it's late. You never know who is going to be out there. I just want to be safe."

So my father was lying to me. I wondered why.

"I should be back in a number of hours. Probably before you leave for your tennis."

With that, my father walked through the kitchen and went outside. I made a hasty decision. As soon as I heard my father start his car, I grabbed my car keys which were on a counter in the kitchen. As soon as he started driving down our drive way, I hurried out the door. I was greeted by a blast of cold air, which chilled me to the bones. A robe and slippers didn't do much to combat the freezing temperatures. I leaped into my car and started the engine. With any luck I could catch up to my father, and with more luck, he wouldn't know it was my car behind him.

When I made my way out of our neighborhood I took a guess and turned left on Eagle Point Road. In the far distance I saw some tail lights. Hopefully that was my father's car. By the time I passed Rossford High School on my right, I was close enough to the car to see it was indeed my father ahead of me. He wasn't driving particularly fast, but I stayed fairly far back. As we proceeded down Miami Street I waited to see if my father would really continue driving in the direction of St. Charles Hospital. In light of his lie, I doubted it. And I was right. Instead of staying on Miami Street, my father got on the entrance ramp to I-75 and the South End Bridge. He was crossing the river and heading towards downtown Toledo.

I followed up the entrance ramp. Traffic was sparse at that time of night, so I stayed well back. I wasn't too worried that my father would spot me because I was fairly certain he didn't suspect me of following him. He used to go to the hospital late at night quite often, but not anymore. However, I'm sure he thought that his story sounded good and I would think nothing of his late night departure. After he crossed the river my father got on to I-475, which headed in the direction of northwest Toledo and Sylvania. Eventually he got off at the Secor Road exit and turned left. I had to hurry and go through a yellow light, but I was able to keep pace. Soon after the turn, my father entered the parking lot of the Sheraton Hotel. I pulled into the same parking lot and waited to see what my father was going to do.

Eventually he parked and entered the front door of the hotel. The parking lot wasn't very full so I parked my car fairly far away from where my father was parked, but I also made sure that I had a decent view of the front door and also my father's car. I looked at the clock. It was now getting close to midnight. I waited for what seemed like forever, mainly because I was anxious to see what my father was up to. Then I saw them.

My father, walking out the door with Ricardo Diaz. It was just a few minutes after midnight.

Obviously Diaz had called my father to arrange this rendezvous. Maybe Diaz was more of a friend to my father than he chose to admit. On the other hand, maybe my father wasn't all that thrilled to be meeting Diaz in the middle of the night. They got into my father's car and took a right out of the parking lot onto Secor Road. They continued going straight through Monroe Street and kept going until they reached Laskey. On Laskey they took a left and I started to figure out where they were going. The Bier Stube, my father's favorite drinking hole. He stopped there fairly often after he played tennis because the bar was located near the Toledo Tennis Club and also had a nice variety of beers, including several German brands.

I drove past the bar but then turned around shortly after that. As I was driving back I could see Diaz and my father entering the bar. I pulled into the parking lot and tried to decide what to do. For whatever reason my father had lied to me and didn't want me to know he was meeting with Ricardo Diaz. Maybe he didn't want me to know that he was going out for a late beer. And why did he bring his revolver? I never knew my father to carry his firearm out in public. Not only would that be potentially dangerous, it was against the law. After sitting in my car until after one o'clock, I decided I would gain nothing by sitting there any longer. Plus what was I really going to do. All I had on was a pair of shorts, my robe, and my slippers. I wasn't about to go outside in that outfit. And I was starting to get tired. I reluctantly started my car up and drove back home.

When I got home I grabbed a quick glass of water and tiredly plodded downstairs. I'd had enough sleuthing for the day. Apparently I wasn't really cut out to be a detective. Not one who had to participate in stakeouts, in any case. Although I was really tired, my mind was restless. I wanted to know right now why my father was meeting with Ricardo Diaz, and I wanted to know right now why he lied to me. Eventually my mind petered out and I reached the same level of exhaustion with my mind that I already had with my body. I fell into a deep sleep.

Ring! Ring! I was startled out of a deep sleep. The phone in the adjoining den was ringing again. It was after three o'clock in the morning. The phone kept ringing. Why wasn't my father answering? That's right. He was out with Ricardo Diaz. The bars close at two o'clock, so he must still be making his way home. My muddled brain jolted out of its deep sleep and I scrambled to the den to pick up the phone.

I grabbed for the phone, fumbled it, and regained hold of it.

"Hello," I answered loudly, perhaps thinking I had to speak louder at this time of night so the person on the other end would hear me better.

"Hello," came the reply, in a screechy and scratchy voice. "Is this the Iskersky residence?"

"It is," I answered, while feeling a bit uneasy that someone would be calling our house at this hour, unless there was bad news. "May I ask who's calling?"

"Yes, this is Officer Shelley Coslowski, with the Toledo Police Department. Please don't get alarmed. May I speak with Mrs. Iskersky?"

"She's not home. She's in New Jersey."

"Are you, by chance, Vladimir Iskersky's son?"

"Yes, I'm Erick. Why are you calling? How do you know my father?" I asked with a sense of dread in my voice.

"Look, please stay calm. Take a deep breath."

By now I was on pins and needles. There was no way I was taking a deep breath.

"I'm sorry to have to report to you that your father has been shot."

What I was told didn't immediately register. Or I didn't want to hear it.

"What do you mean he was shot?"

"I know it's a shock to you, but your father was shot in the parking lot of the Bier Stube bar. But at least he's alive. He's here at Mercy Hospital in downtown. He's being operated on as we speak."

My mind shifted into panic mode, at a hundred miles an hour. I couldn't think straight. Why didn't I stay at the Bier Stube instead of coming home? Why didn't I confront my father and insist that he tell me what was going on? Why did I try to play detective?

"How's he doing? Is he alright?"

"I'm sorry. I don't know. You'll have to get an update from the hospital."

I didn't bother to say goodbye. I ran to my bedroom and hastefully got dressed. In a matter of moments I was barreling down the road, heading down Miami Street towards the Cherry Street Bridge. This time I wasn't following my father, this time I was racing to the hospital to see if my father would live. I crossed the Cherry Street Bridge and immediately looked for the entrance to Mercy Hospital. I spotted the entrance and turned into the parking lot reserved for visitors. I jumped out of my car and ran to the emergency room entrance.

At this time of night the emergency room was swarming with people. Some were obviously hurt and waiting in line to get treatment. Those in line were not the serious cases. Most of the people in line looked a bit dirty and unsavory. Maybe they had been in a bar fight, maybe they were homeless, or maybe they didn't have insurance and the only way to get treated was at an emergency room. It didn't matter to me. I needed to find out what was happening to my father.

I saw the information desk that was nestled in the corner of the emergency waiting room. I hustled over to the desk and addressed the young lady sitting there. Her name tag indicated she was Emma Deaver, Receptionist.

By this time I was a bit breathless, both because I had been running around like a mad man, and because I was nervous and worried as hell. "Emma, my name is Erick Iskersky. My father has been shot and is being operated on. Who can I talk to in order to find out how my father is doing?"

"Oh, yes, Officer Coslowski told me you would be coming in. There is another waiting room in the east wing of the hospital for relatives of those being operated on. I'll have one of the orderlies take you over there."

It seemed like we were taking a tour of the entire hospital as I followed Jerry the Orderly. The hallways were like a maze to me. I kept thinking we were finally there, and then we would take another turn, down another hall way. Eventually we got to the waiting room and there was another information desk, although this one was unoccupied.

"Who do I talk to Jerry?" I pleaded, "there's no one there."

"I'll go find one of the nurses."

Jerry used his key to get through a set of double doors leading into a hallway. The waiting room itself was occupied by a handful of people. All looked tired. Some were drinking coffee. At this hour there could only be emergency surgeries. It was apparent that, like me, these people were nervously waiting to get news about their loved ones. Then I spotted a police officer standing by her self near one of the coffee vending machines. I walked over to her and took a look at her name tag. In so doing I couldn't help but notice she was rather well endowed. Even her uniform couldn't hide that fact. And when I looked up to see her face, I was surprised to see how young and pretty she was. That caused me to stammer.

"Officer Coslowski. Erick Iskersky. You spoke to me on the phone."

"You made it here pretty quick. Do you live near here?" There was that screechy voice again.

"Yeah, just across the river in Rossford. But I was flying here. Any news on my father?"

"Not yet, I'm afraid. If you're up to it, I'd like to ask you a few questions."

Right then, Jerry walked up to me with a nurse.

"I'm Nurse Meltzer. I understand you need to see someone."

Jerry walked off after I thanked him. I asked Officer Coslowski to wait while I talked to Nurse Meltzer. Nurse Meltzer looked exactly like I expected a nurse to look like. She was relatively short and stocky. Her hair was up in a bun. Her figure was not svelte. Her eyes looked worn out – she'd probably been on duty most of the night. She was business like, but friendly.

"Yes, my name is Erick Iskersky. Officer Coslowski called me to tell me my father was shot and is being operated on. Can you tell me how he's doing?"

"Unfortunately Erick, I can't tell you anything yet. He was only taken into surgery about two hours ago. I'm praying for him. Your father is on staff here at the hospital. I know he does most of his work at St. Charles, but I see him here on occasion. He's really nice to the nurses. I'll let you know as soon as we find out anything."

The waiting and not knowing was gnawing at me. I wanted to know something. Good or bad. I couldn't take much more of this. I tried to calm myself. I took some deep breaths and let them out. I closed my eyes and for the first time thought about what life might be like if my father died. The pictures in my mind of life without my father were unbearable. To avoid the thoughts I said a little prayer. I prayed for my father and for my mother. I prayed that all would be good, but it didn't make me feel a lot better.

"Are you alright?" Officer Coslowski had quietly waited while I was talking to Nurse Meltzer and her voice startled me a bit.

"I'm as good as I can be I guess. Can we sit down? Suddenly I'm feeling kind of tired. I suppose the adrenaline is wearing off."

We sat across from each other at a small table covered with old mgazines. Now I got a really good look at Officer Coslowski. She couldn't have been older than twenty two, tops. Her hair was relatively short, somewhat wavy. Her eyes looked gorgeous, deep aqua with a sweet melancholy gaze. Her skin was smooth in texture. Her facial features were almost perfect. Gorgeous face, luscious lips, nose and ears perfectly symmetrical. For a brief moment I was distracted away from my troubles. Her look had a way of mesmerizing me.

I blurted out without thinking. "How old are you and how did someone as beautiful as you become a police woman?"

She blushed and looked away. She quickly regained her composure and returned my eye contact. "I've always dreamed of being a police woman. My father is a lawyer and has been for years. He didn't want me to become a cop, but now he's quite proud of me. I'm twenty three but I've only been a police woman for about one year." Her squeaky voice was completely incongruous with her appearance.

Unfortunately the brief interlude of peacefulness in my mind disappeared and the realization that my father might be fighting for his life hit me like a ton of bricks. I felt the need to cry, but I felt embarrassed to do it in front of Officer Coslowski.

"Is there any way you can tell me what happened to my father?"

"Here's what we know so far. The detectives are still on the scene. Sometime after 1:30, right around last call at the Bier Stube, a man ran into the bar and shouted that there was a shooting. No one inside the bar had heard anything, as far as we know, because someone had turned on the juke box and the music was playing pretty loudly. There weren't that many people in the bar. The bar tender called 911 and so we were summoned to the scene." That means I had left the parking lot no more than twenty minutes before my father got shot.

"Where was my father shot?"

"Out in the parking lot. Not that close to the entrance to the bar. He might have been leaving, we don't know. There was another man shot too. Based on the ID we found on him, we think the other man is named Ricardo Diaz. And he didn't make it. He died at the scene. Do you know who Ricardo Diaz is?"

My mouth dropped open. The man who I barely knew and who I had come to despise in a very short time, was dead. Suddenly I felt some pangs of guilt. Maybe he wasn't such a bad guy after all. Maybe I should have given him the benefit of the doubt. And then I also realized I shouldn't have been totally shocked. After all, my father and Diaz had driven to the Bier Stube together.

"Well yes. I just met him. He's a friend of my father's who lives in Mexico. They weren't close friends, I don't think, but this is the first time I've ever heard of Diaz. I have to admit I didn't like him much, although I met him only briefly. He just seemed kind of slimy."

For the next hour or so I spoke with Officer Coslowski. Her manner was very comforting and helped to calm me down. I'm sure she could have done something more useful, although she indicated that she was to wait at the hospital until a determination was made by the doctors about my father's condition. I asked her a lot of questions about the incident at the Bier Stube, but she had only been at the scene of the crime for a short period before she drove over to the hospital.

Certain facts seemed clear. My father and Ricardo Diaz had been shot in the parking lot of the Bier Stube. Diaz was dead. Potentially there was a witness to the crime, or at least someone who was at the scene immediately after the shooting – namely the man who ran into the bar and reported the shooting. Officer Coslowski had also mentioned that the "witness" was no where to be found after the shooting. It had also been established that multiple shots were fired at both my father and Diaz. Other than that, Officer Coslowski could not tell me much more.

It was approaching 6:00 am. Despite my worries I was getting so tired that I found myself drifting off for short naps. Before I called my mother in New Jersey and Boris in Germany, I wanted to find out exactly what my father's condition was – and whether he would survive the shooting or not. Officer Coslowski (or Shelley, which is what she eventually asked me to call her) maintained a level of alertness that surprised me. She was up for as long as I had been, but except for occasional sips of coffee, did nothing to indicate that she might be tired.

Sometime after 6:00 am, I felt myself being shaken. Apparently I had drifted off yet again. Shelley and Nurse Meltzer were standing over me, looking down. Next to them stood a tall, gray haired man with spectacles. Their faces looked grim and I steeled myself for the worst.

"Alright, Erick. Your father is finally out of surgery. This is Dr. Addison Whyte, who performed the surgery."

I felt some sense of relief. They were not talking about my father in the past tense. Just in case I asked the question I was so scared of asking. "Is my father alive?"

CHAPTER 8

Dr. Whyte hesitated a bit before he answered my question, and his face looked tired and worn out. "Yes, he is alive."

That's all I heard. My heart beat faster and I felt a surge of adrenaline at the unbelievable news. It had been hours of tense waiting and now I at least knew that my father was alive.

"I'm sure these past few hours have been tough on you. The surgery was very difficult and took more time than I anticipated. Fortunately your father is in good physical shape and he's a real fighter. He was shot three times and lost a lot of blood. Because of the shock and the loss of blood, he is in a coma and in very serious condition. But I am very optimistic he will make a full recovery."

"Thank God," I said. It took me a few moments to regain my composure and continue speaking. "I'm sure you are very tired yourself, Dr. Whyte. I appreciate your effort very much. When will you know for sure the prognosis for a full recovery?"

"I would think that within a couple of days we'll know for sure how well your father will recover. As I said, I am very optimistic."

I thanked Nurse Meltzer and Dr. Whyte one more time and asked them if there was a phone I could use to call my mother. And then I realized that I didn't have Aunt Vera's phone number. I would have to go home first and find my godmother's phone number. Needless to say I was still quite shaken up and exhausted. At this point, Shelley indicated that she had a few more questions she had to ask and quite generously, I thought, offered to drive me home. Even though I had my car at the hospital, it was easy to accept the gracious offer. Somehow I didn't want to be alone and I wasn't yet ready to say good bye to Shelley. Despite the grueling circumstances, I actually was worried I would never see her again, which of course was quite likely.

We left the hospital. By now it was almost eight o'clock in the morning. Despite my weariness and worry, Shelley's presence gave me some comfort and as she drove me home it was difficult to keep my eyes off her beautiful face. She must have sensed my unease, but at the same time I could tell she knew I was glancing at her quite often. I felt rather despicable. Here my father was on the verge of death, and I was captivated by a gorgeous young woman with a voice that resembled Edith Bunker's voice from All In The Family fame.

When we arrived I invited Shelley inside and told her I would call my mother and then she could take me back to the hospital. During our drive from the hospital she had asked me a couple more questions about my father's evening and if I knew why he had gone to see Ricardo Diaz. I answered as truthfully as I could, but I didn't mention the fact that my father had lied to me about having to fill in at St. Charles' Hospital emergency room.

Aunt Vera answered the phone on the third ring. "Good morning, Aunt Vera," I said in rather less than perfect Russian. "It's Erick. I really need to talk to Mom. She's there, isn't she?"

"Hey, Erick, it's nice to hear from you. Of course Helen is here. Are you doing well?"

"As well as can be expected. There was an accident. Father was injured. That's why I need to talk to Mom."

"Oh no!" Aunt Vera blurted out, with grave concern in her voice. "Is Vladimir alright?"

"I think he'll be fine, so don't say anything to Mom yet. I don't want her to worry."

Aunt Vera called my mother who came to the phone in a matter of seconds. From the tone of her voice I could tell she must have seen Aunt Vera's face and realized something was wrong.

"Erick, what happened? Are you doing okay?"

"Mom, I'm doing okay but try not to get too worried when I tell you what happened last night."

With that I gave my mother a detailed account of what had transpired in the early morning hours, leading up to the shooting, the surgery, and the prognosis for my father's recovery. My mother remained relatively calm when I assured her that my father would have a full recovery. Although that wasn't a certainty, I didn't want my mother to lose control of her emotions and experience any unnecessary anguish. She really only got very upset twice. When I first told her that my father had been shot, and when I mentioned Ricardo Diaz. It was obvious he was not well liked by either of my parents. Even though she expressed regret that he was killed, she did not express approval of the fact Diaz had visited in the first place.

By the time I was done with my call, we had agreed my mother would take the first flight she could find back to Toledo, instead of taking the Amtrak train. Shelley was admiring the view of the Maumee River from our living room and didn't mind waiting around for a call back from my mother informing me when her flight would arrive. By the time we got into Shelley's patrol car it was almost nine thirty.

I decided to be bold. I was hungry and I didn't want to say good bye to Shelley. I knew we were both tired and, although I didn't smell my under arm, I was quite sure my level of hygiene had deteriorated considerably through the night. Nevertheless I asked Shelley if she was hungry and wanted to grab a bite at Moe's Cafe, in Rossford. To my great and shocking surprise, she agreed. Again I felt guilty that I was actually thinking romantic thoughts while my father was fighting for his life. But I needed to distract my mind, and Shelley was the perfect remedy for that task.

Under the circumstances, we had a good breakfast. Moe's Cafe catered to the workers who worked at the Libbey Owens Ford glass factory just down the street. Most of the patrons who ate breakfast had done so earlier. The remaining customers were clearly factory workers who had gotten off the over night shift at seven that morning. By the time

Shelley and I were seated, these guys had obviously had a few beers and were quite boisterous. When Shelley and I had entered the place, there was the initial turning of heads just to see who was coming into the local joint. The turning of heads became the craning of necks, which led to full fledged staring. Not only because of Shelley's looks and her captivating walk, the walk that seemed to accentuate the gentle swaying of her hips, but the fact that this absolutely stunning specimen was wearing a police uniform.

We sat down in a booth and grabbed the menus that were wedged between the salt and pepper shakers and the napkin holder. Surprisingly I was quite hungry. Even though my concern for my father was tremendously high, I was also somewhat relieved and very optimistic because of Dr. Whyte's prognosis. I ordered two scrambled eggs with ham and cheese, one pancake, and hash browns. Shelley ordered a western omelette, toast, and hash browns. Because of her figure, I didn't expect Shelley to order so much food. Obviously she had a fast metabolism.

Our conversation seemed to flow easily, as if we had known each other for a longer period of time. It was just what I needed to keep my mind occupied. It turned out that Shelley was a rather good athlete during her high school days. She played basketball in the winter and ran track in the spring. She had grown up in Ottawa Hills, a well to do suburb of Toledo located near the University of Toledo. Both her parents were professionals so Shelley's decision to fore-go college and attend the police academy was not well received. Luckily, over time, her parents had accepted her decision and any fracture in the relationship caused by her becoming a policewoman was healed.

As we were finishing up our breakfast, one of the workers who had been sitting at the bar strolled over to our booth. From his attitude you could tell two things. First, he was probably fairly inebriated. Second, he thought he was cool. He was dressed in dirty jeans and a dark t-shirt, but you could see he had sweated a lot when he was working. His odor was not pleasant. His face looked circular, almost pudgy, so one would expect him to be fat. But his body really didn't match his facial features. He seemed quite fit and walked with that sliding shuffle that he thought made him look like a stud. My guess was that he was around thirty years old.

"Hey baby," he said with somewhat slurred speech, "whatcha doin' over here? Is this your kid brother?" The second question was said with a sneer. "You getting off duty soon? Maybe you and I can have a drink." He continued to talk without even waiting for an answer to any of his questions. Finally he stopped babbling, apparently convinced he had made his point.

"Sir," Shelley replied with extreme politeness, "I'm afraid I am in a middle of a criminal investigation and am only taking a breakfast break. It's obvious you've had a bit too much to drink, so if you don't mind I'd appreciate it if you went back to your seat. My friend and I have some matters we have to discuss."

He started laughing. He turned to his buddies at the bar. "Hey guys, this police chick claims she's working and has some business she has to take care of with this bozo, instead of having a drink with me." His buddies joined in the laughter.

Shelley's face started to get a bit red and her soft features hardened. Sternly, but certainly not in a loud voice Shelley retorted, "Look buddy, just quietly go back to your seat and leave us alone. Don't turn this into an ugly situation."

"Hell, this ain't no ugly situation. You're real pretty and I think you're just playing a little hard to get because you want some from me, don'tcha?"

What happened next, happened so fast that I barely had time to flinch. Shelley leaped out of the booth, kneed the jerk in the groin, spun him around as he doubled over, and cuffed him from behind. He was in pain and quite shocked, but then he started cursing. Meanwhile his buddies at the bar started to hoot and holler.

"Hey, look what happened to old Tommy. He got roughed up by that pretty policewoman. You not gonna start crying now, are you?"

The men kept making fun of Tommy. Shelley pushed Tommy down onto the seat of the booth and waited until Tommy calmed down. Eventually he realized he was in no position to resist and he sat there glumly while his friends kept laughing. In a matter of minutes Shelley talked some sense into the lout, uncuffed him, and let him go back to the bar. Shelley and I left after paying our bill.

"That was something Shelley," I said admiringly. "I was scared of that guy. I'm glad he didn't come after me because he thought I was a wimp."

"Usually these guys make a lot of noise and nothing else. They work hard and their jobs aren't all that fun, so I think they just need to blow off some steam sometimes."

By the time Shelley dropped me off at the hospital, it was around eleven o'clock. I hadn't slept a wink except for the fitful dozing off at the hospital waiting on word about my father. I felt grimy and desperately needed a shower. But spending the last few hours with Shelley had kept me calm and occupied. Plus, the incident at Moe's had provided some additional entertainment.

"Shelley, thanks so much for everything. I don't know if I would have made it through the night without you."

"Hey, my pleasure. I'm glad it looks promising for your father's recovery. I'm just doing my job."

"If that's what they mean when they talk about police hospitality, I'm all for it," I intoned.

Shelley laughed. "I don't usually have breakfast with the people I'm helping. But you're nice. Under the circumstances, I hope it kept your mind off things."

Little did Shelley know that at that moment I was thinking like an eighteen year old male, dreaming of her in my arms, kissing me. Telling me what a stud I am. Telling me how she needed me more than anything in the world. My thoughts became so graphic I almost could feel myself blush. Luckily, Shelley snapped me out of it.

"Erick, you hear me?"

"Sure I did," I lied. "Whatever you say."

"No, I was just saying I'll give you my phone number in case you want to talk sometime about what happened. Or if you need any help."

"That's really nice of you Shelley. I'd like that."

She wrote down her phone number in a note pad, ripped out the sheet, and handed it to me. I grabbed the slip of paper and thanked her again for everything. And then she drove off. I wondered if I would ever see her again. She had been very nice to me and I wished so much at that moment that I was not an eighteen year old kid. If only I was twenty two or three. I could ask her out. Then I laughed to myself. Fat chance she would go out with someone like me. She was truly gorgeous.

I drove straight home from the hospital and took my long awaited shower. My mother's flight was coming in at 2:15 so I still had a couple of hours. Earlier we had decided to delay calling Boris until later that day, or even the next day, when we got a better idea of what my father's progress was like. I had to leave for the airport by about 1:15, which really didn't leave me enough time for a nap. So I watched TV for a short time and then hopped into my car for the ride to the airport. Amazingly I was no longer that tired. I was probably surviving on adrenaline and still too jumpy to really fall asleep. I knew I had to be strong, for my mother's sake. On the other hand, my parents had gone through a lot of horrible times in their lives when they lived in Russia and had faced much despair. This situation would just be another situation they would meet head on.

Because traffic was heavier than I expected, I only arrived at the airport at 2:00. But the Toledo airport is small, and parking was easy. I made it to the arrival gate with minutes to spare. My mother's flight was on time, so in a few minutes I could see my mother come out of the arrival ramp and enter the arrival lobby. I quickly ran over to her and yelled out.

"Hey, Mom, over here."

She recognized my voice and turned in my direction. She looked worried but tried to smile. I ran over and gave her a big hug. "It will be alright Mom, it will be alright. Pa is going to pull through."

I filled her in as we drove to Mercy Hospital. After what my mom had gone through when she was a young woman, I was confident that she would be able to handle the adversity we now faced with great strength. In fact I was more worried that I would be the one who would break down and fall apart if my father didn't recover from his injuries. By the time we got to the hospital my mom knew everything that I knew and we were certainly prepared for the worst as we headed up to the intensive care unit. We were directed to my father's room and made our way to his bed side.

I was shocked. I wasn't adequately prepared for what I saw. Neither was my mom. My father had tubes sticking out of various parts of his body and he was hooked up to some machines. His face looked sallow and his eyes were closed. His breathing seemed weak, which was probably why he had an oxygen tube inserted through his nostrils. He looked vulnerable and defenseless, which he obviously was. But I wasn't used to seeing him that way. He had always been strong and had a commanding presence. But not now.

My mother started to cry softly but then immediately turned to me and said that it was time to pray. "Your father and I survived much horror and uncertainty. But God has always been good to us. Things could have been much worse, but I truly believe in my heart that without God's help and guidance we never would have made it."

With that, we got down on our knees and prayed. The prayer my mother said was in Russian. Boris and I were raised in the Russian Orthodox faith, which is very similar to Catholicism. However hundreds of years ago the Orthodox Church separated from the Catholic Church. There were differences in the doctrines of the two churches, and in addition, we did not believe in the Pope. During my high school years I attended mass at Toledo St. John's High School during the week. When I was younger, we attended a Bulgarian Orthodox church because there were no Russian Orthodox churches in Toledo. Now, more than ever, my pleas to God were fervent and desperate. It did not seem fair to me that my father had survived The Second World War but was now fighting for his life. Apparently the victim of a random shooting.

After we prayed, we sat in the room for at least an hour and simply wanted to be in my father's presence. I started to feel some peace creep into my body. Perhaps our prayers had helped to soothe our nerves and my outlook had become a bit more optimistic. I also started to get hungry, which meant my body was beginning to function more normally. We both started to feel even better when Doctor Whyte stopped by and gave us a fairly upbeat assessment of my father's up-to-the-minute condition. He encouraged us not to focus on what my father looked like as he lay in the hospital bed. All the tubes and machines were there to stabilize my father's well being. Once he got stronger and stronger, he would eventually be unhooked. Then everything depended upon how soon he came out of his coma. If everything went as Doctor Whyte anticipated, within a number of days my father would come out of his coma and start to make substantial progress.

As evening approached, we ate dinner in the hospital cafeteria and visited my father's bed side one more time. I was finally getting exhausted. Because I hadn't really slept all night, I was ready to hit the sack. My body had been running on adrenaline fumes for the past few hours, now there were no fumes left. We headed home and I went to sleep almost immediately. But not until I prayed one more time.

The next morning when I woke up, I could smell something good in the kitchen. My mom was making apple pancakes, served with fruit syrup and sour cream. She also was serving hard boiled eggs. My appetite was large that morning and I felt good. I was convinced that my father was going to pull through. He had to. There was so much more I wanted to do in life to make him proud of me, so I couldn't accept the fact that he would die so soon. My mother looked like she was holding up fairly well. "Remember," my mother said, "Russians love to have a good breakfast. A big breakfast. It will give us energy and help us make it through these tough times." And she was right. I felt ready to go.

Before we left for the hospital, we called Boris in Munich. His immediate reaction, after the shock had worn off, was to insist on flying back home. But Mom talked him out of it. "Father would insist that you continue your studies. Your future is too important. Father is strong. He will live. He knows that you love him. That's what will help him pull through. He knows his family loves him."

After convincing Boris to stay in Germany, we drove to the hospital. We followed the same routine for the next few days. Mornings at the hospital. Home for lunch. Back to the hospital for more visiting and dinner in the hospital cafeteria. It was obvious even to a casual observer that my father was getting stronger. Although I didn't play any tennis, I needed to do something physical. Both to keep my body fit and to keep my mind sharp. Dr. Whyte continued to give us more and more promising news, but I was still not feeling at ease. The exercising helped me immensely.

I also called Shelley a couple of times to give her updates and, of course, just to talk to her. I certainly didn't let her know how I felt about her. I tried not to sound too eager when I talked to her. For the most part we discussed her job and what her aspirations were for the future. I steered clear of discussing her personal life because I knew I would be crushed if I learned that she had a boyfriend. Even though it was ludicrous for me to think that Shelley would want to go out with an eighteen year old, in my dreams I pretended that I would ask her out and she would say yes.

Ten days after my father was shot, the miracles of miracles finally happened. My father came out of his coma. We were at home when it happened. But a nurse from the hospital called us right after he woke up. What unmitigated joy. We called Boris in Germany, Aunt Vera and Uncle Erik in New Jersey, and my mom's Uncle Dmitri in New York. After we made all of the calls we literally leaped into the car like we were on cloud nine and drove to the hospital. When we got to my father's room we weren't quite sure what to expect, but our spirits were soaring. The tubes were no longer protruding from my father's body, nor was he hooked up to any machines. He was back to the living.

A nurse was in the room when we walked in. Her name was Emma Lovejoy, but she hardly looked like she was loving, nor did she look joyful. She had a very stern look on a very taut looking face – as if she had plastic surgery in the past. But that was doubtful. She couldn't have been more than forty years old. She was somewhat pretty, but her expression was so mean looking that her beauty was hidden by her scowl.

"Who are you?" she barked out at us. Before there was even time for a reply my mother ran over to my father's bed side, leaned over and gave him a big kiss. Immediately she started talking to him in Russian with expressions of love and kindness. I didn't see such displays of affection by my parents very often, so I was truly touched.

My father still looked pale and he had lost a considerable amount of weight. But his jaw still looked strong and the look in his eyes, although not fully alert, indicated that he was quite cognizant of his surroundings. Obviously we were simply thrilled that he was with us once again, so his looks were not a priority in our mind.

Surprisingly Nurse Lovejoy's tone softened considerably. "You must be Mrs. Iskersky. We are so ecstatic that Dr. Iskersky has made such wonderful progress. And to see him out of his coma is simply fantastic. Don't talk to him too much. We don't want him to get too tired."

My father spoke haltingly, but clearly. "How wonderful to see you both. Where is Boris? Why isn't he here?"

"Boris is in Germany, studying," my mother replied.

"Why is that?"

"Because he could get into medical school over in Germany and have it paid for," explained my mother. "He has one year of pre-med studies to finish and then he'll have three years of medical school."

My father nodded. "I guess I remember some of that. But my mind is foggy. I don't really know why I'm here exactly."

It took us a fair amount of time, but we explained everything that had happened as best as we could. We didn't mention the shooting of Ricardo Diaz and his death, just in case it would greatly disturb my father. The way he had talked about Diaz made me doubt that he would have been all that upset that Diaz was dead. Nonetheless, we were careful not to say anything to my father that might make him too emotional.

While we were still in the room a man wearing a frumpy suit with a loosened tie walked in. He had a bulbous nose, with a face that must have been covered with acne when he was a youth. He wore a hat and I didn't see any hair below the brim of his hat so I surmised that he might be bald. I realized I was right when he removed his hat to display a gleaming, bald pate, smooth as a bowling ball. His head was awkwardly shaped, as if a doctor had to pull him out of the womb with tongs and had accidentally applied too much pressure to his skull. His eyes were jet black. His lips seemed too small for his face and were so red that initially I thought he might actually have lipstick on. If I'd met him in a dark alley, I would have been terrified.

"I'm Detective Brad Pascoe," he exclaimed, talking out of the side of his mouth while tilting his head. He had a deep baritone, a voice that resonated strongly. "I'm assuming you are Mrs. Iskersky. Doctor, it's good to see you are out of your coma." He said it with little emotion. "I'm in charge of the case involving your shooting," he said as he turned to my father, "and I'm certainly hoping you will be able to answer some questions."

"Detective Pascoe, please don't take very long or ask too many questions," interjected Nurse Lovejoy. "Dr. Iskersky is still very weak and his memory is still not completely normal."

"Don't worry Nurse," and he looked at her nameplate, "Lovejoy, I'll be brief this time and come back another time for a more thorough session."

With that Pascoe started asking my father a number of questions. At first he couldn't even remember why he was in the hospital, but with some prompting he gradually was able to provide a minimum body of information. It was clear that Pascoe was getting quite frustrated. After no more than fifteen minutes, he growled about how useless this visit was and stated he would come back another day when my father's memory started to improve. We were all quite relieved when he left. Thankfully Pascoe's job didn't require a high degree of charm, because that's one thing he certainly didn't have.

We left the hospital a short while later. Through all of the stress and turmoil we didn't even realize it was Thursday, November 25. My mother was worn out, even though she was as happy as could be. We made plans to visit my father in the evening and then go out for Thanksgiving dinner. Very few places were open because of the holiday, so we ended up at Denny's, which never closed. Who knows if the dinner was good. My mother and I enjoyed it immensely, simply because our mood was so great.

Even a lousy meal couldn't have spoiled our feelings of joy and happiness, but we definitely proclaimed this one of the best Thanksgivings of all time. For us, it truly was a time to be thankful.

Now that my father was out of his coma and on the road to recovery, I started to plan my trip to Germany to visit Boris. Of course in the back of my mind was the mission of discovering more about Gunter Gruber and the "Inner Circle of Five". Somewhere in the books that Dr. Berry recommended I look through at the University of Munich Library and Munich Museum of War, I was convinced that I would find out something that would help solve the mystery surrounding Gruber. I also vowed to press my father for more details about his Second World War experience. Clearly that had something to do with the Gruber incident in New York. For some reason Gruber wanted to talk to me, or perhaps even kidnap me. So I was excited about the prospect of going to Germany.

Over the next two weeks my father got better and better. His memory sharpened, he gained weight once he started eating solid food, and he was antsy, ready to come back home. Detective Pascoe made another visit. And he also questioned me about my account of the night Ricardo Diaz was shot. I was very wary of Pascoe and wasn't sure about one thing. Do I tell Pascoe my father took his gun with him the night he went to the Bier Stube with Diaz? I wasn't sure if it was legal for my father to do so.

As it turns out, I had a lot to worry about. Pascoe relayed to me what my father had told him. Apparently, as Diaz and my father had left the Bier Stube and were by my father's car, two black youths with a gun accosted them. They proceeded to rob them. Then, afraid perhaps of being identified, they shot Diaz and my father. Ballistic tests had confirmed that the bullets retrieved out of Diaz's and my father's bodies were from the same gun. Pascoe didn't mention anything about a gun found on my father. Nor did he say that my father told him about a gun. This put me in a quandary.

Pascoe pressed me for details of that evening. I told him everything I could remember. How I followed my father to the Sheraton, and then the Bier Stube. How I left when Diaz and my father went into the Bier Stube.

I couldn't get myself to tell Pascoe that my father had a gun when he left the house. I didn't want to get my father in trouble. Plus I wondered why no gun was found on my father. Could it be the two young robbers had taken it? In any case, until I talked to my father, I wasn't going to say anything.

My father was scheduled to come home around December 10 and I was scheduled to leave for Germany on December 12 and to return on December 22. I would have roughly nine days to research the "Inner Circle of Five". Then I would come home with Boris, and we would spend Christmas with my parents. After New Year's Day we would both be off to school. Boris to return to the University of Munich. Me, to start my studies at Trinity University. I was definitely getting bored and needed to compete on the tennis court once again. Because of everything that had happened, and because I was stuck in Toledo with no good practice partners, my game was not sharp. I was worried that I wouldn't play real great when I got to San Antonio.

My father actually got out of the hospital a day early, on December 9. He looked almost like himself, but was still a bit weak. His memory was completely back. His recovery was phenomenal. When he came home I said a prayer of thanks. I don't know if I would say that my faith was real strong or that my belief in God was overwhelming. But the fact that my father came home in such good condition certainly enforced the notion in my heart that there is a God and He is a good God. On the other hand, tell that to those who have lost loved ones in random acts of violence or in accidents. Their prayers were never answered. Why is that?

The night before I left for Germany, I sat down with my father in the living room. My mother was cleaning up in the kitchen after dinner.

"Pa, why didn't you tell Detective Pascoe that you had a gun with you when you went to see Diaz? And what happened to the gun? I know you had it because I saw it under your coat when you were leaving the house that evening."

"Erick. It is very tricky. I have a license for the gun, but I am not allowed by law to carry it in public places. Stupidly I forgot to leave the gun in the glove compartment of the car when we went into the Bier Stube. I was so surprised when we were attacked that I didn't have time to take out the gun and try to use it. When the two thugs discovered I had a gun as they were robbing us, I think they panicked and decided to shoot us. I'm assuming they took my gun after they shot us."

"And why did you tell me you were going to St. Charles Hospital the night you were shot, instead of telling me you were going to see Ricardo Diaz?"

"I didn't want you to know that I was going to see him late at night. You know he bothered me and always wanted something. I thought it would be easier to just tell you I was going to the hospital."

Presumably that solved the mystery of the disappearance of my father's gun. Reporting that to the police would change nothing. At least that was my opinion. Other than the fact that the two assailants were black, and seemed to be young, my father had been unable to provide much of a description to the police about his attackers. More than likely, unless they were somehow apprehended by accident and confessed, the two black youths who had killed Ricardo Diaz and gravely wounded my father, would never be caught.

CHAPTER 9

My flight to Munich left on time on December 12. I was booked on a non-stop flight on Lufthansa that left Detroit International Airport at 8:45pm Eastern Standard Time and was due to arrive at the Munich International Airport by 9:00am local time. Boris was going to meet me at the airport. The flight itself was uneventful except I would be arriving in Munich at 3:00am Eastern Standard Time so I knew I was not going to get a full night of sleep. Our arrival was punctual.

It took me about an hour to get my luggage and get through customs. As I entered the arrival area outside customs I spotted Boris, standing near one of the exits to the parking lot. He waved to me and hurried over to give me a big hug. His hair was considerably longer than when he had left Toledo a few months before. Other than that he looked pretty much the same. Because he was wearing a heavy coat, I surmised that it was quite cold in Munich. I was definitely right. When we walked out the doors we were hit by a cold blast of air. I could see a bunch of snow piled high in the parking lot where it had been pushed to the side by snow plows.

We headed across the many lanes of traffic in front of the arrival entrance and walked up to a bus stop. I knew from previous conversations with Boris that Munich had an excellent public transportation system. It was so good that Boris could easily live in Munich without a car. We boarded the next bus that pulled in at our stop and headed toward downtown.

I had read up on the history of Munich at the Toledo Public Library when it was decided I would visit Boris. I knew it was the third largest city in West Germany and was situated only thirty miles from the edge of the Alps. In the 1920's Adolph Hitler had begun his political activities there and it was there that he had organized the first Nazi Party army. During The Second World War nearly half of the buildings in Munich were destroyed by bombing, but by 1970 most of the damage was repaired. By 1976 the population was 1,300,000 inhabitants.

We remained on one bus until after we crossed the Isar River. After that we boarded a bus that would take us to Marienplatz, which is the main square of Munich. From there, Boris indicated, we would take one more bus to Ludwigstrasse, which was a street only several blocks from where Boris lived in his one room apartment. Boris lived very near the University of Munich, so it was very convenient for him to attend his classes. The University of Munich is a large university with over 23,000 students. Based on my previous conversations with Boris I knew that I would also be near the Munich Museum of War. There are several more museums in the same area of the city, namely the Bavarian National Museum and the Residenzmuseum.

Boris lived on Munsterstrasse. His apartment was on the top floor of a three story building. The apartment was sparsely furnished, but very comfortable. It faced the street below, so a lot of the street noise filtered through the walls and reminded me that we were in the middle of a big city. By now I was quite sleepy and exhausted, but Victor convinced me not to take a nap. "If you take a nap now," he explained, "you won't want to go to bed at night. Remember, we are six hours ahead of your time. You have to stay awake until night time." I grudgingly acquiesced.

Instead we took a walk toward the university, where Boris had a class later that afternoon. We stopped in at a local cafe named Maximilian's Kaffeehaus. We had a typical German breakfast. Fruit to begin. Crispy rolls with butter and jam. German cold cuts, mainly ham and salami, and plenty of cheese, served on an open faced sandwich. And hard boiled eggs. Topped off with hot chocolate for me, coffee for Boris.

The plan for the day was simple. Boris would attend his class in the afternoon. I would explore the area around the university and the campus itself. At three o'clock in the afternoon, we would meet at the University of Munich Library to search through the books Professor Berry recommended that I study to find out more about Gunter Gruber and the "Inner Circle of Five". Naturally the books were published in the German language. Fortunately, Boris is fluent in German. Boris was excited as I was about figuring out what Gunter Gruber had really been up to in the United States and why he had pursued me during the summer. I was convinced I would find much more information here in Germany than I had found in my library searches in Toledo.

As I walked around through the area near the university I was fascinated by the architecture. It was a combination of the very old, not destroyed by the bombing of World War II, and the new. The old consisted of churches with cupola-capped towers and huge columns. The old buildings were ornate and I could only imagine the history connected with these buildings. Some of the buildings which were destroyed during the war had been re-built very much in their original form. This created a fantastic combination of architectural styles that immediately surrounded the University of Munich campus. Old buildings that were really old, new buildings that looked old except they were spiffy and clean looking, and new buildings built from steel and mortar.

The university itself was constructed by the impetus of King Louis I, in the 19th century. Like much of the city, it had also been partially destroyed by the bombing. Many of the buildings originally built in the 1800's were still standing. But many had been built after The Second World War ended. Consequently, the architectural design of the university buildings showed great variance. Because it is an urban campus, I didn't see much landscaping, but it was still a gorgeous setting.

I met Boris at the entrance to the library a little after three o'clock. The library had escaped the war unscathed. The building was magnificent. It looked like two castles had been built together. There were two majestic towers at opposite ends of the building. Between the two towers was the main body of the structure, a two story rectangular building. It was made out of a reddish stone with irregularly shaped brick-like pieces.

Ornate carvings stretched across the walls between the first and second stories. The windows were huge and every other window was glass stained like one would see in a church. The entrance doors were made of heavy wood, were very thick, and were at least ten feet tall. They were not that easy to open.

Because of Boris' fluency in German, we found the first of the books that Dr. Berry had listed in no time. Boris translated the title as "War Criminals of The Second World War". I told Boris we were looking for any reference to the "Inner Circle of Five" or the Munich Tribunals. There must have been a reason this book was first on Dr. Berry's list. According to Boris, there were several chapters listed about the "Inner Circle of Five" and the Munich Tribunals. While Boris read the relevant chapters and took notes, I killed time by looking at other books about the war. Unfortunately, my poor grasp of the German language precluded me from understanding most of which I read. I satisfied myself mainly by looking at the pictures in the books.

There were three other books that Boris looked at from Dr. Berry's list that afternoon but by seven o'clock we were both quite hungry and Boris had enough, for the moment at least, of reading and taking notes. He admitted that he had quite a bit of studying to do himself, so we called it a day and headed back to his apartment. We grabbed some leftovers he had in his refrigerator and sat down to eat.

"I have to say Erick, the "Inner Circle of Five" was a gruesome organization. This Gunter Gruber fellow was truly a horrible person and a sadist. I think all of those guys were." As my brother continued to speak, I could tell he had really been affected by reading the history behind the "Inner Circle of Five". "They enjoyed the sexual exploitation of the young girls they were kidnapping. They weren't even participating in the cruel and inhumane treatment of the girls. They simply enjoyed capturing these girls and then watching Hitler's goons sexually abuse the girls. It really was sick. I can see why so many of those connected in any way to the "Inner Circle of Five" were convicted and sentenced to long prison terms at the Munich Tribunals."

It was getting fairly late, so Boris went to his bedroom to finish his studies for the night. Buoyed by the adrenaline I felt in learning more about the "Inner Circle of Five", I was no longer tired or sleepy. Instead I settled down in a chair in the living room and read through my brother's notes. As I had learned earlier from my reading, Gunter Gruber was the only member of the "Inner Circle of Five" who had been convicted at the Munich Tribunals. The other four members were either never captured, or in the case of Dr. Hans Friedrich had been confirmed as dead.

Friedrich had been a brilliant surgeon in his youth, but by the time The Second World War had started he was getting fairly old. Apparently getting involved with Hitler was his way of stimulating his life at a time when all excitement had vanished. For a time he became one of Hitler's personal physicians, but then he was assigned to be the chief medical officer of the "Inner Circle of Five". In addition to becoming the personal physician for all those individuals associated with the "Inner Circle of Five", it was his duty to perform abortions on the girls who were being raped and abused by Hitler's cronies. Many of the men were married and didn't want to bother with having any children out of wedlock. It was also his duty to carry out the execution of any of the girls who tried to resist the rapings. This was done by lethal injection. It was quite certain he would have been convicted and sentenced to death by the Munich Tribunals had he not died.

Joseph Erdmeister, the man who killed my father's brother Ivan, was born in 1921 according to Boris' notes. His father was one of the early members of the Nazi Party so it was only natural that Erdmeister would work his way up the ladder and eventually become one of Hitler's confidants. Although he spent a considerable amount of time on the eastern war front during the war, he ended up being one of the primary thugs involved with the "Inner Circle of Five". He was last seen by a witness in the Russian sector of Berlin as the war was coming to an end. For that reason it was speculated that he was either killed or captured by the Russians.

I continued to read Boris' notes. Unfortunately, because four of the five members of the "Inner Circle of Five" were never able to be prosecuted, many details of their "exploits" were not available. Gruber denied that he was guilty of any crimes at his trial so all of the information about the "Inner Circle of Five" was provided by various witnesses. However, these witnesses provided quite a lot of information about those tangentially involved with the rapings and exploitation of the kidnapped. Of the 428 individuals who were convicted at the Munich Tribunals, 103 of them were connected to the "Inner Circle of Five."

Now I began to speculate. Could the man with the scar who shot and killed Gruber have had a connection with one of Gruber's victims? Or perhaps he was himself involved with the "Inner Circle of Five"? Maybe he was one of the 103 individuals convicted by the Munich Tribunals who were somehow involved in the rapings of those unfortunate young girls preyed upon by Hitler's goons. If he was one of the 103, it seemed very unlikely that I would be able to identify him. So far Boris had noted, there were photos of Gruber and Erdmeister in the books we'd looked at, along with one of Dr. Friedrich. But for the most part, there were no photos available of the 103 other individuals who were convicted by the Munich Tribunals for their involvement with the kidnappings and rapings. Thus, I had no ideas on how I could identify the mystery slayer of Gruber.

Gruber himself had been born in 1916. He was born in Frankfurt and after he graduated from Brahms University in Essen he became a teacher. He taught students at the high school level. In 1940 he was drafted into the German army and from there he rose quickly in the ranks. Apparently he was a very avid Nazi and within a very short period of time had caught the eye of General Hans Schiller. Schiller promoted Gruber to the rank of captain and eventually sent him to the eastern front. It was there that Gruber continued his meteoric rise and ended up in charge of a prisoner of war camp in Poland. From there he had ended up in Berlin, on the recommendation of General Schiller. After serving as the top attache under General Rolf Maurer for a number of months, Gruber was instructed by Ernst Kaltenbrunner to create and organize the kidnapping and rape "club" for the benefit of Hitler's associates and comrades. That organization eventually was administered by the "Inner Circle of Five".

It was obvious, based on the notes Boris wrote down, that Gruber was very much in charge of this organization, which became known as the Meister Personen Verbindung, which translated to English as the Fraternity of the Master Race. Hitler believed that the Germans were indeed the Master Race, superior to all others in the world. Gruber believed the Nazi propaganda, and he did all he could to ingratiate himself to those in power. It was not clear whether or not Gruber had much personal contact with Hitler himself, but he was definitely very close to some of Hitler's top henchmen.

As the war was coming to an end, Gruber realized that he would be in grave danger if he remained in Berlin near Hitler's compound. At some point he decided to try to escape. He did not go far. Because of his notorious reputation, it was not easy for him to hide. There were a considerable number of witnesses who had been mistreated by Gruber. In addition, many parents of the girls who had been victims of the Fraternity of the Master Race, were extremely eager to have Gruber captured and punished. Consequently before he could escape from Berlin as the Allies closed in on the embattled city, Gruber was captured by the English forces. He was able to elude capture by the Russians, which would have resulted in certain death. However, he was caught at a checkpoint that was manned by English soldiers. The man in charge of his capture was Colonel James McMillan. McMillan was viewed as a war hero, famous for his participation in the Normandy Invasion. After the Normandy Invasion, McMillan advanced with the English and American troops towards Germany and ended up being in charge of one of the battalions responsible for capturing suspected war criminals.

At this point Boris came into the living room. He was done studying for the night and the time change was finally catching up to me. Although it was only ten o'clock at night in Germany, I had been up since three am United States time. I was definitely ready for some sleep. Fortunately Boris had a fold-out couch, so my night of rest was pleasant indeed. In fact I slept so soundly that I awoke to the clanging of dishes the next morning. Boris was preparing breakfast and getting ready to go to his morning classes.

"How'd you sleep?" Boris asked me.

"I slept great! Waiting all day before I went to sleep was really a good idea. I can't imagine what would have happened if I had taken a long nap right after I arrived here. I probably would have been up all night."

I got up from the couch and joined my brother for breakfast. He'd prepared some eggs with ham on the side, toast with jam, and a delicious medley of fried potatoes, cheese, onions and green peppers. I felt famished so it was very easy for me to finish everything on my plate. I washed it all down with some cold orange juice.

After breakfast Boris headed to class. I headed to the Munich Museum of War. I took the underground train that had been completed only five years before in 1971. The museum was located on the outskirts of the city, near the municipal soccer stadium. I didn't expect to find much that would help me track down the history of Gruber. Professor Berry indicated that most of the books at the museum would have a lot of photos but might not have much useful information. But I was also looking forward to seeing some of the war artifacts that were on display at the museum.

When I arrived I was struck by the sheer size of the building. It had been built in the late 1960's. There was quite a bit of controversy in connection with the creation of the museum. Much of the controversy centered around the fact that Germans born after The Second World War felt ashamed about the period from the early 1900's to the mid-1940's when Germany was an aggressor in the world stage. Germany caused great pain and anguish to millions of people, all in the name of imperialism and world dominance. Now the citizens of the present wanted to forget that ugly chapter of German history. They believed that building a museum would not allow that to happen. The cost of the museum was also in the millions of dollars so many Germans questioned the wisdom of spending such a huge amount of money on what, they at least viewed, as a totally unnecessary project.

As I entered the building I could see why it was so huge. There was a gigantic convention hall in the middle of the building. It must have been the size of two football fields. According to the diagram posted at the entrance, there were a series of rooms located around the perimeter of the building which contained various historical artifacts arranged by subject matter. The convention hall contained all sorts of machinery and weaponry used during the war.

In the front of the convention hall was an impressive array of tanks. There was a Panzer I which was originally designed as a training vehicle. Nonetheless over 1,400 of these tanks were produced and were used in actual combat though that was not the original intent of the designers. It was plagued by weapon and armor shortcomings through its entire life in World War II. There was a Panzer III that was intended to be the main core of the German armored divisions. Over 5,700 were built during the war. Unfortunately for the Germans, its 37 mm and 50 mm guns were over matched by the Russian tanks. For that reason, the Germans designed the Panzer IV. Over 8,000 of these tanks were built and these tanks became the real workhorse of the German tank force. This tank was armed with a larger 75 mm gun, which made this a very effective weapon against the Russian tanks.

It was quite eerie standing by these large weapons of mass destruction. I thought of the thousands upon thousands of men who lost their lives battling against these war machines. It must have been terrifying facing these machines in battle, particularly if they were bearing down on you at a high rate of speed and you had nowhere left to hide. The armor was thick and could shrug off most firepower used by the enemy forces.

Parked behind the Panzer tanks in the convention hall were the Tiger tanks. These tanks were even larger and heavier than the Panzer tanks but were plagued by mechanical problems. Apparently the development of these tanks was greatly rushed by the designers because the Germans were starting to lose the war. To try to counter-act the onslaught of the Allied advance on Germany, these Tiger tanks were produced too quickly, without enough research. Consequently they were not a real factor in the war.

I continued to wander throughout the remainder of the convention hall of the museum. As a history buff, I was enthralled with what I was experiencing. Yet I felt a sense of foreboding. Everything I was looking at was created to kill. Everything I was looking at was created because a mad man decided he wanted to dominate and control the world. And millions of Germans supported his quest. Because of that support, Hitler was able to stay in power and bring the world to the brink of destruction.

There were hundreds of weapons on display behind the area where the tanks were located. There were 75 mm field guns, large weapons used to penetrate and destroy the enemy infantry forces that advanced on the German troops. There were antiaircraft guns that were used to shoot enemy airplanes out of the sky. There were tank guns, used by the various tanks to inflict as much damage as possible. Then there were anti-tank guns, which were used against advancing armor plated tanks. These guns were of limited use unless fired in conjunction with antitank rocket launchers.

From the convention hall I proceeded to the various rooms located around the perimeter of the museum. Displayed in these rooms were items that were much more personal in nature. Revolvers and rifles. Uniforms and hats. Diaries written by soldiers and their loved ones. Books with photographs. Pipes for smoking tobacco. Medical instruments used during the war. All reminding me of the grim nature of war. How unnecessary it all was. The waste of human life. The destruction of cities. The temporary destruction of societies. My trip through the Munich Museum of War humanized the war for me in a way that no history class could.

I was particularly touched by the photographs I viewed. Many displayed death and anguish. Many displayed courage and the spirit of fighting on. It made me think of what my parents must have faced during the war. Like those I viewed in the books, my parents had faced the unthinkable. It made me realize how lucky I was that my parents were able to flee Russia and survive The Second World War. It made me realize how lucky I was to be an American.

Then I hit pay dirt. One of the rooms was devoted to those who were victims of war atrocities and inhumane treatment. The photos I saw in this room were quite horrible. Much of the room was dedicated to the victims of the Holocaust. I could barely glance at the photos that showed some of the unspeakable cruelty the Nazis had inflicted upon the Jews. But there was also a section of the room dedicated to prisoner of war camps and other instances of crimes against humanity. One photograph was of Gunter Gruber, apparently taken at the prisoner of war camp where he had been in charge. He was wearing a Nazi uniform. His pose was one of arrogance. Chin thrust upwards, a smirk on his face, his left hand resting on his hip. His eyes looked beady and cruel. Or maybe I imagined that simply because I knew what he had done. Behind him you could see the interior of the prison grounds. Hundreds of bodies could be seen in the background. Some were standing, some seemed to be lying on the ground. It made me wonder if some of those on the ground were dead prisoners of war.

There was one other photo that caught my eye. It was a photo of Adolph Hitler. Standing next to him was none other than Gunter Gruber. So Gruber was indeed personally acquainted with Hitler. At least enough to have a photo taken with him. The other man in the photo was identified as Alfred Rheingold. From Boris' notes I remembered that he was the fifth member of the "Inner Circle of Five". I was startled by how young he looked in the photo. He looked no older than eighteen years old. His face was child-like and pallid. His skin looked smooth. He looked quite happy in the photograph. Bright blond hair, combed back, accentuated the facial features. He was taller than both Hitler and Gruber. The photo had a date of 1943 marked on it. It had a heading written below it, with a paragraph presumably describing the photograph. But I couldn't understand the writing. I could only make out a couple of the words and also the fact that the photo was taken in Berlin.

Now I had seen photos of four of the members of the "Inner Circle of Five". With luck I might even find a photo of the fifth member of the group, Peter Brenner. But it didn't matter all that much. I knew Gruber and Friedrich were dead. Erdmeister, Rheingold, and Brenner were dead or missing. Could it be the man with the scar who shot Gruber was Peter Brenner? If I found his photo I might be able to discover the identity of the man with the scar. Perhaps Brenner had some sort of grudge against Gruber and tracked him down to kill him. That still wouldn't explain why Gruber was pursuing me during the summer.

The trip to the museum energized me. I felt like I was learning more and more about the "Inner Circle of Five" and what they had been about. Whether I would ever know what Gruber was up to in New York was open to wide conjecture. But I felt a real adrenaline rush. In my own little world I believed I was a detective, working hard to solve a mystery. A mystery I was personally involved in.

The museum allowed patrons to photocopy books and documents in its possession. I photocopied all of the photos that included Gruber. Boris and I had done the same with the photos we found at the University of Munich Library. I now had a small collection of photos and some notes to start a file. In the next few days I hoped Boris would be able to look through the rest of the books from Dr. Berry's list and add more information to what I already knew.

I got on the underground train and sat patiently looking out the window at the darkened passageways as we passed under the streets of Munich. Within the hour I was back up on the streets. The cold crisp air felt good on my face. The sun was bright and the snow that had piled up on the streets and sidewalks of the city was starting to melt. I realized I was quite hungry so I hurried back to Boris' apartment for some food. I climbed the stairs to the third floor apartment and opened the door with the spare key Boris gave me. It was nearing two o'clock. Boris wouldn't be home until six o'clock because he had some group study sessions he had to attend.

I found some bread and potato salad in the refrigerator. I also spotted some liverwurst, one of my favorite lunch meats. It was strange. I couldn't stand to eat liver, but I loved liverwurst. I added some mustard to my sandwich, found a bottle of carbonated black currant juice, and sat down to a tasty lunch. Fully satiated, I sat down on the couch and propped my feet up on the coffee table. In a matter of minutes I dozed off. By the time I woke up, it was almost five o'clock. I decided to go for a jog. I didn't want to get out of shape while I was on my trip. Soon after I returned home I would be off to college. I wanted to make sure when I arrived in San Antonio I would be physically ready to perform at my best. If I wasn't in great shape, it was doubtful I would fulfill my potential on the tennis court. The jog really invigorated me. I pushed myself. I envisioned myself hoisting the winner's trophy at the US Open, or at Wimbledon. That's what I always loved about tennis. It let me dream big. I could imagine whatever I wanted to. Being third in the nation as an eighteen year old was something I was really proud of. But how would I do in college? Time would tell, but for the moment I needed to stay sharp physically. I wasn't going to be playing any tennis while in Germany so I hoped my game wouldn't suffer too much while I was visiting Boris.

When Boris returned from the university we sat around and talked about what we would do for the next few days. Boris had three more days of classes and then he was off for the weekend. After the weekend he would have no more classes and then we were returning to Toledo on Wednesday. We had plenty of time to continue our research into the "Inner Circle of Five" and the Fraternity of the Master Race. We would also have plenty of time to see the sights in Munich and the surrounding area.

That night we went to a restaurant that was known for its sausages and sauerkraut. I had a delicious bratwurst served on a home-made bun, slathered with a spicy brown mustard. Boris had a knockwurst. We both had a huge serving of the sauerkraut, which had the perfect combination of sour and sweet. We topped off our meal with a slab of apple strudel. Quite a treat.

The next few days passed quickly. When Boris had the time we would go to the university library and Boris would look through the books Dr. Berry had recommended. There was a considerable amount of information about the Fraternity of the Master Race. I was convinced that the man with the scar was involved with the organization, but I had no clear evidence to prove it. Of the 103 members of the organization that were convicted at the Munich Tribunals, 21 of them had died while in prison. Gruber, and a small handful of those convicted, were sentenced to thirty years in prison. The others were sentenced to shorter sentences ranging from 5 to 20 years. Consequently, none of the fraternity's members were still in prison.

Unfortunately I didn't have the resources nor the time to try to track down the 82 members of the fraternity who might still be alive. Not all of them would be living in or near Munich, so I couldn't adequately pursue my theory that the man with the scar had been a member of the fraternity for logistical reasons. However, Boris had a friend from school, Karl Lubeck, whose father was an administrator with the German Department of Defense. We were able to utilize that connection in an effort to find the former members of the fraternity who lived in the Munich area.

After explaining the situation to Mr. Lubeck, he agreed to check the data base that listed those convicted of war crimes and provide us with any current information on former members of the Fraternity of the Master Race who lived in the Munich area. Of the 82 names that we provided to Mr. Lubeck, only 23 lived in the Munich area. I spent the next few days going to the addresses given to us by Mr. Lubeck and trying to meet those on the list. Of the 23, only 18 still lived at the addresses we were provided. Eventually, with persistence, I actually met all 18.

The process was a bit awkward. I would knock on the door and ask to see Mr. So and So. If the man in question answered the door and identified himself as Mr. So and So, I would take a close look at the man and determine if it was the man with the scar. Then I would simply say thank you and stroll away. If the man in question wasn't at home, I would come back later. Ultimately none of the 18 men that I met was the man with the scar. That meant potentially there were still 64 former members of the fraternity who I hadn't identified. It was quite discouraging because I realized I would never find the man with the scar under the scenario I was pursuing.

In the meantime, Boris and I tried to enjoy ourselves as much as possible. One day we took a tour bus to the foot of the Alps, located roughly thirty miles from Munich. The mountains were majestic and amazingly high. I had never seen anything like it in my life. They were covered in snow and clouds hovered over their peaks. We were able to hike up the side of the foothills, probably reaching an elevation of no more than two thousand feet. It was tough going, trudging through the snow, but well worth the experience. I couldn't imagine climbing one of those peaks to the very top.

We also visited my father's cousin Sergei, and his wife Anna. Sergei was a dairy farmer who lived on the outskirts of Stuttgart. It was good to see him again after so many years. I really didn't remember much about him because I was so young when he visited us years ago in Ohio. It was also nice to meet Anna, who was not yet married to Sergei at the time of his visit to Ohio. He described how he escaped from Russia to Germany, but his trip was much less harrowing than my parents' experience. I also told him how my father initially claimed that Sergei had testified against Gunter Gruber and that explained why Gruber had come after me in New York. Sergei laughed quite heartily about it. He knew nothing about Gruber and surmised that my father simply didn't want to burden me with details about the horrible events of a terrible war.

Boris also showed me the sights of Munich. We saw the Frauenkirche, a cathedral dating from 1488. I saw three of the original town gates that were not destroyed during the war that dated from the 14th century. We walked through the former arsenal of Munich at Jakobsplatz, which was now the municipal museum. I was really excited to see all of the old architecture and to imagine what life was like hundreds of years ago. To me, it was fascinating to think that I was treading on the same ground that historically significant individuals had tread on years before.

The 22nd of December arrived quickly and it was time for my visit to come to an end. I had a great time and learned a lot of important information. Boris had compiled forty pages of notes for me so I had quite a bit of material to study. Hopefully it would help me to come up with a hypothesis as to why Gunter Gruber had pursued me in New York. I also had a list of potential suspects. One of those 64 names I had might be the one who shot Gruber. With all of that on my mind, Boris and I headed to the Munich International Airport and boarded the Lufthansa flight headed for Detroit. Within a number of hours we would be home. For Boris, this would be the first time he would see our father since he had been shot.

CHAPTER 10

It was brutally cold. Snow was on the ground. The wind howled much of the time. Gray skies were the norm. But we didn't care. We were together again as a family for the first time in months. And with Boris studying in Germany, and me going to San Antonio to study, it was unlikely we would spend much time together in future years to come. My father had recovered beautifully from the shooting and was ready to go back to work after the New Year's holiday.

We had a fantastic Christmas. Because my parents were in such a festive mood, they gave us all sorts of great presents. Not necessarily all expensive gifts, but electronic gadgets, and books, and clothes. They also got me a nice big suit case so I could pack a lot of stuff for my trip to Trinity University. It was a Christmas full of good memories and of thanks that my father had survived a dangerous shooting.

I also got bold and called Shelley Coslowski. I invited her over for dinner so she could meet my family. Of course my parents had no idea that I had a secret crush on Shelley. They also would not have approved that I was eighteen (almost nineteen) and thinking of asking a young woman four years older than me out on a date. On the other hand I was too chicken to ask her out and because I was leaving for school in just a few days I could justify my cowardice. After all, why ask Shelley out when I knew I would be over one thousand miles away at school and very unlikely to see her again. Instead, I would have to be satisfied with merely dreaming about her, and nothing more.

Before I left for San Antonio I called Detective Jason in New York and asked him for an update on the Gruber investigation. Dead end. Jason explained that in a final bid to identify the man with the scar the police had scoured the list of passengers who had flown into New York in early June and then flown out in the weeks immediately after Gruber was shot. The list of names was in the hundreds and there was no realistic way of reducing that number to a workable list. With great regret Jason informed me that the case was officially going into the cold case file and nothing more would be done unless a witness stepped forward who could further the progress of the case.

The day arrived. I was off to San Antonio. My parents and Boris saw me off at the airport in Toledo. My connection was through Chicago and by late afternoon I arrived in Texas. My coach, Bob McKinley, greeted me at the airport and drove me to the Trinity University campus. I expected the weather to be balmy and the skies to be sunny. As I quickly learned, January in Texas is not always warm and sunny. It was in the low 50's and cloudy. Still it was a lot better than the weather in Ohio.

I quickly settled into the school routine. My room mate was a junior named Bob Eckelman. One of my suite mates was Tony Giammalva, who was also on the tennis team. I had three classes scheduled in the morning on Monday, Wednesday, and Friday. On Tuesday and Thursday I had two classes in the morning. As I quickly discovered, the afternoon was reserved for tennis practice. Everyday from Monday through Friday we practiced from two o'clock until six o'clock. That included conditioning at the end of practice. I was not use to that much practicing, but my game needed it. The rest of the players on the team had been practicing that way the entire fall and their games were much sharper than mine. By the time we were ready to play our first match, the line-up was pretty much set. Larry Gottfried, who finished his junior career ranked first in the nation, and Tony Giammalva, who finished fifth, would share duties playing at #1 and #2 singles. Ben McKown, who finished third in the nation a year earlier and then sat out from school for a year to play tournaments, would play #3 singles. Me, having finished third in the nation right behind John

McEnroe, would be playing #4 singles. Unfortunately my game was not sharp. Rounding out the line-up were Eddie Reese at #5 singles, and Mike Davidson and Dave Benson, who alternated playing at #6 singles.

Our very first team competition, with four freshmen on the team, was the National Collegiate Team Indoor Championships. The event was to be held at the Nielsen Tennis Center at the University of Wisconsin in Madison. We didn't have indoor courts at Trinity University (and it really was never cold enough to prevent us from playing outside) so it was uncertain how Larry and Ben, who were from Florida would adjust to indoor tennis. In the first round we were pitted against the University of Alabama, a good team ranked in the top 20, but not a powerhouse. Based on the reputation of our individual national rankings, Trinity was seeded fourth behind Stanford, USC, and SMU.

Individually my first collegiate match was a stinker. I played tentatively and scared. I had barely played any tournaments in recent weeks and performed terribly. I choked my match away in three sets. At that moment Bob McKinley probably wondered if he made a mistake when he recruited me. Fortunately everybody else played up to par and we won rather easily by a score of 7-2, taking four out of six singles and winning all three doubles.

In the quarterfinals we took on the host team, the University of Wisconsin. They were one of the top teams in the Big Ten, however the Big Ten was not particularly strong in tennis. The University of Michigan was perennially ranked in the top 20 and often in the top 10. But other than that, the Big Ten was nothing to write home about. We easily beat Wisconsin and I won my first collegiate match over Ken Thomas who I had beaten before during my junior tennis days.

On to the semi-finals. We were matched against Stanford. They were always one of the top teams in the nation and had a line-up much more experienced than we had. Once again I played #4 singles. I was playing Peter Rennert. We split the first two sets and then we reached six games all in the third set. Now we had to play a tie-breaker to decide the match. The best five out of nine points would win. Now the nerves became frayed. This was a crucial match. If I won, we went up 4 matches to 2. If I lost, we went into the doubles tied at 3 apiece. Stanford most likely had the superior doubles line-up. Rennert and I both were battling hard, knowing how important the match was. We reached 4 points each. The next point would determine the match! After a relatively long rally I came to the net. In reply to my volley Rennert tried to lob over me. I ran back as fast as I could, but, Hallelujah!!, his shot landed several inches out. I pulled the match out in the clutch. Now I really felt like I was part of the team and that Bob McKinley had been justified in recruiting me. We ended up winning one of the doubles matches, and with four freshmen in our very first national event, we reached the finals to play against USC.

USC was coached by the legendary George Toley. Their top player, Bruce Manson, was unavailable at this tournament, but nonetheless USC reached the finals. The night before our match Ben McKown, my doubles partner, got sick and would be unable to play. At the pre-match introduction you could almost see a smirk of confident joy when Toley discovered Ben was not going to play. As it turned out, it didn't matter.

We played inspired tennis that day. I won my match again, this time over Buzz Strode. We were both playing one spot higher in the line-up because of the absences of Manson and McKown. Despite our youth, we'd all played years of junior tennis. Tony, Larry, Eddie, Mike and I all won our matches. The doubles didn't matter. We shocked everyone and clinched the match by winning five out of the six singles. Truly a special moment. Our very first tournament and we were now national champions. Trinity University had claimed its first national championship since 1972. In that year the team was led by Brian Gottfried (Larry's older brother) who became top 10 in the world, Dick Stockton, who also became top 10 in the world, and my current coach, Bob McKinley, who reached top 50 in the world. What a very special feeling it was to play college team tennis and to win a national championship. At that moment, all of the hard work I had put in through the years really seemed worth it.

The next couple of weeks we played some home matches and Bob put me at #1 singles to see if I had raised the level of my game. I won against the University of Tennessee and the University of Houston. But I was still not playing anywhere near my best when we took a west coast trip to play against UCLA and USC. UCLA was a tennis power and was always ranked in the top 5 in the nation. Against UCLA I lost to Bruce Nichols at #4 singles. We ended up losing our first dual match of the year. Against USC I won at #4 singles and we managed to beat the Trojans for the second time that season.

We returned to Texas and played in the Corpus Christi Invitational. At this tournament I learned what it was like to play in the howling wind. Corpus Christi is located on the Gulf of Mexico and in March the wind is constantly blowing at twenty miles per hour, gusting to fifty miles per hour. Playing tennis in those conditions is not fun. Sometimes you could literally hit a lob into the wind as hard as possible, and it would blow back onto your side of the court. Nonetheless we reached the finals and had to face our arch-rival, SMU. Things did not go well for us that day. Everybody was struggling in the wind and the players from SMU handled the conditions much better and were clearly mentally tougher than we were. I lost at #4 singles to Dave Bohrnstedt, who was not highly touted nor was he anything more than a "pusher". He got every ball back but rarely did anything with it. Losing to a player with such a defensive style was particularly galling. After the match you could almost see steam rising from Bob's head he was so furious. Bob did not take losing well and was very competitive. His competitiveness carried over to us as a team so we were all very disappointed with our performance. We looked forward to a little revenge in the near future.

I limped into the Rice Invitational with an 8-4 record. The Rice Invitational was a prestigious tournament played at Rice University in Houston. The draw consisted of 64 players. Each player competed individually but for each match won, points were awarded to the school the player represented. Thus, at the end of the tournament there was both an individual champion and a team champion.

In the first round I played a player from Oklahoma City University who was from Australia and was balding. He looked like he was at least

25 years old. I struggled mightily against this less than stellar opponent. With Bob's coaching and encouragement, I pulled out a tough three set match. Then something clicked. For no apparent reason I finally loosened up and started to play up to my capabilities. In the third round I upset Jai DiLouie, seeded third and SMU's #1 player. I came back from a 5-1 deficit in the first set to win in straight sets. Then I upended fifth seeded Gary Plock, Texas' #1 player in the quarterfinals. In the semifinals I knocked off Chris Delaney of SMU, 7-5, 6-1. I now had to face my team mate, Larry Gottfried, in the finals. Larry had knocked off Tony Giammalva, another team mate of mine, in the other semifinals.

By virtue of the fact we had three semifinalists in the event, we clinched the team title. It was the eleventh time Trinity had won the Rice Invitational, an event which was started in 1959 by Tony Giammalva's father when he was the Rice University coach. I lost to Larry in the finals, but I really wasn't very disappointed. I had finally got my game and confidence back. I now knew I was as good as Larry, Tony, and Ben and was capable of playing #1 singles when needed. The remainder of my freshman season turned around dramatically after the Rice Invitational.

We beat our rival SMU twice during the regular season to avenge our defeat at Corpus Christi. After the loss to SMU at Corpus Christi we didn't lose any more dual matches the rest of the season. I only lost one more dual match when I lost to Mark Turpin of SMU. But it didn't matter. We still beat them in our season finale at SMU and headed off to the NCAA Championships seeded second behind Stanford University. The NCAA tournament was being held at the University of Georgia in Athens. For the first time in its history, there would be a team championship followed by individual singles and doubles events. In the past, the team champion had been determined by awarding points to teams based on the individual performances of players in singles and doubles, much like the format at the Rice Invitational. One thing we knew – it would be hot and humid in the middle of May. And that was fine with us, we were used to it because the weather in San Antonio was also hot and humid.

In the first round we knocked off Oklahoma University without any problems. They were the best team to come out of the Big 8 region, but were not highly ranked. The big match came in the next round, the quarterfinals, against USC. It was obvious they wanted revenge against us big time. With four freshmen we had knocked them off twice that season. They had a veteran team led by junior Bruce Manson, sophomore Chris Lewis, and two seniors, Mike Newberry and Andy Lucchesi. This would be a big challenge. It would not be easy to knock them off three times in one season.

As predicted, the match turned out to be a real dog fight. After the singles we managed to pull out to a 4-2 lead. I had played well enough to beat Andy Lucchesi at #3 singles. All we needed was to win one of the three doubles matches to clinch the victory. Unfortunately the weather turned nasty and we had to complete the match in the University of Georgia basketball arena. Two temporary courts had been put down inside the arena. It was huge and cavernous, designed for basketball or holding concerts. It was unique playing in such an environment, but it was still exciting and nerve wracking.

We quickly lost at # 1 doubles. Ben McKown and I were playing #2 doubles against Andy Lucchesi and Mike Newberry. Meanwhile, our #3 doubles team of Eddie Reese and Dave Benson were being hammered. By the time we reached the beginning of our third set, it was apparent Eddie and Dave were going to lose. The outcome of the match now hinged on Ben and me. We were up against two veteran players who were acting cocky and trying to intimidate us. The pressure was on. The question was who would fold – them or us?

The tension mounted. No one could take charge. We reached six games all. Now it was time for a nine point sudden death tiebreaker. Whoever won 5 out of 9 points would be the winner of the doubles match and vault their team into the semifinals of the NCAA National Championships against SMU. We were knotted at three points each. Lucchesi served to me and I hit a fairly weak return. They put the volley away. From the add court Ben hit a great return and Newberry made the error that tied it up.

Everything came down to one point. After all of the matches we played that season, and after all of the hard work, literally one shot was going to determine the success or failure of our season. Because Ben's return of serve was outstanding, we chose to have Newberry serve to Ben. It was definitely the most tension I had ever felt in a tennis match. We were playing not only for ourselves – we were playing for the entire team.

Everything seemed to be in slow motion. Ben made the return. I hit a backhand ground stroke but as nervous as I was I wouldn't say it was all that good a shot. It turned out to be good enough. Lucchesi, obviously feeling the heat as much as me, hit a tentative volley and it drifted long. We were stunned, ecstatic, feeling as lucky as could be. Our team mates ran onto the court excitedly and we all celebrated our amazing good fortune. We were headed to the semifinals. It was particularly sweet because USC was a cocky team and I'm certain Coach Toley never believed we could beat them three times in one season. But we did.

The next day the weather was rainy again. Both our match and the UCLA versus Stanford match would have to be played indoors on two courts. Because of that it would likely take all day. After waiting at the hotel for a couple of hours, I was summoned for my match against Mark Turpin at #3 singles. I had lost to Turpin in our last dual match of the regular season. This time I turned the table and came through to beat him in straight sets. After what happened against USC the day before, I figured there could be no way our match against SMU could be any tighter or more nerve wracking. I was wrong.

After the singles matches we were tied 3-3. The weather had improved so we now played the doubles outside. Ben and I won our doubles match at #2 doubles. Tony and Larry lost their match at #1 doubles. It all came down to our #3 team of Eddie Reese and Dave Benson against Pem Guerry and Mark Vines. Like yesterday, Eddie and Dave were getting thumped. They lost the first set and were serving at 1-4 in the second set. SMU had three break points to go up 5-1 in the second set and pretty much seal the deal. I couldn't take it. I started walking back to the hotel. I was crushed. We were going to lose to our arch rival and miss making the finals.

At the hotel I paced nervously in my room on the third floor. I expected the rest of the team to arrive back at any moment. But they didn't. I kept waiting and kept glancing out the window. What was going on? Although it was ridiculous, I actually began to think something miraculous was going on. Then I saw the SMU van pull into the parking lot. I saw the players climb out of the van. My heart and mood lightened a bit. None of the players looked that happy. I saw no laughter. Could Eddie and Dave have pulled one of the greatest comebacks in the most important match of their lives? Conversely, was it really possible the duo from SMU pulled one of the greatest chokes in history?

When I saw our van pull into the parking lot a few minutes later, my belief got stronger. At least from the third floor window, my team mates looked happy. They had a spring in their step. When they arrived on the third floor they confirmed what I thought was impossible. Eddie and Dave had come back to win the second set in a tiebreaker and then easily won the third set. After nearly nine hours of tennis we beat SMU 5-4 and were in the finals.

Against Stanford in the finals, we were tied at three matches each after the singles for the second straight day. I won my match against Perry Wright at #3 singles in straight sets by winning the second set in a tiebreaker. Larry won at #2 singles against Bill Maze and Ben won at #4 singles. After the singles the weather turned nasty once again. This time there would be no drama. Tony and Larry lost to Matt Mitchell and Perry Wright at #1 doubles. Eddie and Dave were losing their match by the time Ben and I took the court. Eddie and Dave were out of magic and lost in straight sets. Ben and I didn't even get started. Our remarkable run in the NCAA tournament came to an end. We won the indoor championships, but were all despondent that we couldn't win it all in the outdoor championships. Still, it was somewhat satisfying that we were able to accomplish what we did with four freshman in the line-up. Emotionally it was the most draining experience I had encountered in my tennis career. The ups and downs were incredible. Exhilarating, yet devastating.

The next day the individual singles and doubles portion of the NCAA Championships began. After winning my first round I faced fourth seeded Bill Maze of Stanford. He had a long three set match against Mark Turpin of SMU and was not all that energized for his match against me. I took advantage of the situation and beat him in straight sets. I had reached the round of 16. That meant I was automatically awarded a spot on the 1977 All-American Team. As a freshman. I was pretty thrilled. Even my loss to Tony Graham of UCLA the next day didn't dampen my spirits. Growing up in Toledo I had always dreamed of what was happening to me at that very moment. I was actually an All-American and I still had three more years of college tennis to play. Now I had to re-set my goals for even bigger and better things.

That summer I made my first foray into the world of professional tennis. And not too successfully. All my excitement and enthusiasm had to be put on hold temporarily. I played several qualifying events for the American Express Circuit in Raleigh, North Carolina; Pinehurst, North Carolina; and Concord, New Hampshire. The American Express Circuit was a step below the major tennis circuit called the Grand Prix Circuit. I didn't qualify for the main draw in any of the events I played. I also played the qualifying tournament for three Grand Prix events in Columbus, Toronto, and North Conway, New Hampshire. Once again I failed to qualify. As the summer came to an end my unbridled enthusiasm had turned to discouragement. Maybe my dream of becoming a professional tennis player was premature. Or maybe I just had to be patient.

I headed back to school in late August. My father had fully recovered from his injuries. Boris was just starting his first year of medical school in Munich. I'd pretty much resigned myself to the fact that I would never know why Gunter Gruber had pursued me. I would never figure out who the man with the scar was nor why he shot Gruber. My father would say nothing more about the situation when I asked him about it. He insisted that Gruber was merely carrying out an act of revenge in retaliation for my father's act of testifying against him at the Munich Tribunals. Perhaps it was that simple and I just had to accept the reality that my sleuthing days were over and there was no mystery to solve. On the other hand I didn't throw away the file that contained all of the notes Boris and I had compiled during my trip to Germany. Maybe there was a clue I had missed.

We continued to work hard my sophomore season. I was really getting into the groove of practicing four hours a day ending at 6:00, eating dinner, and then studying. After that, three times a week around 9:00 my room mate, Ky Cauble from Abilene, and I would do additional conditioning. Ky was a freshman and was on the junior varsity team. Usually we either jumped rope for 45 minutes to the disco sounds of Donna Summer or did intervals over a distance of three miles. The disco beat was perfect for gaining a rhythm while jumping rope. For the intervals we would sprint the straight away on the school track and then jog the turns. By the time the winter season came around I was in great shape.

This had to be the most enjoyable time of my life. I was playing the sport I loved at a high level, the weather was gorgeous most of the time, and my major was history, a subject I really enjoyed. Trinity was a good school academically and the classes were small because the total enrollment was only around 2,500 students. As a team we got along quite well with each other and we were all driven to succeed. I could not have been happier.

We played two big tournaments in the winter of 1978 getting ready for the dual match season. I won both of them. First I won the 1st Annual National Collegiate Indoor Singles Championships over USC's Robert Van't Hof by a score of 6-4, 6-1. In the semis I defeated John Austin of UCLA, who beat defending NCAA singles champion Matt Mitchell of Stanford. My match with Austin was a long three setter, 4-6, 6-3, 6-2. Winning this event was a real thrill for several reasons. It was my very first individual college national championship. It was also held at the Metropolitan Club in Houston, Texas. It was a beautiful facility located on top of a several story high parking complex in downtown. It was definitely a first class club that was run by Tony Giammalva's father Sam, the same Sam who had been the Rice coach and who started the Rice Invitational. First prize for winning the tournament was a 19 inch color television. That was fantastic because I didn't have a television in my dorm room and always had to go to the student union to watch TV. Now I could watch in my room.

I also won the $3500 Rookie Pro Tennis Tournament that was held at our Trinity courts and run by Bobby Riggs' son Larry. Bobby, of course, had been labeled as the infamous "chauvinistic pig" who played the number one ranked woman in the world, Margaret Court, on Mother's Day a few years back. Although he was 55 years old he defeated her in straight sets. He then lost to Billie Jean King in the "Battle of the Sexes" tennis match. Rumor had it he tanked the match because the Las Vegas bookies had him listed as a heavy favorite. By betting on Billie Jean King and throwing the match he was said to have profited quite handsomely. The weather was cold and nasty for the tournament. But it didn't matter. In the finals I met my team mate Larry Gottfried and beat him 6-2, 7-6, 2-6, 6-3. It was a real boost to my confidence to win these two tournaments back to back.

At the National Indoor Team Championships we played a super match in the semifinals against USC and beat them 9-0. It probably was one of the best matches we had ever played. We were now 4-0 in our career against USC. I beat Robert Van't Hof again, at #1 singles. We headed into the finals with a great deal of momentum. The only problem was that we had to play Stanford in the finals. Not only did all of their players return from the previous championship season, including defending singles champion Matt Mitchell, but they had one very important addition to their team. John McEnroe, who was now a bona fide star. In the summer of 1977, a year after I had beaten him in the finals of the Western Open, he got all the way to the semifinals of Wimbledon. Now, as a college freshman, he was ranked top 25 in the world. We were really going to face a stiff challenge.

I played a decent match but was beaten in straight sets. Needless to say, McEnroe had improved dramatically since I had played him in the summer of 1976. His lefty serve was even tougher and indoors his serve and volley game was quite devastating. I managed to hang in there but I just couldn't break through on his serve. It was not a great performance by Trinity that day, and Stanford clobbered us to prevent us from winning back to back national indoor championships. Now, it was time for the out door season to begin.

Meanwhile, I actually had something to distract me from my tennis that also made me quite happy. In fact it made me feel like I was walking on cloud nine. Shelley Coslowski and I had seen quite a bit of each other during the summer and when I had come home during the Christmas break. Although she was honest about the fact she was dating other men, she admitted she really liked me and enjoyed the idea of seeing someone young like me. Obviously I didn't object, particularly because I was quite a neophyte when it came to the dating game. I was flabbergasted that Shelley was interested in me and also flattered. At this young stage of my life I didn't care if she dated other men, I was just happy to see her once in awhile. Shelley was going to come down to visit me in early May right after our exams were over and before we were going to leave for the NCAA Championships. I was definitely looking forward to that trip.

The rest of our season continued with a great deal of success. We only lost four times during the season. Two of our losses were to Stanford. The second time we played Stanford was at our Trinity University tennis courts. It was a two day match that included the women's teams playing against each other. Bob McKinley threw Larry Gottfried into the #1 singles slot against McEnroe, mainly because Larry had quite a bit of success against John in the juniors. The strategy paid off. In front of a screaming crowd of over 1,500 people Larry beat John. It was only the second loss of the season for McEnroe and it would be his last. I also won my singles match against Perry Wright and Ben won his match. But we couldn't prevail in the doubles and once again we lost to Stanford and their legendary coach, Dick Gould.

We ended the season ranked fourth in the nation behind Stanford, UCLA and Pepperdine. The next order of business was finishing our semester and taking our exams. Then we would have about ten days to practice and prepare for the NCAA Championships. It was somewhat weird when we did that because we were the only students left on campus except for a few international students who also stayed in the dorms while they waited for the summer session of classes to begin. I looked forward to the end of exams, to practicing for the NCAA tournament, and to Shelley's visit. All was good.

CHAPTER 11

My last exam was on a Tuesday. We would leave for the NCAA Championships held at the University of Georgia a week from Saturday. Between now and when we left we would practice twice a day, except on Sunday and on the day we traveled. I was looking forward to our practices and being out of school, but I was more excited about Shelley's visit. She was arriving on Friday and would leave on the following Wednesday.

I didn't have a car but Tony let me borrow his so I could pick up Shelley at the airport. Her flight was coming in at 6:15 in the evening so I got to the airport and parked in the short term lot. I walked over to baggage claim and checked for her flight. It was on time. I sat down near the baggage carousels and nervously waited for her arrival.

When I saw her, I momentarily lost my breath. I hadn't seen her since early January. She looked stunning. Her hair cascaded over her shoulders and accentuated the beautiful shape of her face. As always, her figure was impeccable and even from a distance I could see the special twinkle in her eyes, which always gave me a warm feeling inside. For that moment I was totally lost in lust and rapture. I couldn't believe this gorgeous creature was here to see me. When she spotted me she ran over enthusiastically to greet me.

"Hey Erick! Wow. It's great to see you again. It's been too long."

By now I had gotten used to her squeaky voice and ignored the incongruity of such a beautiful young lady talking like some middle aged woman pumped up on helium. Everything else about her well made up for this minor flaw. And with all my flaws, who was I to complain about her voice. We embraced and then she planted a long and luscious kiss on my lips.

The next couple of days were like a dream. When I wasn't playing tennis we took the bus and viewed the various sites of San Antonio. The Alamo and the Riverwalk were particularly memorable. So was the HemisFair Park which was built for the 1968 World's Fair. We ate at the top of the Tower of Americas, a 750 foot tall building that was a favorite of out of town visitors. But mainly we just enjoyed each other's company. I had no illusions about our relationship. I knew it was unlikely that our relationship would ever grow serious and I knew I was way too young to consider a romantic future. But Shelley was so much fun to be around and she made me feel so special, that I ignored any jealous thoughts that tried to creep in. I knew that I was almost like a toy to her that she could easily wind up and manipulate. But boy did she make being manipulated a wonderful experience.

Monday night we went out to grab some burgers from Olmos Pharmacy, which was walking distance from the Trinity campus. It still had the old fashioned lunch counter inside a pharmacy with great food and great shakes. We walked back to campus hand in hand and I felt a twinge of sadness. I was having such a great time and yet I knew Shelley was leaving the day after tomorrow. I probably wouldn't get to see her very much at all in the summer because of my tennis schedule. That evening, the reality of the situation hit me like a ton of bricks. I realized that I really cared for Shelley much more than I previously was willing to admit.

We approached "B" Dorm, where my room was located on the third floor. My side of "B" Dorm faced the city skyline and at night I could see downtown all aglow from the lighted skyscrapers. Downtown was no more than five miles away from our campus. My dorm had elevators but the building was designed with hallways that were actually outside, really more like sidewalks with guard rails. The entrance to my room was from this outside hallway.

It was a bit eerie in our dorm now. Except for Tony and me, all the other students had left home for the summer break. The lights in the hallways were on, but all of the windows were dark. Shelley and I rode the elevator up to the third floor and made a right turn to head toward my room. As we approached the room I saw a shadowy figure lurking in the entrance way of the room located next to mine. Obviously no one should have been around except Tony, and I very much doubted that Tony was going to be hiding and waiting for us. The figure moved quickly onto the hallway in front of us where he became visible in the lights. He was no more than twenty feet away from us and he held a long knife that glinted like an icicle being hit by bright sunlight.

We froze in our tracks. We weren't sure what to do. The man approached us slowly in a menacing fashion with the knife held in front of him. He got closer and closer. In fact he got so close that I could smell alcohol on his breath. He had piercing blue eyes with smooth skin. His face almost looked child-like and I got the impression from his features that he was quite happy to see us – the knife not withstanding. Although he looked lean and strong, and despite his young looking face, he had graying hair and obviously must have been in his fifties. For some reason, he looked familiar.

"Hello Erick," he said in heavily accented English. "Who might this young lady be?" he inquired. Although he had an accent he seemed to have a strong command of the English language. Before I could answer, he spoke again. "I'm afraid I'm going to have to ask you to come with me. The young lady will stay, but first we will tie her up so she can't follow us."

At this point Shelley spoke up. "What makes you think Erick is going to go with you, and what makes you think I'm going to let you tie me up?"

"Now, now, Miss, there is no need to be difficult." He grinned and then waved the knife in our faces. "I would prefer that we do things my way in an orderly fashion, and then no one will get hurt. Now let's go into your room and I'll take care of tying the young lady up and then you and I will be going away." He motioned for us to walk to the entrance of my room.

By now I was quite petrified and visibly shaking. I also felt rather embarrassed because out of the corner of my eye I could see Shelley. Shelley looked as cool as a cucumber. Despite the situation her face looked serene. We slowly turned in the direction of my room with the knife wielding man following close behind. Suddenly, and in a moment of great stupidity, I whirled around and tried to kick the man in the groin. He was caught by surprise, and perhaps because he had been drinking, his first swipe of the knife just missed clipping me in the arm.

That's the opening Shelley needed. Much like at Moe's Place in Rossford when the drunk worker had come on to her, Shelley moved with lightning speed. But this time her attack was much more aggressive and vicious. She swung her leg around with a classic karate kick to the stomach of our attacker. As he hunched over in pain she quickly followed that up with a kick to his bent over head. The kick sent him sprawling backwards suddenly and with great force. He flew up against the guardrail and then centrifugal force took control. Teetering, he lost his balance and plunged over the guardrail.

We ran to the edge of the guardrail and looked down. The man's body was sprawled grotesquely on the sidewalk below. There was some light shining from the adjacent hallway, but it was difficult to see clear details of the body's condition. For the moment at least the body was not moving.

"Quick, Erick, we have to hurry down there and find his knife just in case he's only unconscious. Then we'll call the police."

We skipped taking the elevator and ran full speed down the stairs. As we got closer we could tell it was unlikely the man was ever going to move again. One side of his face was bashed in, which must have meant he had landed on his head. He was on his stomach but one of his legs had somehow awkwardly got caught under his body and probably was broken based on the weird configuration of the limb. Shelley spotted the knife lying just a few feet from the body. Then she walked right up to the body to make sure the man was dead.

Meanwhile, I hung back a little. I was very shaken by the incident and was not used to seeing dead bodies. Even though I had seen Gunter Gruber's dead body up close and personal, this incident was no easier to take. I had to regain my composure and fight hard not to faint because the sight of all of the blood was making me dizzy. Shelley noticed my discomfort, but because of her training she immediately sprang into police mode.

"Erick get up to your room and call the police. This guy isn't going anywhere. Tell them we'll need an ambulance and that we have a dead body on our hands. Don't tell them anything else other than where we are."

I nodded and hurried back up the stairs. Once in my room I dialed 911 and got the emergency operator to send the police. Then I took a few long breaths and went back down to see what Shelley was doing. Frankly I was still scared and didn't want to be all alone. When I got back to Shelley she was holding something in her hand. Upon closer inspection, it looked like a passport.

"I didn't touch anything else," Shelley explained, "but I saw this sticking out of his pants pocket and I couldn't resist. Obviously the guy knew you since he called out your name. Do you know who he is?" With that she handed me the passport. I opened the passport and looked at the name and picture of the man who accosted us. It was then that I realized why he looked familiar.

It was Alfred Rheingold, another member of the "Inner Circle of Five". I had seen his picture in one of the many books I had looked through while at the Munich Museum of War. Of course the picture was from over thirty years ago and I had made a copy of it for my notes. But there was no mistaking those piercing eyes and child-like face. The man may have been a vicious war criminal, but you would never have guessed it from his appearance.

The passport was issued by Brazil. It now made sense. Rheingold was able to escape to Brazil, which for some reason was willing to harbor Nazi war criminals after the war. And they refused to extradite the war criminals to countries that were pursuing these criminals. More than likely, Rheingold was able to live out his life in virtual anonymity because the post-war enforcers of justice didn't know to where Rheingold escaped. His crimes were also mainly against Germans themselves. Had his crimes been committed against Jews the result would probably have been different. The Jewish Nazi hunters were unstoppable and would go to any lengths to track down their prey and bring them to justice. Rheingold had been lucky – he wasn't notorious enough to be hunted down.

Shelley slipped the passport back into Rheingold's pocket. She turned to me and gave me a big hug, followed by a warm kiss. "You know, it was really stupid of you to try to kick the guy. I was petrified that you were going to get hurt."

"Shelley, trust me, you weren't nearly as petrified as I was. I just wasn't thinking. Thank God my girlfriend is a cop." And I laughed, while realizing how nice it sounded to call Shelley my girlfriend. If she noticed that I called her that, she didn't acknowledge that in any way. In my mind I could hear her saying that she was happy that she was able to save "one of her boyfriends".

"It's kind of bizarre. This guy from Brazil tracks you down in San Antonio and tries to kidnap you. What's the deal? Do you know?"

"It's a long story Shelley. Why don't I tell you all about it tomorrow morning. The police will probably be here any minute and I'm really tired after all of this commotion. Can it wait till tomorrow?"

"Sure it can. And if it's something really personal you can't share with me, I'll understand."

With that we waited for the police. In a matter of minutes two squad cars with sirens blaring and lights gyrating pulled up to the roadway in front of "B" dorm. Out of each car alighted two policemen. Luckily they were carrying bright flashlights because the lights from the dorm were not bright enough to sufficiently illuminate the spot where Rheingold had landed.

Ignoring any pleasantries, one of the cops, who was obviously the senior officer, stepped up to us. "I'm Officer Fodor. I assume you called this in?" He looked at me, but I turned to Shelley and hoped she would intervene. Luckily she did.

"Hi, I'm Shelley Coslowski. This is my friend Erick Iskersky. He made the actual 911 call. Not that it matters but I'm a police officer from Toledo, Ohio. I'm just a visitor."

When she stated that she was a police officer I could see looks of doubt on the faces of the four policemen. Clearly they were not used to cops looking quite as delicate and beautiful as Shelley. Inside myself I smirked. If only they had seen the way Shelley took care of business with her physicality. She may not have looked it, but she could be a real brute when she needed to be.

Fodor started to question me while one of the other officers by the name of Tom Rainkin started to question Shelley. I suppose they did that to make sure our stories were the same. While they were questioning us the coroner arrived on the scene and started to go through his procedures. It was at least an hour before they were done questioning us. We had nothing to hide. I revealed everything I knew about Rheingold and provided an explanation for why he had accosted us. At times I wondered if we should have talked to a lawyer before we answered any questions. On the other hand, we weren't being treated as suspects nor were we being arrested. Consequently I felt fairly comfortable with the situation.

By the time everything was wrapped up it was around eleven o'clock. I was getting tired but I still wanted to call my parents. Unfortunately it was midnight in Ohio. I decided to wait until the morning to call them. The police finally left and told us the detective assigned to the case might be getting in touch with us. I had explained that Shelley was leaving on Wednesday and I was leaving on Saturday. For the moment everything seemed alright as far as the police were concerned and I was confident that we would both be allowed to leave San Antonio with no difficulty. It took some time for me to get sleepy that night even though I was tired. Luckily Shelley wasn't real sleepy either. Even though she didn't show it, I was sure that Shelley was also shaken up by the Rheingold attack.

The next morning I called my parents with a report on what happened to Shelley and me. They were very concerned but also relieved that we were not hurt. My father apologized profusely for the way his past was causing me so much trouble. He had never been so emotional before. He acknowledged that he knew who Rheingold was, but had assumed that he died at the end of the war or had somehow escaped from Germany. Never did he think Rheingold would become a threat.

"He was a member of the "Inner Circle of Five" I learned about in my research," I explained to my father. "Obviously he was somehow involved with Gunter Gruber, or in contact with him before he died. Why else would he have come after me in San Antonio? And how did he know I was here?"

"Of course he was involved with Gunter Gruber," my father agreed. "But, because he disappeared at the end of the war, I never testified against him at the Munich Tribunals. It is so difficult to guess why he tried to kidnap you. Gruber was obviously seeking some sort of revenge against me. Rheingold – who knows? I don't know what he thought he would gain by going after you."

On the plus side, at least three members of the "Inner Circle of Five" were dead. Dr. Friedrich, who died during the war, Gruber, and Rheingold had all perished. Joseph Erdmeister was thought to be dead or had been captured by the Russians. And Peter Brenner's whereabouts were unknown. Presumably my odds of being attacked again were very small. Of course my odds of being hit by lightning were real small also, but the odds were irrelevant if I actually got struck.

After I got off the phone with my parents, I talked to Shelley. I told her the whole story from the beginning. She was fascinated by the ordeal my parents had gone through during The Second World War. In Shelley's opinion my father originally shielded me from the truth about Gruber and the "Inner Circle of Five" because he was very embarrassed about his involvement with the Germans during the war. She also thought he wanted to spare me the pain of knowing that, rightly or wrongly, my father might be branded as a "Nazi". And she was right. I never viewed my father as anything but a refugee who was forced to serve in the German army. Perhaps if I found out my father was involved, however tangentially, with the "Inner Circle of Five", I would have viewed my father much differently.

On Tuesday I had to miss tennis practice while we were interviewed by the lead detective on the case. Hector Flores was a brutish looking human being. Big and lumpy, he had a scowl that seemed to be permanent. His clothes was frumpy and out of style. He spoke with just a trace of a Spanish accent, but his command of the English language was strong. He spoke with the confidence of someone who had years of experience and who expected immediate cooperation.

At first he treated us a bit rudely and wondered out loud if our story made sense. After peering at Shelley while she gave her account of last night's event, he snickered a bit. He didn't believe someone that beautiful and fragile looking could be such an aggressive fighter. His attitude changed dramatically when he learned that Shelley was a cop. He treated us with new found respect and suddenly he seemed to believe everything we told him. The rest of the interview went well. It was quite certain after the interview with Flores that we would not be charged with any crime.

That night Shelley and I went out for our last dinner during her visit. She would fly out the next morning. We went to Earl Abel's, a restaurant near the Trinity campus that had been around since 1933. It was a San Antonio tradition that serves a large variety of diner type food. It was also open 24 hours a day and served alcohol. For those reasons it attracted a rather diverse clientele. Some of the customers were quite normal, some were not. We thoroughly enjoyed our meal and were looking forward to our last evening together.

I felt very much in love with Shelley yet I had a real aching in my heart knowing that I might never see her again. Who knew. Perhaps she felt the same way about me, but if she did she didn't say so. I wanted to tell her I was in love with her and never wanted to be with another woman again, but I knew that was not the right thing to do. I had to accept our relationship for what it was. If Shelley ever decided she wanted it to become more serious, I knew she would let me know.

Of course it was sad to see Shelley off to the airport. We had a morning practice that I couldn't get out of, so Shelley took a taxi from my dorm.

As soon as she left I missed her. I realized then how much in love with her I really was. Not the best thing to happen. I would always be traveling a lot with my tennis commitments, at least if I planned to pursue my dream of becoming a professional tennis player. And that was one dream I wasn't giving up. Tennis was my priority. Shelley could not be. It was certain Shelley would slip away from me.

After a couple more days of practice it was time to depart for Athens, Georgia. We left on Saturday and were scheduled to practice on Sunday. The NCAA Championship would begin on Monday. We were seeded fourth behind Stanford, UCLA, and Pepperdine. The draw was certainly going to be tough. Assuming we both won our first round, we would face our nemesis USC in the quarterfinals. Although we had beaten them 9-0 earlier that season, this was going to be a much tougher task. We were playing outdoors, for one thing, and the earlier result was certainly an aberration.

As usual the weather in Georgia was hot and steamy in late May. Both USC and Trinity took care of business in the first round, so there we were. The re-match. I was playing #3 singles in the match and was up against Buzz Strode, who had a quirky game. He utilized a lot of spin and his strokes were a bit unorthodox. Based on seasonal results I was clearly favored to win. But this was the NCAA Championship. The pressure was immense. The best player didn't always win. Sometimes the player who didn't choke ultimately prevailed. I won the first set but stumbled in the second set. I was going to have to pull out a three setter. Thankfully, even though I didn't play my best tennis, Buzz didn't take advantage of the situation. I pulled out an unimpressive three set win. Little did I know how crucial it was that I took so long to win.

We entered the doubles tied at three apiece. In addition to my win, Ben McKown won at #2 singles and John Benson won at #5 singles. Unfortunately Larry Gottfried lost to Robert Van't Hof at #1 singles and Mike Davidson lost at #6 singles. The turning point came at #4 singles where Tony Giammalva started cramping in the heat and lost a tough three setter.

And that's why my three setter became so vital. The long three setter took a lot out of me and I played a horrible doubles match with John Benson's older brother Dave at #3 doubles. I was on the verge of cramping throughout the match and was unable to muster enough reserve energy to adequately perform. In addition, Dave played fairly tight in the match with the realization that our match was incredibly crucial.

One year before we were jubilant. We had pulled out a nail biter over USC. A year later, we were emotionally crushed. Dave and I lost. At #2 doubles, Tony played miraculously well considering he was recovering from cramps. John and Tony won to even the match at 4-4. It came down to Ben's and Larry's #1 doubles match against Van't Hof and Chris Lewis. We all sat in agony as we watched our dreams of reaching the finals for the second straight year go down the tubes. Larry and Ben could not pull out their match and we lost 5-4.

It was hard to believe that losing a tennis match could hurt so much. After all, we were all just playing a game. Nothing more. How could it be so painful? But I knew. We were a close knit team. We were all competitors. Nothing, absolutely nothing, can be worse than losing under those circumstances. We now only had two more years to try to win the outdoor national championship. Our indoor national championship from the previous year was meaningless. We were living in the here and now – and it stunk.

The loss to USC was hard to swallow. We hated losing to that team. It was the first time we lost to them, and as it turns out, it was the last time we lost to them in my career, although we only played them a couple more times. All we could do was lick our wounds and get ready for the individual championship, which would start after the team title was decided. Larry, Ben, Tony and I all qualified for the singles draw. We had a couple of days to rest and get ready. Meanwhile, as expected, Stanford, led by John McEnroe won the NCAA Team Championship in 1978 when they beat UCLA in the finals. It was now time for us to forget the team tournament and to get selfish. Now we were playing only for ourselves.

I won my first two matches with relative ease. The pressure of having to win my first two matches in the main draw to repeat as an All-American was not on me this year. Because of my regular season record and my National Indoor Collegiate Singles title, I was seeded in the top eight in the NCAA Singles Championship. The top 16 seeds automatically were named All-Americans.

In the round of 16 I had to face Leo Palin from Pepperdine. He played #2 singles for Pepperdine behind Eddie Edwards, the only other player beside my team mate Larry Gottfried to beat McEnroe during the season. Things started very poorly for me against Palin. I was nervous and played very tentatively, dropping the first set 6-1. Fortunately I started playing better in the second set and Leo and I had a nip and tuck battle going before I edged him out for a 7-5 triumph. Suddenly, with the momentum of the second set driving me, I found my groove and won the third set in easy fashion, 6-2. Now I got to face John McEnroe for the second time this season. I definitely was going to have my hands full in the quarterfinals.

I did not get off to a good start against McEnroe. The one thing going for me was the fact that we were playing outside in the heat and humidity. Unlike when I played him indoors earlier in the season, McEnroe's serve and volley game wouldn't be quite as effective outside and our rallies would probably last longer. The longer I could keep him out on the court, the better chance I had of frustrating him and perhaps pulling the major upset. Consequently, after I lost the first set 6-2, I still felt like I had a chance. I just had to do a better job of holding serve.

My plan seemed to be working. I jumped out to a 5-2 lead in the second set and McEnroe started to get angry. He started behaving like the McEnroe I knew in the juniors. Unlike most players who lost their cool, McEnroe usually started playing better when he lost his emotional control. And so it was. He started playing better and I started to wilt under the pressure of having a big lead against the top college player in the nation who just happened to be ranked in the top 25 in the world. Soon my lead was gone and we were tied 5-5. McEnroe held serve to win his fourth straight game. At 5-6 I somehow held serve to stave off elimination and at least somewhat slow McEnroe down.

The tie-breaker I played was one of the most exciting moments in my tennis career. With the raucous crowd cheering against McEnroe and cheering for the underdog, I managed to win one out of two points on McEnroe's serve to start the tie-breaker. Then I won both points on my serve and I gained a 3-1 lead as the crowd got louder and McEnroe got testier. He quieted the crowd by winning the next two points. Then I served again and after an unforced error by McEnroe I actually had a set point at 4-3. But McEnroe came through in the clutch with a great shot to even the tie-breaker at 4-4. If McEnroe won the next point, the match was over. If I won the point, we would go to a third set. McEnroe chose to receive serve in the ad court. This was about as good as it would ever get for me. The pressure was on, the atmosphere was electric and I could either fold or come through.

I hit a good first serve and served and volleyed. McEnroe's return was fairly high and not that strong. I hit an aggressive volley to his forehand corner. It was the right move because it caught McEnroe leaning the wrong way. He quickly changed direction and was forced to hit a forehand passing shot on the run. I momentarily held my breath as he drilled the ball down the line. The surge of excitement hit me as soon as I saw the ball clip the top of the net and fall back. I'd done it. I was heading to a third set against John McEnroe.

The momentum had shifted. I easily held serve to start the third set and McEnroe was starting to unravel. Then McEnroe pulled a classic McEnroe outburst, and the match would never be the same. As we changed sides after that first game, McEnroe started yelling at a spectator who was cheering against him. Play stopped for at least 10 minutes. Ridiculously, the umpire, Joe Frierson, got out of his chair and became embroiled in the bickering instead of making McEnroe resume play. Like an idiot I sat and waited and did nothing. My coach, Bob McKinley was seething but was unable to get Frierson to do anything to resume play. When we finally started playing again, my momentum had been lost. The juices weren't flowing the same way anymore. Courtesy of McEnroe's well-timed out-burst, my game fell apart and his got better. I lost six straight games and never threatened in the third set after the McEnroe spectacle. As usual, McEnroe got rewarded for his antics and intimidated the officials. What a shame a player who was that great and that talented had to resort to seamy outbursts to help him win matches. Personally I was dejected that I was unable to keep my composure and continue to play well even after the outburst and delay.

It turned out to be a great lesson for the future. And all was not lost. Because of my performance during the season and during the NCAA Championships, I was named to the College Junior Davis Cup team. Now my dream of playing professional tennis might become a reality. Along with eleven other top college players, including my team mate Larry Gottfried, I would be playing professional tournaments all sum-mer. And if any of us played well enough by playing through the qualify-ing draws to get into the main draws we would gain a spot in the world rankings. And better yet, all of this would be paid for by the generosity of the United States Tennis Association. For that moment at least I had forgotten about Shelley Coslowski and was thinking only of my tennis.

CHAPTER 12

My summer began at an American Express Circuit tournament in Birmingham, Alabama. I managed to make my way through the qualifying rounds. This meant I would now have a world ranking and would be playing my very first main draw professional match. I won rather easily over Hugh Thomson in straight sets and I was thrilled that my professional career had started. In the second round I ran into Keith Richardson, who was ranked around #100 in the world and was one of the top seeds. I lost 7-5 in the third set. This match provided me with a great deal of confidence. It let me know I could be competitive with a player of Richardson's caliber. Perhaps my dream of becoming a professional tennis player was not that far fetched.

The next week I found myself down in the last round of qualifying to Ricardo Acuna by one set and 5-2 in the second set. The tournament was another American Express Circuit tournament being held in Asheville, North Carolina. I survived multiple match points in the second set, including a few in the tie-breaker. After fighting off a total of eight match points, I ended up pulling out the tie-breaker and headed to a third set. In what was definitely my greatest comeback to date, I won the third set and qualified for the main draw. That match provided me with a great deal of momentum.

In the main draw I won four matches over Ali Madani, Bernard Fritz, Woody Blocher, and Joe Meyers. Now I was in the semifinals facing a familiar foe – Eliot Teltscher, my former Junior Davis Cup team mate. Eliot had turned pro after one year at UCLA. He was seeded second at the

NCAA Championship and was predicted to meet McEnroe in the finals, but was upset by John Sadri in the quarterfinals. This I knew would be a tough match, and it was. Teltscher beat me in straight sets but I headed to our next tournament in Raleigh with a lot of confidence.

Once again I had a good deal of success. I defeated Sashi Menon, Kevin Curren, and Rick Meyer before losing to Alvaro Betancur of Colombia in the quarterfinals. The first three tournaments of the summer helped me start climbing the world rankings and because of my results the USTA awarded me a wild card into the Western Open in Cincinnati, Ohio. This meant I received a spot in the main draw of the tournament even though my ranking wasn't high enough to get me in. This would be my first main draw match in a Grand Prix Circuit tournament. The Grand Prix Circuit was the highest professional level in the world.

My first round opponent was Ricardo Cano, who was ranked #68 in the world and seeded eleventh in the event. To my surprise (and delight) I destroyed Cano 6-2, 6-0. This was my first win over a player ranked in the top 100 in the world. I was particularly shocked because I won the match so easily. Perhaps Cano was over confident because he had no idea who I was. It didn't matter to me. In the second round I played Rick Fagel, a player with a huge forehand and a lot of speed. He was ranked #120 and had reached the semifinals of last year's Western Open. Once again I got off to a fast start and led 6-3, 5-3. My nerves got the better of me when I realized I was about to reach the third round of the event. Luckily, I somehow managed to keep it together and pulled out the second set 7-5.

Now I was in the round of 16 against Pat Dupre, who was about four years older than me and had played at Stanford. He was ranked #55 in the world and was seeded eighth. Other than McEnroe, this was the highest ranked player I had ever faced. Luckily for me the tournament was being played on clay. DuPre was more of a hard court player. I lost the first set 6-3 but didn't feel that I was totally outclassed. I reminded myself about my win over Cano in the first round, who was not ranked much lower than DuPre. I turned things around in the second set and won 6-3. The third set was nip and tuck all the way. Neither one of us could get up a break. We ended up going to a tie-breaker. Because I was from Ohio and was trying to pull an upset, the crowd, though not big, was pulling for me. After a series of nerve wracking points filled with good shots but also tense errors, I somehow prevailed. I was in the quarterfinals of my very first Grand Prix tournament!

The next day I was quickly brought back to earth. My opponent was Eddie Dibbs, ranked in the top ten in the world and seeded first. His specialty was clay and along with Harold Solomon he was considered one of the very best on that surface. I was no match for him as he crushed me by a score of 6-2, 6-0. That match made me realize what a long way I had to go to become a successful professional player. The gap between a player ranked around 50 in the world and one ranked top 10 in the world was substantial. I had a lot of work to do.

It was now the middle of July and we headed for the Grand Prix event being held in Washington D.C. It was hot and muggy, typical summer weather in the Mid-Atlantic region. I was in the qualifying event. If I won three matches I would be one of eight qualifiers to make it into the 64 player tournament. When I looked at the main draw I couldn't help but notice that one of the eight qualifiers would play John Austin, formerly from UCLA and now a pro ranked in the top 100. If that qualifier beat John Austin, he would play Ken Rosewall, from Australia, assuming Rosewall won his first round match. Although he was over 40 years old, Rosewall was still ranked 15th in the world and one of the high seeds at the event. He was also one of my tennis idols when I was growing up as a kid. If I could qualify I had a one in eight chance of getting the spot I needed in the main draw.

When I was ten years old Ken Rosewall, Rod Laver, Fred Stolle, and Roy Emerson had come to Toledo to play an exhibition at the Toledo Racquet Club, the first indoor tennis club in Toledo. They were all ranked in the top ten in the world and Laver was the number one player in the world. I absolutely was thrilled to be a ball boy at the exhibition and Rosewall and

Laver were my favorite players. They were classy and elegant. They were extremely talented, but both were fairly short. Now ten years later I might have the chance to play one of the great legends of all time.

Despite the tremendous pressure I felt in the qualifying event because I so desperately wanted to play Rosewall, I was able to hang in there and win three matches. I was now in the main draw. Now I had a one in eight chance that my name would be drawn to play against John Austin. Sure enough, as if fate intervened, my name was drawn in exactly the slot I wanted to be in. My first round match against Austin would be played the next day.

The next day I was extremely nervous. I couldn't keep the thought of playing against Ken Rosewall out of my mind. I quickly lost the first set against Austin by a score of 6-2. Austin had improved quite a bit since I had beaten him in college at the National Indoors a few months before, but I felt like I had a good chance to beat him on the clay court surface. I pulled out the very tight second set by a score of 6-4. My dream was still alive. Despite the heat and humidity, and despite the fact I had played three qualifying matches the previous two days, I felt vigorous. My adrenaline was pumping at the potential of playing Ken Rosewall. In the third set I played outstanding tennis and cruised to a 6-3 win. I quickly rushed over to the draw to see if Rosewll had won his first round match. To my great relief, he did.

Tuesday was an off day for me so I put in a short but intense practice session and anxiously waited for the next day. When I walked onto the court the next day with Ken Rosewall and started warming up for our match, everything seemed surreal. Here I was, some kid from Toledo playing a professional tennis match against a player I had grown up watching. A player who as recently as four years ago had reached the finals of Wimbledon and the US Open. A player who had played one of the greatest five set tennis matches of all time when he defeated Laver at the WCT Championships in Dallas. A player I idolized. And I was playing against him! I couldn't believe it.

For a while I hung in there with Rosewall. He had the greatest slice backhand in the history of the game. It was piercing and skidded unmercifully, even on the clay. I tried to keep it to his forehand as much as possible. Even at his age, Rosewall was still quick, and he had great volleys. Although his serve was not powerful, he had an uncanny knack of placing his serve and varying the spin. He kept me off guard the entire match. I gamely fought as hard as I could, but still dropped the first set 6-4. I hoped that the heat and humidity might start getting to Rosewall, but that hope started to fade quickly as he jumped to a 3-0 lead in the second set. He broke me again at 3-0 and the match was all but over. I only managed to win a single game in the second set and my dream match ended. But what a thrill while it lasted. How many kids get to play one of their sports idols? Not many I would venture to say.

The summer continued and got tougher and tougher. Of course being part of the Collegiate Junior Davis Cup team was a tremendous honor and opportunity. And because of my results, I was now ranked in the top 200 in the world. But it was draining. We never got a week off, which probably would have made a lot of sense – at least for a player like myself who was having fairly good success and playing quite a few matches. The strain was more mental than physical, but I tried to focus on the ultimate goal. I wanted to get ranked as high as possible in the world so the next summer I could get into the main draw of the Grand Prix events without having to qualify.

I qualified for the Grand Prix event in South Orange, New Jersey and lost a three setter to Peter McNamara from Australia in the first round of the main draw. Then it was off to Wall, New Jersey for an American Express event. I was actually seeded at that event because the draw was comprised of players ranked lower than those at Grand Prix events. I defeated Robert Van't Hof from USC once again in the first round. For some reason, after losing to him the very first time I played him, I had great success against him after that. In the second round I beat Joao Soares of Brazil in straight sets and followed that up with a three set win over Chris Sylvan of the United States. My tournament ended when I was beaten by the 1977 NCAA Champion from Stanford, Matt Michell.

At this point I didn't think my summer could get any better, but it did. We were playing the Grand Prix event in Columbus, Ohio. Columbus was where I had won my state high school championships and it was neat to be playing a professional tournament in my home state. I beat Chris Lewis from USC in the last round of qualifying and, lo and behold, I got an immediate chance for revenge when I drew Peter McNamara in the first round, having just played him two weeks earlier in New Jersey. This time I turned the tables on him and beat him in straight sets, 6-1, 6-4.

In the second round I got to play another all-time legend when I faced Arthur Ashe. I had played McNamara on Monday while Ashe played his first round on Tuesday. We were scheduled to play the Thursday night feature match. On Wednesday afternoon I went out to the courts to practice. It just so happened that Ashe was also at the courts looking for some practice and he walked up to me and asked me if I wanted to hit some. It surprised me, because I was going to be playing him the next day. Then it hit me. He had no idea who I was, and why would he? I was still in college playing my first real summer of professional tennis.

I casually mentioned to him that I was playing him tomorrow and would gladly hit if he didn't care about practicing with a next day foe. Ashe, in a generous gesture, acted like he knew something about me. Naturally he didn't care that he was playing against me the next day. Even though he was past his prime, he was still ranked in the top 20 in the world so I'm sure he felt I was not much of a threat. In any case, for the first time in my career I practiced with my next day opponent. It was certainly well worth it. I had the pleasure of practicing with one of the all-time greats.

The next day, however, was not all that pleasurable. Ashe applied a lot of pressure on my game. Even though it was on clay, he still attacked the net relentlessly. His serve was still exceptional and his volleys were crisp. Even at the age of 35 he was still graceful and quick. I tried my best to keep him away from the net by playing a more aggressive style than I normally played. But it didn't work. He beat me 6-3, 6-2. Ashe was very gracious to me after the match and displayed no arrogance that a player of his caliber had every right to display. He was a true gentleman and a true champion. It was hard to believe that in just over a year Ashe would suffer a heart attack. Just four years after he won his Wimbledon title in 1975, Ashe would have quadruple by-pass surgery and be forced to retire from the game he loved.

After I lost I was flown by private plane to Poughkeepsie, New York to play the sectional Junior Davis Cup Championship. The flight was gorgeous as we flew over the mountains of Pennsylvania and eventually over the Hudson River. Because I was from Ohio I represented the Western Tennis Association, which was comprised of Ohio, Michigan, Illinois, Wisconsin, and Indiana. Why it wasn't called the Midwest Section I have no idea. From Poughkeepsie we traveled to New Jersey for a national amateur event. By this stage of the season I was getting exhausted. I lost to a player whose name I can't even remember in the first round. It actually was a blessing in disguise. I took off a few days and didn't pick up a racket. It was a chance to re-charge my batteries.

By now I was ranked in the top 125 in the world. I was granted a wild card slot into the main draw at the Grand Prix event in Boston, held at the historic Longwood Cricket Club. This was an old club that had both clay and grass courts. The tournament was played on the clay. In the first round I drew none other than Arthur Ashe. This time I fared better because I got the first set to a tie-breaker. Ashe's game was too much for me in the tie-breaker and then he romped over me in the second set, 6-1. After wards, in the locker room, Ashe spoke with me about my future and gave me words of advice and encouragement. There was no need for him to take the time to be nice to me, but he was. A truly classy individual.

The summer was now almost over. I had one tournament left to play. Based on my performance during the summer, the United States Tennis Association thrilled me by awarding me a wild card slot into the main draw of the US Open. I was exuberant. At the age of 20 I was going to get to play in my first grand slam event. For the first time ever, in 1978, the US Open would be played on hard courts and would be played at Flushing

Meadows in Queens, New York. The facility was located right by Shea Stadium, where the Mets played their baseball games.

My entire summer seemed like a long and exciting dream. I got to play some of the legends of the game. I got to play players ranked in the top 10 in the world. My ranking had climbed to near 100 in the world. If I won my first round match I would crack the top 100 for the first time ever after only playing in ten professional tournaments. And my first round was winnable. I was pitted against Ricardo Ycaza from Ecuador, a young pro ranked around 90 in the world. I anxiously waited for my first glimpse at the US Open site as we made our way from the hotel in Manhattan to Flushing Meadows.

We arrived by tournament bus and pulled up right near the main stadium. The Louis Armstrong stadium was huge, seating nearly 20,000 fans. It was a fantastic feeling as I pulled out my player pass and showed it to the guard at the gate. I got to walk right through. I was actually a participant in the US Open. It was a special moment for me and that day my practice went really well. I was on cloud nine. Hanging out in the locker room. Seeing many of the players I grew up reading about. Feeling like I truly belonged because my ranking was good enough to get me into a Grand Slam event.

The next day, playing on an outside court in the shadows of Armstrong Stadium, I discovered to my pleasant surprise that I wasn't that nervous. Ycaza, who once was one of the top juniors in the world, had beaten me in an international junior event on clay when I was 18. But things were different now. We were on hard courts and he hadn't quite lived up to his junior days hype. We both held serve four times. At 4-4 the tide of the match changed dramatically. I broke Ycaza's serve and then held to win the first set. I immediately broke Ycaza's serve again to start the second set and his spirit seemed to sag. The second set was 6-2. I'd done it. I won a match at the US Open and in doing so would crack the top 100 in the world.

Now I would face a familiar foe. Eliot Teltscher. The same Eliot Teltscher who beat me earlier in the summer in Asheville. By now

Teltscher was ranked in the top 70 in the world. He was a feisty competitor and it would be a very tough match. But I was familiar with his game from our junior playing days and it was actually a good draw considering there were a lot of players I could have faced who were ranked much higher than Teltscher. However, what followed was one of the most bizarre endings to a match I had ever encountered.

I started out strong and won the first set 6-4. If I could just win one more set I would get to play Roscoe Tanner in the third round. But Teltscher fought back. He broke me twice in the second set and beat me 6-3. Then we played a nip and tuck third set, with neither of us being able to gain a real foot hold. Even though we were playing at an outside court a decent crowd started to gather. The fans tended to gravitate to courts where the matches were tight and in the third set, or to courts where the big names were playing. It reached 4-5 in the third set, my serve. At 30-all I made an unforced error and suddenly I faced match point. It was now or never.

On match point we had a groundstroke rally before Teltscher hit a short ball. I ran in and struck a forehand down the line out of Teltscher's reach. A winner. I saved the match point. Suddenly Teltscher started yelling at the linesman and then at the umpire. He was making quite a scene and was complaining loudly that my shot was out. The next thing I knew the umpire was asking the linesman if he was sure of his call. Then the linesman blurted out that he was unsighted, meaning his view had been blocked. Without warning, or discussion, the umpire yelled out, "The ball hit by Mr. Iskersky was out. Game, set, and match to Mr. Teltscher."

My memory of that ending is vivid. I was stunned and stood at the net arguing with the umpire. Teltscher, in what I always considered a classless display, ran off the court without shaking my hand. Once he left the court my goose was cooked. Despite my protestations the umpire insisted that he'd made the right decision. I knew otherwise. He was intimidated by Teltscher's antics and succumbed to the pressure. My chance to get to the third round of the US Open was dead.

That evening I was quite depressed during dinner. But as the evening wore on, I reflected about my entire summer experience and realized it couldn't have been much better. I now knew, based on my performance, that I really did have a shot at becoming a successful professional tennis player. Right now I was one of the best 100 tennis players in the world. No one could take that away from me. All that hard work had paid off.

My parents were of course thrilled to see me when I finally got home. They knew I would be leaving almost immediately back to San Antonio to start my junior year of college. For a brief moment I thought of turning professional and foregoing my college tennis career. But I couldn't turn my back on my team mates. We had unfinished business. I spent a lot of time with my parents and friends during the days I was home, and then I was off. Back to school.

That fall I played our usual fall tennis tournaments and it felt a bit strange because, not only was I one of the top college players in the nation on one of the top teams, I also had a world ranking of #95. Now I was the target of all of my competitors. Everyone wanted to knock me off and I wasn't entirely used to such pressure. I may have been a good college tennis player before I earned my world ranking, but now I was one of the elite players in the world of college tennis. I was expected to win most of my matches. When I was beaten, it would usually be considered an upset. Nonetheless I had a decent fall and also played one professional tournament, held in Hartford, Connecticut. McEnroe was seeded first at the indoor event and I was actually seeded seventh. The first time I was ever seeded in a Grand Prix event. I ended up losing in the first round to Australian Dick Crealy in three sets.

I had a wonderful Christmas at home. Boris came home from Germany and we got to spend this Christmas together. His studies were going well in medical school and he had met a German girl named Greta, and based on what he was telling me they were getting rather serious. My parents were much more interested in Boris' future medical career and so they were not all that enthralled with the romantic developments in his life. Overall it didn't matter. We had a great time together and the time flew quickly. Although I loved being with my family I longed to get back to the warmer weather in Texas and to get back to playing competitive tennis. My goodbyes were bittersweet, but tinged with excitement at the thought of going back to school.

I arrived back in Texas by the middle of January. The first big tournament we were scheduled to play was the National Collegiate Indoor Singles Championship. Once again it was being played at the Metropolitan Racquet Club in Houston. Because I was the defending champion I felt excited about the opportunity to repeat my title. But I knew it wouldn't be easy.

I won my first three rounds. Now I was in the semi finals only two matches away from becoming a two-time national champion in this event. In my way stood a familiar opponent – Robert Van't Hof from USC. I played a really good match and won with relative ease. I had made it to the finals. Once again I was facing a familiar foe.

Ricardo Acuna, who played for Northwest Louisiana University had gotten into the event when Kevin Curren, seeded second behind me, of the University of Texas, pulled out of the event. Acuna took full advantage of getting in the tournament and had knocked off third seeded Andy Kohlberg from the University of Tennessee in the semi finals. In light of the fact Acuna had blown eight match points against me when we met in the summer at the Asheville event, I'm sure he was eager to gain some revenge.

Because the finals of the NCAA Championship was played in a 3 out of 5 set format, Acuna and I agreed to play the same format in this event when asked to do so by Sammy Giammalva, the tournament director. It was a decision that I would regret. The match was tight from the beginning. Acuna had a huge serve, even though he was fairly short, well below six feet tall. We got to a first set tie-breaker which I pulled out by a 5-4 sudden death victory. In the second set Acuna returned the favor when he won a 5-4 sudden death tie-breaker. Now we headed to the all important third set. The winner of the third set would have a two set to one lead and a huge turn in momentum.

And so it was. I played a strong third set and was able to break Acuna's serve twice. I won the set 6-2 and felt a wave of confidence. But Acuna didn't wither. And I also started to feel a bit tired as we reached the middle of the fourth set. Suddenly I wished I hadn't agreed to play three out of five sets. I also realized that I was not in peak physical shape. That meant I had to work harder on my conditioning. However, I managed to break Acuna twice, while he broke my serve only once, as we headed into the tenth game of the fourth set. I was serving at 5-4, serving to become the defending National Indoor Champion. And I choked. All of a sudden we were even. I was tiring and starting to make too many mistakes. I was losing my poise. Then I steadied myself. Acuna made a couple of unforced errors and I broke his serve right back. At 6-5 I managed to hold serve and the match was over. I did it! I was the repeat winner of the National Collegiate Indoor Singles Championship. And to make it even sweeter, my prize for winning was a huge boom box. Last year I won a TV and now a boom box. I was all set for my video and audio entertainment.

Next we headed to the National Collegiate Indoor Doubles Championship in Wichita, Kansas. In my freshman year I had played with Ben McKown, but in my sophomore year Bob McKinley split us up. Now in my junior year we were back together, trying to prove to Bob that we could be a very successful team. And we did. At the end of the tournament we were crowned the winners. Even though we were playing second doubles on our own team behind Tony Giammalva and John Benson, we were good enough to take the national title. It was my third collegiate national title.

The rest of the season went very well. I only lost four dual matches all season and continued to be ranked among the top six players in the nation. As a team we stayed ranked in the top four throughout the season and it looked like we would have a great chance to finally win it all. Meanwhile I also found the time to take advantage of my world ranking and played in three Grand Prix tournaments in Baltimore, Little Rock, and San Jose. Unfortunately things didn't go well as I lost in the first round of all three events to Bruce Manson, Johan Kriek, and Terry Moor respectively. All were seasoned pros and ranked in the top 70. In fact Kriek was in the top 30.

I also got to experience yet another thrill of a life time. IMG, one of the major sports management companies in the world, whose first client was Arnold Palmer, invited me to play in a tournament they were running in Jacksonville. There were eight players invited. Rod Laver, John Newcombe, Vitas Gerulaitis, Sandy Mayer, Eliot Teltscher, Bill Scanlon, and Ben Testerman. Amazing what company I was in. All-time legends and Grand Slam winners. And in the first round I would get to play my other idol, Rod Laver. Only a few years earlier I had ball boy-ed for him in an exhibition held in Toledo. I had also read his very entertaining tennis book which chronicled his successful quest to win all four Grand Slam events in 1969. Now I actually would get to be on the same court. Admittedly he was now 39 years old and past his prime, but I didn't care.

As expected he exuded great class. When we first met on court he treated me with respect, which of course most top tennis players would not have done. I jumped off to a fast 5-1 lead and then started thinking. Here I was trouncing the greatest tennis player of all time. Plus, I remembered reading in his book that he tended to be a slow starter. All of that was too much. Laver started to play much better and I faltered. He won four straight games to even the set at 5-5. But then miracles of miracles. I held it together. The great Laver was no longer great. He missed shots he never would have missed in his prime. I won the next two games and the set 7-5. In the second set I prevailed 6-4. There it was. I had just beaten the greatest tennis player of all time. I was thrilled, but in my heart I felt saddened that Laver was no longer able to be the player he once was. Age had caught up with him.

My thrill ride continued, however. After the match Laver asked if I was willing to practice with him. Coincidentally he was going to Toledo after this event to play an exhibition with John Newcombe. He wanted to get in some extra hitting to sharpen up his game. What followed was pure ecstasy. For two hours we drilled. And we drilled some more. And he gave me some advice and tips. Me, some kid from Toledo, practicing on the court like old buddies with Rod Laver. Unbelievable. Afterward he drove me back to our hotel. Rod Laver actually asked me if I wanted to join him for dinner that evening. Like an idiot, because I was so shy, I said thanks but I was going to just get room service. What a moron! It is one of the greatest regrets of my life. Turning down an invitation to join the great Rod Laver for dinner.

The next day I played Sandy Mayer, who was ranked tenth in the world. It was the highest ranked player I had ever faced other than Eddie Dibbs, who was ranked fifth when I played him. Mayer was a hard court player so I thought that maybe I would have a chance on the clay court surface. It sure looked like it in the beginning. I won the first three games of the match. But then I hit a stone wall. Mayer started to assert himself. He won the next 11 of 12 games and at 5-1 in the second set was up 40-love. Triple match point. It was all but over. Then something miraculous happened. I saved all three match points and, lo and behold, I won the next eight games. I won the second set and was actually up 2-0 in the third set against the 10th ranked player in the world. At that point Mayer must have decided he'd had enough. He raised his level of play considerably and won the next six games. The tournament organizers were thrilled. Just what they didn't need was some no-name like me in the finals.

That was March. Now it was May and we were getting ready for the NCAA Championship, which once again was being held at the University of Georgia. Unfortunately for me Shelley Coslowski was not visiting me in San Antonio like she did the previous year. In April Shelley called me to inform me that she was engaged to be married. I felt lousy. Even though Shelley made it quite clear our future was not going to be long term, in the back of my mind, in the tiniest way possible, I'd hoped that Shelley really loved me. And that she would wait for me patiently while I pursued my professional tennis dreams and then would be there for me when I was ready.

Once again we had a strong season as a team and we were seeded second going into the NCAA Team Championship. UCLA was seeded first, our arch-rival SMU was seeded third, and defending champion Stanford was seeded fourth. We won our first round match rather easily and then toppled a tough California-Berkeley team in the quarter finals. Like two years ago we faced SMU in the semi finals. And like two years ago we barely beat SMU by a score of 5-4. Now we had our chance again – the chance to be national champions.

We faced top seeded UCLA in the finals. I really believed we should win the match. At #2 singles I defeated Mike Harrington in straight sets. Mike's father Pat Harrington was an actor and was one of the stars in the TV sitcom "One Day At A Time". If he was watching his son play, I didn't see him. As expected, we lost at #6 singles. However, painfully and unexpectedly, Larry Gottfried, one time national junior champion, lost to Dick Metz in an upset at #4 singles. Also, somewhat shockingly, Tony Giammalva lost in three sets to Blaine Willenborg. Unfortunately, as was often the case in Athens, Georgia, Tony struggled with the hot conditions in late May. Now we were down 3-1, and both Ben McKown, at #1 singles, and John Benson, at #5 singles, were battling it out in third set matches. Ben went up a break in the third against Fritz Buehning, who in a couple of years would be ranked as high as #21 in the world. Unfortunately for us Ben could not hold the lead and we were now down 4-1. Luckily, John pulled out his match against Marcel Freeman in dramatic fashion, and we were still alive, though down 4-2.

When the doubles began, Ben and I gave Trinity renewed hope as we beat Harrington and Freeman at #2 doubles in straight sets. But then the tide started turning against us as John and Tony, at #1 doubles fell behind early, as did Mike Davidson and Eddie Reese at #3 doubles. Soon our dreams were crushed again, as Tony and John couldn't come back. We failed again. For the second time in our college careers we were runners-up in the NCAA National Championship.

Words cannot describe how low we felt as we drove back to the hotel. We were almost in tears. At the hotel we had an emotional team meeting. Bob McKinley, our coach, did the best he could to avoid getting emotional, but he couldn't. Tears flowed as he tried to put our effort into perspective and as he encouraged us to be proud of what we had accomplished.

But it didn't work. We felt like real failures that evening. It wasn't easy to swallow such a defeat. It just seemed like we had a better team and should never have lost three of the top four singles matches. We might never have such a chance again. That's probably what hurt the most.

The very next day the individual singles and doubles portion of the NCAA Championship began. I was still very distressed as I walked on the court against an unheralded opponent from a mid-western school. It looked like I was going to have a disastrous day. I dropped the first set. Because I was seeded sixth I already knew I would be an All-American for a third straight year, but that certainly didn't mean I didn't want to win the singles crown. It was tough because I kept moping about, thinking about the previous day. Fortunately Bob came out onto the court after I lost the first set and told me there was nothing I could do about our loss to UCLA, and if I kept playing as badly as I was, I would lose this match and feel even worse. His words got me going and I ended up pulling out a three setter.

Later that day I beat Leif Shiras, from Princeton, who was very talented and would one day be ranked in the top 50 in the world. The long day was capped off by Ben's and mine first round doubles match. We were seeded seventh and won in convincing fashion. Although it was hot and humid, we still felt eager and motivated. I felt like getting through the first day was a real boost to my confidence and helped me forget about our loss to UCLA in the finals.

In the final 16, I had to face California-Berkeley's #1 player, Larry Stefanki. He would be ranked in the top 50 in the world in the future. At that time, however, I was a better player than he was. For whatever reason he peaked later in his career, so I ended up beating him 6-3, 6-4. And now I faced a very familiar foe in the quarterfinals – Robert Van't Hof. Our last meeting had taken place a few months earlier at the National Collegiate Indoor Singles Championship, where I beat him in the semi finals. We had played several times in our junior and college career, and I had the upper hand losing to Robert only once. But now we would see what would happen under the extreme pressure of the NCAA Championship.

The match was tight all the way. We both wanted to win so badly. I managed to squeak by in the first set by a score of 7-5. Van't Hof turned the tables on me in the second set by 6-4. Now we headed to the third set as the tension mounted. I was both nervous and confident. I had a strong, winning record against Van't Hof so it seemed like I would have a lot of reasons to believe I should win. On the other hand, what happened before was probably irrelevant. Neither one of us could gain an advantage in the third set. Eventually it reached 5-5 and Van't Hof held serve. I was serving at 5-6 and was up 40-30, but blew that point. I was down to my last gasp. Because of no-ad scoring it was now game point for me to get to the tie-breaker, but more crucially it was match point for Van't Hof. I was one shot away from losing.

We had a long rally and Van't Hof came to the net when I hit a short ball. My backhand passing shot clipped the top of the net and, in what seemed like slow motion, plopped upwards in a high arc. Van't Hof reached for the ball with a backhand volley. Unbelievably enough, he dumped the shot in the net. I was momentarily saved. In one split second, I was given new life and a chance to get to the semis. Boosted by my good fortune, I went ahead in the tie-breaker 4-2. On my first match point, Van't Hof hit his service return long and I had done it. I was in the semis. One lucky break gave me a chance at winning the NCAA national title. Without that break, I would have lost in the quarter finals for the second straight year.

Late that afternoon Ben and I defeated Jeff Etterbeek and Matt Horwitch from Michigan in the second round of the doubles tournament. I was so happy because of my singles, that I was loose as a goose in the doubles match. That looseness carried over to my singles match the next day when I faced Juan Farrow who was seeded 15th. Once ranked #1 in the nation as a junior, his career had revived when he attended Southern Illinois-Edwardsville. Earlier in the tournament he had beaten my team mate Larry Gottfried. Larry had upset second seeded Andy Kohlberg of Tennessee. On a cloudy and humid day I beat Farrow with relative ease 7-5, 6-1. Everything seemed surreal. Here I was in the finals of the NCAA Singles Championship. I never would have believed that my dreams could be coming true. Little did I know, which I unfortunately learned in the future, your dreams can be destroyed in no time and you can be at the very bottom, looking up. But for now, I was enjoying myself immensely.

Ben and I then had some business to do in the doubles. In the quarter finals we faced Van't Hof and Roger Knapp. We beat them 7-6, 7-5. Needless to say I was playing as good as ever, like I didn't have a care in the world. Each win in doubles was just adding to my adrenaline. In the semi finals we probably played the best doubles match of our lives. We whipped Peter Rennert and Lloyd Bourne of Stanford, 6-1, 6-0. I had accomplished something even John McEnroe couldn't do – reach the finals of the NCAA Team, Singles, and Doubles Championship (in fairness to McEnroe his team won the title, he won the singles, and he lost in the semis of the doubles). But it does sound good to boast about doing something the great McEnroe couldn't do.

You would think I would be tired by now. I had played 17 matches in 7 days. But I didn't care. I was on cloud nine. Tomorrow I would have to play two 3 out of 5 set matches and I was looking forward to it. My opponent in the finals was Kevin Curren of Texas, who one day would reach the finals of Wimbledon. Our doubles opponents were Andy Kohlberg and Michael Fancutt from Tennessee.

Bob McKinley warmed me up for my match the next morning but I could never gain an edge in my match against Curren. I played tight. Curren's big serve and powerful forehand were causing me all kinds of difficulty. Earlier in his career I had beaten him a couple of times and back then he was not all that strong mentally. But he'd worked on his mental game and I couldn't count on him to collapse. He simply played a lot better than I did and crushed me by a score of 6-2, 6-2, 6-3. Curren became the first non-American (he is from South Africa) to win the NCAA singles crown since 1969. Naturally I was dejected but I simply didn't deserve to win. All I could do now was to go back to the hotel, shower and eat, rest up for a bit, and come back to play the doubles.

In the afternoon it was hot. Because we were playing 3 out of 5 sets, I hoped we wouldn't have a long doubles match. I didn't know how well I would hold up after playing three sets in the morning. But luckily, Ben played great. We jumped to a 3-0 lead in the first set and never looked back. We won the first set 6-2. We were up 3-1 in the second set, but stumbled. Kohlberg and Fancutt won four straight games and suddenly we were behind 5-3. The big moment in the match occurred right then and there. We broke Fancutt and returned the favor by winning four straight games and the second set, 7-5. We jumped out to a 5-1 lead in the third and eventually won 6-3 when Ben hit a winner. We reacted with uncharacteristic emotion when we jumped up in the air and hugged. It was a real thrill. Although Trinity had teams that had reached the doubles finals, none had ever won. Ben and I were the first. And it felt great.

The 1979 NCAA Championship was really a special moment in time for me. As a kid growing up, it was what I was dreaming about. I never really thought I could accomplish what I did and I kept pinching myself to make sure it was real. And it was. The last year of my life had truly been magical. Most people never have the good fortune of dreaming big and then accomplishing much of what they dream about. I was lucky. Because of a fortunate net cord shot against Van't Hof and because I happened to play some good tennis when it really counted, my childhood dreams were, for the most part, fulfilled. Now came my next fantasy. I was on my way to play at Wimbledon. The dream was living on.

CHAPTER 13

I was very excited about playing at Wimbledon, but I didn't realize how difficult it would be to prepare for the tournament. The main reason it was hard to prepare for the tournament was that I had a really challenging time finding any grass courts to practice on in Ohio. Through the tennis rumor mill I heard that a professor at Bowling Green State University had a grass court in his back yard. Bowling Green was only about fifteen miles from our house, so I figured I would be able to practice at the professor's house, if he let me. And fortunately, after I called him, he was gracious enough to let me try out his court.

I drove down with Gary Driftmeyer, a friend of mine who was several years older than me and who had played for the University of Toledo. We arrived at the professor's house and I introduced ourselves. He led us to the back yard and then sat down to watch us practice. What followed was rather comical. His "grass court" was simply a normal lawn that was cut very short and had chalk lines drawn on the surface. It was nothing like a real grass court. It wasn't rolled, the grass was not anything like the grass used on a grass court, and the bounces were horrific. Because the professor was watching, Gary and I tried to keep a straight face as we played, but it was very hard to do so. After our practice I thanked the professor but needless to say I wasn't planning on returning.

Next I discovered that Mayfield Country Club in Cleveland had grass courts. Fortunately I knew Jim Twigg, who was the head professional at the club. I called him and he invited me to the club for some practice. It was about a two hour drive but it was definitely worth it. I needed some practice on grass before I played Wimbledon, and I was quite certain Mayfield Country Club would have legitimate grass courts. On my way there I had the misfortune of getting a speeding ticket, but all in all the trip went fine.

The courts at Mayfield were quite plush. The ground underneath was fairly firm but the surface itself was spongy. The ball bounced very low and skidded so I realized, after playing against Jim for awhile, that it was best to get to the net as much as possible. Rallies were very limited because of the unpredictability of the bounce and because of the speed with which the ball skidded. I learned rather quickly that my game was not very well suited for a grass surface. In addition I only practiced with Jim a couple of times because I couldn't drive to Cleveland every day. Consequently I wasn't sure I was going to have much of a shot at being sharp on the courts of Wimbledon. But I really didn't care. I wanted to live out my dream of playing at the true mecca of tennis.

My flight to London was a non-stop flight from Detroit. My parents saw me off at the airport with warm wishes for success. They were a bit nervous because this was my first flight overseas and I was flying solo. On the other hand they realized I was now twenty-one years old and should be able to handle myself well enough. I wasn't worried about the trip and was looking forward to visiting Boris after I played at Wimbledon. After I visited Boris I was playing one more tournament in Europe, at Gstaad, Switzerland. It would be a fascinating tournament to play because it was located in the Alps. The flight itself was uneventful. We left Detroit in the late evening and arrived in London by nine o'clock local time. It was then that I made my first mistake.

I arrived at the tournament hotel, The Gloucester, and checked in. The Gloucester was located in the heart of down town London. I was exhausted because I really didn't sleep very well on the plane and it was five o'clock in the morning Ohio time. I immediately went up to my room and plopped on the bed. Within minutes I was out like a light. I slept soundly. Too soundly as it turns out. When I awoke it was well past dinner time. I got out of bed and showered before hurrying out the door to grab a bite to eat. It was odd crossing the streets because the English drive on the left side of the street. I avoided getting run over and had a rather drab meal at a fast food restaurant. So far the cliché seemed true. English food sucks and it's always raining. On my way back to the hotel I got drenched by a sudden down pour.

Then I paid for my decision to sleep during the day. I was wide awake and remained so almost the entire night. I had been stupid. I should have stayed awake all day after I arrived so I would get used to a new sleep pattern. Instead it was likely I would never get sleepy until the middle of the night. I finally got to sleep after hours of boredom. There were no late night TV channels and I got fed up with the book I was reading. Not an auspicious start to my trip.

The next morning, rather late in the morning, I got up and opened my curtains. I was on the third floor and had a good look below of Midsomer Street, the main street running in front of the hotel. The weather was gloomy again. I looked up and down the street. It was a Sunday morning so the streets weren't very crowded. I couldn't help but notice one man, who was pacing back and forth. He was on the other side of the street but my eyes were attracted to him because he had a pronounced limp. In itself I suppose it meant nothing. But when he turned and walked in one direction I could swear that I saw an ugly scar on his right cheek. The distance was too far to say for sure. The more I looked at the man, the more I was sure. It was the man who had shot Gunter Gruber! Perhaps I was hallucinating. I don't know. But I was going to make sure.

I hurriedly threw on some clothes and rushed down to the lobby. I bolted out the front door and looked in the direction where I had seen the man with the scar. He was leaning against a building near the corner of Midsomer and Covington. Haphazardly, without remembering to look, I crossed the street. Luckily the cars in the street were far enough away from me that they really didn't have to brake very hard to avoid me. At that moment the man with the scar seemed to gaze in my direction. A couple of people suddenly were in my way, but I could see the man I was pursuing start to walk quickly toward the corner. Next thing I knew he was disappearing around the side of the building located at the corner. I started to run as fast as I could. It had to be the man with the scar. Why else would he be trying to get away from me.

As I raced around the corner I craned my head back and forth, looking at both sides of Covington. Then I spotted him. He was just beginning to hurry down the stairs leading to a London Underground Station. Apparently, if he really was trying to elude me, he was going to do so by subway. The entrance to the Underground could not have been more than one hundred feet away so I was certain I would be able to catch up to the man. I got to the stairs and barreled my way past people making their way up the stairs.

At the bottom of the stairs I saw the token booth. Almost simultaneously I saw the man with the scar limping toward the subway platform. He glanced over his shoulder and moved even faster. I heard the sound of an approaching subway train. Then it hit me. I didn't bring any money with me. In my haste, I'd forgotten to take my key and wallet with me. I couldn't buy a token. I rudely pushed past the people in front of me in line and started yelling at the token seller.

"I need to get on that next subway," I yelled at the token seller. "It's an emergency and I forgot my money in my hotel room. I need to get on that subway." Out of the corner of my eye I could see the moving cars of the subway as they started to arrive at the station.

At first the token seller ignored me with a stony stare. Then he pretty much blew me off. "You can't get on that subway without a token," he snarled in a thick sounding English accent. "There are no exceptions. What's the big emergency anyway? I don't see anything going on."

The people behind me started to yell at me. I yelled back. I wasn't getting anywhere. I quickly got out of line and ran toward the token structures. The machines had revolving gates that one could only push successfully after a token was inserted into the slot adjacent to the entrance to the platform. Between the structures was chain link fencing. The only way through to the platforms was through the structures. I looked through the fence. By now the subway was stopped. I desperately looked for the man with the scar. I spotted him just as the doors to the subway slid open. The passengers getting off at this station got out of the subway cars and headed toward the exits.

This was my last chance. I ran to the exit structures hoping to squeeze through the exit gates to the platform area when the departing passengers made their way through the revolving gates. But it couldn't be that simple. The gates revolved in only one direction. What an idiot! Obviously the revolving gates were designed to let people exiting get out – they were also designed to keep people on my side of the structures from getting in. One last look at the subway and I spotted the man with the scar getting on the subway. He didn't look back. I felt unbelievably frustrated. I was certain the man I chased was the man who shot Gruber. And I was certain that it could not be coincidence that he was in London, and obviously even more unlikely that he was near The Gloucester. I was livid. I just blew my chance to unravel the mystery surrounding the man with the scar.

I hurried back to The Gloucester and asked to be let into my room, explaining I forgot my key. Even though I had no ID on me I convinced the front desk manager that I was a legit guest and they gave me a spare key. The very first thing I did was to call my father. Luckily he was home.

"Pa, I just saw the man with the scar who shot Gruber," I exclaimed with a combination of excitement and anger. "Why in the world would he be here other than he is following me?" I had started talking as soon as my father had answered the phone so it took him a minute to grasp what I was saying.

"Are you sure it was the man with the scar?"

By now I knew I couldn't really trust everything my father had told me about the past and the events of the war that were connected to Gruber and his co-horts. Who knew anymore what was true and what wasn't true.

"Of course I'm sure. He started to run away when he saw me coming after him and he had that limp. There is no doubt that was him. Now why was he here and what do you know about it?" I demanded in an angry tone.

"Erick, you have got to believe me. I don't know why he is there. Obviously he doesn't want to harm you, because he protected you from Gruber. Perhaps he thinks he must protect you further, but I can't imagine from whom. Gruber and Rheingold are dead. As you yourself discovered, Peter Brenner is presumed dead as is Joseph Erdmeister. Dr. Friedrich died years ago. All members of the "Inner Circle of Five" are most certainly dead. You must try to forget about all of this from my past and concentrate on your tennis."

And my father was right. I had to focus on my appearance at Wimbledon. It might be a once in a life time opportunity and I didn't want to play poorly because I was concentrating all my energy on the mystery surrounding the "Inner Circle of Five". If my father knew more, and I suspected he did, he was not going to tell me. It was also true that, more than likely, all the members of the "Inner Circle of Five" were dead. Perhaps Peter Brenner had escaped from Germany at the end of the war, but so far he hadn't surfaced. And if Joseph Erdmeister was captured by the Russians, it would seem certain that he was killed as retribution for his treatment of captured Russians. I knew my father loved me and would not jeopardize my life. If he thought I was in danger, I'm sure he would have taken the necessary steps to protect me.

Soon after I got off the phone, it started raining quite hard. I picked up a copy of "The Daily Telegraph", England's main newspaper, and turned to the sports section. I scoured the paper for the order of play at Wimbledon scheduled for Monday, June 25, 1979. And there I saw it. The third match of the day, on court 12. V.E. Iskersky vs J. James. Although my first name was Waldemar, the Germanized version of Vladimir, I entered Wimbledon as Vladimir Erick Iskersky. Why my parents named me Waldemar, rather than Vladimir, I never knew and for some reason never asked. Needless to say, from an early age I went by my middle name.

I hardly slept that Sunday night in anticipation of my match. I finally drifted off but was awakened by my alarm at 10:00. I was in no hurry. Traditionally the opening matches at Wimbledon began at 2:00pm. At this time of year, play could go on as late as 10:00pm. The courts were also too wet in the morning for play – the dew had to dry off before play could start. After a large breakfast, I was taken to Wimbledon by a courtesy car.

When I arrived on the hallowed grounds of Wimbledon for "The Championships", as the tournament was known in England, I got chills running up and down my spine. I was going to play at the mecca for tennis, the most famous tennis facility in the world bar none. I went through the mobs of spectators waiting in line to get into the tournament and was shown to my locker. I was assigned to the locker room for unseeded players. The top 16 seeds had their own locker room.

Unfortunately my excitement and anticipation, which was at an extremely high level, was dampened significantly, both literally and figuratively. By 2:00pm the rains came. By 6:00pm it was still raining. All third matches on court were canceled for the day. I got my ride back to the hotel. By the time I got back to the hotel and turned on the TV, it was announced that all play for the day at Wimbledon was canceled for Monday.

Remarkably I went through the same ritual for two more days. Some matches were played, but the rain played havoc with the schedule. By the time it was my turn to play my match, either the rains came again or the match in front of me was unable to finish because of the darkness. Finally, on Thursday, the fourth day of the tournament, the weather cooperated and the forecast was good. I hadn't hit a tennis ball in days and now I had to play a match on grass after practicing no more than three times on the grass in Cleveland. It did not seem like an auspicious start to my Wimbledon.

That Thursday morning I got a ride to the Queen's Club, which had indoor wooden courts to practice on. With three other players, we were allotted a half hour of court time. After that brief hit, I headed over to Wimbledon. I was the second match scheduled on court 12. I had a light lunch in the players' dining room and spent my time watching some of Bjorn Borg's second round match on center court against Vijay Amritraj.

As it turned out, it took Borg five sets to win and he had to pull out a tie-breaker to even make it to the fifth set.

Finally my match was called in the late afternoon. I walked out through the crowd back toward the far end of Wimbledon's grounds with my opponent, John James from Australia. He was ranked right around #100 in the world, which presumably meant I had a good draw. The only problem was that he was quite adept on grass and was an experienced player. As we warmed up I felt my nerves. I could see my name on the score board and just felt like I was in a surreal dream. I was actually playing a match at Wimbledon! My journey through my tennis dream had taken me this far and it was thrilling.

The thrill wore off when the match started. My lack of experience on grass became evident right away. Not only was I nervous, I had trouble with the bounces on grass and wasn't comfortable with serving and volleying on every point when it was my turn to serve. If I stayed back, James immediately came to net and forced the issue. I felt totally out of my element. The surface at Wimbledon was much firmer than the courts I had practiced on in Cleveland, but the bounces were no less unstable. In no time, the first set was over, 6-2.

The match only got worse. In the second set James started playing even better, and I had no answer. My serve wasn't good enough to win me a lot of free points and my attempts at serving and volleying were fairly futile. My returns were floating way too much because I was tentative and I couldn't think of an alternative strategy that would get me back in the game. Soon, I lost the second set, 6-1.

Maybe playing Wimbledon wasn't such a good idea. My attitude changed a bit in the third set when I managed to stay even with James for the first six games. I was playing somewhat better, and I finally started to get a higher percentage of my serves in play. I loosened up because in the back of my mind I had no chance to win. Could this be the start of a stirring comeback? Unfortunately no. At 3-3 my serve was broken by James. He held serve easily and at 3-5 I at least managed to hold serve one more time. James served out the match in the next game with little resistance from me, and the match was over. I was drubbed in my Wimbledon debut by a score of 6-2, 6-1, 6-4. I left the court quite discouraged.

As I made my way back to the locker room I could only chastise myself for playing so horribly. It hurt to think that I had come all this way to fulfill a dream of mine, and then totally fell flat on my face. I knew I could play better, but I also learned a valuable lesson. If I was going to play professional tennis at a high level, I had to be better prepared. Most of the players were pros and not amateurs. They were playing for their livelihood. I arrived at Wimbledon with no grass court experience, virtually no practice time on grass, and without advice from any of my mentors on how to handle the situation. Certainly not a good recipe for success.

I was brought out of my stupor by a shout from behind. "Erick, Erick Iskersky," bellowed a voice with a strong English accent. "May I chat with you?" the man to whom the voice belonged inquired. As he walked closer to me in my direction I surveyed his appearance. I certainly didn't recognize him and had no idea who he was. He hurried impatiently toward me and finally pushed around a couple of spectators and ended up uncomfortably close to me. Then he stuck out his hand to shake mine.

I have to admit that he seemed rather ugly as men go. He had lousy, tobacco stained teeth that were quite crooked. He was of average height and looked to be in his fifties. His hair was frizzy, his lips thin and dull red. His eyes darted nervously about, as if he were searching for someone in the crowd around us. My first thought, from the way he was dressed, was that he was a common laborer who was working at Wimbledon as some sort of maintenance man. I timidly stuck out my hand in response to his gesture.

"Colonel James McMillan, at your service," he said with an accent that seemed rough around the edges. "If I do say so, it is a real pleasure to meet you. I'm a friend of your father's so to speak. I'm sorry the match didn't go better."

At first I was puzzled. How could an Englishman be a friend of my father's. As far as I knew my father had never been to England. Then it hit me. Colonel James McMillan was the legendary war hero who had captured so many of the Nazi war criminals in Berlin as the war was coming to an end. As I remembered from my research, he was the one who captured Gunter Gruber.

"Yes, I know who you are. I was doing some research about the end of World War II and I came across your name. You actually captured a man by the name of Gunter Gruber. I had a most unpleasant experience with Gunter Gruber about three years ago. My father has never mentioned you."

"Well, yes, yes. That's understandable. Calling myself a friend of Vladimir would probably be stretching the truth a bit. He happened to be one of the soldiers we captured in one of our forays within Berlin, but eventually he was released. Many soldiers were released unless they were suspected Nazis or refused to cooperate with our interrogations. I remember your father well because he was very cooperative with us and even helped out some of the wounded during our incursions into Berlin. Yes, his bravery stands out in my mind, and when I saw the name Iskersky in the draw at Wimbledon I just had to believe it was Vladimir's son. I called your father and confirmed it."

"It's my pleasure to meet you Colonel. As I said I've read about you and it's almost as if history is coming alive right in front of my eyes. I've never met a war hero before."

"You're too kind, you're too kind. I only did what any well meaning soldier would have done. Those were horrible times and I'm glad the war ended when it did."

We chatted for close to one hour. I had all kinds of questions for the Colonel. It was fascinating to talk to someone so intimately involved in The Second World War. Of course it was a bit strange in that I had never really sat down with my father and had a long conversation with him about his war experiences. After talking with Colonel McMillan, I realized how much my father must have gone through during the war. At least, as a medic he was not involved in the killing of others and was typically behind the front. Nonetheless, I more fully appreciated what my father encountered during one of the greatest tragedies in world history.

By the time I was done conversing with the Colonel, it was agreed that I would meet him for dinner at his flat the next evening. He gave me directions and assured me that I would find his residence without any problems. He lived near an underground tube station not more than thirty minutes from The Gloucester. We parted ways and I finished my day with a shower and dinner at the players' dining room. By now I was less gloomy about my defeat and was actually looking forward to my visit with the Colonel the next day.

By the time I got back to The Gloucester it was nearly ten o'clock. I'd stayed to watch some of the matches at Wimbledon and hoped that I would some day return to the hallowed grounds of tennis. I excitedly called my father that night around midnight to tell him about my encounter with Colonel McMillan, even though it was only 6:00am in Ohio. I expected him to be quite happy that I was able to meet the Colonel, but quickly found out otherwise.

"Yes, that Colonel McMillan called me to see if you were indeed my son. I'm sure he acted as if we were great friends and that I owe him because I was released from custody, soon after I was captured. I'm not really going to get into it, but he really wasn't the reason I was released. Suffice it to say, in my eyes he is not a real hero. There is much the public doesn't know."

When pressed for details, I could get nothing out of my father. Knowing how he felt about McMillan, I didn't tell him I was visiting the Colonel the very next day. Something really bothered my father about McMillan, but I didn't pressure my father any further. Plus, I really didn't know if I could fully trust my father anymore. Clearly he was hiding something from me about Gunter Gruber and the "Inner Circle of Five". Of that I was certain. I made up my mind to question Colonel McMillan thoroughly about anything he knew about the "Inner Circle of Five".

The next day was a leisurely one. All I did was have a nice breakfast, walk around the areas of London near the hotel, and watch some TV. The weather stayed fairly warm and it would have been a good day to be at Wimbledon. But after losing the day before, I didn't feel like traveling out to the club to watch others playing. I longed deeply to still be in the event and thought dreamily about what it would be like to hoist the championship trophy. I made up my mind to try to work even harder and to see if I could one day return to Wimbledon and perform better. For now, I had to get ready to have dinner at Colonel McMillan's flat.

McMillan lived at 1520 Kennington Court. He had given me directions on how to get there by the inner tube and told me it would take about 45 minutes to get to his flat from The Gloucester. Just in case he had also given me his phone number. I was expected at 6:00, so I left The Gloucester around 5:00. Fortunately the directions were concise and easy to follow because I had to make two changes of trains. When we arrived at the Frost Boulevard station I got off the tube and proceeded up the stairs to the street above.

Frost Boulevard turned out to be a quiet, residential street. There were a few shops and cafes near the station, but for the most part it was obvious I was in the suburbs of London. I followed McMillan's directions and turned left on Abbey Street. After a few blocks I saw the sign for Kennington Court and turned right. Kennington Court had a number of large, four story buildings on it. McMillan called his place a flat, but to me it looked like these were what we would consider luxury condominiums in the United States. Soon enough I found 1520. McMillan's flat number was 42, located on the fourth floor. When I entered the building, I saw the bank of elevators and pressed the up button.

In a matter of moments I was riding up to the fourth floor. My exhilaration started to build as I wondered if McMillan had some connection with the "Inner Circle of Five" or knew something that my father knew but was unwilling to tell me. Of course it was more likely that McMillan knew very little and was simply a war hero living a quiet life in the suburbs of London.

When I got to the door of McMillan's flat I rang the door bell and could hear the loud chime. I waited for what seemed like a rather long time but there was no response. I rang the bell again. And waited. Still nothing. This time I knocked loudly and shouted out McMillan's name.

There was absolute silence. I was puzzled. What should I do I wondered? I decided to ring the door bell of flat 41 located directly across the hall. This time I got an immediate response as an older woman, probably in her late sixties with pepper colored hair and a substantial paunch, opened her door and peered out.

"Yes, may I help you?" she asked me in a raspy voice.

"Yes, please, if you could that would be great," I replied. "I was supposed to meet Colonel McMillan at 6:00 and there is no answer. I was just wondering if you have seen him at all."

"I've not see James since yesterday morning. I have to admit we are not very close friends, but I see him about and we chat fairly often. Generally I've always thought of him as a very fastidious and organized fellow, so it would surprise me if he forgot that he was to meet with you."

"Yeah, it does seem a bit odd because he only invited me to his flat yesterday, so I don't see how he could forget. If you happen to see him could you tell him that Erick came by and ask him to call me at The Gloucester."

"I'll do that laddy," the lady exclaimed and closed her door.

The next day I went over to Wimbledon to watch some of the matches. I planned to leave the following day to Munich and visit Boris before going to Gstaad, Switzerland, the site of my next tournament. I enjoyed hanging out at Wimbledon that day because I never knew if I would be back to play the event or not. I certainly hoped I would get the chance again. I also tried calling Colonel McMillan a couple of times while I was at Wimbledon, but there was no answer. It seemed odd to me that he would stand me up in such a rude manner, particularly since he was the one who went through such pains to meet me. Just in case I called him one more time at night after I ate dinner, but I still didn't get an answer.

I woke up quite early the next morning. My flight wasn't until the afternoon but I was anxious and ready to go. I hadn't seen Boris in quite some time so it would be good to visit him and see how his medical studies were going. I went down to the lobby and grabbed the newspaper and ambled over to get some breakfast at The Gloucester coffee shop.

The headline of the front page startled me and grabbed my immediate attention. "World War II Hero Found Dead In Flat", screamed the headline. And below that, "Colonel James McMillan Murdered In His Own Living Quarters". I couldn't believe it. I quickly started to read the article.

"Colonel James McMillan, a war hero from World War II, who was renowned for capturing enemy combatants in Germany at the end of the war, was found dead yesterday evening. Several friends of his, who were to meet at McMillan's flat for a card game were concerned when he didn't answer the door and persuaded the land lord to let them in. To their disbelief and horror they discovered McMillan dead in the living room, the victim of what police described as a 'vicious stabbing'. According to sources, it was obvious that McMillan had put up a fight and that he did not die easily."

From there the article went on to describe McMillan's accomplishments and what he had done after the war. Surprisingly he hadn't done much. He served for roughly ten more years in the army after the war and then abruptly resigned his commission and never worked again. It seemed hard to believe he could live comfortably after only serving a total of 20 years in the army, but I certainly had no idea what his pension was. The newspaper article implied that he must have had an outside source of income beyond his pension in order to live in the neighborhood and flat where he was residing.

This development sent my mind reeling. It seemed obvious that the presence of the man with the scar and the death of McMillan were somehow connected. I was certainly convinced that I had indeed been chasing Gruber's killer and that he was watching or following me. Now Colonel McMillan, another individual with some sort of connection to my father, however remote, was dead. And once again the man with the scar was present. I knew trying to get anymore information out of my father was hopeless. He was definitely not telling me something and the only way I could find out, was to find out by myself. Unfortunately, I had no strategy I could think of. I had already done all the research I could about the "Inner Circle of Five" and could only conclude that the man with the scar and McMillan had some connection to that group. But none of the group seemed to be alive, to the best of my knowledge, based on my research. Although, I had to admit, only Gruber, Alfred Rheingold who attacked Shelley Coslowski and me in San Antonio, and Dr. Hans Friedrich, were confirmed dead. Joseph Erdmeister was presumed dead or captured by the Russians, and Peter Brenner was never found dead or alive. The mystery seemed to grow, but the answers were elusive and seemingly unattainable. I headed to Munich that afternoon with much on my mind, but clarity was not forthcoming.

CHAPTER 14

I arrived in Munich and was greeted warmly by Boris. We hadn't seen each other in quite sometime so we were both excited about spending a few days together. It was the perfect remedy for the way I felt after losing at Wimbledon. It also helped take my mind off the mystery surrounding Gunter Gruber and the "Inner Circle of Five". It seemed like the more that happened, the cloudier the mystery became. And I knew full well my father was not going to provide any additional information if he had any to provide.

The time spent in Munich went quickly and was a lot of fun. Boris was on break from his medical school studies so we had much free time to eat, to exercise, and to rekindle fond memories of our childhood. Luckily Boris was able to get me situated at a club in Munich that had red clay courts and I got a fair amount of practice in preparation for the tournament in Gstaad. After a few days it was time to say goodbye. Boris would be finishing medical school by May of 1981, so it was possible I wouldn't visit him in Munich again. That was a shame because I really enjoyed my time in Munich.

I boarded the train for my trip to Gstaad. I had to make several transfers because Gstaad was a resort town located high in the mountains. The scenery was some of the most beautiful I had ever seen, jagged mountain peaks that could be seen from the railroad car, with the train snaking its way upwards ever so slowly. I marveled at the engineering exploits that resulted in this magnificent feat of human perseverance. I was a bit nervous because this was the first time I was alone in a country whose first language was not English. And my German was so poor that it didn't do me much good, even though I was in the German region of Switzerland.

Even though in the scheme of things I was a nobody, at the Gstaad tournament all of the players were treated quite well. My hotel room was provided for free and we were given meals at the hotel for breakfast and dinner, while lunch was at the club. My first round opponent was Jeff Borowiak, an American who had played at UCLA and was once ranked as high as #25 in the world, but now was ranked right around #100. Unfortunately this match began a string of horrible matches I played throughout the summer. I played tight and was so worried about how my performances would affect my ranking. Ranking points stayed on the computer for 52 weeks. After the drubbing by Borowiak all my points from the successful Challengers and Cincinnati from the previous summer came off the computer – to be replaced by one ATP point for each of my first round losses at Wimbledon and Gstaad. Quickly my ranking started to plummet.

I lost three more first round matches after Gstaad. First to Victor Pecci in Washington D.C., which was certainly not a bad loss since he was ranked top 15 in the world and seeded very high. At Louisville I lost to Rejean Genois from Canada who was ranked around #90. At South Orange I lost to Gene Malin, who was a real journeyman ranked #160. Finally in Boston I broke through with a win over David Schneider of South Africa, before losing in the second round to Hans Gildemeister, who was ranked #14 and very proficient on the clay courts at Longwood Cricket Club. By the time the summer was over I was discouraged and tired. I had only played 6 tournaments and lost first round in five of them. My ranking had dropped precipitously.

In an effort to regain some ranking points I signed up for three Challenger events in Charlotte; Lincoln, Nebraska; and Austin. I made the round of 16 in one of the tournaments and had a win over teammate Tony Giammalva. Tony returned the favor when he beat me in the quarterfinals in Austin. In between, I lost to former NCAA Champion Matt

Mitchell in the second round in Lincoln. By the time the year was over, my ranking had dropped all the way to #216.

As January 1980 arrived, the last semester of my college career, I was hit with a shock. My doubles partner, Ben McKown, decided to quit school and turn pro. It was devastating to our team and also to me. One of the main reasons I stayed in school for my senior year was to see if we could win the team NCAA Championships. Being runner-ups twice was not fun. Now, without Ben in the line-up, we really didn't stand much of a chance. He was one of our top four players, and was reliable beyond belief. He had once compiled a winning streak of 30 dual match wins in a row and had lost only 8 dual matches in three seasons. When he left, my attitude inexcusably turned negative. Because of my attitude and a sense of burnout, my senior year was my worst of my college career. I also developed tendonitis in my wrist. When all was said and done, we lost in the quarterfinals of the NCAA Team Championships to Cal-Berkeley and I lost in the second round of the singles tournament. For the first time in my four year career, I failed to make All-American. My entire senior season turned out to be a real blow to my confidence and ego.

My summer was no different. I lost in several qualifying events for Grand Prix tournaments and was so desperate I decided to travel to Brazil and play four Challenger events. In those events I only managed to reach the third round of two of the events and the second round of another one. My ranking kept dropping, almost to 350 in the world. To try to salvage something, I returned to the United States and signed up to play in the USTA Satellite Circuit to be held in Texas. This was about as bad as it could get. I was back to playing the absolute lowest level of professional tennis available on the ATP tour. In fact I had so much early success when I started to play professional tournaments, that I had never even played a satellite circuit. Basically, players signed up to play four tournaments with 64 draws. After four tournaments, the 32 players with the best records moved on to a fifth and final "Master" event. Based on the standings after the final event, players were awarded ATP points and rewarded with one tournament on the computer. Needless to say, the satellite circuits were the true "minor leagues" of professional tennis. It took five weeks to get points and credit for one tournament. In effect, I was starting over at the very bottom. The question was simple. Would I ever succeed as a professional tennis player again? Or, was my career over?

The USTA/Texas Satellite Circuit started in El Paso and I got off to a horrible start losing in the first round of the first tournament. From there we went to Midland, where I lost in the second round. The same thing happened in Abilene. Things couldn't have gotten any worse. Not only was I playing horribly, I was traveling by Greyhound bus and skimping on my expenses because the prize money in satellite circuits is really negligible, unless you are winning the events. My entire professional career was on the brink. As I traveled to Beaumont for the fourth tournament I really began questioning myself. Was it time to give up my dream of being a successful professional tennis player?

Beaumont was do or die. If I didn't do well I was unlikely to make the "Master" event and would earn zero ATP points. For whatever reason, which I certainly couldn't pinpoint, I played well that week and gained some confidence. I ended up reaching the finals. This earned me a spot in the "Master" event in Wichita Falls. In Wichita Falls I came through in the clutch one more time and reached the finals for two weeks in a row. I earned some valuable ATP points and finished the 1980 season ranked #302 in the world. Not very good, but at least I had some confidence restored from my performance in Texas.

I began the 1981 season with little success. I lost in the qualifying events for the Grand Prix tournaments in Memphis and Richmond. After that it was off to Germany for Boris' wedding. He was finished with medical school and was marrying his German fiance Greta. From there they would move to Charleston, South Carolina. The wedding was a huge affair because Greta had a large family. It was held in a small town not far from Munich. I rarely saw Boris anymore so it was good to see him again and attend his wedding. For the first time I met Greta's parents and brothers, and her extended family. Needless to say it was a joyous occasion.

Boris and Greta were going to honeymoon in Paris and so I joined them on the train for their trip. I was going to disembark in Nancy, France where a Grand Prix tournament was being held. I had no idea what to expect. This was my first trip back to Europe since 1979 when I played Wimbledon and Gstaad and it was my first experience in France. I also hadn't played any tennis at all for a week.

Amazingly enough I played quite well. I won three matches in the qualifying rounds, beating Jan Gunnarson of Sweden in the final round. Because I qualified I now received free accommodations and food, and of course prize money and ATP points depending on how I performed. Unfortunately I drew Guillermo Vilas in the first round, who was the top seed and ranked sixth in the world. It didn't matter much that we were playing indoors (it was still cold in the middle of March) because the surface was called "Greenset", which was a very slow surface. It was a temporary surface set up in indoor venues that were not tennis specific. Vilas was at his best on slow surfaces, so I was even in more trouble than I normally would have been in against the sixth best player in the world. I hung in there in the first set losing only 6-4. In the second set I got drubbed 6-0.

After that event, I lost in qualifying tournaments in Nice, France and Barcelona, Spain. My last tournament of this trip was in West Berlin. It was a Challenger event, a step below the Grand Prix level. The trip to West Berlin was eerie. I was on a train that passed through communist East Germany that made its way to the divided city of Berlin. Although I didn't go to see the Berlin Wall, I was very aware of the historic nature of my location. My parents escaped communism and eventually made it to Germany. Once again God must have smiled down on them because they ended up living in West Germany, where the people were free and not in East Germany, where the people suffered under a communistic regime. How ironic it would have been had my parents gone through the travails they faced escaping Russia, only to be caught in the web of communism once again in East Germany. If they had settled in what became East Germany, they never would have made it to the United States.

The tournament in West Berlin went great. It was held in late April, so it was outside and on clay. I defeated seventh seeded Steve Krulevitz of the United States in the second round. After disposing of Fernando Maynetto of Peru I defeated top seeded Andreas Maurer of Germany, who ended the 1981 season ranked #47 in the world. I lost to Werner Zirngibl of Germany in the finals. I picked up some ATP points, $2500 in prize money, and a boost in confidence as I headed back to the United States for a break.

After practicing for over a month I was back in Europe by the end of June. There were more tournaments for me to play overseas so I decided to stay for a few weeks. Little did I know at that time that I would end up staying for almost six months. My quest to get back into the top 100 in the world continued in Germany once again. Both events were Challenger events and both went miserably. I lost in the first round in Travemunde and Essen to lowly ranked players. The confidence I had gained by my performance in Berlin didn't seem to carry over. I still recall watching Wimbledon on TV in Essen, remembering how I was once ranked high enough to play there in the main draw. It was a very painful memory.

I qualified for the Stuttgart Grand Prix event. The highlight was getting to watch Bjorn Borg play his first round match. However, I had a decent performance. I lost in three sets to Mark Edmonson from Australia, who ended up ranked #20 in the world at year's end. The most notable thing that occurred was when I was practicing a couple of days later. Edmonson was practicing next to me with some of his Australian buddies. He didn't know I was near him and he told one of his friends what a pleasure it was playing someone in the second round who "actually hit the ball, not like in my first match". Obviously he was insulting me because he thought I pushed the ball. Years later when Edmonson's skill had declined I beat him in the qualifier at the ATP Championships. The memory of his words remained with me and I used it as motivation during my match. Needless to say he had no idea that I heard what he said years before, nor did he even remember that we had played before. But I certainly enjoyed beating him.

I had a great result at the Hilversum, Netherlands Grand Prix event, which again I had to qualify for. I beat Ramesh Krishnan, who was seeded and ranked in the top 70 and then beat Eric Deblicker of France. In the quarterfinals I lost to Wojtek Fibak of Poland, ranked in the top 20. I continued my long trek in Europe playing five Challenger events in France, Italy, and Belgium. In the Brussels event I lost in the finals after being up 7-6, 5-3. A total choke. It was one of the biggest disappointments of my professional career. But on the bright side, my game was really picking up.

In Bordeaux, France I got into the main draw of the Grand Prix tournament. I took full advantage of the situation by beating Loic Courteau and future top tenner Anders Jarryd, before losing to #37 ranked Andres Gomez in the quarterfinals. From there I flew to Athens to play in a Challenger event. I reached the semifinals where I lost to movie star and pro tennis player Vince Van Patten.

It was now the end of September. I had now been playing in Europe for three straight months. My ranking had climbed to the top 200. If I went home I would have to start the 1982 season playing qualifying events in Grand Prix tournaments, or play Challenger events. If I stayed in Europe for two more months I could continue to play tournaments and hope to climb back up in the rankings. Even though I was getting mentally drained, I decided to stick it out. I desperately wanted to get back into the top 100.

Rather than play qualifying events for Grand Prix tournaments, I chose to play two Satellite Circuits in Holland and Belgium. It would be 10 consecutive weeks of tennis and because of my ranking in the top 200 I would be seeded quite high in each tournament. But the pay-off could be valuable. If I won both of the circuits, I might very well break back into the top 100 in the world.

My strategy paid off. In Holland I won two of the five events, and lost in the finals of a third tournament. I finished second in that particular circuit. Then, off to Belgium. I won three out of five events and finished first overall in the circuit. With the ATP points I picked up in these two circuits, when I went home in December my ranking was back up.

I finished 1981 ranked #113 in the world. I was mentally and physically exhausted, but I now would have a great chance of getting into the main draws of some of the Grand Prix events. My dream of returning to the top 100 was nearly fulfilled.

I returned home to a well deserved rest. All thoughts of Gruber and Nazis were out of my mind. It no longer was a factor in my life. My energy was now devoted to tennis and fulfilling my dreams. I loved playing tennis and making a living doing something I loved was fantastic. Although it had become fairly apparent I wasn't going to be a superstar or be good enough to win a Grand Slam event, I still was highly motivated. In the back of my mind I still had a dream of being in the top 10, but realistically I knew that wouldn't happen. But, I still hoped I could crack the top 50.

1982 got off to a decent start. I had a wonderful rest during Christmas spending time with my family. I played almost no tennis for an entire month because I was still exhausted from my months long trip to Europe. During the holiday season I realized how truly lucky I was that my father escaped Russia, eventually settled in the United States, and was able to become a successful doctor. All of those factors contributed to me being able to become the tennis player I now was. Without all of the good fortune, there was no way I could have become a world class tennis player.

My first tournament of the season was in Palm Springs, California held at the La Quinta Resort. I had been practicing indoors in Toledo, where needless to say it was cold and snowy. I had to play Thierry Tulasne from France, who once was the best junior tennis player in the world having won the Junior Wimbledon title in 1980. As a pro he was now ranked #51 in the world, so I would definitely have my hands full. It was really hot so I was very pleased when I won the first set 7-5. It was nip and tuck in the second set. Unfortunately I wilted under both the pressure and the heat, dropping the second set 7-5. Tulasne cruised to a 6-1 victory in the third as I labored mightily in the heat and offered little resistance. Clearly my conditioning had to improve.

From the glamor of Palm Springs I headed to the smog and altitude of Monterrey, Mexico. I played Skip Strode, a lowly ranked player at #438 in the world (although by year's end he would reach his career high ranking of #127). He had a big serve and I couldn't find a way to break him in the speed of the high altitude and the fast courts. After such a promising end to the 1981 season, I started out with two straight first round losses. Now off to Europe to see if my fortunes would change.

In Brussels I ran into Sammy Giammalva, the younger brother of my former college team mate Tony. Although Sammy had turned pro right after high school and was five years younger than me, he had a fair amount of success in his young career. He was ranked #58 in the world and I played a really good match to beat him in straight sets 7-6, 6-3. It was my first win of 1982 and felt great. That win pushed me back into the top 100 in the world after almost a three years absence. Brian Teacher, #16 in the world and one of the top seeds in the tournament, dispatched me to the sidelines in the second round 6-3, 6-4.

The tour in Europe then headed to the Grand Prix event in Metz, France. The tournament was known as the Lorraine Open. My first round opponent was the seventh seed, Jose Lopez-Maseo from Spain. He was ranked #78 in the world so he was certainly going to be tough. Luckily for me he was more of a clay court player. Although the Greenset indoor surface in the arena was quite slow, the speed of play on a hard court versus clay court surface suited me versus an opponent like Lopez-Maseo. I got off to a fast start and won the first set 6-4. I was on the verge of victory 5-3 in the second set when Lopez-Maseo twisted his ankle. He decide he couldn't continue and I moved into the second round.

Karl Meiler from Germany was my second round opponent. Meiler was 33 years old and near the end of his career. I knew him because he once was a highly ranked player when I was a youngster, but in the last few years his ranking had not cracked the top 100. Currently he was #142 so I felt a good deal of confidence. I won the first set rather easily but got too confident and Meiler played much better in the second set and beat me 6-3. in the third set I think my youth was an advantage and Meiler petered out and I prevailed 6-3.

Now I was getting pumped up. I was in the quarterfinals of a Grand Prix event for the first time since Bordeaux in September, 1981. My opponent was Jan Gunnarson from Sweden who was ranked right around #100 in the world. Although I had two previous losses to him in main draws, in last year's Lorraine Open I defeated him in the last round of qualifying. Fortunately his mind did not seem to be on our match. I easily won the first set 6-2 and in the second set it became apparent Gunnarson wanted to head back to Sweden. I bageled him 6-0 and was in my very first Grand Prix semifinal. Blocking my path to the finals was the young up and coming French player Henri Leconte who would end the year ranked #28 in the world.

His current ranking of #170 was not indicative of his talent. He was young and on the rise and I knew I would have a very difficult match. We held serve all the way through in the first set until 4-5 with Leconte serving. I came through in the clutch and broke his serve to win the set. The second set saw more of the same. The crowd was raucous and cheering for their fellow Frenchman and at one point late in the second set Leconte hit a spectacular shot and wildly pumped his fist. Although in general my poise was not bad, I lost control and swore directly at Leconte. Luckily the crowd was making a lot of noise and neither Leconte nor the umpire heard my outburst. I regained my composure enough to break Leconte's serve once in the second set and that was all I needed. I won 6-4, 6-4 to advance to my first ever Grand Prix final.

In the finals I was a definite underdog. I faced Steve Denton, who was an American who played at the University of Texas when I was at Trinity University. He had a good deal of success in college, but did not have as good a college career as I did. In the pros, however, he had vaulted past me. He reached the finals of the Australian Open in 1981 and was ranked #15. If I won this match it would be the biggest win of my professional career and my first Grand Prix singles title. Not only that! I would also earn $15,000 out of the $75,000 total prize money, my biggest paycheck by far. My odds of winning seemed slim. Denton had a huge serve so I would be under a lot of pressure to hold my own serve.

I would be lucky to break his serve even once in the match. Although my ground strokes were more consistent, Denton would hit more winners. He would also be at the net more than me and put additional pressure on me in that way. I had two slight edges. Everyone would expect Denton to win because he was ranked so much higher than me. Also, although he had reached the finals of a Grand Slam event and several other finals, he had never sealed the deal. Like me, he was looking for his first tournament title. Overall, he had more to lose in this match than I did. From an expectations viewpoint, I had nothing to lose and everything to gain.

The tennis gods were good to me that day. Denton did not serve well and he definitely felt the pressure of being the favorite. Somehow I broke his serve once in the first set and pulled it out 6-4. I was playing well but not necessarily great. It was more that I was being consistent and Denton was spraying the ball around. I had to be ready for when he started to play better. But he never really did. I broke his serve to begin the second set, and broke his serve again to go up 3-0. But then it happened.

Never before did I encounter the sudden feeling of pressure like I did at that moment. At the changeover my legs started to shake. I realized that I was on the verge of achieving one of my childhood dreams. I was going to win a high level professional tennis tournament and beat one of the top 20 players in the world. Instead of focusing on playing one point at a time, the moment got to me. Denton broke my serve, held his own serve, and then at 3-2 I was down 15-30. Second serve. This was the real turning point of the match. I hit a tentative second serve which, thank God, found the service box. Even more unbelievably, Denton missed the return. Somehow I held serve that game and went up 4-2. I was up 5-3 when Denton served to stay in the match. In the most important moment of my tennis career I played one great game and broke Denton's serve. I was a champion! Thousands of world class tennis players would never win a Grand Prix tennis title. In fact in 1982 there would only be 40 such players (although some of the top players would win multiple titles). No one could ever take that away from me. Along with Connors, McEnroe, and

Borg, the name Iskersky would be etched in the history of 1982 professional tennis. I too would be a tournament champion. Even though there were times during my match with Denton when I let the pressure get to me, I came through when it mattered.

I was literally on cloud 9 when I left Metz for the tour stop in Milan. My ranking would climb to #66 in the world. I would have been in the qualifying event for the Milan tournament but instead I was awarded a special exemption. That meant I was automatically placed in the main draw in Milan, even though my ranking wasn't high enough, because I was still playing in the semifinals of the Lorraine Open in Metz when the qualifier began in Milan. Milan was a top tier Grand Prix event, with big prize money. Not only that, my first round opponent in Milan was Italian Gianni Ocleppo, once ranked as high as #31. However, because of injuries his ranking had dropped to #200 so he was granted a "wild card" into the main draw in Milan. That meant he was awarded one of the two spots in the main draw that were the tournament director's choice, regardless of the player's ranking. My luck just kept getting better.

I quickly discovered winning my first tournament wouldn't automatically make me a better player. I played very tentatively against Ocleppo, realizing that a win would earn me a good deal of ranking points and money. After playing for almost three hours our match came down to a final set tiebreaker. I had won the first set in a tiebreaker before losing the second set 6-4. Both of us played the final few points of the match like our lives depended on the outcome. We both played scared. Somehow I managed to squeeze out the victory. I now would face Sandy Mayer, #16 in the world.

Mayer dispatched me with little trouble. His serve and volley game put me under a lot of pressure on the fast indoor surface and I mounted little resistance. Although my performance was quite woeful I earned a good deal of money and my ranking went up to #64 by virtue of my win over Ocleppo in the first round. That would be the peak ranking of my life. Not bad for a kid from Toledo but certainly well short of the dreams I had growing up.

Before I left Europe, I had one last tournament to play. It was the last indoor tournament of the winter season and was held in Zurich. It was a World Championship Event which meant there were no ATP world ranking points on the line. Only money. The WCT Tour, started by Lamar Hunt, a rich businessman, was a competitor of the ATP Tour. Because the tournaments were not sanctioned by the ATP, results from these tournaments were not recognized for ranking purposes. Nevertheless the tournaments were popular because the prize money was big.

Like in Milan, I played poorly and was drubbed by Wojtek Fibak, one of the top seeds at the tournament. He was from Poland and was ranked #20 in the world. He wasn't a powerful player but had a fantastic slice backhand with great volleys. I could never get my rhythm going and lost 6-2, 6-1. I learned a very valuable lesson after Milan and Zurich. Even though I had won a Grand Prix event, my game had to get a lot better if I was going to compete successfully against the top players in the world. My win over Denton in Metz was great, but there were too many holes in my game. My matches against Mayer and Fibak proved that.

My parents were glad to see me but my father already was showing some early signs of dementia even though he was only 62 years old. It was always bittersweet when I saw him because he was no longer sharp mentally, and I wondered if his reluctance to discuss the entire Gunter Gruber fiasco had something to do with his memory loss. I was sure he knew more than he would tell me but at this stage of his life I decided not to push things. It seemed certain I would never learn the entire truth and would have to accept it. Nothing had happened for a couple of years to help me figure out the mystery surrounding Gruber and it seemed unlikely that I had any avenues to pursue further beyond the ones I had already tried. My research of the matter could only take me so far.

Only two weeks after I came home I was off to Houston to play in the Grand Prix event held at historic River Oaks on red clay. In the first round I faced Terry Moor, a familiar foe who I had played before. He ended the 1981 season ranked #51 but was struggling a bit in the early part of 1982. I played a good solid match and beat him 7-6, 6-4.

In the second round I had to face Peter McNamara, also a familiar foe. In 1978 I split matches with him. I beat him in Columbus, but three weeks earlier he had beaten me in South Orange, New Jersey. The only problem was he was ranked around #70 in the world back then – now he was #10. His career had flourished and he was one of the best players in the world. In what would have been the biggest win of my career, I played great in the first set and pulled out a tiebreaker. McNamara re-established his superiority in the second set and drubbed me 6-1. Unfortunately he started to play like the tenth ranked player in the world. I tried my best in the third set to pull the upset but lost 6-3. My performance encouraged me because I went toe to toe with one of the world's best and, even though I didn't win, I held my own.

In Tampa my encouraging results from Houston were both solidified and tempered. I beat qualifier Cliff Letcher in the first round in straight sets like I was supposed to. In fact I beat him 6-2 and then 6-1. However, in the second round Mel Purcell, the third seed in the tournament and ranked #27 destroyed me 6-3, 6-1. Mel was a familiar player from my junior and college days and had made a real splash as the ATP Tour Rookie of the Year in 1980. It was obvious I was still way too inconsistent in my play and, unless I drastically improved my serve and my backhand return, I wasn't going to move up in the rankings too far.

As a result of my performance in the early stages of the 1982 season, I got into the main draw of the WCT Tournament of Champions held at the iconic Forest Hills Lawn and Tennis Club, the former site of the US Open. In what had to be described as a mathematically improbable stroke of bad luck I had to play Vitas Gerulaitis in the first round for the first time of three consecutive meetings in three weeks. I also ended up having to play him in the first round at the Italian Open and the French Open. From 1977-1982 Gerulaitis was ranked in the top 10 in the world and currently was ranked #5. Needless to say I didn't want to play an opponent of that caliber in the first round for three straight weeks.

In a real thrill I got to play Gerulaitis in the featured night match on the historic center court at Forest Hills. My great aunt Dortha Duckworth, by virtue of being the second wife of my mother's uncle Dmitri, was in attendance. She was an actress and lived in New York. Dmitri had died a number of years ago but my mother always stayed in touch with aunt Dortha so I enjoyed seeing her. She appeared in a number of movies during her career including Murphy's Romance starring James Garner and The Man With One Red Shoe starring Tom Hanks. Her friend, William Prince, an actor who I knew from his hundreds of television roles, most recently in Hart to Hart, Dynasty, and Trapper John, M.D., also was there.

Although Gerulaitis was ranked #5 my ground strokes were comparable to his. What made him such a great player were volleys, his amazing quickness, his ability to put pressure on his opponent, and his confident attitude. He took the first set 6-4 and, most importantly, I wasn't that nervous so I played well. Gerulaitis probably lost focus in the second set and I toppled him 6-4. Could I pull the biggest upset of my life? The answer was a resounding no. Gerulaitis raised the level of his game and trounced me 6-0.

In my next tournament, the Italian Open, I was naturally dismayed to see that I had to play Gerulaitis in the first round again. This time I didn't play all that well. The most intriguing aspect of the match for me, which I lost 6-2, 6-3 on the fabled Foro Italico stadium court, was the boisterous behavior of the Italian fans. The Italians were known for their rowdy behavior and did not disappoint. If an easy shot was missed, they booed. Yelling during points was par for the course. And because my match against Gerulaitis was not close and he was a popular figure in Italy, the crowd was against me and enjoyed ripping me to shreds.

During my stay in Rome a very significant incident occurred, which I learned by accident when reading the International Herald Tribune, an English language newspaper available throughout Europe. Imagine my shock when I read a tiny article that announced that German war criminal Joseph Erdmeister, the man who killed my father's brother Ivan during World War II, was released from a Siberian Prison by the Soviet Union. He had spent 37 years in prison. Although he was supposed to be tried by the War Tribunal for his involvement with the infamous "Inner Circle of Five", he was never found and had been presumed dead. The article went on to say that it was unlikely he would face further legal action in Germany because of his long incarceration at the hands of the Russians.

I felt very torn about this development. I wanted to tell my father about the information but decided I would say nothing. If he found out through another source that was fine, but I believed the knowledge that Erdmeister was still alive would simply dredge up very unpleasant memories for my father about his brother and the war. I kept my mouth shut but briefly thought about traveling to Germany and confronting Erdmeister. Perhaps I could get him to tell me more about the "Inner Circle of Five" and what he knew about Gunter Gruber. Ultimately, to avoid pursuing the matter further and to avoid finding out things about my father I might not want to know, I did nothing. It was tempting to resume my amateur sleuthing, but I didn't do it.

From Rome I traveled to Paris to play in the French Open. The nearly impossible odds happened as I drew Vitas Gerulaitis for the third straight tournament in the first round. Of course I was ticked off. I was playing well but facing the #5 player in the world week after week in the first round was not a good way of improving my ranking. I tried to be positive when I stepped on the court against Gerulaitis. One good thing was that I was no longer intimidated playing him because I was used to seeing him on the other side of the court. It was almost like I was practicing against him. What followed was the most disappointing match of my professional career.

We were playing on one of the outside courts, not in the stadium court. That was good for me. My nerves would not be as much of a problem outside of the spotlight of the main stage. It was crucial that I perform at my best if I stood a chance. In fact the first set was one of the best sets I ever played. It was nip and tuck all the way. I came through with a couple of clutch shots and pulled out a dramatic first set tiebreaker. Could this be the day I finally beat a player ranked in the top 10?

In the second set Gerulaitis established control early and cruised to a 6-3 win. This was a three out of five set match so the third set was pivotal. Whoever won the third set was going to have a huge advantage. In what was the best seven games I ever played, I jumped out to a 5-2 lead and I was serving. I was up two breaks of serve. I had a real chance to beat one of the best players in the world. The pressure suddenly became unbearable. The stands were packed. One of the top players in the world was on the ropes in the first round of the French Open and the word had spread.

And I collapsed. In a devastating display of tentativeness I did exactly what I could not afford to do. I played "not to lose" instead of "playing to win". Gerulaitis quickly broke me back twice with a combination of better play and my self induced destruction. We were tied 5-5. The moment of truth. Would I roll over without a fight now that I blew the lead, or would I put up some resistance? My pride was at stake and I actually delivered. It seemed that I was relaxed once again now that I accepted the fact I'd blown such a big advantage and I played a fantastic game to break Gerulaitis for the third time in the set. At 6-5 I served for the third set and went up 40-30. I now had set point!

In my mind my entire career came down to one shot. At set point I netted an easy backhand ground stroke. I simply choked. All those hours of practice. All those years of playing tournaments. All those years of dreaming of a moment just like this. The chance to beat a top player at a Grand Slam event. That shot could have changed everything! And I missed it. Gerulaitis broke my serve again and now we were in the tie-breaker. Now Gerulaitis sensed that the edge had dramatically shifted in his direction. I played a decent tiebreaker but with less zeal than necessary. My dream faded as Gerulaitis won the tiebreaker and closed out the match by beating me 6-3 in the fourth set. It was the most depressing moment of my tennis career. I sat in the locker room for at least two hours after the match, pretty much not moving and licking my wounds.

On to what should have been real excitement. Another chance to play at Wimbledon. Unfortunately I was not a good grass court player and after getting destroyed by Marcos Hocevar at Queen's Club, I decided to withdraw from Wimbledon. Perhaps it was a stupid decision because I never knew how many chances I would get to play in Grand Slam events, but at the time I thought it was the best thing for me to do.

The summer season leading up to the US Open did not go well for me. I played six tournaments in Boston; Washington D.C.; South Orange, New Jersey; Columbus; Toronto; and Cincinnati and lost in the first round four times. I lost to Claudio Panatta, David Pate, and Stanislav Birner all in three sets and to Brian Teacher in straight sets. In the other two tournaments I won my first round matches over Chris Dunk and Tim Wilkison respectively, but lost second round matches to Mark Dickson and Mario Martinez. Needless to say I was limping into the US Open with little confidence and a ranking hovering around #100 in the world.

I had about ten days to train for my first round match at the US Open after my loss in Cincinnati and I tried to play at least three hours a day and do a lot of conditioning. Potentially the weather in New York could be extremely hot at the end of August so I wanted to be in great shape for the three out of five set format I would be facing. My opponent was going to be Stefan Simonsson, a Swede who was ranked around #110 and whose best surface was clay, not fast courts like the US Open. It was certainly a good first round draw.

I was training for the US Open in Toledo so I was spending a good deal of time home with my parents. Although I was extremely tempted to bring up Joseph Erdmeister's arrival in Germany and ask my father if he knew anything about it, I kept my mouth shut. It was true I had originally decided to ignore the matter but I could not completely sweep everything that had happened to my father in the past under the rug. I resolved to explore the Erdmeister situation further when I went back to Europe in the fall to play more tournaments. I wouldn't let my father know about anything I was going to do, but I was going to carry out a more intensive investigation and get to the bottom of the "Inner Circle of Five". What kind of connection did my father really have to Gruber? Did he know something about the "Inner Circle of Five" that he wouldn't tell me about, and if so, why not? I had to learn the truth without upsetting my parents.

I arrived for the US Open on a Saturday and was scheduled to play on Monday, August 31 at 11:00 am. Because I was the first match of the day scheduled on my court I wouldn't have to wait around for the completion of a previous match. Saturday was hot and humid and Monday would turn out to be no different. The excitement in the air was palpable when I arrived at the facility Monday morning. There is definitely a special atmosphere at each of the Grand Slam events. Each of the events is unique in their own way, but all are exciting and spectacular. The US Open is all New York. Noisy and boisterous. Hot and humid most of the time, but occasionally rainy and cool. The fans are loud, obnoxious, excited to be part of the event. The facility huge, concrete, and located in Queens right by Shea Stadium.

My first set against Simonsson was long and precarious. Neither one of us could gain an advantage and both of us started out nervously. Both of us knew we had a very winnable first round. There were no breaks of serve in the first set and I forced a tie breaker when I held serve at 5-6. The tie breaker was also nip and tuck. Winning the first set in a three out of five set match is a huge advantage and when I finally prevailed in the tie breaker 8-6 when Simonsson missed an easy backhand, I felt great. I released a huge sigh of relief. Now I had to consolidate my advantage.

It wasn't going to happen. I started thinking about winning the match in straight sets because I wanted to get it over with. It was starting to get really hot and there was virtually no cloud cover. Unfortunately Simonsson wouldn't cooperate. He kept up the battle and went up a break in the second set. Although I broke his serve when he was serving at 4-2, he broke me right back and served out the second set in routine fashion for a 6-3 win. Now it came down to who had the stamina and the mental toughness to win the third set and take charge of the match.

As I sat down on the changeover after I dropped the second set, the reality of the situation hit me. I was living my dream, playing in the US Open and battling it out in a dramatic three out of five set match. Although there were not that many fans watching my match on one of the outer courts, the fans who were there encouraged me. They were cheering for the American. Patriotism in sports is a fantastic thing and makes competitors like myself try even harder. It was a great moment. My resolve to win the third set grew exponentially with each cheer from the sparse, but vocal crowd.

Even though I lost the second set, my dream like experience at the changeover seemed to inspire me. I held serve and immediately broke Simonsson to go up 2-0 in the third set. I pumped myself up and tried to forget about my match against Gerulaitis at the French Open where I lost the lead in the all important third set. I did my best to go for my shots and not play tentatively and it paid off. I couldn't break Simonsson's serve again, but he couldn't break me either. There I was serving for the set at 5-3. Once again the moment of truth. And, deja vu!! I couldn't do it. I folded when it counted the most. I played a scared game and Simonsson promptly broke my serve and held his own. Now we were tied 5-5.

Incredibly enough I maintained my composure and held serve to go up 6-5. At the changeover I tried to breathe slowly, in and out, in and out. I needed to relax. And relax I did. I played an aggressive game, trying to attack the net. Finally it paid off. I went up 40-15 on Simonsson's serve. In what I considered just a small dose of redemption for my blown third set against Gerulaitis, I played a clutch volley that Simonsson couldn't reach, and the third set was mine.

Who knew that would end up being the highlight of the match for me. After just three games of the fourth set it became apparent the heat and humidity had gotten to me. My legs started to cramp. I stopped trying to run and basically threw the fourth set intentionally. I ate a couple of bananas and drank water, hoping like hell that the cramps would subside and I could battle it out in the fifth set.

It didn't happen. I really felt like crying. I wasn't going to win my first round at the US Open like I did in 1978. I finished the match but without being able to run at all. I basically pushed the ball into the court and could watch only helplessly as Simonsson simply hit the ball a few steps away from me. I could do nothing. The cramps were extremely painful and I couldn't do a damn thing about it. I lost the last two sets 6-1, 6-1. What had started as a glorious opportunity to advance in the US Open ended ignominiously. There would be no second round match against sixth seed Gene Mayer. I couldn't feel any worse.

Some joy did emerge from my appearance at the 1982 US Open. My doubles partner, Jiri Granat, from Czechoslovakia, was an acquaintance but not someone I had played doubles with before. We decided to pair up and won our first round easily. In the second round we had to play against Robert Van't Hof, my old nemesis from USC, and John Lloyd, Chris Evert's husband (we jokingly called him John Lloyd Evert). They were seeded so it was definitely going to be a tough match. In one of the best doubles matches I ever played, we ended up pulling the upset. Now in the round of 16 we had to face the best doubles team in the world, John McEnroe and his partner Peter Fleming. Fleming was a great singles player but was more known for teaming up with McEnroe.

We played a night match on the Grandstand Court. It was a lot of fun but we were definitely out of our league. We lost 6-3, 6-2 but I didn't feel too bad about it. Doing well in the doubles helped ease some of the pain from my singles defeat and it brought in some decent prize money. It was also my best doubles performance in a major tournament.

I headed back to Toledo with mixed emotions. My singles game wasn't all that sharp, yet I wasn't really going to take any time off to practice my weaknesses. My ranking was still high enough to get me into the main draws of Grand Prix events throughout the world. In fact, one week after the US Open ended I headed to San Francisco to play in the Trans America Open. Unfortunately I drew Brian Teacher, ranked #18 in the world. His serve and volley game was tough for me to handle, particularly on the indoor carpet surface. I lost 6-2, 6-3. I flew to San Antonio for a couple weeks of practice with the Trinity University team. From there I was off to Europe for the rest of the fall season.

I vowed to do two things. Improve on my performance from the last few months. If I didn't start doing better I might very well drop out of the top 150 in the world. That would mean I would start the 1983 season in qualifying instead of the main draw of the Grand Prix events. I also vowed to further investigate the "Inner Circle of Five" and find out once and for all what my father's connection to Gunther Gruber was all about. Perhaps I would try to find and confront Joseph Erdmeister. He definitely knew something important about the past and was also responsible for the death of the man who would have been my uncle.

CHAPTER 15

I flew to Basel, Switzerland in early October to begin my European fall tournament schedule. My first round opponent was Eric Fromm, a very familiar foe. I knew Eric from junior and college tennis and he was making his way up the rankings. He was ranked around #70 in the world so both of us, I'm sure, were looking forward to this match. This was winnable for either one of us. For me this match would turn out to be a real lesson about the need for emotional control in the heat of the moment.

In this particular match our umpire was a young man, probably no more than 19 years old. For some reason he felt the need to interject himself in the action way too often. Several times he needlessly and incorrectly overruled calls of the linesmen. This put me in a horrible state of mind and it shouldn't have. I wasn't playing great and instead of focusing more on my play I let myself get upset with the umpire. This was particularly stupid because the calls were bad for both players so I should have accepted things and moved on. But I didn't.

I lost the first set 6-3, not because of the calls but because Eric was playing better than me. I turned things around in the second set by playing better and improving my level of composure. In the third set I jumped out to an early break but got broken back. Then I let all hell break loose and it probably helped lead to my demise.

Fromm hit a shot that was at least one foot inside the baseline. I missed the shot but in the meantime the umpire called the ball out. In my favor! What did I do? I decided to be the honorable sportsman and informed the umpire his call was wrong. Instead of playing the point over (which was what I expected would happen), the umpire awarded the point to Fromm on the basis that I missed the shot and his overrule did not interrupt play (which was true). I went nuts. First, I was stupid to intervene. I was playing for my living – now wasn't the time to have some sportsmanship spiritual awakening. Second, it was a crucial point. And third, because I went berserk I once again lost my way emotionally in this match.

To compound matters, the umpire made another overrule on a close call, this time against me, and it further exacerbated the disaster. I totally lost control and partially because of my mental state I lost some very important points. Eventually I dropped the match 7-5 in the third set. My European swing was off to a horrendous start.

The next day I was in a foul mood. I had several days to practice before I left for the next tournament in Vienna, Austria. I couldn't resist the temptation to track down Joseph Erdmeister. I had no idea if I could find him or what I would say to him if I did find him. But I felt a strong urge to play the role of a private investigator and track down the only person I knew was in the "Inner Circle of Five" and was still alive. The first step I took was to call Boris in South Carolina and clue him in on what I was doing.

After we made our preliminary greetings and small talk, I focused on what I really wanted.

"Boris, I need your help again. It concerns the "Inner Circle of Five". I never told you, but the guy who killed Ivan in the war was released from a prison in Russia, where apparently he has been for the last 35 or more years. I want to confront him. But I don't want Father to know about it."

"What am I supposed to do?" inquired Boris. "I don't know nearly as much as you do and I'm not sure we should drum up all of this old stuff. Maybe we'll just end up hurting Father somehow. Is what you're trying to do really worth it?"

"I think it is. All I want to do is find out more information about this "Inner Circle of Five" and why Gunter Gruber, and then Alfred Rheingold were after me. Father has to know more than he is willing to tell me. And then that English Colonel McMillan gets killed and he knew Father from the war. Too much has happened to let it go. I'm not going to tell Father about any of this or hurt him in anyway. I just have to know the truth."

"Okay, so what do you want from me?" Boris demanded to know in an increasingly irritated voice.

"I want you to call your friend Karl Lubeck, the one whose father was an administrator in the German Department of Defense. Mr. Lubeck was able to get us information on current whereabouts of living former members of the Fraternity of the Master Race. Maybe he can track down Joseph Erdmeister for me."

Hesitatingly Boris agreed to talk to Karl and convince him to have Mr. Lubeck do some research and find out where Erdmeister now lived. I also convinced Boris to give me Karl's phone number in Munich if I needed to get in touch with him. Karl had already completed his medical studies and was now a resident at a hospital.

The days in Basel seemed to crawl. Even though I had a doubles match to play in which my partner Marco Ostoja and I lost to Yannick Noah and Henri Leconte, I couldn't stop thinking of the possibility of confronting Erdmeister. I tried to calm myself by deciding that even if Mr. Lubeck didn't let me know where Erdmeister lived, I could find out on my own. It would just take a bit more effort on my part. However, on October 15, the day before I was to leave for my next tournament in Vienna, I received a call from Boris.

"Well, Mr. Lubeck came through for you. He gave me Erdmeister's address. But he also told me to warn you not to do anything stupid. Erdmeister spent 36 years in a Siberian prison. Who knows what his mental state will be? He's probably around Father's age and based on his history he might still be a dangerous man."

"I'm not going to do anything dramatic. I just want to confront him and try to make him tell me what he knows about the "Inner Circle of Five" and Gunter Gruber. Maybe this can lead to some sort of closure and a final resolution. I want to find out what Father really knows and why in the world Gruber came after me in New York. There has to be a reason."

ERICK ISKERSKY

Boris wished me luck and once again emphasized that I should do nothing that could hurt Father in anyway and that I should be careful when confronting Erdmeister. I assured him everything would be fine but I also didn't really know how I would react when I finally saw Erdmeister. Of course he might refuse to even see me or his memory could be greatly damaged if his imprisonment was traumatic. Whatever was going to happen, I tried to prepare myself mentally for either the best or worst outcome.

By coincidence Erdmeister lived in Stuttgart, where my father's cousin Sergei lived. I decided it would be a good time to visit Sergei and his wife Anna. It would save me the cost of a hotel and I would have a place to go to and from Erdmeister's residence. I called Sergei and luckily he was going to be around in late October, after I played the tournament in Vienna. I made arrangements for my flights from Basel to Vienna, and then to Stuttgart.

I was excited when I flew into Vienna. My first round opponent was Stan Smith, one of the great players of his era. He'd won both Wimbledon and the U.S. Open in singles and the U.S. Open in doubles. Unfortunately he developed tennis elbow and never reached the heights of greatness for which he was destined, but he still had a great career. By the time I was playing him in Vienna his career was winding down so I really believed I had a great chance to beat him.

It was, however, not to be. I played tentatively because of the circumstances of being the feature night match on stadium court. In addition, Smith's attacking style gave me a lot of trouble and I couldn't get into any sort of rhythm. I kept hoping I would loosen up and do something dramatic to turn things around but it never happened. I lost 6-2, 6-3 and was very disappointed by my performance. But I also realized how lucky I was to get to play some of the game's greatest players during my career. So far, in addition to Stan Smith I had played Laver, Rosewall, Ashe, and McEnroe. That wasn't all bad.

I was now on pins and needles as I prepared to fly to Stuttgart, under the guise of visiting Sergei and Anna. My real mission was, of course, to get to the bottom of the "Inner Circle of Five" and the reasons my father seemed to have some sort of connection to Gruber. In my heart I believed there was a stronger connection than merely the fact that my father testified against Gruber at the Munich Tribunals. I didn't know what I would find out, but I felt like I'd rather find out the truth, even if the truth was painful, than being in the dark. The flight was a short one and as soon as I got to baggage claim Sergei spotted me and came over to greet me.

"So good to see you again Erick," Sergei proclaimed speaking in Russian. It was not always easy to communicate with Sergei and Anna because they spoke Russian to me but my Russian was not quite up to snuff. Sergei didn't speak English so we had no other choice than to plod our way along as I tried my best at speaking Russian. The last time I had seen Sergei was during my visit to Boris when I did my research in Munich about the "Inner Circle of Five".

Although I had a two week break between the tournament in Vienna and my next tournament in Paris, I didn't waste time in making my plans known to Sergei. At first he didn't want to get involved in anyway, but finally he agreed to drive me from his farm to Stuttgart so that I could confront Erdmeister. I convinced him that I needed him with me, which was true. Because he was now a German citizen and had lived in Germany for years, Sergei's German was flawless and I would need an interpreter in order to communicate with Erdmeister. I doubted that he spoke English.

We decided to leave for Stuttgart early Wednesday morning. Mr. Lubeck also obtained Erdmeister's phone number for me but I thought it would be best if we surprised Erdmeister, in hopes of getting a more un-rehearsed reaction. It took nearly an hour for us to arrive in Stuttgart. It turned out that Erdmeister lived in an industrial area where the buildings were old and the streets were dirty. The air was foul from the smoke billowing from the nearby factories. Sergei explained to me that the factory workers, many of whom were immigrants, lived in the area because it was cheap and near where they worked.

Erdmeister's apartment building was several stories high and there was no security of any kind at the entrance, which I assumed was normal in the old and rundown apartment buildings in the area. There were also no elevators so we trudged up the stairs. Erdmeister lived on the third floor toward the end of the hallway. I'm sure Sergei felt nothing, but to me the tension was palpable, almost a thickness that hung in the air by Erdmeister's door. We stood in front of the door and after some hesitation I knocked loudly.

Initially I heard nothing. Then footsteps and a loud voice yelled out in German, "Who is it?" That much I could understand. Then we put our plan into motion. Sergei would do the talking because his German was excellent as opposed to my high school learned skills. We were going to tell Erdmeister that we were friends of one of his past acquaintances and simply wanted to ask him some information about the past. I didn't know if that would be enough to get him to open the door but it seemed better than telling him the absolute truth.

Then he asked what was the name of this acquaintance. Sergei looked at me and I whispered to him, "Go ahead and tell him Father's name. I guess that will be the most direct way and we'll know right now whether he'll see us."

Sergei said that it was from a long time ago, from during the war and then he loudly stated that the acquaintance was Vladimir Iskersky. There was a prolonged period of silence. We breathlessly waited. Then there was a slight squeaking sound as the door knob began to slowly turn. The door opened part way and a man stuck his head out through the opening. He said nothing but stared menacingly at us. Then unexpectedly his gaze mellowed, he fully opened the door, and waved us in.

Erdmeister shuffled, more than walked, towards a beat up chair and sat down. Then he gestured to a couch situated across from the chair separated by an antique looking coffee table. Sergei and I sat down and then I uttered a greeting in my horrible German. Erdmeister chuckled. He said something to Sergei that I didn't understand. They spoke back and forth in German for several minutes. Erdmeister's voice was gruff. He looked disheveled. And old. Spending 36 years in a Russian prison probably had that effect.

Even though he was certainly in his late fifties by now, I still recognized his face from the photos Boris and I had looked at during our
visit to the University of Munich library. His face looked evil, probably
because I knew the history about the atrocities the "Inner Circle of Five"
had committed. If I saw him on the street, who knows? I might just
think he was a withered looking older man. He was not an unpleasant
looking man. In the photos he looked somewhat handsome. There was
a fire in his eyes, his skin wrinkled and pale. That contrast made his
eyes stand out even more. A full head of hair, charcoal gray, combed
back like some gangster from the thirties. He wasn't frail but he didn't
look overly strong.

Suddenly he started speaking to me in Russian. He explained, with
bitterness in his voice, that he had plenty of time while sitting in a Siberian
prison to learn the Russian language. Sergei had explained to him that
my German was very poor and apparently they established that they both
knew Russian, so it was agreed that we would all speak Russian. Erdmeister
spoke no English.

I was quite stunned by Erdmeister's candor once we started talking.
His Russian was better than mine even though I had grown up speaking
the language so there was no chance that our conversation was somehow
a conglomeration of mistaken notions. He told me many stories about his
participation in assisting Gunter Gruber with the administration of the
prison camp in Poland. Even now he seemed like a thoroughly despicable
human being. Thirty six years in prison made him bitter, but it sounded
like he was also bitter when he was a member of the "Inner Circle of Five"
and a fully participating Nazi.

As with many Nazis he claimed he was merely following orders, although he did not apologize for his heinous conduct. Anything he did in
the prison he did in accordance with Gruber's orders. Anything he did
as a member of the "Inner Circle of Five" he also did in accordance with
commands he received. I pressed him for details about my father but he
initially said he had little interaction with him. I also asked him questions about Gruber and he provided me with a scenario of a man who was

obsessed and who believed in Hitler with his heart and soul. We engaged in conversation for over one hour when I finally told him that I knew he killed my father's brother.

His reaction was at first subdued. Then he came apart at the seams. He screamed that my father's brother deserved to die because he wouldn't fall in line with the other prisoners and wouldn't buy into the greatness of Nazism. Unlike my father, who cooperated and eventually bought into the message being delivered by Gruber and his cohorts, Ivan had refused. Because of that, Erdmeister shot and killed Ivan.

Now my blood started to boil. Erdmeister accused my father of turning on his own people and converting to the Nazi ideology in order to save his own skin. On the one hand I could understand how prisoners faced with extinction would convert their beliefs to save their lives, but I also wanted to believe my father was brave and mighty. He would never sell out, would he?

I started screaming back. "You're just a murderer. I know what you Nazis did and how your "Inner Circle of Five" raped all sorts of girls. You deserved to be in prison for all these years!"

He shouted back as Sergei tried to calm us down. "Your father was a part of our "Inner Circle of Five". You didn't know that, did you? Who do you think replaced Dr. Friedrich when he died?"

I was shocked. Did my father really participate in the activities associated with that evil group? Was he secretly a Nazi? I just couldn't believe it. I felt rage, shame, betrayed and saddened all at the same time. Had my father lived a double life all of these years?

As if on cue, Erdmiester got up and pointed at me. "Is your father alive?"

Before Sergei could stop me, I blurted out an affirmation.

"Ask him then. What did he do during the war? You think he was some innocent medic in the German army? I don't think so. And I do have a strong reason to hate your father. At the end of the war he turned me over to the Russians. I could have disappeared into the German countryside. I wasn't known like Gruber. I never would have been captured. Your father cost me 36 years of my life."

With that he held up his hand, signifying that we should wait. He hurried into the bedroom and after a couple of minutes he returned. In his hand he held up what looked like a photograph. "I still have some mementos from the war. My brother kept them for me. Your father was so kind to let my brother know that I was in the hands of the Russians," he said with biting sarcasm. "My brother was the only one who knew I was turned over to the Russians. He never let the German authorities know because he was afraid the Americans would try to put me into a sham trial and try to execute me. So for 36 years I sat in prison while my brother hoped to hear from me. He never did because the Russians never even let me write a letter."

He threw the photograph at me. "Find your father in the photo. He was a full fledged Nazi."

The photograph floated to the floor. I gingerly picked it up. With a feeling of foreboding I looked at it. It was a photograph of about twenty people, standing in various poses in a semi-circle. In the center stood Adolph Hitler. Next to him stood Gunter Gruber. I recognized him almost immediately, both from the photos Boris and I saw at the University of Munich library and because even as a young man he was short and fat. Just like when I encountered him in New York.

I examined the photo closely. I noticed a young man who, at first, I thought looked a bit like me. Then I realized with revulsion that the man looked like a younger version of Ricardo Diaz, my father's so-called friend who was shot and killed in Toledo. Upon further examination I found my father in the photo. He was standing near Diaz. I also recognized a couple other members of the "Inner Circle of Five". There was Alfred Rheingold, the man who accosted Shelley Coslowski and me in San Antonio, who we inadvertently killed. And from library photos I also recognized Dr. Hans Friedrich, the doctor who performed abortions on victims of the "Inner Circle of Five", or helped to kill them when necessary.

And, of course, Erdmeister was right there, standing no more than five feet from my father.

"Now do you believe me?" proclaimed Erdmeister.

Needless to say, I was shocked. But I had the presence of mind to point to Ricardo Diaz and ask Erdmeister what Diaz did during the war.

Erdmeister laughed. "Who is Diaz? This man is Peter Brenner. I heard that he was able to escape, maybe to Brazil or somewhere else in South America. Of course, soon after that your father betrayed me and I don't really know for sure. Brenner was in our "Inner Circle of Five."

So now I knew who all five members were. I thought I recognized a couple of other men from the University of Munich library photos but I wasn't sure. Was the man with the scar who killed Gruber in the photo? "So there was you, Brenner, Rheingold, Gruber, and Friedrich. Why would Gunter Gruber want to kidnap me? And who would want to kill Gruber?"

I told Erdmeister about what happened in New York and he howled with laughter. "I have no idea why Gruber wanted to kidnap you or why he was killed. Remember I was in prison all of these years. Perhaps your father also betrayed Gruber and he wanted revenge." I shuddered a bit at that statement because I knew that could possibly be true because my father testified against Gruber in the Munich Tribunals. But it also gave me hope. If my father really replaced Dr. Friedrich as a member of the "Inner Circle of Five", why wasn't he arrested and imprisoned along with many other Nazi war criminals? Instead he testified against Gruber and was used by the prosecutors for his knowledge. Or maybe my father made a deal to testify in exchange for some sort of immunity.

I pointed out seven men in the photo who I thought I remembered from the University of Munich library photos and asked Erdmeister if he could remember their names. He remembered six names. Herbert Probst, Andrei Anhaus, Franz Maier, Ludwig Dachwurst, Markus Mortkopf, and Johann Schwartz. I resolved to utilize Mr. Lubeck's help again. Perhaps one of these men had a reason to pursue and kill Gunter Gruber. Although I was sure my father wouldn't admit it, maybe he knew one of these men and through that connection there was knowledge about why Gruber was killed. I admit my excitement level grew exponentially as I wrote the six names down.

But I was also really depressed. My father obviously had lied to me about a lot of things, including about who Ricardo Diaz was. Reality started to sink in. Things were not what they seemed. What should I do? I could no longer trust my father. Worse yet, did I really want to confront him and find out the ultimate truth, assuming I could get it out of my father? I had to think. I decided after pausing for a moment not to ask too many questions just yet. I would let Erdmeister ramble a bit if he felt like it. And he did. He told me all about his love of Hitler and the Nazi way. Clearly he believed in what he did in the past and really wasn't remorseful. However he also seemed to regain his composure as he told his tales. In his mind the exploits of the "Inner Circle of Five" were quite laudable and worthy of recognition. It was difficult to sit in the same room with the man who killed the man I would have known as my uncle.

Eventually I had heard enough. But then Erdmeister surprised me further and told me he had more photos he could show me, but they were still in possession of his brother. He suggested he bring them to me. His motivation, according to this sinister war criminal, was to prove to me my father was no different then he was. I bristled at the suggestion and in a heat of passion agreed with his plan. I assured him my father was nothing like him, although the conviction in my heart was somewhat fading. Sergei was not thrilled with the idea, but I begged him to acquiesce. It was agreed Erdmeister would come out to Sergei's farm the next day with the pictures. I guess I saw this as my opportunity to learn as much as I could. My father had treated me remarkably well throughout my lifetime and I decided that even if any of what Erdmeister said was true my father still loved me. And I still loved him. I could not abandon him just because he may have done some horrible things in his past. Plus I hoped to ask Ermeister even more questions about Gunter Gruber to see if his answers could help me figure out why he confronted me in New York. Hopefully I could figure it out without having to confront my father. I wanted to discover everything for myself and not face the emotional crisis head on.

Did my father become a full fledged Nazi after he was captured and forced into the German army as a medic? I wanted to know but without making me feel any less about my father.

With that we agreed to a meeting time for the next day. Sergei gave Erdmeister directions to the farm, and we left. During our drive back Sergei tried to comfort me and explained that a lot of people did things during the war they didn't want to do – but circumstances forced them into situations they couldn't get out of. Sergei pointed out to me that my father was a doctor and had spent most of his life healing and helping people. The war was a crazy time. Sergei himself remembered some of the things he did during the war and wasn't proud of. For survival he stole food from people and ratted out friends to the communists. He even hid like a coward in his village while other men confronted the invading Germans and were killed for their bravery.

"Imagine how I feel. Because I was a coward I survived. Then when I was eventually captured and brought to Germany I got to start life over after the Nazis fell. But I actually was forced into the German army and fought against fellow Russians. I killed my own countrymen simply because I wanted to live and I definitely didn't want to go back to Russia once I got out."

As he told this story tears started forming in his eyes. "So give your father a break. No matter what you find out. It was a horrific time and survival was all that mattered."

And I had to agree. The past was very difficult for my parents. My life was relatively easy. Who was I to judge my father's actions over thirty years later? I wanted to find out the truth and as many facts as I could, but I didn't want to destroy my relationship with my parents nor jeopardize our lives. Selfishly I loved my life and anything that I discovered and revealed could negatively affect my great situation. As the cliché went "knowledge is power" and perhaps in this case it was true. But it was definitely a power I would never try to use in anyway. I loved my parents and my life too much to do anything, even if I found out the worst.

Now I felt energized in the respect that I believed my sleuthing finally had gotten me somewhere and I was, perhaps, on the verge of finding out some really important information. I swore Sergei to secrecy. He agreed it would be best not to reveal anything to my father about our meeting with Erdmeister. After Erdmeister visited us with the rest of the photos I planned on calling Karl Lubeck and ask for his father's help once again. I truly believed I was getting closer and closer to the truth.

CHAPTER 16

As agreed upon, Erdmeister arrived at 10:00 in the morning. Sergei and his wife Anna decided to leave us alone for a few hours so they left to go to Stuttgart for the day around 9:30. Erdmeister arrived with a satchel in his hand, presumably containing the photos. I greeted him and offered him something to drink, but he declined. I asked him to follow me into the study and he obliged. He asked about Sergei and I told him where my father's cousin and his wife went.

"That's probably best – that will give us some quiet time to discuss matters."

"I don't think we'll need that much time," I replied. "I just want to learn all I can about the "Inner Circle of Five" from your photos. I really don't believe my father was one of you. Your group was evil. My father is not."

"That is where you are so wrong. But here is the photo from yesterday. Why don't you keep it and show it to your father? I'm sure that will bring back many sweet memories." With that Erdmeister burst out with derisive laughter. The scene seemed a bit surreal. Here I was talking in Russian to a German war criminal who clearly loathed my father. Yet I felt like I was going back in time and experiencing a piece of history.

Then he reached into his satchel and pulled out a bunch of photographs and threw them in my direction. They scattered all over the floor at my feet. I leaned over to pick them up.

"There is all you need to see about our group. We were going to change history. And we did. We ruled the world for a number of years.

Europe was lucky that America stuck it's nose into Germany's business and helped in the war. Without America's help all Europeans would be speaking German and there wouldn't be any Jews left. Your father was going to help with that. And he helped us take care of any medical needs we had when we brought those young girls in for a little fun. You should have been there. All those girls providing such fun and pleasure for the officers and your father right there with them."

I said nothing but compiled all of the photos and started looking at them. What I saw shocked and sickened me. These must have been photos from prisoner of war camps and probably some from concentration camps. There were photos of piled up dead bodies and prisoners who were skin and bones. The brutality of World War II and the Nazis came alive right in front of my eyes. There weren't any photos with my father in them. Every photo was a horrible photo depicting death, the morbidness of war, and the cruelty of Nazis.

"My father isn't even in these photos. You lied. This proves nothing except that the Nazis were despicable and cruel. You were one of those despicable people. You deserved to be in prison. You deserved to die." I was outraged and infuriated. Clearly Erdmeister wanted to torment me with the photos and he had no proof that my father had participated in the activities of the "Inner Circle of Five".

"I read about your group and what they did. My father wasn't mentioned in any of the documents I read nor was he mentioned in the transcripts of the Munich Tribunals. In fact he testified against Gunter Gruber."

"I'm sure that was to save his skin," replied Erdmeister. "After Dr. Friedrich died your father took over his duties. He performed abortions on many of the young girls and probably helped kill a lot of them."

"You're a war criminal. I don't believe anything you say," I yelled back loudly.

"Enough," growled Erdmeister. "Let me take care of business now."

With that Erdmeister reached into his satchel and pulled out a gun. Immediately I was petrified. This I hadn't planned on.

As he pointed the gun at me Erdmeister nonchalantly proclaimed, "I really do hate your father. If he didn't betray me I could have escaped from Germany like many did. I could have lived a nice life. Your father prevented that. Because of him I spent most of my life holed up in a terrible prison. Now he will pay for it. But so will you."

Obviously I had totally misjudged Erdmeister's intentions. I assumed he was a bitter man who would simply be satisfied to be back in Germany to live out his life. I never even considered the possibility that he might do something that would send him back to prison. Whatever he planned on doing to me would certainly put him in trouble with the law and deprive him of his freedom. On the other hand I should have realized that he was an unstable individual. Perhaps he was capable of doing anything and not worrying about the consequences. The fear inside of me grew substantially. In a way I wished I hadn't sent Sergei and Anna away. But on the other hand, Erdmeister might have done the same thing even with them around. Had they stayed they would also have been in danger and I would have felt considerable guilt about that. It didn't really matter. I needed to focus on the present situation and figure a way out.

"You see, my plan is very simple. I need to inflict as much pain on your father as possible. Killing him would be wonderful. But killing his son would be even better. That way he'll have to live with the realization that his actions resulted in the death of his son."

"Look Erdmeister," I pleaded, "if you kill me Sergei will know who did it and you will eventually be caught and go back to prison. Is that what you want? Now you at least have your freedom. Killing me will eliminate your freedom."

"That is a nice speech," intoned Erdmeister, "but you have things a bit confused. Sergei will not know what happened to you because I will kill he and his wife when they return. They certainly suspect nothing and are bound to return just in time to be killed themselves. After I kill all three of you I will head back to Stuutgart. No one knows I'm here and there will be no clues to find. In due time I'll send your father a nice letter, anonymous of course, but he will certainly know who killed his son. The hints

I drop in the letter will make it obvious to him who killed you, but there will be nothing that the police will be able to use. What is really nice is that I will reveal that your father was a Nazi to the American media, also anonymously, but with information they will be able to research. Not only will your father be responsible for your death, his life will be ruined when all the facts about his past come out."

Now I was really in trouble. Erdmeister had thought things out and Sergei probably made it easier for him by leaving with Anna. Erdmeister could kill me and then take his time waiting for Sergei and Anna to come back. I desperately tried to think of an escape plan, but nothing came to mind. Suddenly I knew what real pressure was. Playing a tennis match was pressure, but it was an invigorating pressure. A truly stimulating event. Facing the prospect of death at the hands of a scoundrel like Erdmeister was terrifying. My only option seemed to be to keep Erdmeister talking and hope that I could distract him. Or perhaps he had a grandiose plan for my death and if Sergei and Anna returned sooner than later they would interrupt his scheme. That might at least give me a chance to warn them. Maybe they could survive and let the police know who was my killer.

It became quite clear my scheming would do me no good. Erdmeister pulled his gun up, moved closer to me, and in a very menacing manner said, "Good bye. It has been really nice knowing you. Thank you for finding me and making all of this possible. Without you it would have been a lot of work to find out where your father is and without you it wouldn't be possible for me to inflict such catastrophic pain on your father. You have made it so easy for me to exact revenge upon your father."

Suddenly I heard a sound behind me, as if something was bouncing along the floor and then there was a crashing sound to my left, where the living room was. Erdmeister was momentarily distracted as he glanced towards the living room and he lowered his weapon. I immediately dived for the floor. Erdmeister had a choice. Shoot me now, then investigate the noise. Or wait until he looked in the living room, while keeping the gun trained on me. He raised his gun back up, pointed it at me, and prepared to shoot. Obviously he wasn't going to worry about the commotion just yet.

Boom!! A loud explosion shattered the air. I was confused. The noise came from my right, where the kitchen was and I felt no pain. Erdmeister must have missed. But why did the sound come from the kitchen. I looked up. Erdmeister was on the ground, clutching his chest. One more shot rang out. He was no longer clutching his chest. Part of his head was missing and his body simply collapsed on the floor and was still. I had a sudden rush of emotions. On the one hand, I was sickened by the gruesome sight. On the other hand, I was happy to be alive. Someone saved my life and I was elated about that. I scampered up off the floor and ran through the kitchen. I felt completely safe now. Whoever shot Erdmeister was obviously my benefactor and wouldn't harm me. At least that's what I believed.

I bolted through the kitchen door. In front of me was the barn and a detached garage building next to it. The driveway leading to those buildings was to my right so I ran in that direction and looked around the corner of the house. I saw someone running at the end of the driveway and turning left around some hedges. I pursued the person as fast as I could. When I reached the end of the driveway I looked around the hedges and saw my savior opening the door to a red car. The person gave me a quick glance. He had a ski mask on.

"Hey," I yelled. "Don't go! I want to talk to you. You saved me, why are you running away?"

The car started. As I rushed towards the car, it made a quick u-turn and careened down the road in the opposite direction. I was going to memorize the license number of the car except it had no license plate. Obviously whoever was in the car wanted to make sure the car couldn't be tracked down. Once again it looked like I was going to be frustrated.

One thing I was sure about. The man with the scar who saved me in New York had a limp. Erdmeister's shooter did not have a limp. Plus, Erdmeister's shooter seemed faster and smaller than the man in New York. I surmised, with my brilliant sleuthing mind, that it was likely someone other than the man with the scar who shot Erdmeister.

I trudged back towards the house. I was still shaking from the experience, being so close to death, but thrilled to be alive. And though I wasn't sure what it meant, I now had several clues to ponder. First and foremost, who was the shooter? How did he know that Erdmeister would be at Sergei's house with me? I was very suspicious that Sergei must have somehow participated in the scenario that occurred. There could be no other way that the shooter knew Erdmeister would be here unless he was tipped off by Sergei. But I vowed not to accuse Sergei of anything just yet. If things kept on as they had, he would deny knowing anything, as would my father. I had to find things out on my own.

As I walked up the driveway in a calmer state, I looked towards the barn. The barn door was open and it looked like someone was trying to slither out through the opening. From a distance I couldn't tell why he or she wasn't walking, so I approached with caution. As I got closer I could see that the person was a man and that his hands and feet were tied up. And his mouth was covered with tape. What was going on?

He notice me and stopped slithering. I walked up to him and told him I would remove the tape but that I wasn't going to untie him because I had no idea who he was. I asked him if he understood. He nodded, so obviously he spoke English. With that I ripped the tape off and he yelped in pain.

"Ow. That hurt. Now untie me at once." His English was accented, but I couldn't tell what kind of accent it was.

"I'll do no such thing. I have no idea who you are, why you're here, and if you have anything to do with what just happened."

"Look, I was simply coming to this house to get directions when somebody with a gun accosted me and tied me up. I'm just a tourist."

"I don't know if I believe you or not," I replied, "but I think I'll call the police and let them figure out who you are."

I hurried back into the house. My plan was simple. I'd get all my stuff together, leave a note for Sergei explaining that there was a shooting, that I was safe, and that I would call him later. Because I was fairly sure Sergei was somehow involved, I didn't think he would be totally shocked when he found Erdmeister's body. I would let him call the police. Then I would call a taxi. I didn't want to be around when the police showed up. I had no interest in helping the police apprehend the shooter. I had a thought in my mind. If it panned out I might discover who the shooter was. Or at least I might figure out whether the car belonged to the shooter or someone connected to the shooter. Somehow, the man with the scar had to be involved. He had saved me before.

As disgusting as it was, I walked over to Erdmeister's body. I tried not to look at the bloody mess as I reached over to pick up his satchel. I looked inside. There weren't any other photographs. Erdmeister probably had lied. He probably didn't have any other photographs to show me that implicated my father. So there would be no more clues to investigate. However, I still had one thought left. Maybe the odds were remote, but perhaps I could make use of the photograph Erdmeister showed me the day before.

First I called Karl Lubeck. Luckily he was just waking up after a long shift at the hospital where he was a resident. He was sleepy but I told him I was in a desperate situation and needed his father's help. With that I gave him the names of the six people from the Erdmeister photograph that I had written down. Men I thought I recognized from the University of Munich library photographs. I told Karl I needed to know which of the men, if any, were still alive. Of those who were alive I needed their addresses, and most importantly, I needed to know if any of them owned a red car. I begged Karl to get me the information as soon as possible. I also promised that I would never bother him again if he helped this time. I told him I would call him tomorrow.

Then, after I called for a taxi, I hurriedly packed my things. Before I called I looked out at the barn area because I remembered about the tied up stranger. I didn't see him. I wasn't too worried because he was tied up quite securely and I didn't think he could be much of a threat. Although I was definitely curious about why he was on the premises. Was he really just a tourist?

I grabbed my luggage and went outside. I went back towards the barn area and searched around but didn't see the stranger. I did see the cords with which his hands and feet were tied, but somehow it looked like they had been cut. It puzzled me, but I couldn't worry about it now. I had to get out of there. I went back around to the front of the house where my luggage was and waited for the taxi. I had a bit of trepidation in my mind about when Sergei would arrive home. He would encounter a horrible scene and would probably be quite shocked. Or would he? If he tipped off the shooter about Erdmeister's visit, he had to know there was potential for something to happen. I decided to stick with my plan and leave Sergei's house.

Impatiently I waited for the taxi. Because Sergei's house was in a rural area it took nearly an hour for the taxi to arrive. I clambered in and told the driver to take me to Stuttgart. I needed to stay at a hotel for the night and the driver knew a good hotel that wasn't too expensive. I still had a few days before I had to leave for the Paris Indoor event so that would give me time to let my plan play out. This might be my last chance. If this didn't work I would either confront my father one final time or simply drop everything.

I wasn't able to relax the rest of the day. I finally decided to call Sergei in the evening. "Sergei, it's Erick. I hope you weren't too shocked when you got home. Unless I totally misread everything, somehow somebody knew that Erdmeister was coming to your house. You must have told. There could be no other way. That's why I left. If I didn't think you knew anything about this I wouldn't have left."

Sergei didn't reply right away. Then I heard a sigh. "I can't say much now Erick. Tell me where you are and I'll pick you up. Then we'll go from there. It's a very delicate situation. Perhaps you should call your father."

"Right now Sergei I'm going to stay where I am. I'll think about calling my father but it seems I've been lied to way too often. Did you call the police?"

"For the moment, you don't have to worry. I am going to take care of everything. Leave it at that. I think it is best not to involve the police."

We said good night and I knew I was reaching the end of the trail. My father would be in an awkward position. He obviously knew much more than he was willing to tell me, but he might think telling me more would forever change our relationship. Did I want to know more? Would I hate my father if I learned the truth? I wanted to know everything, but in my heart I felt doubt. Would it really be worth it or would I become disillusioned? I decided I would try to find out everything I could the next day, and then regardless of what I learned, I would then call my father. Of course it was quite possible I would learn nothing new.

I slept fitfully. I knew that tomorrow was going to be the do or die day. If I learned nothing from Mr. Lubeck I had no other alternative but to call my father and demand to know everything he knew. But I was also excited. It seemed that with Erdmeister's death I was now safe from any more attacks. All the members of the "Inner Circle of Five" were now dead. Dr. Friedrich died during the war. Gruber was killed by the man with the scar. Brenner, or as I knew him Ricardo Diaz, died in Toledo during the supposed robbery. I now had the feeling my father had to be somehow involved in Brenner's death. It strained the imagination to believe my father and Brenner had been randomly robbed late at night near the Bier Stube in Toledo. Rheingold died when he fell off the balcony in San Antonio. And obviously Erdmeister was just killed by the mystery shooter. I believed I was safe but still I needed to know why I was involved in the first place.

The next morning I woke up and had a quick breakfast. Right after that I called Karl. There was no answer. From that moment I called him every hour on the hour. He wasn't home. Now I became tense. I needed to know! It wasn't until 4:00 that Karl finally answered.

"Karl, it's Erick. I hope your father found something out for me. This is really important."

"Hello Erick. I just got home about thirty minutes ago. From the hospital. I haven't had time to call my father back to see what he found out. Let me have your phone number and I'll call you back."

It seemed like hours but it really was no more than fifteen minutes. The phone rang in my hotel room and I snatched it up. "Karl?" I nearly yelled at the top of my lungs into the phone.

"Yes, Erick. I was able to talk to my father. He gave me the information you wanted."

I held my breath. "Four of the six men are still alive. Do you want all four names?"

"Yes, yes," I impatiently replied. "Do any of them own a red car?"

"Herbert Probst doesn't own a red car. Marcus Mortkopf doesn't own a car. He is in a nursing home. Franz Maier owns a red car and a white car. Andrei Anhaus also owns a red car."

"That's great information. I don't know cars very well but what kind of red cars do Maier and Anhaus own?"

"Maier owns a Volvo sedan. Anhaus owns a Volkswagen station wagon."

"I know the car I saw wasn't a station wagon so give me Maier's address if you have it. Just in case give me all four of the addresses."

Karl gave me all of the addresses and I thanked him profusely. My first target had to be Maier. He had a red car and it wasn't a station wagon. Of course it didn't seem likely that he could have shot Erdmeister if he was the man with the scar because the shooter was fairly small and had no limp. Granted, someone could recover from a limp but he couldn't change his physique. Still, it was the best clue I had and so I prepared to check out of the hotel and head to Munich where Maier lived. I arranged for a rental car and within the hour I was on my way. Munich was about 120 miles southeast of Stuttgart so it took me almost three hours to get to the city and find a hotel. It was nearly 10:00 by the time I finished dinner so I decided to hit the sack. Tomorrow I would get a map of Munich and find out how to get to Maier's home.

I woke up early the next morning and asked the hotel concierge where I could buy a map of Munich. After breakfast I walked to the tourist center the concierge had recommended and bought the map.

Maier lived at 1033 Renastrasse in the southwest part of the city. My hotel was pretty much on the western outskirts of Munich. It would probably take me no more than thirty minutes to get to Maier's house. With both excitement and trepidation I headed back to the hotel and got my car out of the hotel garage. I left the map open on the passenger front seat and started to drive to Maier's house. I guess I assumed it was a house because there was no apartment number, but of course I really had no idea what kind of residence it was.

I realized it was morning so Maier could be at work. But perhaps he was retired and was at home. In any case I didn't have the patience to wait. I would go to the house and see what was up. It was also very possible that this was going to be a total waste of time and it was total coincidence that Maier was in the photo Erdmeister showed me. Just because he was in the photo and owned a red car really didn't mean anything. Unless, of course, he was connected to Erdmeister's shooter.

1033 Renastrasse was located in a modest neighborhood. The houses were relatively small, but were neat. The yards were well kept and most of the houses had a garage. In front of Maier's house a white car was parked by the curb. The garage door was closed so I didn't know if a red car might be inside. So I drove a couple of houses past Maier's house and parked at the curb.

By now my hands were sweaty and I was nervous. But I also felt very safe. If this was who I was looking for he had been involved with saving my life. The threat to me, whatever it had been, was probably extinguished with Erdmeister's death. I walked up the pathway leading to the front door. I hesitated and then I rang the doorbell. It sounded like a chime. Initially I heard nothing. There was a solid wooden door without a screen so there was no way to look into the house. The front drapes were also drawn so there was no hint whether someone was home or not. I waited a bit longer and then my impatience took over. I pushed the doorbell button two times in succession. I didn't hear anything for a few seconds, but then the door opened a crack. I stood and waited. I felt like a fool for that instant and so I tentatively said, "Hello. Who is there? I came to see Mr. Maier."

Finally the door opened all the way. Standing in front of me was a young lady dressed in a uniform. Whether it was a police uniform or army uniform I really had no idea. My jaw dropped when our eyes met. The young lady looked just like me except she had long hair! I was flabbergasted. I was speechless for a good while, but finally was able to blurt something.

"Who are you?" is all I could manage to mutter.

The young lady didn't seem quite as stunned as I was, even though it must have also been obvious to her that we looked almost identical. She finally smiled, and without further ado motioned me to follow her inside. I did so and closed the door behind me.

"I am Marta," she said with an accent. "I don't speak the best English, but I can get by. I know you are Erick. I just didn't think we would ever meet. Did Sergei send you here?"

"No, I did some investigating after what happened at Sergei's house and found out that a man named Franz Maier owns a red car and this is his address. It's a long story and it involved a lot of luck. But I saw a photograph recently and one of the men in the photograph was Franz Maier. Through a process of elimination I figured out that I had to come to this address and see if Mr. Maier could provide me with some information. Do you know Mr. Maier?"

"Yes."

"I mean you do know we look the same, right? And you know me. So, although I am absolutely shocked, it appears you are my sister."

"Yes, of course I know we look the same. And I have known about you for over two years. Mr. Maier, as you call him, is my father."

Now I was even more stunned if that was possible. "You're saying Mr. Maier is my father? All of these years I've lived in America and not with my father?"

"Let's go sit down. I think it is time you learned the entire story. There doesn't seem to be a reason to keep it from you now. Come, meet my father."

We walked into what was most likely the living room. A man in a wheelchair sat facing the window. I could only see his left profile. He gradually turned the wheelchair so he faced me. On his right cheek was a jagged scar. There he was, right in front of me. Mr. Maier had to be the man who killed Gunter Gruber. He had saved me from being kidnapped. Or, who knows, perhaps he saved my life. It was obvious from his condition that he did not shoot Joseph Erdmeister yesterday.

"This is my father, Franz Maier." Marta grabbed my hand and pulled me towards the crippled man. He looked rather gaunt and he seemed to move with some difficulty as he stuck out his hand to shake mine. I gladly shook his hand, although his grip was weak.

Tears started to well up in Marta's eyes. "Unfortunately Father developed ALS over two years ago. I believe you call it Lou Gehrig's Disease in America. Father doesn't speak English. I know you must have many, many questions. When Father developed the disease he decided it was time to tell me the truth about everything. I thing I liked things just as they were, but now perhaps it is for the better that I know the truth. And I think it is better that you now know the truth. Perhaps after I tell you the entire story of who we are and why things happened as they did, you can tell us how you found us. I know Father would be interested to know, because he was very proud of helping you but he also wanted to follow your father's wishes and not be discovered."

"Please tell me everything. I am still absolutely amazed. Who is our father? Obviously we're twins. Is Mr. Maier my father, or is the man I love as my father, also your father?"

"Sit down, sit down," Marta encouraged me. "I will tell you everything. Let me call work and tell them I can't come in today. I am a police woman in Munich. I will call and tell them I have an emergency. I think they will understand. They know about Father's condition so I will tell them I have to take care of him today."

With that Marta picked up the phone in the living room and made a quick call. She hung up a couple minutes later and sat on the chair across from the sofa I was sitting on. Mr. Maier rolled his wheel chair over by Marta.

"It is a long story Erick, but I will do my best to tell you all I know. Father will try to help if you have any questions. It really is rather exciting to meet you."

Marta began telling my history from the very beginning. All the way back to World War II. My father first met Mr. Maier when Erdmeister killed my father's brother Ivan. He was in Erdmeister's unit. Eventually my father started to cooperate with the Nazis in order to make things easier on himself. Enough trust was established that my father was made a medic in the army. My father recognized the fact that he had to stay alive and cooperate in order to have any chance of ever reuniting with my mother. At that time he had no idea that she was going to try to escape Russia and head towards Germany. Over time Maier and my father became friends and Maier taught my father to speak German.

As the war turned bad for the Germans on the Eastern front, many of the army units were sent back to Germany in preparation for setting up defenses against the approaching Allies. Maier and my father were sent to Berlin with their unit. During this time Maier and my father started to support the cause of the Nazis. My father, because he thought it would be a better alternative than having the Soviet Union win the war and take over Germany. Plus the Soviets might view him as a traitor and kill him. My father viewed Naziisim as the lesser of two evils. Maier, because he feared that millions of Germans would be killed by the Soviets if they conquered Germany and took over the country. Their real fear was that the Soviet Union would take over.

"Their fear of the Soviet Union is what really put them in an awkward situation. By fully embracing the ideology of Naziism, at least outwardly, our fathers believed they would survive. Thus began their participation with the organization known as the Fraternity of the Master Race which was controlled by the "Inner Circle of Five".

At this point I explained to Marta that I had done extensive research about the "Inner Circle of Five" and knew about all of the members and what they had been doing during the war. I also decided, before she continued to tell her story, that I would tell her all that had happened to me, starting with the death of Gunter Gruber in New York. She listened patiently and then spoke to her father for a few minutes.

"Father said that you will understand all after I finish telling this story. But he wants you to know that your father loves you very much and no matter what you are told about the past, that will never change."

Marta informed me that after the death of Dr. Friedrich, my father was entrusted with carrying out many of the horrific duties involving the girls who were kidnapped and raped by the Fraternity of the Master Race. He had to perform abortions as ordered and treat the girls when the rapists brutalized them. Maier assisted in some of the kidnappings but never participated in any of the rapes. The same was true of my father. They did what they had to, to survive, and felt terrible about it. Through that time period they grew closer and closer. They became the best of friends.

Then the Allies and Soviets started closing in on Germany from the west and from the east. In one of the battles Maier was gravely injured. Apparently my father saved his life with his quick thinking and medical skills. That was how Maier sustained the scar on his right cheek and how he developed his limp. His leg was horribly damaged by a bullet wound and his face was disfigured by shrapnel. Because of that, Maier felt forever indebted to my father.

As the war came to an end there was of course much chaos. Circumstances developed that forever intertwined Maier and my father. A unit led by Colonel James McMillan, the British soldier I met in London, captured many members of the Fraternity of the Master Race, as well as Gunter Gruber. The other members of the "Inner Circle of Five", namely Peter Brenner (or as I knew him, Ricardo Diaz) and Alfred Rheingold escaped capture. Marta explained that my father had turned Joseph Erdmeister over to the Russians as a matter of revenge for killing Ivan. This, of course, I already had learned from Erdmeister himself.

Now I began to see a picture of intertwining elements. Colonel McMillan wanted to visit with me in London while I was playing

Wimbledon. Of course after I saw him at Wimbledon, and before I had a chance to see him at his home, he was killed. Rheingold died at Trinity University when he fell from my dorm balcony. Brenner was killed in Toledo during an apparent robbery. Now, it became somewhat obvious, all of these killings were connected in one way or another. It could not all be coincidence.

Marta continued telling the story. My father and Maier escaped capture, but at a price. McMillan, it turned out, had discovered documents that implicated my father and Maier as being involved with the "Inner Circle of Five". For reasons that only became clear in the future, McMillan let my father and Maier go, but he reminded them that he possessed documents that would create extreme difficulties for my father and Maier if they ever ended up in the wrong hands.

Meanwhile, before all of this happened, Gruber and Brenner put my father and Maier in charge of taking care of several girls who were born as a result of the rapes perpetrated by the Master Race Fraternity. These were daughters of girls who were raped by high ranking Nazi officials. The disgusting plan Gruber and Brenner came up with was to place these girls with various sympathizers and continue the bloodlines of those high ranking Nazis. At some point they wanted to have those girls impregnated. Those who bore male babies would have these babies taken from them. In the future Gruber and Brenner wanted these boys to become the new Nazi leaders that Gruber and Brenner would train.

"Obviously the plan seemed one that only lunatics could think of," Marta exclaimed, "but that meant that my father and your father had to play along with the plan. At the time that seemed the safest route they could take."

Maier and my father apparently placed many of these girls with Nazi sympathizers. One young girl was kept by my father, and adoption papers prepared. It was then expected that my father would take care of this girl until she became old enough to be impregnated. The girl my father adopted was born to a young woman who was raped by Heinrich Himmler, the dreaded leader of the infamous SS, or Gestapo. The arm of the Nazi war machine responsible for the extermination of Jews and any other individuals who opposed the Nazis. The Gestapo tortured, brutalized, and killed millions.

Marta pointed out that the young women were raped by not only Himmler, but other infamous Nazis like Martin Bormann, Nazi Party Secretary. Wilhelm Frick, Hitler's Minister of the Interior. Hermann Goring, commander of the Luftwaffe (the Nazi Air Force), and Ernst Kaltenbrunner, Himmler's associate who helped Gruber's rise in the Nazi party. There were many more and even Hitler was rumored to have raped one of the young women. Somewhere out there, it was possible that there was a direct descendant of Adolph Hitler alive and well.

With Gruber's capture it seemed the plan could not continue. For the most part that was true. Unfortunately Brenner was crazy enough to believe Nazi Germany would rise again, and it would be led by the offspring of one of the girls born as a result of the rapings. Most of the girls were eventually assimilated into German society. The Nazi sympathizers with whom Maier and my father had placed these girls realized that Gruber's plan was really sheer madness and there would be no future Nazi uprising. Thus the plan died.

"But, unfortunately my father and your father were still being haunted by their connection to Gruber and Brenner," Marta explained further. "And by their connection to Colonel McMillan. Brenner escaped to Brazil, and eventually made his way to Mexico. He had a lot of evidence linking your father and my father to the "Inner Circle of Five". Even though they did everything they did because they felt threatened, our fathers would certainly look quite guilty if evidence of their connection to the "Inner Circle of Five" was revealed."

"So Brenner, and Rheingold, who had also escaped to Brazil, stayed in secret contact with your father and my father. Even though it seemed so crazy, they insisted that Himmler's daughter Maria, who was adopted by your father, would have a son who would then lead the revival of the Nazi dream of world dominance. This created great problems in our fathers' lives. They constantly felt the pressure of being exposed and having their lives destroyed."

At this point Mr. Maier spoke out. Marta and he conversed in German for several minutes and then Marta turned to me.

"My father just wanted to tell you that your father is a very good man. Everything that happened as it did, could not be helped. They never intended to be involved with the "Inner Circle of Five", but simply felt trapped. They did the best they could."

Then Marta continued. The other problem that developed was that Colonel McMillan started to blackmail Maier and my father. The documents he seized during Gruber's capture came in handy. He threatened to expose both my father and Maier to the German and American authorities. That would mean ruination for my father and Maier. Certainly it would have been the end of my father's medical career and possibly his freedom. It would have been the same for Maier, who had become an engineer. Now I began to understand why my father had been so reticent to talk about the past and his connection to Colonel McMillan and the infamous Ricardo Diaz. Apparently Colonel McMillan was able to retire early on his army benefits, but mainly because of the blackmail payments he received from my father and Maier.

"Erick, now I must tell you some things that are not pleasant," Marta said. "At first I hated my father when he told me what happened. Then I realized he did these things because he loved me and wanted to keep my life as happy and normal as possible. Your father did everything because he loved you and wants the best for your future. I will not stretch out the story. I will simply tell you what happened, even if it causes some pain."

After my parents came to the United States with Himmler's daughter Maria, life became fairly normal and good. However, Brenner and Rheingold kept the pressure on my father and Maier, ever reminding them that Naziism would rise again when a new leader was born. That leader would be Maria's son. In what was a heart wrenching decision for

Maier and my father, they took Maria to Mexico in 1957 when she was 16. Boris was already two years old by then. They left Maria with Brenner in Mexico. They knew what would happen next. They could not forgive themselves for what they had done, but the alternative seemed to be ruination of their lives and the lives of their families. If the truth came out about their involvement in the "Inner Circle of Five" they would probably be thrown in jail for a long time and their wives left all alone. Life would be over as they knew it. At this time Maier was married to Uma, who unfortunately died of cancer in the early 1960's.

"It was very sad," Marta continued. "Brenner had sex with Maria. No doubt it was rape. What 16 year old would willingly have sex with a stranger who was over 20 years older than her? She didn't even know what sex was. She eventually became pregnant and your father then went to Mexico when Maria had been pregnant for several months. You can probably guess by now. Your father delivered the babies. They were twins. We were the twins."

Now it hit me. Marta and I were grandchildren of one of the most despicable Nazi leaders, Heinrich Himmler. And we were children of Peter Brenner, another despicable Nazi who had raped our mother. For the moment, at least, I was disgusted.

"What happened to our mother?" I asked.

"Unfortunately, she died at child birth. Apparently the strain of delivering twins was too much for her young body to take."

Marta resumed telling the rest of the story. Brenner, being the ultimate slime that he was, had built up many connections with politicians in Mexico. It was easy to bribe the political officials as needed. Maria's death was listed as an accident on the official death certificate and my father took her body back to Toledo, where she was buried. Brenner arranged adoption papers so that eventually my parents were able to adopt me, and Maier was able to adopt Marta.

Everything after that went well except for the terrible guilt my father and Maier lived with. The thought that their decision to preserve their own lives led to the ultimate death of Maria was unthinkable. My parents loved Maria and they gave her up to be raped by Brenner. Rationalizations that they had to do it, or the lives of my father's and Maier's families, would be destroyed, didn't help. But it had been done and they would now have to live with it forever. They continued ruing the day that Gruber would get out of prison and join forces with Brenner and Rheingold. Brenner openly admitted that, by the time I turned 18, Gruber would be out of prison and then it would be time. Gruber, Brenner and Rheingold would take me from my family and prepare me to become the next great Nazi leader. Craziness, yes. But unfortunately they really believed they could revive the Third Reich.

"Our fathers decided they could not let you be taken by Gruber, Brenner and Rheingold," Marta explained. "However, they also decided that they would have to continue to play along and let Gruber think that he would be able to take you away from your father. Now you can probably start to guess the rest of the horrible truth."

And indeed I could. I tentatively described to Marta what I believed must have happened next, based on all of my research and thoughts on the matter.

"Obviously I recognize your father as the man who killed Gruber in New York. And I'm guessing that your father may also have been the one who killed Colonel McMillan in London."

"So far you are right," Marta said. "Our fathers decided there was no other way. My father insisted on killing the two men because your father saved his life during the war. And they believed the only way to preserve what they and their families had was to eliminate Gruber and McMillan. Of course you had the misfortune of running into Rheingold. Your father, of course, told my father how Rheingold died."

That left Brenner. I now had the feeling that Brenner did not die in a robbery. If what I thought was correct, Maier and my father orchestrated the killing of my biological father. I had to admit that I was not saddened in any way by the thought. The only thing that saddened me was that my father had to involve himself in the killings of four men. Simply because they were crazy or greedy. He didn't ask to be put in that situation. I sought confirmation from Marta.

"Brenner's death in Toledo wasn't a result of a robbery, was it?" I asked Marta.

"No. Our fathers knew there would be no reasonable way to deal with Brenner once he came to Toledo in hopes of taking you with him to Mexico. They had to kill him to end his threats."

All of this information hit me like a ton of bricks. I suspected that my father knew much more than he would tell me and that he somehow might have had some involvement with Gruber. But I had no idea that the story was going to be so shocking and involved.

"What about Erdmeister?" I asked Marta with great interest. "Clearly your father is in no condition to run around and shoot a gun. And the man who shot Erdmeister seemed fairly small in stature so I don't think it was Cousin Sergei."

"The shooter was not a man. It was me," Marta said with little emotion. "Remember I am a police officer and very well trained. My father and I decided I would have to kill Erdmeister. There was no choice once Sergei told us what Erdmeister might be up to. We weren't sure that he might try to kill you, but we thought there was that chance."

Now I was absolutely flabbergasted. The twin sister I never knew I had, saved my life. I was the grandson of a Nazi war criminal. My father was at least indirectly involved in the killing of four men. Even if there was justification it was hard to swallow. And my biological father had been a crazy, Nazi war criminal himself. Now I began to see why my father had not wanted to tell me the truth. My mind was churning. How would I ever reconcile all of this and live a normal life? There just seemed too much bizarreness to deal with. But ultimately I knew I loved my parents. They had been through hell to get to where they were in life. As distasteful as it was that four killings occurred, perhaps there was no other way. Of course, even I had been involved with the killing of a man, Alfred Rheingold, not by choice but by necessity.

I spent the rest of the day with Marta and Mr. Maier. It seemed that the best way to handle the situation was to get to know them. They had saved my life. I also decided to continue my tournament swing through Europe. I had three tournaments left. The best way to ease my mind as much as possible was to continue playing. I promised them I would come back to visit them after my tournament in Helsinki. And I also asked them to promise not to talk to my father until I called him. That's what I did that evening from my hotel. It was definitely one of the hardest things I ever had to do in my life.

CHAPTER 17

That evening, when I got back to my hotel, I relaxed for a few minutes. I pondered what I would tell my father when I called him. It was a lot to take in. I knew one thing for sure. Even though my father may have done many things that would be considered horrible, he did them for good reasons. He did what he had to do to survive during the war. And he also did what he had to do in recent years to take care of the problems created by Gruber, as well as McMillan. I loved my parents and nothing that Marta told me would change that.

I couldn't really sleep very well and decided I would call around 2:00am German time so my father would still be home when I called. I knew he wouldn't leave before 8:00am Ohio time. The phone rang three times before it was picked up.

"Hello," my father answered. There was some tentativeness in his voice.

"Hi Pa," I said as casually as I could. "I guess we should talk about a few things."

"Yes, I think it is time," my father agreed.

What followed was a long and honest conversation. My father began by apologizing for not telling me the truth. But he said he wanted to protect me and not hurt me. He also made it clear that my parents always loved me like their very own. He started crying when he brought up Maria and how terrible he felt about her death. And especially how terrible he felt that my parents had taken Maria to Brenner and allowed him to rape her. Maria was their adopted daughter. Even though they brought her to the United States knowing that Brenner would eventually want the plan to impregnate Maria carried out, they had hoped Brenner would get captured. Or die. Or realize how crazy the whole plan was. But unfortunately none of that happened. So my parents did what they thought would be best in the long run.

I told my father how much I loved my parents. That I understood what they went through during the war. Mainly because of all the research I did when I was investigating the "Inner Circle of Five". I learned how horrible World War II really was. And I told my father I would never reveal the dark secrets that were a part of his life. And I also told him that I understood why he never wanted to tell me about the past. For the rest of my life I would be affected by what had happened. If I knew less, or better yet, nothing at all, it would have been for the better. Unfortunately, once Gruber entered my life things were bound to change for the worse. But, by being so insistent on pursuing the truth, I probably exacerbated the situation even more. The truth doesn't always set you free.

My mother also came on the phone. She wept throughout the conversation, but also expressed her love and her remorse for what had happened. Mainly she was so very happy that I was safe. With the death of Erdmeister would come final peace. Life would be lived without the constant fear and turmoil brought about by the circumstances of war and its aftermath. My mother said that she had been inclined through the years to let Brenner reveal all and see what would happen. But my father was certain that would lead to disaster. And once McMillan started to blackmail my father and he paid the blackmail money, there was really no turning back.

I finished the conversation by explaining that my heart was heavy with the realization of the pain the war had caused my parents. But my heart was light with the realization that my parents loved me like their very own child for all these years. Then I joked that I now understood why Boris and I didn't look alike. Finally I told them I couldn't wait to see them again but I was going to finish playing three more tournaments and then go visit Marta and Mr. Maier. They agreed that was a good idea. In fact, they brought up the idea of flying Marta and Mr. Maier to Ohio for the Christmas season. Then we said goodbye. It was both a difficult, yet wonderful, conversation. I felt like a heavy burden had been lifted off my shoulders.

Despite everything that happened and everything that was revealed to me I felt a real eagerness going into the Paris Indoor Championships. Gone was the doubt about my father. Gone was the feeling that my father was being untruthful. Yes, it was difficult to know my biological father had been such a despicable human being. But I was lucky. My life had turned out to be wonderful. There was no reason the past should have any effect on my future. I could look forward, not backward.

My first round opponent was Jerome Potier from France. It was a great first round draw. He was a qualifier. He was ranked only #277 in the world. But his ranking was irrelevant. He played better than I did. I played tentatively knowing that I had a very winnable match in front of me. I dropped the first set 6-2 and barely pulled out the second set 7-5. One would have thought the momentum would shift severely in my direction. But it didn't. I dropped the third set 6-3 and all the positive energy I had going into the tournament was deflated like a leaky balloon.

Now I had to play in the Stockholm Open after a miserable performance in Paris. My confidence was shaky. Worse yet, I drew Roscoe Tanner in the first round. Once ranked as high as #5 in the world he still possessed one of the biggest serves in the game. For seven straight years he was ranked in the top 15 in the world. Now, his ranking was #35, but he was seeded fifth. My prospects didn't look all that great. But the gods of tennis were smiling down on me. Tanner never showed up. He withdrew from the tournament and instead I got to play Christophe Bernelle from France. Bernelle lost in the last round of qualifying. Because he was the highest ranked player who lost in the last round of qualifying he was a "lucky loser". He was put in the draw to replace Tanner.

Of course this good draw meant nothing unless I took advantage of it, something I miserably failed to do in Paris. But this time I played better.

I beat Bernelle rather handily, 6-1,6-4. Needless to say I was thrilled that I didn't have to play Tanner and when I got off to a good start, all my jitters disappeared. My good play continued in the second round against #75 Bruce Manson. In my mind Manson had always been a bit arrogant. At least that's how I remembered him from college days when he played for USC. He was a couple of years older than me. I lost to him in Baltimore three years ago so I saw this as an opportunity for revenge. I pulled out a first set tiebreaker and felt a surge. For me this would be a good win. I played even better in the second set and won 6-2. I was through to the third round.

In the next round I got to play one of the legends of the game, Adriano Panatta of Italy. He was well past his prime and was only ranked #70 in the world. However, in 1976 he had won both the French Open and Italian Open. He was once ranked as high as #4 in the world. He was the only player to beat Bjorn Borg at the French Open, which he did twice. Now he was older, out of shape, and not all that intense on the court. After I won the first set 6-4, Panatta pretty much folded up his tent and signaled he was ready to go home. I was a lot hungrier to win and the second set was 6-1. I was now in the quarterfinals against Wojtek Fibak, from Poland.

Fibak was one of the top seeds. He was perennially ranked in the top 20 from 1976-1981 and was currently #22. Unfortunately I had already lost to him twice in my career. He didn't have a big game but he possessed pin point accuracy, a great slice backhand, and superb volleys. This was enough to overcome his lack of power against all but the very top players. I couldn't muster much of a fight. Fibak toppled me rather easily, 6-2, 6-3. This tournament result gave me a great chance to finish the year in the top 110 in the world, a ranking which would get me into the main draws of the grand slam events if I could maintain it.

Now came the last event of the year for me. It was the $25,000 IBM Open, a Challenger event held in Helsinki, Finland. Unlike a Grand Prix event, which had to have at least $75,000 in prize money, the smaller purses in Challenger events attracted lower ranked players. In fact, even though I was only ranked #125 in the world, I was the top seed. Suddenly I was the one expected to win the tournament. This created a type of pressure I wasn't used to.

In the first round I faced Marc Flur, who had recently graduated from Duke University. He was ranked #200 in the world. Fortunately, or unfortunately, I decided to try a new racket at this tournament. Instead of my conventionally sized wooden Dunlop Maxply Fort, I went with the oversized Wilson Ultra, which I had recently received from a racket representative. It was my first attempt at trying a graphite frame. The graphite and larger head size provided me with more power. But probably also less control.

It seemed like it was a great choice. I won the first set 6-2 and was cruising in the second set 5-2. Then I got tight. I felt like I couldn't hit the ball in the court with the new racket. Which, of course, was absurd because I had done just fine for 15 games. But it became a mental thing. I fell apart and ended up losing the second set 7-6. When we sat down at the changeover I was angry and baffled. How could I play so well with that racket and then just blow it?

I made up my mind to go back to my wooden Dunlop frame, which fortunately I still had with me in my racket bag. Did I play better? Not necessarily, but for some reason I felt more comfortable with that racket. The third set ended up being a nip and tuck affair and we had to settle the match with a third set tiebreaker. Luck was on my side. I prevailed and squeaked through to the second round. For now, my racket experiment was over.

In the second round I beat Billy Nealon, who had played at USC and was ranked #300 in the world. My quarterfinal opponent was Randy Druz, from Houston, who I defeated in straight sets 6-3, 6-3. Then I defeated hometown hero Olli Rahnasto from Finland 6-3, 6-2 to reach the finals. In the finals I was slated to play Amos Mansdorf, from Israel. The irony of that match-up would soon become quite apparent to me.

By now I was playing with a fair amount of confidence and believed I could beat Mansdorf, who was ranked #259, in straight sets if I played well. But Mansdorf would have none of that. Even though I won the first set 6-4, Mansdorf wouldn't budge an inch. He fought tooth and nail in the second set and beat me 6-4. Although this wasn't a Grand Prix event I desperately wanted to win another title to add to my win in Metz, France. Plus, I had lost two previous Challenger event finals so I felt like this was my chance for redemption.

Neck and neck we came down the stretch. No one could gain a real foot hold. I hoped my experience would prevail. Mansdorf was only 18 and was a rookie. I had to stop him. Fortunately I finally gained the edge when I broke him at 5-5 in the third set. At 6-5 I served a good game, Mansdorf made a couple of mistakes for me, and I had my title. And $5,000, which wasn't a bad week of work. If you could call that work.

Needless to say I was elated heading back to the hotel. Even though my doubles partner Richard Lewis and I lost in the doubles finals, all in all I had a really good week and was looking forward to the 1983 season. With a ranking of #112 after the tournament, I would be getting into a fair amount of Grand Prix event main draws and would have the opportunity to try to get my ranking higher. Now I was looking forward to my trip to Munich and a visit with Marta and Mr. Maier.

I went out to dinner at a restaurant near the hotel. It was bitterly cold and snowing, a light, powdery snow. I enjoyed my meal immensely and was quite tired. It had been a long day full of up and down emotions. I needed the mental break I was going to take in the next few weeks. It still was incredible. I was playing a sport I loved and was actually doing it for a living. But even when you love something so much, you need an occasional rest. Now was the perfect time for that period of relaxation. It took me no more than ten minutes to make it back to my hotel from the restaurant and I went up to my room to do some reading.

I turned the key in the lock and pushed the door open. As soon as I turned on the light the door was slammed shut behind me and I was grabbed. Because of the shock I never even tried to resist. Before I knew it, my mouth was covered with duct tape and I was pushed down on my bed. Standing in front of me were three men. Almost immediately I recognized one of the men. It was the man I encountered by Sergei's barn and garage after the Erdmeister shooting. The supposed tourist was now in my hotel room in Helsinki. What in the world could be going on.

There was no point in struggling or thinking of some dramatic escape. There were three of them and only one of me. Plus, the tallest of the three had a gun pointed at me. The man with the gun was the first to speak.

"Well, well," he proclaimed. "We finally have our prey. It took a long time, but this could finally be the end."

I had no idea what he was talking about, but of course with my mouth taped shut there was nothing I could say. He spoke flawless English so I guessed he was American. Then he spoke to the other two men in a foreign language. I wasn't sure but I thought it might be Hebrew.

"You see Erick, we tracked you down with the help of your sister Marta. It was quite easy to make her tell us everything once we threatened to kill her father. Now you will have a chance to, quite possibly, save yourself and your sister. It just depends on how we feel after you tell us your story."

Again I was baffled. What could he want with me and why did he want to hear my story? With Erdmeister's death I was sure everything would be fine. Now with the appearance of these men, especially the one who was at Sergei's farm, it was obvious there was a connection. What the connection was I couldn't say. It seemed unlikely that these men could me friends of Erdmeister. He had been in a Russian prison for over 35 years. I couldn't see how these men would know of him.

"It really is quite simple. We are agents of the Mossad. If you are not aware, it is the national intelligence agency of Israel. Perhaps similar to your C.I.A. We are special agents. We were handed a certain task, a task that has been performed by many agents over the years. In a very unofficial capacity, you understand. Mossad would deny our existence and would deny anything we have done. Very secretive."

He chuckled. With that he spoke to his companions and they quickly grabbed my arms, put them behind my back, and duct taped them.

"There. Now I can lower my gun and we can relax a bit. Basically, Erick, we search out direct descendants of Nazi war criminals and decide whether to eliminate them or not. There were many rumors about the "Inner Circle of Five" and the Fraternity of the Master Race that our intelligence agency picked up on after World War II. After years of research and investigation we came up with many leads about many Nazi war criminals. We discovered Joseph Erdmeister was imprisoned in Russia. But Russia wouldn't deal with us."

The man continued to detail the story of how they had to wait for Erdmeister to get out of prison before they would have a chance to get information out of him. Meanwhile, Alfred Rheingold, who Shelley Coslowski and I had encountered with deadly results in San Antonio, had contacted the Mossad. Apparently he decided he wanted money more than he wanted to carry on the glorious mission of Gruber and Brenner. By then Gruber and Brenner were both dead anyway.

Anonymously, Rheingold contacted the Mossad and told them he would turn over the grandson of Heinrich Himmler in exchange for money. The exchange was apparently to take place in San Antonio. When Rheingold didn't show up the Mossad agents didn't know what to think. After considerable research they discovered that a man named Alfred Rheingold was killed in San Antonio. They knew he had been a member of the "Inner Circle of Five." Now, they at least thought it was possible that there really was a grandson of Heinrich Himmler alive and well. They believed the key was to talk to the last known survivor from the "Inner Circle of Five".

"So," the Mossad agent continued, "we knew Erdmeister was the last connection to the "Inner Circle of Five". Unfortunately you and your sister interfered with our plans. Except, by accident, you actually did all the work for us. After Erdmeister was killed we followed you from that farm and eventually we got the entire story from your sweet sister Marta.

So now it is your chance to tell us the story. If your story matches Marta's, who knows? We might let you and your sister survive. Don't tell a false story. Right now we have Marta and her father being guarded. One call from me and they are done."

I felt a chill run up and down my spine. Ironically, if Erdmeister had not been killed by Marta and was interrogated by these Mossad agents he would have been no use to the agents. He surely was aware of the birth of my biological mother Maria because he was intricately involved with the "Inner Circle of Five". However, he was in prison and had no contact with the outside world by the time Brenner had impregnated Maria. He would never have known I was Himmler's grandson. If I had never contacted Erdmeister, the Mossad agents wouldn't know of my existence and I wouldn't be in the bind I was in. My unrelenting pursuit of the truth was probably going to cost me a great deal.

The threat was very real. I decided the best chance I had was to tell the agents the entire story. If I left things out and it conflicted with what Marta old them, they would know I was lying. If I told them some things that Marta might have left out, it might look like I was simply remembering some parts of the story Marta forgot to tell them. After they removed the duct tape from my mouth, I started telling the story as best I could. They sat there and listened impassively. Once every few minutes one of them would ask a question. The American sounding agent did most of the talking, but the other two occasionally put in their two cents worth. My hope was they would realize how ridiculous it would be to harm me or Marta. Obviously we had no sympathy with Naziism and we never even knew until recently about our bloodline. In addition, Mr. Maier was personally responsible for eliminating Gruber and Brenner, while Marta eliminated Erdmeister. Inadvertently I helped to eliminate Rheingold. Because of our actions, the "Inner Circle of Five" was destroyed.

After I finished with the story the agents briefly conferred in Hebrew. Then without warning, one of the men reached into his coat pocket and took out a bottle. Meanwhile the American sounding agent approached me.

"Your story was very interesting. We shall have to think about what we'll do next. In the meantime..." And his voice trailed off. He suddenly grabbed the duct tape, tore off a piece, and taped my mouth. Then the agent with the bottle soaked a handkerchief with the liquid from the bottle. As I tried to turn away, the other two men grabbed my arms. The agent with the bottle covered my nose with the handkerchief. Soon after, my ability to try to resist totally faded away. I started to see bright lights and seemed to lose feeling in my body. Then I felt nothing.

EPILOGUE

Right after I pulled the rip chord on the parachute, I came to a screeching halt for one brief second. My head jerked backwards and I had an extreme moment of panic. Then my body righted itself and I resumed falling towards the Earth's surface, but not quite as fast as before. I had no idea what to expect after I was pushed out the door, but my descent was faster than I thought it might be when aided by a parachute.

The air was freezing. And it was pitch black all around me. In the distance I could see what I assumed were stars. Down below I could see very little. Perhaps there were some tiny flickers of light, but of that I could not be sure. At times I felt like I was floating through a fog, which meant I was probably flying through some clouds. It was hard to breathe, but as I kept falling, it got easier and easier to do so.

What could my captors have in mind? I thought of my family and also of Marta and Mr. Maier. Was everyone safe or were they in danger? What would the Mossad agents do now? I remembered what the American Mossad agent had said while I was still on the plane. "Your fate is now in the hands of God." But why throw me out a plane with a parachute? It very well may be that they simply intended to scare me, I thought to myself. If that was the case, there would be no reason that they would harm Marta or Mr. Maier. And they never even mentioned hurting my parents. As unpleasant as my downward flight was, I began to have hope.

After a few minutes I began to see what looked like large specks of white, surrounded by large patches of black. I kept drifting down. The

255

white specks became bigger and bigger. The patches of black looked smooth, but I couldn't be sure. Then I became horrified. Could it be the patches of black were water? Helsinki was located on the Gulf of Finland and near the Baltic Sea. The twinkling lights were now brighter and more numerous, but in the distance. The white specks no longer were specks. They loomed larger. Could the white shapes be icebergs? Was I being dropped into the icy cold waters off the coast of Finland? This seemed a lot more like luck, not like the work of God. Apparently I was either going to drown in the freezing waters, or luck out and reach land.

I dropped closer and closer to the darkness below, spotted now with huge looking white objects. At the same time, I was drifting sideways towards the brighter and brighter twinkling lights. Surely, the lights were an indication that land was near. I needed the wind to keep swooshing me in the direction of the lights. The blackness below seemed almost upon me and I saw what definitely was a huge block of ice. The lights were seemingly so close now. I might make land. I might fall into the freezing water below which I could now see clearly. Or would I have the misfortune of plummeting into the top or side of an iceberg?

Suddenly I burst out in prayer. God let me make it to shore. Suddenly I decided I needed more than luck. Don't let me plunge into the freezing water. I would never survive. The water was right below me. With relief I noted that I was no longer above any blocks of ice. Now I just had to float through the air a little farther. I might just make it to the land that I could now see. The lights seemed so very close now. I was drifting, drifting, downwards, ever closer to my salvation. And then...

I crashed on the rocky ground and immediately tumbled over and over. Eventually my body came to a stop. I quickly unharnessed myself from the parachute. I was battered but I was alive. It appeared my ordeal was finally over. It was cold, but I barely felt the chilly air. I survived. I could see lights in the distance and started trudging in that direction.

At the moment I didn't care about anything but getting to a phone and calling my parents. And then Marta. For whatever reason the Mossad agents decided to play a little game with me. They obviously didn't care whether I lived or died. But at least they gave me a chance. Now was the time to be grateful. I guess that was the bottom line.

ABOUT THE AUTHOR

1983 U.S. OPEN

Erick Iskersky is a former professional tennis player, once ranked number sixty-four in the world. A detailed record of his career is available on the ATP Tour website. He used his experiences in tennis as background for his new mystery, *Evils of a Secret Past*.

Iskersky was the #3 ranked junior in the United States and then played college tennis at Trinity University. He won an NCAA Doubles Championship and was runner-up in the NCAA Singles Championship. He also won the ITA National Indoor Singles Championship in back-to-back years as well as the ITA National Indoor Doubles Championship. His team won the NCAA Indoor Team Championship and lost twice in the finals of the NCAA Outdoor Team Championship.

Iskersky was inducted into the Intercollegiate Tennis Hall of Fame and was a National Coach with the United States Tennis Association's Player Development Division. He coached the University of Toledo and the University of Louisiana–Lafayette men's tennis teams.

Iskersky received a BA from Bowling Green State University, a MEd from the University of Toledo, and a Juris Doctor from Louisiana State University. He lives in Columbus, Ohio, with his wife, Cyndee.